THE KILLING SPIRIT

THE KILLING SPIRIT

an anthology of murder for hire

Edited by Jay Hopler

THE OVERLOOK PRESS
WOODSTOCK · NEW YORK

First published in the United States in 1996 by
The Overlook Press
Lewis Hollow Road
Woodstock, New York 12498

Library of Congress Cataloging-in-Publications Data

The killing spirit : an anthology of contractual murder / edited by Jay Hopler.
1. Murder—Literary collections.   2. Murderers—Literary collections.
3. Criminals—Literary collections.   4. American literature—20th century.
I.   Hopler, Jay.
PS509.M83K55   1996   96-3581   810.8′0355—dc20
ISBN 0-87951-661-5

BOOK DESIGN BY BERNARD SCHLEIFER
Printed in the United States of America
First Edition
10   9   8   7   6   5   4   3   2   1

Grateful acknowledgment is made for permission to use the following copyrighted works.

"In Search of the Assassin" by Jay Hopler originally appeared in a longer form in *Pequod.*

From *This Gun for Hire* by Graham Greene. Copyright ©1936 by Graham Greene, renewed. Used by permission of Viking Penguin, a division of Penguin Books USA Inc. Appeared as *A Gun for Sale* in the U.K. Used by permission of David Higham Associates Ltd.

"The Hit Man" by T. Coraghessan Boyle. Copyright ©1980 by T. Coraghessan Boyle. Reprinted by permission of Georges Borchardt, Inc. for the author.

"Gentlemen, The King!" by Damon Runyon, from *Guys & Dolls: Twenty Stories by Damon Runyon.* Copyright ©1956 by Damon Runyon. Reprinted by permission of Penguin Books, U.K.

"Loose Ends" by Bharati Mukherjee, from *The Middleman and Other Stories.* Copyright ©1980 by Bharati Mukherjee. Reprinted by permission of the author.

Acknowledgments

I am indebted to Stephen Dixon, Bill U'Ren, and Dr. Richard Macksey for their comments and suggestions.

# CONTENTS

If it is important to be sublime in anything, it is especially so in evil. You spit on a petty thief, but you can't withhold a certain respect from a great criminal. His courage bowls you over. His brutality makes you shudder. What you value in everything is consistency of character.

— DENIS DIDEROT, *Rameau's Nephew*

Introduction
IN SEARCH OF
THE ASSASSIN

Jay Hopler

It is easier to find a good hit man than it is to find a good hit man
story. In Baltimore, you can have anyone killed for $25 — more if you want
finesse. I knew of a dozen street corners, all within five blocks of my one-
bedroom apartment on Saint Paul Street, where an assassin could be
hired; the only modern hit man story I knew of was Ernest Hemingway's
"The Killers." But the existence of the one argues favorably for the
existence of the other, so I began, one afternoon in a rainy November,
what would turn out to be almost three years of research into the
literature of professional murder.

I read hundreds of short stories, novels, plays, screenplays, songs,
poems and essays all concerned with hired killers only to find that perhaps
one in every twenty met the criteria I had devised. I was looking for an
accurate and compelling literary representation of the assassin and the
margins he so emphatically occupies. Though the modern hit man story is
an independent literary subgenre that had its genesis with Hemingway in a
lonely hotel room in Madrid on May 16, 1926, the psychological profile of
the character predates its modern appearance by at least 320 years, with

Shakespeare's *Macbeth*, the last and darkest of his four great tragedies written most likely in the latter half of 1606. Take lines 91–113 of III.i, in which Macbeth secures the services of two assassins and arranges for Banquo's murder:

> MACBETH: Ay, in the catalogue ye go for men,
> As hounds and greyhounds, mongrels, spaniels, curs
> Shoughs, water-rugs, and demi-wolves are clept
> All by the name of dogs. The valued file
> Distinguishes the swift, the slow, the subtle,
> The housekeeper, the hunter, every one,
> According to the gift which bounteous nature
> Hath in him closed: whereby he does receive
> Particular addition, from the bill
> That writes them alike; and so of men.
> Now, if you have a station in the file,
> Not i'th' worst rank of manhood, say't;
> And I will put that business in your bosoms
> Whose execution takes your enemy off,
> Grapples you to the heart and love of us,
> Who wear our health but sickly in his life,
> Which in his death were perfect.
>
> 2ND MURDERER: *I am one, my liege,*
> *Whom the vile blows and buffets of the world*
> *Have so incensed that I am reckless what*
> *I do to spite the world.*
>
> 1ST MURDERER: *And I another,*
> *So weary with disasters, tugged with fortune,*
> *That I would set my life on any chance*
> *To mend it or be rid on't.*

(the italics are mine)

The specifics change with every author, poet and playwright who appropriates it—that's to be expected—but the core of the character remains essentially the same, a singular feat when you consider it has been employed by authors as diverse as William Shakespeare and Elmore Leonard. Even more amazing is that the narrative structures of these stories have also remained fixed. While professional killers have fascinated writers for centuries, there are for the most part only two kinds of hit man story—each with its own set of variables, each with its own set of rules.

● ● ●

Type one, the "Metamorphosis tale," is the less common of the two and has a scenario much like the sample which follows.

(1) The killer is introduced. Usually a male, blue collar, luckless though still pursuing acceptable means of improving his situation—he is not a killer when the story begins. He has few friends, none very close. If he is married, he is apathetically so. What is most important here is the killer's relationship to his surroundings—*there is no contrast between the two.* Though he is aware of the banality of his situation, he is also perfectly suited to it. This is not to say that he is resigned, quite the contrary. In fiction, as in life, realization rarely connotes acceptance. Take this passage from "When This Man Dies," by Lawrence Block:

> He went on doing his work from one day to the next, working with the quiet desperation of a man who knows his income, while better than nothing, will never quite get around to equaling his expenditures. He went to the track twice, won thirty dollars one night, lost twenty-three the next.

The hero's quiet desperation is suffused with the knowledge of his placement as it relates to the other—he merely survives while those around him thrive. His self-awareness is defined by his inability to act in any decisive way—the climax of a "Metamorphosis tale" is inaction brought to its highest power. In the beginning of all stories told in this mode, the hero embodies one of life's most terrifying prospects (certainly one more terrifying than death!): he is exactly equal to the sum of his parts.

(2) The beginnings of initiation.

> Murder is a negative creation, and every murderer is therefore the rebel who claims the right to be omnipotent. His pathos is his refusal to suffer.   — W.H. Auden

As the banality of the situation verges on suffocating the hero, a way out is presented: murder as vocation. He immediately disregards the possibility, but his arguments against it (which are most often morality arguments used to strengthen the hero's sympathetic bond with the audience) lack conviction. The real obstacle is his fear of the consequences naturally contingent upon the imposition of disorder in order—the wake that focused action inevitably leaves. There is always the possibility, as was the case with Macbeth and his wife, that the world of order will somehow reform and crush that which sought to alter it. Look at these lines from

"The Assassins," a brilliant—if almost completely unknown—prose riff done by Percy Bysshe Shelley in 1814:

> To produce immediate pain or disorder for the sake of future benefit, is consonant, indeed, with the purest religion and philosophy, but never fails to excite invincible repugnance in the feelings of many. Against their predilections and distaste an Assassin, accidentally the inhabitant of a civilized community, would wage unremitting hostility from principle. He would find himself compelled to adopt means which they would abhor, for the sake of an object which they could not conceive that he should propose himself. Secure and self-enshrined in the magnificence and pre-eminence of his conceptions, spotless as the light of heaven, he would be the victim among men of calumny and persecution. Incapable of distinguishing his motives, they would rank him among the vilest and most atrocious criminals.

The professional killer is at ease with the possible consequences of his actions because his forays into the daily world are brief—he is not of that which he alters. The initiate's ultimate success depends largely upon his ability to break from the society of men (Shelley's "civilized community") and survive in the margins. To do that, he must completely embrace what amounts to the nihilist's call to personal responsibility: futile action is no viable means of confronting the world, only action which alters carries weight.

(3) The situation worsens. The hero adheres to his old methods of operation even though the hopelessness of his situation is steadily increasing. It is important to note that there is nothing in the hero's life that can be of any assistance to him in the making of this decision. There is rarely any family and no faith in organized religion. Once the initiation is complete, this lack of faith is replaced by a fanatical belief in his own personal code of conduct. Every decision he makes thereafter is in keeping with his code and, while its strict observance is never enough to subdue the world, it makes his being in the world a gallant gesture.

(4) The killer acts—the murder is completed. The deed done, the killer is nervous and expects arrest (Note: once the transformation is complete, the moral question is never again raised. It is not, *should I have done this thing?* but rather, *can I get away with it?, can I succeed?*). Time passes and when it becomes obvious the job was a success, he relaxes and marvels at how easy it was, the implication being that if he had just *acted in the first place,* he could have saved a great deal of time and trouble. (Macbeth, again, this time from the soliloquy beginning I.vii: "If it were done, when t'is done, then t'were well/it were done quickly.") Here as in the "Utopia tale" (the description of which follows) intellectual contemplation is portrayed as the cause of problems, a hindrance to personal progress. Professional killers are successful men freed from the moral seriousness which necessarily attends contemplative thought. They are pure action—they *do*. This is why so many of these stories are short, written in a sparse—if not exactly hard-boiled, certainly non-lyrical—style.

There is social criticism implicit in the "Metamorphosis tale." The underlying questions in all of the stories written in this mode are these: what kind of society would so neglect its members that they would see murder as a viable means of self-support? How can the danger inherent in the life of a professional murderer pale in comparison to the unremitting banality in which a man lives? Given the desperate situations in which many people live, the evolution from non-entity to killer seems an almost natural progression. These lines from chapter 3 of Shelley's "The Assassins" could well apply to the way in which the hero of the "Metamorphosis tale"—the successful transformation—engages the world by story's end:

> Thy createst—'tis mine to ruin and destroy.—I was thy slave—I am thy equal, and thy foe.

• • •

There are certain elements all hit man stories share, for example, the killer is always a disinterested third party—something that sets hit man fiction apart from standard crime and detective fiction which focuses on the full realization of the bleaker human emotions: hate, fear, jealousy, *et al*. Hit men represent the perfect rupture of the relationship between cause and effect, something regular fiction (and certainly crime and mystery fiction!) cannot tolerate. As Auden makes clear in his essay, "The Guilty Vicarage," the first requirement for a successful detective story is a closed society in a state of grace. Mystery and detective fiction depend upon the society's original (apparent) innocence being altered by the unimaginable act: the murder; and then restored by the apprehension of the fallen member. It falls apart unless every member of the given society is a likely suspect— take the novel, *And Then There Were None*, by Agatha Christie (also published as *Ten Little Indians*). The best example of the kind of closed society that is so crucial to mystery fiction, it features a cast of ten characters stranded on Indian Island, a small, privately-owned rock completely isolated from the Devon coast. All ten have been asked to the island for the weekend by a mysterious host whose motives are completely unknown and who never makes an appearance. Shortly after dinner on the first night, a gruesome phonograph recording is played in which the sins of each member of the party (the perfectly closed society) are detailed. At this point, the apparent innocence of the society is called into question, but not yet altered—accusations of past transgressions, whether true or false, are simply hearsay. The necessary alteration is not achieved until the first confirmed murder occurs—that of young Anthony Marston at the end of chapter four, a victim of poison in his after-dinner drink. As the story progresses, suspicion falls on each one of the surviving characters in turn because it is obvious the murders are being committed by one of them, the breakdown is internal. As a consequence—and this is especially true of *And Then There Were None* though it could be said with equal certainty about almost any decent example of the genre—no one is innocent.

But in the hit man story, the innocence of the affected society is never altered. There is a victim—a body—so it follows by obvious logic that someone is responsible for its appearance, that at least one member of the society has fallen from grace; but, because of the rupture of cause and effect, it is impossible to determine which one, and resolution in the classic sense is impossible. This, of course, is the crux of the most interesting paradox: because hit men are employed as experts in endings, hit man stories are not about conflict—their focus is entirely on resolution.

• • •

The issue of open and closed societies—the profound effect a marginalized other can have on the mainstream—raises the question of open and closed space, the moral implication of distance. The mastery of time-as-space (duration), as has been mentioned in the outline of the "Metamorphosis tale," is a crucial factor in the making of a professional killer—as Lafcadio exclaims near the end of André Gide's novel *Lafcadio's Adventures* (first published as *The Vatican Swindle* in November, 1925), "What a gulf between the imagination and the deed!" In these stories, professional killers are able to eliminate that gulf easily, precisely because of their own marginalization—as Shelley points out, "[t]ime was measured and created by the vices and miseries of men, between whom and the happy nation of the Assassins, there was no analogy nor comparison." But there remains a tension between the hit man and his moral relationship to physical distance. The same situation which allows for such a complete mastery of time—the fact that he is not of that which alters—interferes with his mastery of the deed. The distance between the killer and the victim must be closed completely if the act is to have merit. Take these lines from chapter 21 of the novel, *The Assignment,* by Friedrich Dürrenmatt, in which the post-engagement feelings of Achilles, a bomber pilot who flew missions from *The Kitty Hawk* during Vietnam, are described:

> . . . and after the attack he did not feel himself a hero but a coward, there was a dark suspicion in him sometimes that an SS henchman at Auschwitz had behaved more morally than he, because he had been confronted with his victims, even though he regarded them as subhuman trash, while between himself and his victims no confrontation took place, the victims weren't even subhuman, just an unspecified something, it wasn't very different from exterminating insects, the pilot spraying the vines from his plane couldn't see the mosquitoes either, and no matter what you called it, bombing, destroying, liquidating, pacifying, it was abstract, mechanical, and could only be understood as a sum, probably a financial sum . . .

The more skilled the assassin—the more professionally honest—the closer he can get to the target. This issue was dealt with beautifully by Luc Besson in *The Professional,* his first American film since *La Femme Nikita.* The hit man, Leon (Jean Reno in a role very similar to the one he played in *La Femme Nikita*), against his better judgment, takes in a young girl, Matilda, (played by Natalie Portman) whose family is killed by a gang of rogue DEA agents. To his surprise she is not shocked or repulsed when she finds out what he does for a living. On the contrary, she asks him to teach her how to become an assassin so she can find the men responsible for her four-year-old brother's death (he was the only member of the family she cared for) and right the wrong. After much argument and discussion, he agrees to teach her the theory behind the profession and goes to his middleman (Danny Aiello) to collect the rifle he used as a beginner. The middleman is surprised that such a highly skilled professional would ask for a rifle and, when questioned about it, Leon explains (with no small amount of embarrassment) that he just wants to keep in shape, that the rifle is only for practice. What follows is one of the best scenes in this, or any other movie in this genre. On a roof top in New York City, Leon explains to Matilda the exact meaning of distance and the necessary progression from amateur to professional:

> The rifle is the first weapon you learn how to use because it lets you keep your distance from the client. The closer you get to being a pro, the closer you can get to the client. The knife, for example, is the last thing you learn.

In the hierarchy of murder and its practitioners, hit men are revered as artists. They (and their employers) think of the sniper, the psychopath and the passion killer as unskilled labor, their deeds as the uncouth graffiti slung roughly on an alley wall. Any coward can kill from a distance—it requires no special skill or understanding. Though murder is any form is morally reprehensible, there is something thrilling about the assassin who sneaks unnoticed through ranks of heavily-armed guards and dispatches his mark quickly, quietly, without any wasted motion or fanfare—just as there is something peculiarly pathetic and ugly about the cuckold who disengages the breaks on his wife's car so that it will crash sometime later, miles from home. Regarding this crisis of distance and its effect on the aesthetics of the deed, Thomas De Quincey exclaimed in the first paper on his treatise, "On Murder Considered as One of the Fine Arts," which originally appeared in *Blackwood's Magazine* in February 1827, "Fie on these dealers in poison, say I: can they not keep to the old honest way of cutting throats . . ."

• • •

The second type of hit man story is the "Utopia tale." The hit men of the "Utopia tale" are the modern take on the ideal suggested by Sir Thomas More in 1516—they represent the possibility of regimentation and efficiency without subservience. As Peter, in Book I of *Utopia* exclaims: "Service not servitude. . . ." Heroes here are professionals from the start. They can be, but most likely are not, freelance operators. They are usually affiliated with a crime family or other sub-legal organization. Because the initiations are already complete, this type of story has a simpler narrative than that of the "Metamorphosis tale" and is consistent with the outline below.

(1) **The killer is introduced.** He is usually well-dressed, educated (not necessarily in the traditional sense), with a striking self-awareness and self-assuredness which has its basis in the deed; after all, he is the man who controls life and death. He is usually unmarried and his friends are those he works with, if he works with anyone. As with the "Metamorphosis tale," what is happening on the periphery is of the utmost importance, but for very different reasons. Here, the contrast between the killers and what is going on around them is what provides the punch—the point being that *there is a contrast*. In these stories, normalcy exists in complete ignorance of the irony it provides. The sinister is run gently up against the every-day. In the "Utopia tale" there is no detectable disturbance of the atmosphere one naturally assumes accompanies the presence of those who deal in

human destruction, there is nothing to suggest that all is not well with one's small corner of the world. But this sense of rightness and security is based on the false assumption that there are no killers lurking in the peripheries of the sit-coms. Take these lines from Mark Rudman's book-length poem *Rider* and note the devastating effect the last line, when the margins cozy up to the mainstream:

> the tuna casseroles and macaroni and cheese
>
> making the rounds, apple sauce
> passing from high chair to bib, the Wonder Bread
> on a calcified plate,
> children eating, heads down in silence,
> communicating through eye movements,
> the mother wiping her lips, the father
> grinning stupidly and drooling;
>
> the television quacking in the background,
> the perfect suburban night unfolding
> in bedroom and drive-in and den,
> the sprinkler system ticking.
> The snipers in the tower—.

Notice Rudman's last line is not given any more emphasis than any of the lines that precede it—for all its power, it is their syntactic equal. There is (as yet) no intersection—though complete opposites, the suburban world and the marginal world are pacing each other, each progressing in the same direction, at the same rate, by means of an identical linear framework. The result of this parallelism, which is present in nearly all hit man stories of the "Utopia" variety, is the amplification of presence and credibility of that which is necessarily viewed by the assimilated individual as unreal. Part of the reason hit men are so fascinating is that their actions are continually substantiated by their incredible, rational proximity to our own.

Look at Hemingway's short story, "The Killers." After Nick warns Ole Anderson that there are two men looking to kill him, he talks to Anderson's landlady, a woman whose stubborn normalcy remains unshaken in the face of events. Keep in mind, while this conversation is taking place, a marked man is lying on a cot upstairs waiting for two professional killers to find him.

> "He's been in his room all day," The landlady said down-stairs. "I guess he don't feel well. I said to him: 'Mr. Anderson, you ought to go out and take a walk on a nice fall day like this,' but he didn't feel like it."

"He doesn't want to go out."

"I'm sorry he don't feel well," the woman said. "He's an awfully nice man . . ."

Likewise the dinner scene in *Shelter*: Mrs. Downey, a suburban housewife and mother of three hears a commotion in the den across the hall from where her family is enjoying Christmas dinner (and note that Auden in his essay specifically mentions the Christmas dinner in the country house as one of the perfect examples of a closed society—here, because of the hit man, it is allowed to maintain its state of grace.) She goes to investigate, thinking her daughter's high school boyfriend and his business associate (both of whom have dropped by unexpectedly) might need assistance. What she's hearing: two hit men fighting to the death in her front room.

BOOM!, Sal connects with a sharp blow to Bennie's rib cage, and follows instantaneously with a two-handed uppercut that sends Bennie up and back flattening a Christmas present as he lands. Sal pauses to pick his cigarette back up off the carpet. Bennie crawls toward the fireplace grabbing the Yule log and swinging back with it—connecting hard with Sal's ankle. Sal falls to his knees. Bennie swings again, but Sal grabs the log, using it to throw himself into a sweeping round-house. Sal's loaded fist (*loaded with a pewter figurine of the Christ Child*—my aside) catches Bennie's jaw, knocking him out cold.

MRS. DOWNEY
(through the door)

Is everything okay in there?

Sal grabs his cigarette from the floor again and limps to the door. He opens it a crack, and speaks quietly to Mrs. Downey.

SAL

He's not taking it very well I'm afraid. Give him a minute.

Mrs. Downey nods, and Sal closes the door.

MRS. DOWNEY
(to Bobby)

What a sweet man!

Sal throws the poinsettias from a vase, and splashes the water on Bernie's face. Grabbing him by the collar, he presses a sharp table knife to the groggy man's neck.

Of course, it is possible for the opposite to occur—the mainstream, by some accident, entering the outskirts—but it's rare. Those tales are most closely akin to "Metamorphosis tales" in that they feature an uninitiated other entering the foreign territory. The difference is that the other, in these cases, is able to return to the world he left—changed, to be sure, but not transformed. Of this variety, Robert Lowell's poem "Memories of West Street and Lepke," (and particularly the story behind how it came to be written) is the best example.

The Story: America entered the Second World War (officially) at 4:10 pm Eastern Standard Time on December 8, 1941—one day after the Japanese bombing of Pearl Harbor. Robert Lowell registered for the draft and spent the remainder of that year, as well as the whole of 1942, trying to enlist. He was repeatedly deferred (as Ian Hamilton noted in his biography of Lowell published in 1982, there was even some talk of Lowell being permanently deferred because of poor eyesight). During the summer of 1943, however, he was examined by the draft board for the seventh time and given a date on which to report for induction: September 8, 1943. Lowell spent the remainder of that summer rethinking the prospect of his, now inevitable, military service and in the first week of September he came to the decision that, since the war was essentially over and the position of the allies was no longer a defensive one, he could not serve in good conscience. He wrote a letter to President Roosevelt, along with a statement detailing his position, in which he expressed his deep regret at not being able to accept his country's call to duty. On October 13, 1943, Robert Lowell was arraigned in New York City on the charge of draft evasion and sentenced to one year and one day to be served in the Federal Correctional Center at Danbury, Connecticut. While waiting to be transferred, he was confined at New York's West Street Jail where he met the man who would later become the center of one of his greatest poems. The following is an excerpt from an interview conducted by Ian Hamilton with one of Lowell's fellow inmates at West Street. It ends chapter 6 of Hamilton's biography:

> Lowell was in a cell nest to Lepke, you know, Murder Incorporated, and Lepke says to him: "I'm in for killing. What are you in for?" [*And Lowell says*] "Oh, I'm in for refusing to kill." And Lepke burst out laughing. It was kind of ironic.

(2) The job is outlined. The victim is mentioned, his location, sometimes his background and, occasionally, the reason he is to be killed—though the last, it should be said, is a rarity. Look at this exchange in Bukowski's "Hit Man" and note the necessary rupture of cause and effect:

"Can I ask you one thing?" [Ronnie, the hit man]
"Sure"
"Why?"
"Why?"
"Yes, why?"
"Do you care?"
"No."
"Then why ask?"

The fee is negotiated if it has not been already and a time is decided upon. This is the only contact the hit man has with the person who is contracting the job. His presence is distasteful to his employers—a constant reminder of their own mortality, the fact that their own lives are probably worth no more than their intended victim's, what they are paying the killer for the contract. In a world where success and stability depend—in large part—on who you know and the safe, predictable exchange of favors, the man successful on his own (and because of his dedication and skill!) is a terrific threat, an unknown quantity. One of the most interesting aspects of the professional killer is how at ease he is with his own marginalization; he has no desire to establish anything more that the briefest of working relationships with those in the center of the activity—in short, the feeling is mutual. In Thomas Perry's novel, *The Butcher's Boy*, the hit man flies to Las Vegas after the completion of the contract to await payment and recuperate from wounds sustained in an attempted mugging in Denver. He's not in Las Vegas four hours before the powers-that-be send someone to find out exactly what he's doing there—whether or not he's working. But look as these lines from chapter 29:

It had never occurred to him [the hit man] to wonder where Orloff lived until he'd hired the Cruiser to watch him. He had little interest in the brokers and middlemen. He knew and accepted the fact that he wasn't the sort of man they'd want to spend time with, even if he hadn't been dangerous. And if Orloff had invited him there he would have been insulted. He did the work and took the money, but he would have resented any presumption that he cared who gave it to him, or took any interest in the problems and personalities that provided him with a market for his services.

(3) **The murder is completed.** The victim is eliminated and the killer falls back into the regularity of his life while he waits for another job. There is never any philosophical self-recrimination on the part of the hit man, there is never any moral doubt. And it should be noted that here, as in

the "Metamorphosis tale," the hit man's code of conduct assumes the role otherwise played by organized religion—with one difference: in the "Utopia tale," religion is more than just a regrettable absence. It is portrayed as either a nebulous waymaker to sloppiness and imprecision, or a random malevolent force, something that, quite literally in some cases (don't forget—Sal, in *Shelter*, is using a pewter figurine of the Christ Child as a punching block!), dulls the senses. Look at "In the Beginning," by Ian McEwan, an excerpt from a novel in progress (originally published in *The New Yorker*, June 26, 1995) which is told from the point of view of the intended victim, a man who has been targeted because of lectures he has given regarding the possible genetic basis for religious practice. Notice how he describes the hit men, just before they shoot the wrong person:

> Both men wore black coats that gave them a priestly look. There was ceremony in their stillness.

It is also worth noting that "In the Beginning" is loosely based on historical fact—specifically, the controversy which erupted following the publication of the Harvard biologist E.O. Wilson's *Sociobiology: the New Synthesis*, in the summer of 1975.

The theory behind sociobiology, that human social behavior is genetically based, encountered furious opposition, not the least of which from Wilson's own friends and colleagues. Shortly after *Sociobiology* was published, a number of scientists (including Stephen Jay Gould and Richard Lewontin) formed The Sociobiology Study Group, a group designed to provide a forum for their feelings of outrage. Though they, of course, never thought of hiring hit men, they did publish a letter in *The New York Review of Books* on November 13, 1975, which—perilously close to character assassination as it was—might have done even more damage. In that letter, they stated that Sociobiology was not only bad science but also politically dangerous, going so far as to link Wilson and his theories with racist eugenics and Nazi policies. One of the more notable results of this opposition was that—as Wilson comments in his autobiography, *Naturalist*—it marked perhaps ". . . the only occasion in recent American history on which a scientist was physically attacked, however mildly simply for the expression of an idea." (The episode to which Wilson is referring occurred in January 1978 at the annual meeting of the American Association for the Advancement of Science. Demonstrators seized the stage just as he was about to give a speech, dumped a bucket of ice water on his head and chanted "Wilson, you're all wet!") McEwan makes quick reference to the actual scandal as the story moves away from the beginning:

But anger rose against my assertion that, since religious practice was universal to all known societies, it must have a genetic base and therefore be the product of evolutionary pressure. I invoked E.O. Wilson: "Religions, like all other human institutions, evolve so as to enhance the persistence and influence of their practitioners."

• • •

As mentioned above, the hit men of the "Utopia tale" represent More's "service, not servitude" ideal; the triumph of reason over emotion. Take, for example, the brief explanation of what it is to be a hit man, delivered by Max Von Sydow to Robert Redford at the end of *Three Days of the Condor:*

No need to believe in either side—or any side. There is no cause. There is only yourself. The belief is in your own precision.

Here, too, is an underlying social criticism, but of a different variety than that of the "Metamorphosis tale"—here there is no attempt at laying blame. That the hit men in these tales are victims of societal neglect is, perhaps in some cases, implied but never clear—nor is it important. All transformations are complete before the story begins. The crucial thing to note here is that the hired killers are portrayed as members of cultures in upheaval who have adapted successfully. It is no accident that Jiri Kajanë, an author whose work has never been formally published in his native Albania because of his precarious standing before the revolution and the industrial paralysis which followed, finds the character of the hit man a relevant trope.

Despite Albania's fanatical isolationism (as late as 1984, official business was the only reason Albanian citizens were allowed out of the country) they were not exempt from the economic and political problems which plagued and continue to plague, the former communist countries. Though "The Same, Only Different!" was written after the anti-climactic Albanian revolution of the early 1990s (and Kajanë's view of his native country is constantly touched with anti-climax—notice that the hit woman, the character whose job it is to act decisively, is brought in from Romania), the troubles which lead to it began 12 years earlier, when China withdrew all economic support. This devastating withdrawal was followed three years later—on December 18, 1981—by the mysterious suicide of the Albanian Prime Minister, Mehmet Shehu, which gave rise to an intense clandestine campaign of purges of party leaders which continued through all 1982. Many of those who were close to the former prime minister were murdered or imprisoned. Kajanë, as early as the mid-1980s, was witness to what the article, "The Thrill of the Kill," (*Psychology Today,* January/

February 1993) reports as new information, that contractual murder is the "fastest growing profession in the East."

In a letter written to his American translators shortly after the revolution, Kajanë describes how "The Same Only Different!" came to be written as a means to an answer. During a visit to Vlorë (a small town on the coast of the Adriatic Sea, 100km South/Southwest of the capital, Tiranë), his niece grilled him with questions of the strange spring days which have become synonymous with the onset of the revolution. Her parents, Kajanë's brother and sister-in-law, like so many Albanians, refuse to speak of it. In the final paragraph of the letter, he writes:

> That following week, still trying to formulate some sort of response, I wrote "The Same Only Different!" Of course I never came up with a definite answer—. Was it [the revolution] a beginning? Yes, for some. Was it an end? I suppose. Mostly though, it just felt like a welcome respite from my otherwise monotonous struggle to survive.

JAY HOPLER
Baltimore/Iowa City—1995

from
THIS GUN FOR HIRE

Graham Greene

CHAPTER I

Murder didn't mean much to Raven. It was just a new
job. You had to be careful. You had to use your brains. It was not a
question of hatred. He had only seen the minister once: he had
been pointed out to Raven as he walked down the new housing
estate between the little lit Christmas trees—an old, rather grubby
man without any friends, who was said to love humanity.

The cold wind cut his face in the wide continental street.
It was a good excuse for turning the collar of his coat well up
above his mouth. A harelip was a serious handicap in his profession. It had been badly sewn in infancy, so that now the upper-
lip was twisted and scarred. When you carried about you so easy
an identification you couldn't help becoming ruthless in your
methods. It had always, from the first, been necessary for Raven to
eliminate the evidence.

He carried an attaché case. He looked like any other youngish man going home after his work: his dark overcoat had a clerical air. He moved steadily up the street like hundreds of his kind. A tram went by, lit up in the early dusk: he didn't take it. An economical young man, you might have thought, saving money for his home. Perhaps even now he was on his way to meet his girl.

But Raven had never had a girl. The harelip prevented that. He had learned, when he was very young, how repulsive it was. He turned in to one of the tall gray houses and climbed the stairs, a sour, bitter, screwed-up figure.

Outside the top flat he put down his attaché case and put on gloves. He took a pair of clippers out of his pocket and cut through the telephone wire where it ran out from above the door to the lift shaft. Then he rang the bell.

He hoped to find the minister alone. This little top-floor flat was the socialist's home. He lived in a poor, bare solitary way, and Raven had been told that his secretary always left him at half-past six—he was very considerate with his employees. But Raven was a minute too early and the minister half an hour too late. A woman opened the door, an elderly woman with pince-nez and several gold teeth. She had her hat on, and her coat was over her arm. She had been on the point of leaving, and she was furious at being caught. She didn't allow him to speak, but snapped at him in German, "The minister is engaged."

He wanted to spare her, not because he minded a killing but because his employers might prefer him not to exceed his instructions. He held the letter of introduction out to her silently: as long as she didn't hear his foreign voice or see his harelip she was safe. She took the letter bitterly and held it up close to her pince-nez. Good, he thought, she's shortsighted. "Stay where you are," she said and walked primly back up the passage. He could hear her disapproving governess' voice, then she was back in the passage, saying, "The minister will see you. Follow me, please." He couldn't understand the foreign speech, but he knew what she meant from her behavior.

His eyes, like little concealed cameras, photographed the room instantaneously: the desk, the easy chair, the map on the wall, the door to the bedroom behind, the wide window above the bright cold Christmas street. A little oil stove was all the heating, and the minister was using it now to boil a saucepan. A kitchen alarm clock on the desk marked seven o'clock. A voice said, "Emma, put another egg in the saucepan." The minister came out from the bedroom. He had tried to tidy himself, but he had forgotten the cigarette ash on his trousers. He was old and small and rather dirty. The secretary took an egg out of one of the drawers in the desk. "And the salt. Don't forget the salt," the minister said. He explained in slow English, "It prevents the shell cracking. Sit down, my friend. Make yourself at home. Emma, you can go."

Raven sat down and fixed his eyes on the minister's chest. He thought, I'll give her three minutes by the alarm clock to get well away. He kept his eyes on the minister's chest: Just there I'll shoot. He let his coat collar fall and saw with bitter rage how the old man turned away from the sight of his harelip.

The minister said, "It's years since I heard from him. But I've never forgotten him, never. I can show you his photograph in the other room. It's good of him to think of an old friend. So rich and powerful, too. You must ask him when you go back if he remembers the time—" A bell began to ring furiously.

Raven thought, the telephone. I cut the wire. It shook his nerve. But it was only the alarm clock drumming on the desk. The minister turned it off. "One egg's boiled," he said and stooped for the saucepan. Raven opened his attaché case: in the lid he had fixed his automatic fitted with a silencer. The minister said, "I'm sorry the bell made you jump. You see, I like my egg just four minutes."

Feet ran along the passage. The door opened. Raven turned furiously in his seat, his harelip flushed and raw. It was the secretary. He thought, my God, what a household. They won't let a man do things tidily. He forgot his lip, he was angry; he had a grievance. She came in flashing her gold teeth, prim and ingratiating. She said, "I was just going out when I heard the telephone." Then she winced slightly, looked the other way, showed a clumsy delicacy before his deformity which he couldn't help noticing. It condemned her. He snatched the automatic out of the case and shot the minister twice in the back.

The minister fell across the oil stove; the saucepan upset, and the two eggs broke on the floor. Raven shot the minister once more in the head, leaning across the desk to make quite certain, driving the bullet hard into the base of the skull, smashing it open like a china doll's. Then he turned on the secretary. She moaned at him; she hadn't any words; the old mouth couldn't hold its saliva. He supposed she was begging him for mercy. He pressed the trigger again; she staggered as if she had been kicked by an animal in the side. But he had miscalculated. Her unfashionable dress, the swathes of useless material in which she hid her body, perhaps confused him. And she was tough, so tough he couldn't believe his eyes: she was through the door before he could fire again, slamming it behind her.

But she couldn't lock it: the key was on his side. He twisted the handle and pushed. The elderly woman had amazing strength: it only gave two inches. She began to scream some word at the top of her voice.

There was no time to waste. He stood away from the door and shot twice through the woodwork. He could hear the pince-nez fall on the floor and break. The voice screamed again and stopped: there was a sound outside as if she were sobbing. It was her breath going out through her wounds. Raven was satisfied. He turned back to the minister.

There was a clue he had been ordered to leave; a clue he had to remove. The letter of introduction was on the desk. He put it in his pocket, and between the minister's stiffened fingers he inserted a scrap of paper. Raven had little curiosity: he had only glanced at the introduction, and the nickname at its foot conveyed nothing to him: he was a man who could be depended on. Now he looked round the small bare room to see whether there was any clue he had overlooked. The suitcase and the automatic he was to leave behind. It was all very simple.

He opened the bedroom door. His eyes again photographed the scene: the single bed, the wooden chair, the dusty chest of drawers, a photograph of a young Jew with a small scar on his chin as if he had been struck there with a club, a pair of brown wooden hairbrushes initialed J. K., everywhere cigarette ash—the home of a lonely untidy old man; the home of the minister for war.

A low voice whispered an appeal quite distinctly through the door. Raven picked up the automatic again. Who would have imagined an old woman could be so tough? It touched his nerve a little just in the same way as the bell had done, as if a ghost were interfering with a man's job. He opened the study door—he had to push it against the weight of her body. She looked dead enough, but he made quite sure with his automatic almost touching her eyes.

It was time to be gone. He took the automatic with him.

2

They sat and shivered side by side as the dusk came down. They were borne in their bright small smoky cage above the streets. The bus rocked down to Hammersmith. The shop windows sparkled like ice. "Look," she said, "it's snowing." A few large flakes went drifting by as they crossed the bridge, falling like paper scraps into the dark Thames.

He said, "I'm happy as long as this ride goes on."

"We're seeing each other tomorrow—Jimmy." She always hesitated before his name. It was a silly name for anyone of such bulk and gravity.

He said, "It's the nights that bother me, Anne."

She laughed. "It's going to be wearing." But immediately she became serious. "I'm happy, too." About happiness she was always serious; she preferred to laugh when she was miserable. She couldn't avoid being serious about things she cared for, and happiness made her grave at the thought of all the things that might destroy it. She said, "It would be dreadful now if there was a war."

"There won't be a war."

"The last one started with a murder."

"That was an archduke. This is just an old politician."

She said, "Be careful. You'll break the record—Jimmy."

"Damn the record."

She began to hum the tune she'd bought it for: "It's only Kew to You," and the large flakes fell past the window, melted on the pavement: "a snowflower a man brought from Greenland."

He said, "It's a silly song."

She said, "It's a lovely song—Jimmy. I simply can't call you Jimmy. You aren't Jimmy. You're outsize. Detective Sergeant Mather. You're the reason why people make jokes about policemen's boots."

"What's wrong with dear, anyway?"

"Dear, dear." She tried it out on the tip of her tongue, between lips as vividly stained as a winter berry. "Oh no," she decided, "it's cold. I'll call you that when we've been married ten years."

"Well—darling?"

"Darling, darling. I don't like it. It sounds as if I'd known you a long, long time." The bus went up the hill past the fish-and-chip shops. A brazier glowed, and they could smell the roasting chestnuts. The ride was nearly over; there were only two more streets and a turn to the left by the church, which was already visible, the spire lifted like a long icicle above the houses. The nearer they got to home the more miserable she became, the nearer they got to home the more lightly she talked. She was keeping things off and out of mind: the peeling wallpaper, the long flights to her room, cold supper with Mrs Brewer and next day the walk to the agent's, perhaps a job again in the provinces away from him.

Mather said heavily, "You don't care for me like I care for you. It's nearly twenty-four hours before I see you again."

"It'll be more than that if I get a job."

"You don't care. You simply don't care."

She clutched his arm. "Look. Look at that poster." But it was gone before he could see it through the steamy pane. "Europe Mobilizing" lay like a weight on her heart.

"What was it?"

"Oh, just the same old murder again."

"You've got that murder on your mind. It's a week old now. It's got nothing to do with us."

"No, it hasn't, has it?"

"If it had happened here, we'd have caught him by now."

"I wonder why he did it."

"Politics. Patriotism."

"Well. Here we are. It might be a good thing to get off. Don't look so miserable. I thought you said you were happy?"

"That was five minutes ago."

"Oh," she said out of her light and heavy heart, "one lives quickly these days." They kissed under the lamp; she had to stretch to reach him. He was comforting like a large dog, even when he was sullen and stupid, but one didn't have to send away a dog alone in the cold dark night.

"Anne," he said, "we'll be married, won't we, after Christmas?"

"We haven't a penny," she said, "you know. Not a penny—Jimmy."

"I'll get a rise."

"You'll be late for duty."

"Damn it, you don't care."

She jeered at him, "Not a scrap—dear," and walked away from him up the street to number 54, praying, Let me get some money quick; let *this* go on *this* time. She hadn't any faith in herself. A man passed her going up the road. He looked cold and strung-up as he passed in his black overcoat. He had a harelip. Poor devil, she thought, and forgot him, opening the door of 54, climbing the long flights to the top floor (the carpet stopped on the first). Putting on the new record, hugging to her heart the silly, senseless words, the slow, sleepy tune:

It's only Kew
To you,
But to me
It's Paradise.
They are only blue
Petunias to you,
But to me
They are your eyes.

The man with the harelip came back down the street. Fast walking hadn't made him warm; like Kay in *The Snow Queen* he bore the cold within him as he walked. The flakes went on falling, melting into slush on the pavement: the words of a song dropped from the lit room on the third floor, the scrape of a used needle.

They say that's a snowflower
A man brought from Greenland.
I say it's the lightness, the coolness, the whiteness
Of your hand.

The man hardly paused. He went on down the street, walking fast. He felt no pain from the chip of ice in his breast.

3

Raven sat at an empty table in the Corner House near a marble pillar. He stared with distaste at the long list of sweet iced drinks, of parfaits and sundaes and coupes and splits. Somebody at the next little table was eating brown bread and butter and drinking Horlick's. He wilted under Raven's gaze and put up his newspaper. One word, "Ultimatum," ran across the top line.

Mr Cholmondeley picked his way between the tables.

He was fat and wore an emerald ring. His wide square face fell in folds over his collar. He looked like a real-estate man or perhaps a man more than usually successful in selling women's belts. He sat down at Raven's table and said, "Good evening."

Raven said, "I thought you were never coming, Mr Chol-mon-deley," pronouncing every syllable.

"Chumley, my dear man, Chumley," Mr Cholmondeley corrected him.

"It doesn't matter how it's pronounced. I don't suppose it's your own name."

"After all, I chose it," Mr Cholmondeley said. His ring flashed under the great inverted bowls of light as he turned the pages of the menu. "Have a parfait."

"It's odd wanting to eat ice in this weather. You've only got to stay outside if you're hot. I don't want to waste any time, Mr Chol-mon-deley. Have you brought the money? I'm broke."

Mr Cholmondeley said, "They do a very good Maiden's Dream. Not to speak of Alpine Glow. Or the Knickerbocker Glory."

"I haven't had a thing since Calais."

"Give me the letter," Mr Cholmondeley said. "Thank you." He told the waitress, "I'll have an Alpine Glow with a glass of kümmel over it."

"The money," Raven said.

"Here in this case."

"They are all fivers."

"You can't expect to be paid two hundred in small change. And it's nothing to do with me," Mr Cholmondeley said. "I'm merely the agent." His eyes softened as they rested on a Raspberry Split at the next table. He confessed wistfully to Raven, "I've got a sweet tooth."

"Don't you want to hear about it?" Raven said. "The old woman—"

"Please, please," Mr Cholmondeley said, "I want to hear nothing. I'm just an agent. I take no responsibility. My clients—"

Raven twisted his harelip at him with sour contempt. "That's a fine name for them."

"How long the waitress is with my parfait," Mr Cholmondeley complained. "My clients are really quite the best people. These acts of violence—they regard them as war."

"And I and the old man . . ." Raven said.

"Are in the front trench." He began to laugh softly at his own humor. His great white open face was like a curtain on which you can throw grotesque images: a rabbit, a man with horns. His small eyes twinkled with pleasure at the mass of iced cream that was borne toward him in a tall glass. He said, "You did your work very well, very neatly. They are quite satisfied with you. You'll be able to take a long holiday now." He was fat, he was vulgar, he was false, but he gave an impression of great power as he sat there with the cream dripping from his mouth. He was prosperity, he was one of those who possessed things; but Raven possessed nothing but the contents of the wallet, the clothes he stood up in, the harelip, the automatic he should have left behind.

He said, "I'll be moving."

"Good-bye, my man, good-bye," Mr Cholmondeley said, sucking through a straw.

Raven rose and went. Dark and thin and made for destruction, he wasn't at ease among the little tables, among the bright fruit drinks. He went out into the Circus and up Shaftesbury Avenue. The shop windows were full of tinsel and hard red Christmas berries. It maddened him, the sentiment of it. His hands clenched in his pockets. He leaned his face against a modiste's window and jeered silently through the glass. A Jewish girl with a neat curved figure bent over a dummy. He fed his eyes contemptuously on her legs and hips; so much flesh, he thought, on sale in the Christmas window.

A kind of subdued cruelty drove him into the shop. He let his harelip loose on the girl when she came toward him with the same pleasure that he might have turned a machine gun on a picture gallery. He said, "That dress in the window. How much?"

She said, "Five guineas." She wouldn't "sir" him. His lip was like a badge of class. It revealed the poverty of parents who couldn't afford a clever surgeon.

He said, "It's pretty, isn't it?"

She lisped at him genteely, "It's been vewwy much admired."

"Soft. Thin. You'd have to take care of a dress like that, eh? Do for someone pretty and well off?"

She lied without interest, "It's a model." She was a woman; she knew all about it; she knew how cheap and vulgar the little shop really was.

"It's got class, eh?"

"Oh yes," she said, catching the eye of a dago in a purple suit through the pane, "it's got class."

"All right," he said. "I'll give you five pounds for it." He took a note from Mr Cholmondeley's wallet.

"Shall I pack it up?"

"No," he said. "The girl'll fetch it." He grinned at her with his raw lip. "You see, she's class. This the best dress you have?" And when she nodded and took the note away he said, "It'll just suit Alice then."

And so out into the avenue with a little of his scorn expressed, out into Frith Street and round the corner into the German café where he kept a room. A shock awaited him there, a little fir tree in a tub hung with colored glass, a crib. He said to the old man who owned the café, "You believe in this? This junk?"

"Is there going to be war again?" the old man said. "It's terrible what you read."

"All this business of no room in the inn. They used to give us plum pudding. A decree from Caesar Augustus. You see I know the stuff, I'm educated. We used to have it read us once a year."

"I have seen one war."

"I hate the sentiment."

"Well," the old man said, "it's good for business."

Raven picked up the bambino. The cradle came with it all of a piece: cheap painted plaster. "They put him on the spot, eh? You see I know the whole story. I'm educated."

He went upstairs to his room. It hadn't been seen to: there was still dirty water in the basin, and the ewer was empty. He remembered the fat man saying, "Chumley, my man, Chumley. It's pronounced Chumley," flashing his emerald ring. He called furiously, "Alice," over the banisters.

She came out of the next room, a slattern, one shoulder too high, with wisps of fair bleached hair over her face. She said, "You needn't shout."

He said, "It's a pigsty in there. You can't treat me like that. Go in and clean it." He hit her on the side of the head, and she cringed away from him, not daring to say anything but, "Who do you think you are?"

"Get on," he said, "you humpbacked bitch." He began to laugh at her when she crouched over the bed. "I've bought you a Christmas dress, Alice. Here's the receipt. Go and fetch it. It's a lovely dress. It'll suit you."

"You think you're funny," she said.

"I've paid a fiver for this joke. Hurry, Alice, or the shop'll be shut." But she got her own back calling up the stairs, "I won't look worse than what you do with that split lip." Everyone in the house could hear her: the old man in the café, his wife in the parlor, the customers at the counter. He imagined their smiles. "Go it, Alice, what an ugly pair you are." He didn't really suffer: he had been fed the poison from boyhood drop by drop; he hardly noticed its bitterness now.

He went to the window and opened it and scratched on the sill. The kitten came to him, making little rushes along the drainpipe, feinting at his hand. "You little bitch," he said, "you little bitch." He took a small two-penny carton of cream out of his overcoat pocket and spilled it in his soap dish. She stopped playing and rushed at him with a tiny cry. He picked her up by the scruff and put her on top of his chest of drawers with the cream. She wriggled from his hand; she was no larger than the rat he'd trained in the home, but softer. He scratched her behind the ear, and she struck back at him in a preoccupied way. Her tongue quivered on the surface of the milk.

Dinnertime, he told himself. With all that money he could go anywhere. He could have a slap-up meal at Simpson's with the businessmen—cut off the joint and any number of vegs.

When he got by the public call box in the dark corner below the stairs he caught his name, "Raven." The old man said, "He always has a room here. He's been away."

"You," a strange voice said. "What's your name—Alice—show me his room. Keep an eye on the door, Saunders."

Raven went on his knees inside the telephone box. He left the door ajar because he never liked to be shut in. He couldn't see out, but he had no need to see the owner of the voice to recognize police, plain clothes, the Yard accent. The man was so near that the floor of the box vibrated to his tread. Then he came down again. "There's no one there. He's taken his hat and coat. He must have gone out."

"He might have," the old man said. "He's a soft-walking sort of fellow."

The stranger began to question them. "What's he like?"

The old man and the girl both said in a breath, "A harelip."

"That's useful," the detective said. "Don't touch his room. I'll be sending a man round to take his fingerprints. What sort of a fellow is he?"

Raven could hear every word. He couldn't imagine what they were after. He knew he'd left no clues: he wasn't a man who imagined things, he knew. He carried the picture of that room and flat in his brain as clearly as if he had the photographs. They had nothing against him. It had been against his orders to keep the automatic, but he could feel it now safe under his armpit. Besides, if they had picked up any clue they'd have stopped him at Dover. He listened to the voices with a dull anger: he wanted his dinner; he hadn't had a square meal for twenty-four hours, and now with two hundred pounds in his pocket he could buy anything, anything.

"I can believe it," the old man said. "Why tonight he even made fun of my poor wife's crib."

"A bloody bully," the girl said. "I shan't be sorry when you've locked him up."

He told himself with surprise, they hate me.

She said, "He's ugly through and through. That lip of his. It gives you the creeps."

"An ugly customer all right."

"I wouldn't have him in the house," the old man said. "But he pays. You can't turn away someone who pays. Not in these days."

"Has he friends?"

"You make me laugh," Alice said. "Him friends. What would he do with friends?"

He began to laugh quietly to himself on the floor of the little dark box: That's me they're talking about, me. He stared up at the pane of glass with his hand on his automatic.

"You seem kind of bitter. What's he been doing to you? He was going to give you a dress, wasn't he?"

"Just his dirty joke."

"You were going to take it, though."

"You bet I wasn't. Do you think I'd take a present from him? I was going to sell it back to them and show him the money, and wasn't I going to laugh?"

He thought again with bitter interest, they hate me. If they open this door I'll shoot the lot.

"I'd like to take a swipe at that lip of his. I'd laugh. I'd say I'd laugh."

"I'll put a man," the strange voice said, "across the road. Tip him the wink if our man comes in." The café door closed.

"Oh," the old man said. "I wish my wife was here. She would not miss this for ten shillings."

"I'll give her a ring," Alice said. "She'll be chatting at Mason's. She can come right over and bring Mrs Mason, too. Let 'em all join in the fun. It was only a week ago Mrs Mason said she didn't want to see his ugly face in her shop again."

"Yes, be a good girl, Alice. Give her a ring."

Raven reached up his hand and took the bulb out of the fitment: he stood up and flattened himself against the wall of the box. Alice opened the door and shut herself in with him. He put his hand over her mouth before she had time to cry.

He said, "Don't you put the pennies in the box. I'll shoot if you do. I'll shoot if you call out. Do what I say." He whispered in her ear. They were as close together as if they were in a single bed. He could feel her crooked shoulder pressed against his chest. He said, "Lift the receiver. Pretend you're talking to the old woman. Go on. I don't care a damn if I shoot you. Say, Hello, Frau Groener."

"Hello, Frau Groener."

"Spill the whole story."

"They are after Raven."

"Why?"

"That five-pound note. They were waiting at the shop."

"What do you mean?"

"They'd got its number. It was stolen."

He'd been double-crossed. His mind worked with mechanical accuracy like a ready-reckoner. You only had to supply it with the figures and it gave you the answer. He was possessed by a deep sullen rage. If Mr Cholmondeley had been in the box with him he would have shot him: he wouldn't have cared a damn.

"Stolen from where?"

"You ought to know that."

"Don't give me any lip. Where from?"

He didn't even know who Cholmondeley's employers were. It was obvious what had happened: they hadn't trusted him. They had arranged this so that he might be put away. A newsboy went by outside calling, "Ultimatum. Ultimatum." His mind registered the fact, but no more; it seemed to have nothing to do with him. He repeated, "Where from?"

"I don't know. I don't remember."

With the automatic stuck against her back he tried to plead with her. "Remember, can't you? It's important. I didn't do it."

"I bet you didn't," she said bitterly into the unconnected phone.

"Give me a break. All I want you to do is remember."

She said, "On your life I won't."

"I gave you that dress, didn't I?"

"You didn't. You tried to plant your money, that's all. You didn't know they'd circulated the numbers to every shop in town. We've even got them in the café."

"If I'd done it, why should I want to know where they came from?"

"It'll be a bigger laugh than ever if you get jugged for something you didn't do."

"Alice," the old man called from the café, "is she coming?"

"I'll give you ten pounds."

"Phony notes. No thank you, Mr Generosity."

"Alice," the old man called again; they could hear him coming along the passage.

"Justice," he said bitterly, jabbing her between the ribs with the automatic.

"You don't need to talk about justice," she said. "Driving me like I was in prison. Hitting me when you feel like it. Spilling ash all over the floor. I've got enough to do with your slops. Milk in the soap dish. Don't talk about justice."

Pressed against him in the tiny dark box she suddenly came alive to him. He was so astonished that he forgot the old man till he had the door of the box open. He whispered passionately, out of the dark, "Don't say a word or I'll plug you." He had them both out of the box in front of him. He said, "Understand this. They aren't going to get me. I'm not going to prison. I don't care a damn if I plug one of you. I don't care if I hang. My father hanged. . . . What's good enough for him . . . Get along in front of me up to my room. There's hell coming to somebody for this."

When he had them there he locked the door. A customer was ringing the café bell over and over again. He turned on them. "I've got a good mind to plug you. Telling them about my harelip. Why can't you play fair?" He went to the window; he knew there was an easy way down: that was why he had chosen the room. The kitten caught his eye, prowling like a toy tiger in a cage up and down the edge of the chest of drawers, afraid to jump. He lifted her up and threw her on his bed; she tried to bite his finger as she went. Then he got through onto the leads. The clouds were massing up across the moon, and the earth seemed to move with them, an icy barren globe, through the vast darkness.

4

Anne Crowder walked up and down the small room in her heavy tweed coat; she didn't want to waste a shilling on the gas meter, because she wouldn't get her shilling's worth before morning. She told herself, I'm lucky to have got that job. I'm glad to be going off to work again. But she wasn't convinced. It was eight now; they would have four hours together till midnight. She would have to deceive him and tell him she was catching the nine-o'clock, not the five-o'clock train, or he would be sending her back to bed early. He was like that. No romance. She smiled with tenderness and blew on her fingers.

The telephone at the bottom of the house was ringing. She thought it was the doorbell and ran to the mirror in the wardrobe. There wasn't enough light from the dull globe to tell her if her makeup would stand the brilliance of the Astoria Dance Hall. She began making up all over again; if she was pale he would take her home early.

The landlady stuck her head in at the door and said, "It's your gentleman. On the phone."

"On the phone?"

"Yes," the landlady said, sidling in for a good chat, "he sounded all of a jump. Impatient, I should say. Half barked my head off when I wished him good evening."

"Oh," she said despairingly, "it's only his way. You mustn't mind him."

"He's going to call off the evening, I suppose," the landlady said. "It's always the same. You girls who go traveling round never get a square deal. You said *Dick Whittington*, didn't you?"

"No, no; *Aladdin*."

She pelted down the stairs. She didn't care a damn who saw her hurry. She said, "Is that you, darling?" There was always something wrong with their telephone. She could hear his voice so hoarsely vibrating against her ear she could hardly realize it was his. He said, "You've been ages. This is a public call box. I've put in my last pennies. Listen, Anne, I can't be with you. I'm sorry. It's work. We're onto the man in that safe robbery I told you about. I shall be out all night on it. We've traced one of the notes." His voice beat excitedly against her ear.

She said, "Oh, that's fine, darling. I know you wanted . . ." But she couldn't keep it up. "Jimmy," she said, "I shan't be seeing you again. For weeks."

He said, "It's tough, I know. I'd been dreaming of . . . Listen. You'd better not catch that early train; what's the point? There isn't a nine-o'clock. I've been looking them up."

"I know. I just said—"

"You'd better go tonight. Then you can get a rest before rehearsals. Midnight from Euston."

"But I haven't packed. . . ."

He took no notice. It was his favorite occupation, planning things, making decisions. He said, "If I'm near the station, I'll try—"

"Your two minutes up."

He said, "Oh hell, I've no coppers. Darling, I love you."

She struggled to bring it out herself, but his name stood in the way, impeded her tongue. She could never bring it out without hesitation. "Ji—" The line went dead on her. She thought bitterly, he oughtn't to go out without coppers. She thought, it's not right, cutting off a detective like that. Then she went back up the stairs. She wasn't crying; it was just as if somebody had died and left her alone and scared, scared of the new faces and the new job, the harsh provincial jokes, the fellows who were fresh; scared of herself, scared of not being able to remember clearly how good it was to be loved.

The landlady said, "I just thought so. Why not come down and have a cup of tea and a good chat? It does you good to talk. Really good. A doctor said to me once it clears the lungs. Stands to reason, don't it? You can't help getting dust up, and a good talk blows it out. I wouldn't bother to pack yet. There's hours and hours. My old man would never of died if he'd talked more. Stands to reason. It was something poisonous in his throat cut him off in his prime. If he'd talked more he'd have blown it out. It's better than spitting."

5

The crime reporter couldn't make himself heard. He kept on trying to say to the chief reporter, "I've got some stuff on that safe robbery."

The chief reporter had had too much to drink. They'd all had too much to drink. He said, "You can go home and read *The Decline and Fall—*"

The crime reporter was a young earnest man who didn't drink and didn't smoke; it shocked him when someone was sick in one of the telephone boxes. He shouted at the top of his voice, "They've traced one of the notes."

"Write it down, write it down, old boy," the chief reporter said, "and then smoke it."

"The man escaped—held up a girl—It's a terribly good story," the earnest young man said. He had an Oxford accent; that was why they had made him crime reporter: it was the news editor's joke.

"Go home and read Gibbon."

The earnest young man caught hold of someone's sleeve. "What's the matter? Are you all crazy? Isn't there going to be any paper or what?"

"War in forty-eight hours," somebody bellowed at him.

"But this is a wonderful story I've got. He held up a girl and an old man, climbed out of a window—"

"Go home. There won't be any room for it."

"They've killed the annual report of the Kensington Kitten Club."

"No 'Round the Shops.' "

"They've made the Limehouse Fire a News in Brief."

"Go home and read Gibbon."

"He got clean away with a policeman watching the front door. The Flying Squad's out. He's armed. The police are taking revolvers. It's a lovely story."

The chief reporter said, "Armed. Go away and put your head in a glass of milk. We'll all be armed in a day or two. They've published their evidence. It's clear as daylight a Serb shot him. Italy's supporting the ultimatum. They've got forty-eight hours to climb down. If you want to buy armament shares hurry and make your fortune."

"You'll be in the army this day week," somebody said.

"Oh no," the young man said. "No, I won't be that. You see, I'm a pacifist."

The man who was sick in the telephone box said, "I'm going home. There isn't any more room in the paper if the Bank of England's blown up."

A little thin piping voice said, "My copy's going in."

"I tell you there isn't any room."

"There'll be room for mine. Gas Masks for All. Special Air Raid Practices for Civilians in every town of more than fifty thousand inhabitants." He giggled.

"The funny thing is—it's—it's—" But nobody ever heard what it was. A boy opened the door and flung them in a pull of the middle page: damp letters on a damp gray sheet; the headlines came off on your hands. "Yugoslavia Asks for Time. Adriatic Fleet at War Stations. Paris Rioters Break into Italian Embassy." Everyone was suddenly quite quiet as an airplane went by, driving low overhead through the dark, heading south, a scarlet tail-light, pale transparent wings in the moonlight. They watched it through the great glass ceiling, and suddenly nobody wanted to have another drink.

The chief reporter said, "I'm tired. I'm going to bed."

"Shall I follow up this story?" the crime reporter said.

"If it'll make you happy, but *that's* the only news from now on."

They stared up at the glass ceiling, the moon, the empty sky.

6

The station clock marked three minutes to midnight. The ticket collector at the barrier said, "There's room in the front."

"A friend's seeing me off," Anne Crowder said. "Can't I get in at this end and go up front when we start?"

"They've locked the doors."

She looked desperately past him. They were turning out the lights in the buffet; no more trains from that platform.

"You'll have to hurry, miss."

The poster of an evening paper caught her eye, and as she ran down the train, looking back as often as she was able, she couldn't help remembering that war might be declared before they met again. He would go to it. He always did what other people did, she told herself with irritation, but she knew that that was the reliability she loved. She wouldn't have loved him if he'd been queer, had his own opinions about things; she lived too closely to thwarted genius, to second touring company actresses who thought they ought to be Cochran stars, to admire difference. She wanted her man to be ordinary, she wanted to be able to know what he'd say next.

A line of lamp-struck faces went by her. The train was full, so full that in the first-class carriages you saw strange shy awkward people who were not at ease in the deep seats, who feared the ticket collector would turn them out. She gave up the search for a third-class carriage, opened a door, dropped her *Woman and Beauty* on the only seat, and struggled back to the window over legs and protruding suitcases. The engine was getting up steam, the smoke blew back up the platform: it was difficult to see as far as the barrier.

A hand pulled at her sleeve. "Excuse me," a fat man said, "if you've quite finished with that window. I want to buy some chocolate."

She said, "Just one moment, please. Somebody's seeing me off."

"He's not here. It's too late. You can't monopolize the window like that. I must have some chocolate." He swept her on one side and waved an emerald ring under the light. She tried to look over his shoulder to the barrier: he almost filled the window. He called, "Boy, boy," waving the emerald ring. He said, "What chocolate have you got? No, not Motorist's, not Mexican. Something sweet."

Suddenly through a crack she saw Mather. He was past the barrier; he was coming down the train looking for her, looking in all the third-class carriages, running past the first-class. She implored the fat man, "Please, please do let me come. I can see my friend."

"In a moment. In a moment. Have you Nestlé's? Give me a shilling packet."

"Please let me."

"Haven't you anything smaller," the boy said, "than a ten-shilling note?"

Mather went by, running past the first-class. She hammered on the window, but he didn't hear her, among the whistles and the beat of trolley wheels, the last packing cases rolling into the van. Doors slammed, a whistle blew, the train began to move.

"Please. Please."

"I must get my change," the fat man said, and the boy ran beside the carriage counting the shillings into his palm. When she got to the window and leaned out they were past the platform: she could only see a small figure on a wedge of asphalt who couldn't see her. An elderly woman said, "You oughtn't to lean out like that. It's dangerous."

She trod on their toes getting back to her seat: she felt unpopularity well up all around her: everyone was thinking, "She oughtn't to be in the carriage. What's the good of our paying first-class fares when . . ." But she wouldn't cry; she was fortified by all the conventional remarks that came automatically to her mind about spilled milk and it will all be the same in fifty years. Nevertheless she noted with deep dislike on the label dangling from the fat man's suitcase his destination, which was the same as hers, Nottwich. He sat opposite her with the *Spectator* and the *Evening News* and the *Financial Times* on his lap eating sweet milk chocolate.

THE HIT MAN

T. Coraghessan Boyle

EARLY YEARS

The hit man's early years are complicated by the black
bag that he wears over his head. Teachers correct his pronuncia-
tion, the coach criticizes his attitude, the principal dresses him
down for branding preschoolers with a lit cigarette. He is a poor
student. At lunch he sits alone, feeding bell peppers and salami into
the dark slot of his mouth. In the hallways, wiry young athletes
snatch at the black hood and slap the back of his head. When he is
thirteen he is approached by the captain of the football team, who
pins him down and attempts to remove the hood. The Hit Man
wastes him. Five years, says the judge.

BACK ON THE STREET

The Hit Man is back on the street in two months.

FIRST DATE

The girl's name is Cynthia. The Hit Man pulls up in front of her apartment in his father's hearse. (The Hit Man's father, whom he loathes and abominates, is a mortician. At breakfast the Hit Man's father had slapped the cornflakes from his son's bowl. The son threatened to waste his father. He did not, restrained no doubt by considerations of filial loyalty and the deep-seated taboos against patricide that permeate the universal unconscious.)

Cynthia's father has silver sideburns and plays tennis. He responds to the Hit Man's knock, expresses surprise at the Hit Man's appearance. The Hit Man takes Cynthia by the elbow, presses a twenty into her father's palm, and disappears into the night.

FATHER'S DEATH

At breakfast the Hit Man slaps the cornflakes from his father's bowl. Then wastes him.

MOTHER'S DEATH

The Hit Man is in his early twenties. He shoots pool, lifts weights and drinks milk from the carton. His mother is in the hospital, dying of cancer or heart disease. The priest wears black. So does the Hit Man.

FIRST JOB

Porfirio Buñoz, a Cuban financier, invites the Hit Man to lunch. I hear you're looking for work, says Buñoz.

That's right, says the Hit Man.

PEAS

The Hit Man does not like peas. They are too difficult to balance on the fork.

TALK SHOW

The Hit Man waits in the wings, the white slash of a cigarette scarring the midnight black of his head and upper torso. The makeup girl has done his mouth and eyes, brushed the nap of his hood. He has been briefed. The guest who precedes him is a pediatrician. A planetary glow washes the stage where the host and the pediatrician, separated by a potted palm, cross their legs and discuss the little disturbances of infants and toddlers.

After the station break the Hit Man finds himself squeezed into a director's chair, white lights in his eyes. The talk-show host is a baby-faced man in his early forties. He smiles like God and all His Angels. Well, he says. So you're a Hit Man. Tell me—I've always wanted to know—what does it feel like to hit someone?

DEATH OF MATEO MARIA BUÑOZ

The body of Mateo Maria Buñoz, the cousin and business associate of a prominent financier, is discovered down by the docks on a hot summer morning. Mist rises from the water like steam, there is the smell of fish. A large black bird perches on the dead man's forehead.

MARRIAGE

Cynthia and the Hit Man stand at the altar, side by side. She is wearing a white satin gown and lace veil. The Hit Man has rented a tuxedo, extra-large, and a silk-lined black-velvet hood.

. . . Till death do you part, says the priest.

MOODS

The Hit Man is moody, unpredictable. Once, in a luncheonette, the waitress brought him the meat loaf special but forgot to eliminate the peas. There was a spot of gravy on the Hit Man's hood, about where his chin should be. He looked up at the waitress, his eyes like pins behind the triangular slots, and wasted her.

Another time he went to the track with $25, came back with $1,800. He stopped at a cigar shop. As he stepped out of the shop a wino tugged at his sleeve and solicited a quarter. The Hit Man reached into his pocket, extracted the $1,800 and handed it to the wino. Then wasted him.

FIRST CHILD

A boy. The Hit Man is delighted. He leans over the edge of the playpen and molds the tiny fingers around the grip of a nickel-plated derringer. The gun is loaded with blanks—the Hit Man wants the boy to get used to the noise. By the time he is four the boy has mastered the rudiments of Tae Kwon Do, can stick a knife in the wall from a distance of ten feet and shoot a moving target with either hand. The Hit Man rests his broad palm on the boy's head. You're going to make the Big Leagues, Tiger, he says.

WORK

He flies to Cincinnati. To L.A. To Boston. To London. The stewardesses get to know him.

HALF AN ACRE AND A GARAGE

The Hit Man is raking leaves, amassing great brittle piles of them. He is wearing a black T-shirt, cut off at the shoulders, and a cotton work hood, also black. Cynthia is edging the flower bed, his son playing in the grass. The Hit Man waves to his neighbors as they drive by. The neighbors wave back.

When he has scoured the lawn to his satisfaction, the Hit Man draws the smaller leaf-hummocks together in a single mound the size of a pickup truck. Then he bends to ignite it with his lighter. Immediately, flames leap back from the leaves, cut channels through the pile, engulf it in a ball of fire. The Hit Man stands back, hands folded beneath the great meaty biceps. At his side is the three-headed dog. He bends to pat each of the heads, smoke and sparks raging against the sky.

STALKING THE STREETS OF THE CITY

He is stalking the streets of the city, collar up, brim down. It is late at night. He stalks past department stores, small businesses, parks, and gas stations. Past apartments, picket fences, picture windows. Dogs growl in the shadows, then slink away. He could hit any of us.

RETIREMENT

A group of businessman-types—sixtyish, seventyish, portly, diamond rings, cigars, liver spots—throws him a party. Porfirio Buñoz, now in his eighties, makes a speech and presents the Hit Man with a gilded scythe. The Hit Man thanks him, then retires to the lake, where he can be seen in his speedboat, skating out over the blue, hood rippling in the breeze.

DEATH

He is stricken, shrunken, half his former self. He lies propped against the pillows at Mercy Hospital, a bank of gentians drooping round the bed. Tubes run into the hood at the nostril openings, his eyes are clouded and red, sunk deep behind the triangular slots. The priest wears black. So does the Hit Man.

On the other side of town the Hit Man's son is standing before the mirror of a shop that specializes in Hit Man attire. Trying on his first hood.

"GENTLEMEN, THE KING!"

Damon Runyon

On Tuesday evenings I always go to Bobby's Chop House to get myself a beef stew, the beef stews in Bobby's being very nourishing, indeed, and quite reasonable. In fact, the beef stews in Bobby's are considered a most fashionable dish by one and all on Broadway on Tuesday evenings.

So on this Tuesday evening I am talking about, I am in Bobby's wrapping myself around a beef stew and reading the race results in the *Journal,* when who comes into the joint but two old friends of mine from Philly, and a third guy I never see before in my life, but who seems to be an old sort of guy, and very fierce looking.

One of these old friends of mine from Philly is a guy by the name of Izzy Cheesecake, who is called Izzy Cheesecake because he is all the time eating cheesecake around delicatessen joints, although of course this is nothing against him, as cheesecake is very popular in some circles, and goes very good with java. Anyway, this Izzy Cheesecake has another name, which is Morris something, and he is slightly Jewish, and has a large beezer, and is considered a handy man in many respects.

The other old friend of mine from Philly is a guy by the name of Kitty Quick, who is maybe thirty-two or three years old, and who is a lively guy in every way. He is a great hand for wearing good clothes, and he is mobbed up with some very good people in Philly in his day, and at one time has plenty of dough, although I hear that lately things are not going so good for Kitty Quick, or for anybody else in Philly, as far as that is concerned.

Now of course I do not rap to these old friends of mine from Philly at once, and in fact I put the *Journal* up in front of my face, because it is never good policy to rap to visitors in this town, especially visitors from Philly, until you know why they are visiting. But it seems that Kitty Quick spies me before I can get the *Journal* up high enough, and he comes over to my table at once, bringing Izzy Cheesecake and the other guy with him, so naturally I give them a big hello, very cordial, and ask them to sit down and have a few beef stews with me, and as they pull up chairs, Kitty Quick says to me like this:

"Do you know Jo-jo from Chicago?" he says, pointing his thumb at the third guy.

Well, of course I know Jo-jo by his reputation, which is very alarming, but I never meet up with him before, and if it is left to me, I will never meet up with him at all, because Jo-jo is considered a very uncouth character, even in Chicago.

He is an Italian, and a short wide guy, very heavy set, and slow moving, and with jowls you can cut steaks off of, and sleepy eyes, and he somehow reminds me of an old lion I once see in a cage in Ringling's circus. He has a black mustache, and he is an old-timer out in Chicago, and is pointed out to visitors to the city as a very remarkable guy because he lives as long as he does, which is maybe forty years.

His right name is Antonio something, and why he is called Jo-jo I never hear, but I suppose it is because Jo-jo is handier than Antonio. He shakes hands with me, and says he is pleased to meet me, and then he sits down and begins taking on beef stew very rapidly while Kitty Quick says to me as follows:

"Listen," he says, "do you know anybody in Europe?"

Well, this is a most unexpected question, and naturally I am not going to reply to unexpected questions by guys from Philly without thinking them over very carefully, so to gain time while I think, I say to Kitty Quick:

"Which Europe do you mean?"

"Why," Kitty says, greatly surprised, "is there more than one Europe? I mean the big Europe on the Atlantic Ocean. This is the Europe where we are going, and if you know anybody there we will be glad to go around and say hello to them for you. We are going to Europe on the biggest proposition anybody ever hears of," he says. "In fact," he says, "it is a proposition that will make us all rich. We are sailing tonight."

Well, offhand I cannot think of anybody I know in Europe, and if I do know anybody there I will certainly not wish such parties as Kitty Quick, and Izzy Cheesecake, and Jo-jo going around saying hello to them, but of course I do not mention such a thought out loud. I only say I hope and trust that they have a very good *bon voyage* and do not suffer too much from seasickness. Naturally I do not ask what their proposition is, because if I ask such a question they may think I wish to find out, and will consider me a very nosy guy, but I figure the chances are they are going to look after some commercial matter, such as Scotch, or maybe cordials.

Anyway, Kitty Quick and Izzy Cheesecake and Jo-jo eat up quite a few beef stews, and leave me to pay the check, and this is the last I see or hear of any of them for several months. Then one day I am in Philly to see a prizefight, and I run into Kitty Quick on Broad Street, looking pretty much the same as usual, and I ask him how he comes out in Europe.

"It is no good," Kitty says. "The trip is something of a bust, although we see many interesting sights, and have quite a few experiences. Maybe," Kitty says, "you will like to hear why we go to

Europe? It is a very unusual story, indeed, and is by no means a lie, and I will be pleased to tell it to someone I think will believe it."

So we go into Walter's restaurant, and sit down in a corner, and order up a little java, and Kitty Quick tells me the story as follows:

It all begins [Kitty says] with a certain big lawyer coming to me here in Philly, and wishing to know if I care to take up a proposition that will make me rich, and naturally I say I can think of nothing that will please me more, because at this time things are very bad indeed in Philly, what with investigations going on here and there, and plenty of heat around and about, and I do not have more than a few bobs in my pants pocket, and can think of no way to get any more.

So this lawyer takes me to the Ritz-Carlton hotel, and there he introduces me to a guy by the name of Count Saro, and the lawyer says he will okay anything Saro has to say to me 100 percent, and then he immediately takes the wind as if he does not care to hear what Saro has to say. But I know this mouthpiece is not putting any proposition away as okay unless he knows it is pretty much okay, because he is a smart guy at his own dodge, and everything else, and has plenty of coconuts.

Now this Count Saro is a little guy with an eyebrow mustache, and he wears striped pants, and white spats, and a cutaway coat, and a monocle in one eye, and he seems to be a foreign nobleman, although he talks English first rate. I do not care much for Count Saro's looks, but I will say one thing for him he is very businesslike, and gets down to cases at once.

He tells me that he is the representative of a political party in his home country in Europe, which has a king, and this country wishes to get rid of the king, because Count Saro says kings are out of style in Europe, and that no country can get anywhere with a king these days. His proposition is for me to take any assistants I figure I may need and go over and get rid of this king, and Count Saro says he will pay two hundred G's for the job in good old American scratch, and will lay twenty-five G's on the line at once, leaving the balance with the lawyer to be paid to me when everything is finished.

Well, this is a most astonishing proposition, indeed, because while I often hear of propositions to get rid of other guys, I never before hear of a proposition to get rid of a king. Furthermore, it does not sound reasonable to me, as getting rid of a king is apt to attract plenty of attention, and criticism, but Count Saro explains to me that his country is a small, out-of-the-way country, and that his political party will take control of the telegraph wires and everything else as soon as I get rid of the king, so nobody will give the news much of a tumble outside the country.

"Everything will be done very quietly, and in good order," Count Saro says, "and there will be no danger to you whatever."

Well, naturally I wish to know from Count Saro why he does not get somebody in his own country to do such a job, especially if he can pay so well for it, and he says to me like this:

"Well," he says, "in the first place there is no one in our country with enough experience in such matters to be trusted, and in the second place we do not wish anyone in our country to seem to be tangled up with getting rid of the king. It will cause internal complications," he says. "An outsider is more logical," he says, "because it is quite well known that in the palace of the king there are many valuable jewels, and it will seem a natural play for outsiders, especially Americans, to break into the palace to get these jewels, and if they happen to get rid of the king while getting the jewels, no one will think it is anything more than an accident, such as often occurs in your country."

Furthermore, Count Saro tells me that everything will be laid out for me in advance by his people, so I will have no great bother getting into the palace to get rid of the king, but he says of course I must not really take the valuable jewels, because his political party wishes to keep them for itself.

Well, I do not care much for the general idea at all, but Count Saro whips out a bundle of scratch, and weeds off twenty-five large coarse notes of a G apiece, and there it is in front of me, and looking at all this dough, and thinking how tough times are, what with banks busting here and there, I am very much tempted indeed, especially as I am commencing to think this Count Saro is some kind of a nut, and is only speaking through his hat about getting rid of a king.

"Listen," I say to Count Saro, as he sits there watching me, "how do you know I will not take this dough off of you and then never do anything whatever for it?"

"Why," he says, much surprised, "you are recommended to me as an honest man, and I accept your references. Anyway," he says, "if you do not carry out your agreement with me, you will only hurt yourself, because you will lose a hundred and seventy-five G's more and the lawyer will make you very hard to catch."

Well, the upshot of it is I shake hands with Count Saro, and then go out to find Izzy Cheesecake, although I am still thinking Count Saro is a little daffy, and while I am looking for Izzy, who do I see but Jo-jo, and Jo-jo tells me that he is on a vacation from Chicago for a while, because it seems somebody out there claims he is a public enemy, which Jo-jo says is nothing but a big lie, as he is really very fond of the public at all times.

Naturally I am glad to come across a guy such as Jo-jo, because he is most trustworthy, and naturally Jo-jo is very glad to hear of a proposition that will turn him an honest dollar while he is on his vacation. So Jo-jo and Izzy and I have a meeting, and we agree that I am to have a hundred G's for finding the plant, while Izzy and Jo-jo are to get fifty G's apiece, and this is how we come to go to Europe.

Well, we land at a certain spot in Europe, and who is there to meet us but another guy with a monocle, who states that his name is Baron von Terp, or some such, and who says he is representing Count Saro, and I am commencing to wonder if Count Saro's country is filled with one-eyed guys. Anyway, this Baron von Terp takes us traveling by trains and automobiles for several days, until finally after an extra-long hop in an automobile we come to the outskirts of a nice-looking little burg, which seems to be the place we are headed for.

Now Baron von Terp drops us in a little hotel on the outskirts of the town, and says he must leave us because he cannot afford to be seen with us, although he explains he does not mean this as a knock to us. In fact, Baron von Terp says he finds us very nice traveling companions, indeed, except for Jo-jo wishing to engage in target practice along the route with his automatic Roscoe, and using such animals as stray dogs and chickens for his targets. He says he does not even mind Izzy Cheesecake's singing, although personally I will always consider this one of the big drawbacks to the journey.

Before he goes, Baron von Terp draws me a rough diagram of the inside of the palace where we are to get rid of the king, giving me a layout of all the rooms and doors. He says usually there are guards in and about this palace, but that his people arrange it so these guards will not be present around nine o'clock this night, except one guy who may be on guard at the door of the king's bedroom, and Baron von Terp says if we guzzle this guy it will be all right with him, because he does not like the guy, anyway.

But the general idea, he says, is for us to work fast and quietly, so as to be in and out of there inside of an hour or so, leaving no trail behind us, and I say this will suit me and Izzy Cheesecake and Jo-jo very well, indeed, as we are getting tired of traveling, and wish to go somewhere and take a long rest.

Well, after explaining all this, Baron von Terp takes the wind, leaving us a big fast car with an ugly-looking guy driving it who does not talk much English, but is supposed to know all the routes, and it is in this car that we leave the little hotel just before nine o'clock as per instructions, and head for the palace, which turns out to be nothing but a large square old building in the middle of a sort of park, with the town around and about, but some distance off.

Ugly-face drives right into this park and up to what seems to be the front door of the building, and the three of us get out of the car, and Ugly-face pulls the car off into the shadow of some trees to wait for us.

Personally, I am looking for plenty of heat when we start to go into the palace, and I have the old equalizer where I can get at it without too much trouble, while Jo-jo and Izzy Cheesecake also have their rods handy. But just as Baron von Terp tells us, there are no guards around, and in fact there is not a soul in sight as we walk into the palace door, and find ourselves in a big hall with paintings, and armor, and old swords, and one thing and another hanging around and about, and I can see that this is a perfect plan, indeed.

I out with my diagram and see where the king's bedroom is located on the second floor, and when we get there, walking very easy, and ready to start blasting away if necessary, who is at the door but a big tall guy in a uniform, who is very much surprised at seeing us, and who starts to holler something or other, but what it is nobody will ever know, because just as he opens his mouth, Izzy Cheesecake taps him on the noggin with the butt of a forty-five, and knocks him cockeyed.

Then Jo-jo grabs some cord off a heavy silk curtain that is hanging across the door, and ties the guy up good and tight, and wads a handkerchief into his kisser in case the guy comes to, and wishes to start hollering again, and when all this is done, I quietly turn the knob of the door to the king's bedroom, and we step into a room that looks more like a young convention hall than it does a bedroom, except that it is hung around and about with silk drapes, and there is much gilt furniture here and there.

Well, who is in this room but a nice-looking doll, and a little kid of maybe eight or nine years old, and the kid is in a big bed with a canopy over it like the entrance to a nightclub, only silk, and the doll is sitting alongside the bed reading to the kid out of a book. It is a very homelike scene, indeed, and causes us to stop and look around in great surprise, for we are certainly not expecting such a scene at all.

As we stand there in the middle of the room somewhat confused the doll turns and looks at us, and the little kid sits up in bed. He is a fat little guy with a chubby face, and a lot of curly hair, and eyes as big as pancakes, and maybe bigger. The doll turns very pale when she sees us, and shakes so the book she is reading falls to the floor, but the kid does not seem scared, and he says to us in very good English like this:

"Who are you?" he says.

Well, this is a fair question, at that, but naturally we do not wish to state who we are at this time, so I say:

"Never mind who we are, where is the king?"

"The king?" the kid says, sitting up straight in the bed. "Why, I am the king."

Now of course this seems a very nonsensical crack to us, because we have brains enough to know that kings do not come as small as this little squirt, and anyway we are in no mood to dicker with him, so I say to the doll as follows:

"Listen," I say, "we do not care for any kidding at this time, because we are in a great hurry. Where is the king?"

"Why," she says, her voice trembling quite some, "this is indeed the king, and I am his governess. Who are you, and what do you want? How do you get in here?" she says. "Where are the guards?"

"Lady," I say, and I am greatly surprised at myself for being so patient with her, "this kid may be a king, but we want the big king. We want the head king himself," I say.

"There is no other," she says, and the little kid chips in like this:

"My father dies two years ago, and I am the king in his place," he says. "Are you English like Miss Peabody here?" he says. "Who is the funny-looking old man back there?"

Well, of course Jo-jo is funny looking, at that, but no one ever before is impolite enough to speak of it to his face, and Jo-jo begins growling quite some, while Izzy Cheesecake speaks as follows:

"Why," Izzy says, "this is a very great outrage. We are sent to get rid of a king, and here the king is nothing but a little punk. Personally," Izzy says, "I am not in favor of getting rid of punks, male or female."

"Well," Jo-jo says, "I am against it myself as a rule, but this is a pretty fresh punk."

"Now," I say, "there seems to be some mistake around here, at that. Let us sit down and talk things over quietly, and see if we cannot get this matter straightened out. It looks to me," I say, "as if this Count Saro is nothing but a swindler."

"Count Saro," the doll says, getting up and coming over to me, and looking very much alarmed. "Count Saro, do you say? Oh, sir, Count Saro is a very bad man. He is the tool of the Grand Duke Gino of this country, who is this little boy's uncle. The grand duke will be king himself if it is not for this boy, and we suspect many plots against the little chap's safety. Oh, gentlemen," she says, "you surely do not mean any harm to this poor orphan child?"

Well, this is about the first time in their lives that Jo-jo and Izzy Cheesecake are ever mentioned by anybody as gentlemen, and I can see that it softens them up quite some, especially as the little kid is grinning at them very cheerful, although of course he will not be so cheerful if he knows who he is grinning at.

"Why," Jo-jo says, "the grand duke is nothing but a rascal for wishing harm to such a little guy as this, although of course," Jo-jo says, "if he is a grown-up king it will be a different matter."

"Who are you?" the little kid says again.

"We are Americans," I say, very proud to mention my home country. "We are from Philly and Chicago, two very good towns, at that."

Well, the little kid's eyes get bigger than ever, and he climbs right out of bed and walks over to us looking very cute in his blue silk pajamas, and his bare feet.

"Chicago?" he says. "Do you know Mr. Capone?"

"Al?" says Jo-jo. "Do I know Al? Why, Al and me are just like this," he says, although personally I do not believe Al Capone will know Jo-jo if he meets him in broad daylight. "Where do you know Al from?" he asks.

"Oh, I do not know him," the kid says. "But I read about him in the magazines, and about the machine guns, and the pineapples. Do you know about the pineapples?" he says.

"Do I know about the pineapples?" Jo-jo says, as if his feelings are hurt by the question. "He asks me do I know about the pineapples. Why," he says, "look here."

And what does Jo-jo do but out with a little round gadget that I recognize at once as a bomb such as these Guineas like to chuck at people they do not like, especially Guineas from Chicago. Of course I never know Jo-jo is packing this article around and about with him, and Jo-jo can see I am much astonished, and by no means pleased, because he says to me like this:

"I bring this along in case of a bear fight," he says. "They are very handy in a bear fight."

Well, the next thing anybody knows we are all talking about this and that very pleasant, especially the little kid and Jo-jo, who is telling lies faster than a horse can trot, about Chicago and Mr. Capone, and I hope and trust that Al never hears some of the lies Jo-jo tells, or he may hold it against me for being with Jo-jo when these lies come off.

I am talking to the doll, whose name seems to be Miss Peabody, and who is not so hard to take, at that, and at the same time I am keeping an eye on Izzy Cheesecake, who is wandering around the room looking things over. The chances are Izzy is trying to find a few of the valuable jewels such as I mention to him when telling him about the proposition of getting rid of the king, and in fact I am taking a stray peek here and there myself, but I do not see anything worth while.

This Miss Peabody is explaining to me about the politics of the country, and it seems the reason the grand duke wishes to get rid of the little kid king and be king himself is because he has a business deal on with a big nation nearby that wishes to control the kid king's country. I judge from what Miss Peabody tells me that this country is no bigger than Delaware county, Pa., and it seems to me a lot of bother about no more country than this, but Miss Peabody says it is a very nice little country, at that.

She says it will be very lovely indeed if it is not for the Grand Duke Gino, because the little kid king stands okay with the people, but it seems the old grand duke is pretty much boss of everything, and Miss Peabody says she is personally long afraid that he will finally try to do something very drastic indeed to get rid of the kid king on account of the kid seeming so healthy. Well, naturally I do not state to her that our middle name is drastic, because I do not wish Miss Peabody to have a bad opinion of us.

Now nothing will do but Jo-jo must show the kid his automatic, which is as long as your arm, and maybe longer, and the kid is greatly delighted, and takes the rod and starts pointing it here and there and saying boom-boom, as kids will do. But what happens but he pulls the trigger, and it seems that Jo-jo does not have the safety on, so the Roscoe really goes boom-boom twice before the kid can take his finger off the trigger.

Well, the first shot smashes a big jar over in one corner of the room, which Miss Peabody afterward tells me is worth fifteen G's if it is worth a dime, and the second slug knocks off Izzy Cheesecake's derby hat, which serves Izzy right, at that, as he is keeping his hat on in the presence of a lady. Naturally these shots are very disturbing to me at the moment, but afterward I learn they are a very good thing indeed, because it seems a lot of guys who are hanging around outside, including Baron von Terp, and several prominent politicians of the country, watching and listening to see what comes off, hurry right home to bed, figuring the king is got rid of as per contract, and wishing to be found in bed if anybody comes around asking questions.

Well, Jo-jo is finally out of lies about Chicago and Mr. Capone, when the little kid seems to get a new idea and goes rummaging around the room looking for something, and just as I am hoping he is about to donate the valuable jewels to us he comes up with a box, and what is in this box but a baseball bat, and a catcher's mitt, and a baseball, and it is very strange indeed to find such homelike articles so far away from home, especially as Babe Ruth's name is on the bat.

"Do you know about these things?" the little kid asks Jo-jo. "They are from America, and they are sent to me by one of our people when he is visiting there, but nobody here seems to know what they are for."

"Do I know about them?" Jo-jo says, fondling them very tenderly, indeed. "He asks me do I know about them. Why," he says, "in my time I am the greatest hitter on the West Side Blues back in dear old Chi."

Well, now nothing will do the kid but we must show him how these baseball articles work, so Izzy Cheesecake, who claims he is once a star back-stopper with the Vine Streets back in Philly, puts on a pad and mask, and Jo-jo takes the bat and lays a small sofa pillow down on the floor for a home plate, and insists that I pitch to him. Now it is years since I handle a baseball, although I wish to say that in my day I am as good an amateur pitcher as there is around Gray's Ferry in Philly, and the chances are I will be with the A's if I do not have other things to do.

So I take off my coat, and get down to the far end of the room, while Jo-jo squares away at the plate, with Izzy Cheesecake behind it. I can see by the way he stands that Jo-jo is bound to be a sucker for a curve, so I take a good windup, and cut loose with the old fadeaway, but of course my arm is not what it used to be, and the ball does not break as I expect, so what happens but Jo-jo belts the old apple right through a high window in what will be right field if the room is laid off like Shibe Park.

Well Jo-jo starts running as if he is going to first, but of course there is no place in particular for him to run, and he almost knocks his brains out against a wall, and the ball is lost, and the game winds up right there, but the little kid is tickled silly over this business, and even Miss Peabody laughs, and she does not look to me like a doll who gets many laughs out of life, at that.

It is now nearly ten o'clock, and Miss Peabody says if she can find anybody around she will get us something to eat, and this sounds very reasonable, indeed, so I step outside the door and bring in the guy we tie up there, who seems to be wide awake by now, and very much surprised, and quite indignant, and Miss Peabody says something to him in a language that I do not understand. When I come to think it all over afterward, I am greatly astonished at the way I trust Miss Peabody, because there is no reason why she shall not tell the guy to get the law, but I suppose I trust her because she seems to have an honest face.

Anyway, the guy in the uniform goes away rubbing his noggin, and pretty soon in comes another guy who seems to be a butler, or some such, and who is also greatly surprised at seeing us, and Miss Peabody rattles off something to him and he starts hustling in tables, and dishes, and sandwiches, and coffee, and one thing and another in no time at all.

Well, there we are, the five of us sitting around the table eating and drinking, because what does the butler do but bring in a couple of bottles of good old prewar champagne, which is very pleasant to the taste, although Izzy Cheesecake embarrasses me no little by telling Miss Peabody that if she can dig up any consider-able quantity of this stuff he will make her plenty of bobs by peddling it in our country, and will also cut the king in.

When the butler fills the wineglasses the first time, Miss Peabody picks hers up, and looks at us, and naturally we have sense enough to pick ours up, too, and then she stands up on her feet and raises her glass high above her head, and says like this:

"Gentlemen, the King!"

Well, I stand up at this, and Jo-jo and Izzy Cheesecake stand up with me, and we say, all together:

"The King!"

And then we swig our champagne, and sit down again and the little kid laughs all over and claps his hands and seems to think it is plenty of fun, which it is, at that, although Miss Peabody does not let him have any wine, and is somewhat indignant when she catches Jo-jo trying to slip him a snort under the table.

Well, finally the kid does not wish us to leave him at all, especially Jo-jo, but Miss Peabody says he must get some sleep, so we tell him we will be back some day, and we take our hats and say good-bye, and leave him standing in the bedroom door with Miss Peabody at his side, and the little kid's arm is around her waist, and I find myself wishing it is my arm, at that.

Of course we never go back again, and in fact we get out of the country this very night, and take the first boat out of the first seaport we hit and return to the United States of America, and the gladdest guy in all the world to see us go is Ugly-face, because he has to drive us about a thousand miles with the muzzle of a rod digging into his ribs.

So [Kitty Quick says] now you know why we go to Europe.

Well, naturally, I am greatly interested in his story, and especially in what Kitty says about the prewar champagne, because I can see that there may be great business opportunities in such a place if a guy can get in with the right people, but one thing Kitty will never tell me is where the country is located, except that it is located in Europe.

"You see," Kitty says, "we are all strong Republicans here in Philly, and I will not get the Republican administration of this country tangled up in any international squabble for the world. You see," he says, "when we land back home I find a little item of cable news in a paper that says the Grand Duke Gino dies as a result of injuries received in an accident in his home some weeks before.

"And," Kitty says, "I am never sure but what these injuries may be caused by Jo-jo insisting on Ugly-face driving us around to the grand duke's house the night we leave and popping his pineapple into the grand duke's bedroom window."

LOOSE ENDS

Bharati Mukherjee

She sends for this Goldilocks doll in April.

"See," she says. The magazine is pressed tight to her T-shirt. "It's porcelain."

I look. The ad calls Goldilocks "the first doll in an enchanting new suite of fairy tale dolls."

"*Bisque* porcelain," she says. She fills out the order form in purple ink. "Look at the pompoms on her shoes. Aren't they darling?"

"You want to blow sixty bucks?" Okay, so I yell that at Jonda. "You have any idea how much I got to work for sixty dollars?"

"Only twenty now," she says. Then she starts bitching. "What's with you and Velásquez these days? You shouldn't even be home in the afternoon."

It's between one and two and I have a right, don't I, to be in my Manufactured Home—as they call it—in Laguna Vista Estates instead of in Mr. Vee's pastel office in the mall? A man's mobile home is his castle, at least in Florida. But I fix her her bourbon and ginger ale with the dash of ReaLemon just the way she likes it. She isn't a mail-order junky; this Goldilocks thing is more complicated.

"It makes me nervous," Jonda goes on. "To have you home, I mean."

I haven't been fired by Mr. Vee; the truth is I've been offered a raise, contingent, of course, on my delivering a forceful message to that greaser goon, Chavez. I don't get into that with Jonda. Jonda doesn't have much of a head for details.

"Learn to like it," I say. "Your boyfriend better learn, too."

She doesn't have anyone but me, but she seems to like the jealousy bit. Her face goes soft and dreamy like the old days. We've seen a lot together.

"Jonda," I start. I just don't get it. What does she want?

"Forget it, Jeb." She licks the stamp on the Goldilocks envelope so gooey it sticks on crooked. "There's no point in us talking. We don't communicate anymore."

I make myself a cocktail. Milk, two ice cubes crushed with a hammer between two squares of paper towel, and Maalox. Got the recipe from a Nam Vets magazine.

"Look at you." She turns on the TV and gets in bed. "I hate to see you like this, at loose ends."

I get in bed with her. Usually afternoons are pure dynamite, when I can get them. I lie down with her for a while, but nothing happens. We're like that until Oprah comes on.

"It's okay," Jonda says. "I'm going to the mall. The guy who opened the new boutique, you know, the little guy with the turban, he said he might be hiring."

I drop a whole ice cube into my Maalox cocktail and watch her change. She shimmies out of khaki shorts—mementoes of my glory days—and pulls a flowery skirt over her head. I still don't feel any urge.

"Who let these guys in?" I say. She doesn't answer. He won't hire her—they come in with half a dozen kids and pay them nothing. We're coolie labor in our own country.

She pretends to look for her car keys which are hanging as usual from their nail. "Don't wait up for me."

"At least let me drive you." I'm not begging, yet.

"No, it's okay." She fixes her wickedly green eyes on me. And suddenly bile pours out in torrents. "Nine years, for God's sake! Nine years, and what do we have?"

"Don't let's get started."

Hey, what we have sounds like the Constitution of the United States. We have freedom and no strings attached. We have no debts. We come and go as we like. She wants a kid but I don't think I have the makings of a good father. That's part of what the Goldilocks thing is.

But I know what she means. By the time Goldilocks arrives in the mail, she'll have moved her stuff out of Laguna Vista Estates.

I like Miami. I like the heat. You can smell the fecund rot of the jungle in every headline. You can park your car in the shopping mall and watch the dope change hands, the Goldilockses and Peter Pans go off with new daddies, the dishwashers and short-order cooks haggle over fake passports, the Mr. Vees in limos huddle over arms-shopping lists, all the while gull guano drops on your car with the soothing steadiness of rain.

Don't get me wrong. I liked the green spaces of Nam, too. In spite of the consequences. I was the Pit Bull—even the marines backed off. I was Jesse James hunched tight in the gunship, trolling the jungle for hidden wonders.

"If you want to stay alive," Doc Healy cautioned me the first day, "just keep consuming and moving like a locust. Do that, Jeb m'boy, and you'll survive to die a natural death." Last winter a judge put a vet away for thirty-five years for sinking his teeth into sweet, succulent coed flesh. The judge said, *when gangrene sets in, the doctor has no choice but to amputate.* But I'm here to testify, Your Honor, the appetite remains, after the easy targets have all been eaten. The whirring of our locust jaws is what keeps you awake.

I take care of Chavez for Mr. Vee and come home to stale tangled sheets. Jonda's been gone nine days.

I'm not whining. Last night in the parking lot of the mall a swami with blond dreadlocks treated us to a levitation. We spied him on the roof of a discount clothing store, nudging his flying mat into liftoff position. We were the usual tourists and weirdos and murderous cubanos. First he played his sinuses OM-OOM-OOM-PAH-OOM, then he pushed off from the roof in the lotus position. His bare feet sprouted like orchids from his knees. We watched him wheel and flutter for maybe two or three minutes before the cops pulled up and caught him in a safety net.

They took him away in handcuffs. Who knows how many killers and felons and honest nut cases watched it and politely went back to their cars? I love Miami.

This morning I lean on Mr. Vee's doorbell. I need money. Auguste, the bouncer he picked up in the back streets of Montreal, squeezes my windbreaker before letting me in.

I suck in my gut and make the palm trees on my shirt ripple. "You're blonder than you were. Blond's definitely your color."

"Don't start with me, Marshall," he says. He helps himself to a mint from a fancy glass bowl on the coffee table.

Mr. Vee sidles into the room; he's one hundred and seventy-five pounds of jiggling paranoia.

"You look like hell, Marshall," is the first thing he says.

"I could say the same to you, Haysoos," I say.

His face turns mean. I scoop up a mint and flip it like a quarter.

"The last job caused me some embarrassment," he says.

My job, I try to remind him, is to show up at a time and place of his choosing and perform a simple operation. I'm the gun-ship Mr. Vee calls in. He pinpoints the target, I attempt to neutral-ize it. It's all a matter of instrumentation and precise coordinates. With more surveillance, a longer lead time, a neutral setting, mishaps can be minimized. But not on the money Mr. Vee pays. He's itchy and impulsive; he wants a quick hit, publicity, and some sort of ego boost. I served under second looies just like him, and sooner or later most of them got blown away, after losing half their men.

The story was, Chavez had been sampling too much of Mr. Vee's product line. He was, as a result, inoperative with women. He lived in a little green house in a postwar development on the fringes of Liberty City, a step up, in some minds, from a trailer park. By all indications, he should have been alone. I get a little sick when wives and kids are involved, old folks, neighbors, repairmen—I'm not a monster, except when I'm being careful.

I gained entry through a window—thank God for cheap air conditioners. First surprise: he wasn't alone. I could hear that drug-deep double-breathing. Even in the dark before I open a door, I can tell a woman from a man, middle age from adolescence, a sleeping Cuban from a sleeping American. They were entwined; it looked like at long last love for poor old Chavez. She might have been fourteen, brassy-haired with wide black roots, baby-fat-bodied with a pinched, Appalachian face. I did what I was paid for; I eliminated the primary target and left no traces. Doc Healy used to teach us: torch the whole hut and make sure you get the kids, the grannies, cringing on the sleeping mat—or else you'll meet them on the trail with fire in their eyes.

Truth be told, I was never much of a marksman. My game is getting close, working the body, where accuracy doesn't count for much. We're the guys who survived that war.

The carnage at Chavez's cost me, too. You get a reputation, especially if young women are involved. You don't look so good anymore to sweatier clients.

I lean over and flick an imaginary fruit fly off Haysoos Velásquez's shiny lapel. Auguste twitches.

"What did you do that for?" he shrieks.

"I could get you deported real easy." I smile. I want him to know that for all his flash and jangle and elocution lessons so he won't go around like an underworld Ricky Ricardo, to me he's just another boat person. "You got something good for me today?"

A laugh leaks out of him. "You're so burned out, Marshall, you couldn't fuck a whore." He extracts limp bills from a safe. Two thousand to blow town for a while, till it cools.

"*Gracias, amigo.*" At least this month the trailer's safe, if not the car. Which leaves me free to hotwire a newer model.

Where did America go? I want to know. Down the rabbit hole, Doc Healy used to say. Alice knows, but she took it with her. Hard to know which one's the Wonderland. Back when me and my buddies were barricading the front door, who left the back door open?

And just look at what Alice left behind.

She left behind a pastel house, lime-sherbet color, a little south and a little west of Miami, with sprinklers batting water across a yard the size of a badminton court. In the back bedroom there's a dripping old air conditioner. The window barely closes over it. It's an old development, they don't have outside security, wire fences, patrol dogs. It's a retirement bungalow like they used to advertise in the comic pages of the Sunday papers. No one was around in those days to warn the old folks that the lots hadn't quite surfaced from the slime, and the soil was too salty to take a planting. And twenty years later there'd still be that odor—gamey, fishy, sour rot—of a tropical city on unrinsed water, where the blue air shimmers with diesel fumes and the gray water thickens like syrup from saturated waste.

Chavez, stewing in his juices.

And when your mammy and pappy die off and it's time to sell off the lime-sherbet bungalow, who's there to buy it? A nice big friendly greaser like Mr. Chavez.

Twenty years ago I missed the meaning of things around me. I was seventeen years old, in Heidelberg, Germany, about to be shipped out to Vietnam. We had guys on the base selling passages to Sweden. And I had a weekend pass and a free flight to London. Held them in my hand: Sweden forever, or a weekend pass. Wise up, kid, choose life, whispered the cook, a twenty-year lifer with a quarter million stashed in Arizona. Seventeen years old and guys are offering me life or death, only I didn't see it then.

When you're a teenage buckaroo from Ocala, Florida, in London for the first time, where do you go? I went to the London Zoo. Okay, so I was a kid checking out the snakes and gators of my childhood. You learn to love a languid, ugly target.

I found myself in front of the reticulated python. This was one huge serpent. It squeezed out jaguars and crocodiles like dishrags. It was twenty-eight feet long and as thick as my waist, with a snout as long and wide as a croc's. The *scale* of the thing was beyond impressive, beyond incredible. If you ever want to feel helpless or see what the odds look like when they're stacked against you, imagine the embrace of the reticulated python. The tip of its tail at the far end of the concrete pool could have been in a different county. Its head was out of water, resting on the tub's front edge. The head is what got me, that broad, patient, intelligent face, those eyes brown and passionless as all of Vietnam.

Dead rabbits were plowed in a corner. I felt nothing for the bunnies.

Then I noticed the snake shit. Python turds, dozens of turds, light as cork and thick as a tree, riding high in the water. Once you'd seen them, you couldn't help thinking you'd smelled them all along. *That's* what I mean about Florida, about all the hot-water ports like Bangkok, Manila and Bombay, living on water where the shit's so thick it's a kind of cash crop.

Behind me, one of those frosty British matrons whispered to her husband, "I didn't know they *did* such things!"

"Believe it, Queenie," I said.

That snake shit—all that coiled power—stays with me, always. That's what happened to us in the paddy fields. We drowned in our shit. An inscrutable humanoid python sleeping on a bed of turds: that's what I never want to be.

So I keep two things in mind nowadays. First, Florida was built for your pappy and grammie. I remember them, I was a kid here, I remember the good Florida when only the pioneers came down and it was considered too hot and wet and buggy to ever come to much. I knew your pappy and grammie, I mowed their lawn, trimmed their hedges, washed their cars. I toted their golf bags. Nice people—they deserved a few years of golf, a garden to show off when their kids came down to visit, a white car that justified its extravagant air conditioning and never seemed to get dirty. That's the first thing about Florida; the nice thing. The second is this: Florida is run by locusts and behind them are sharks and even pythons and they've pretty well chewed up your mom and pop and all the other lawn bowlers and blue-haired ladies. On the outside, life goes on in Florida courtesy of middlemen who bring in things that people are willing to pay a premium to obtain.

Acapulco, Tijuana, Freeport, Miami—it doesn't matter where the pimping happens. Mr. Vee in his nostalgic moments tells me Havana used to be like that, a city of touts and pimps—the fat young men in sunglasses parked at a corner in an idling Buick, waiting for a payoff, a delivery, a contact. Havana has shifted its corporate headquarters. Beirut has come west. And now, it's Miami that gives me warm memories of always-Christmas Saigon.

It's life in the procurement belt, between those lines of tropical latitudes, where the world shops for its illicit goods and dumps its surplus parts, where it prefers to fight its wars, and once you've settled into its give and take, you find it's impossible to live any-where else. It's the coke-and-caffeine jangle of being seventeen and readier to kill than be killed and to know that Job One is to secure your objective and after that it's unsupervised play till the next order comes down.

In this mood, and in a Civic newly liberated from a protesting coed, I am heading west out of Miami, thinking first of driving up to Pensacola when I am sideswiped off the highway. Two men get in the Civic. They sit on either side of me and light up cigarettes.

"Someone say something," I finally say.

They riffle through the papers in the glove compartment. They quickly surmise that my name is not Mindy Robles. "We know all about this morning. Assault. Grand theft auto."

"Let's talk," I say.

I wait for the rough stuff. When it comes, it's an armlock on the throat that cuts air supply. When they let me speak, I cut a deal. They spot me for a vet; we exchange some dates, names, firefights. Turns out they didn't like Mindy Robles, didn't appreciate the pressure her old man tried to put on the police department. They look at our names—Robles and Marshall—and I can read their minds. We're in some of these things together and no one's linked me to Chavez—these guys are small time, auto-detail. They keep the car. They filch a wad of Mr. Vee's bills, the wad I'd stuffed into my wallet. They don't know there's another wad of Mr. Vee's money in a secret place. And fifty bucks in my boots.

Instead of an air-conditioned nighttime run up the Gulf coast, it's the thumb on the interstate. I pass up a roadside rest area, a happy hunting ground for new cars and ready cash. I hitch a ride to the farthest cheap motel.

The first automobile I crouch behind in the dark parking lot of the Dunes Motel is an Impala with Alabama license plates. The next one is Broward County. Two more out-of-staters: Live Free or Die and Land of Lincoln. The farther from Florida the better for me. I look in the windows of the Topaz from New Hampshire. There's a rug in the back seat, and under the rug I make out a shiny sliver of Samsonite. Maybe they're just eating. Clothes hang on one side: two sports jackets for a small man or an adolescent, and what looks to me like lengths of silk. On the rearview mirror, where you or I might hang a kid's booties or a plastic Jesus and rosaries, is an alien deity with four arms or legs. I don't know about borrowing this little beauty. These people travel a little too heavy.

The Dunes isn't an absolute dump. The pool has water in it. The neon VACANCY sign above the door of the office has blown only one letter. The annex to the left of the office has its own separate entrance: SANDALWOOD RESTAURANT.

I stroke the highway dust out of my hair, so the office won't guess my present automobileless state, tuck my shirt into my Levis and walk in from the parking lot. The trouble is there's nobody behind the desk. It's 11:03; late but not late enough for even a junior high jailbait nightclerk to have taken to her cot.

Another guest might have rung the bell and waited, or rung the bell and banged his fist on the counter and done some swearing. What I do is count on the element of surprise. I vault into the staff area and kick open a door that says: STRICTLY PRIVATE.

Inside, in a room reeking of incense, are people eating. There are a lot of them. There are a lot of little brown people sitting cross-legged on the floor of a regular motel room and eating with their hands. Pappies with white beards, grammies swaddled in silk, men in dark suits, kids, and one luscious jailbait in blue jeans.

They look at me. A bunch of aliens and they stare like I'm the freak.

One of the aliens tries to uncross his legs, but all he manages is a backward flop. He holds his right hand stiff and away from his body so it won't drip gravy on his suit. "Are you wanting a room?"

I've never liked the high, whiny Asian male voice. "Let's put it this way. Are you running a motel or what?"

The rest of the aliens look at me, look at each other, look down at their food. I stare at them too. They seem to have been partying. I wouldn't mind a Jack Daniel's and a plate of their rice and yellow stew stuff brought to me by room service in blue jeans.

"Some people here say we are running a 'po-tel'." A greasy grin floats off his face. "Get it? My name is Patel, that's P-A-T-E-L. A Patel owning a motel, get it?"

"Rich," I say.

The jailbait springs up off the floor. With a gecko-fast tongue tip, she chases a gravy drop on her wrist. "I can go. I'm done." But she doesn't make a move. "You people enjoy the meal."

The women jabber, but not in English. They flash gold bracelets. An organized raid could clean up in that room, right down to the rubies and diamonds in their noses. They're all wrapped in silk, like brightly colored mummies. Pappy shakes his head, but doesn't rise. "She eats like a bird. Who'll marry her?" he says in English to one of his buddies.

"You should advertise," says the other man, probably the Living Free or Dying. They've forgotten me. I feel left out, left behind. While we were nailing up that big front door, these guys were sneaking in around back. They got their money, their family networks, and their secretive languages.

I verbalize a little seething, and when none of the aliens take notice, I dent the prefab wall with my fist. "Hey," I yell. "I need a room for the night. Don't any of you dummies speak American?"

Now she swings toward me apologetically. She has a braid that snakes all the way down to her knees. "Sorry for the inconvenience," she says. She rinses gravy off her hands. "It's our biggest family reunion to date. That's why things are so hectic." She says something about a brother getting married, leaving them short at the desk. I think of Jonda and the turbaned guy. He fired her when some new turbaned guy showed up.

"Let's just go," I say. "I don't give a damn about reunions." I don't know where Jonda ended up. The Goldilocks doll wasn't delivered to Laguna Vista Estates, though I had a welcome planned for it.

This kid's got a ripe body. I follow the ripe body up a flight of outdoor stairs. Lizards scurry, big waterbugs drag across the landings.

"This is it," she says. She checks the air-conditioning and the TV. She makes sure there are towels in the bathroom. If she feels a little uneasy being in a motel room with a guy like me who's dusty and scruffy and who kills for a living, she doesn't show it. Not till she looks back at the door and realizes I'm not carrying any bags.

She's a pro. "You'll have to pay in cash now," she says. "I'll make out a receipt."

"What if I were to pull out a knife instead?" I joke. I turn slightly away from her and count the balance of Haysoos's bills. Not enough in there, after the shakedown. The fifty stays put, my new nest egg. "Where were you born, honey? Bombay? I been to Bombay."

"New Jersey," she says. "You can pay half tonight, and the rest before you check out tomorrow. I am not unreasonable."

"I'll just bet you're not. Neither am I. But who says I'm leaving tomorrow. You got some sort of policy?"

That's when I catch the look on her face. Disgust, isn't that what it is? Distaste for the likes of me.

"You can discuss that with my father and uncle tomorrow morning." She sashays just out of my reach. She's aiming to race back to the motel room not much different from this except that it's jammed with family.

I pounce on Alice before she can drop down below, and take America with her. The hardware comes in handy, especially the kris. Alice lays hot fingers on my eyes and nose, but it's no use and once she knows it, Alice submits.

I choose me the car with the Land of Lincoln plates. I make a double switch with Broward County. I drive the old Tamiami Trail across the remains of the Everglades. Used to be no cars, a narrow ridge of two-lane concrete with swamps on either side, gators sunning themselves by day, splattered by night. Black snakes and mocassins every few hundred yards. Clouds of mosquitoes.

This is what I've become. I want to squeeze this state dry and swallow it whole.

from
THE BUTCHER'S BOY

Thomas Perry

1

The union meeting, thought Al Veasy, had gone as well
as could be expected, all things considered. He had finally figured
out why the retirement fund was in such trouble all the time, when
everybody else in the whole country with anything to invest
seemed to be making money. And he had explained what he knew,
and the union members had understood it right away, because it
wasn't anything surprising if you read the newspapers. The big
unions had been getting caught in similar situations for years.
Low-interest loans to Fieldston Growth Enterprises—hell of an impressive name, but zero return so far on almost five million dollars.
If the company was as bad as it looked, there would be no more
Fieldston than there was growth. Just a name and a fancy address.
When the union started to apply pressure some lawyer nobody ever
heard of would quietly file bankruptcy papers. Probably in New

York or someplace where it would take weeks before the union here in Ventura, California, heard of it. Just a notice by certified mail to O'Connell, the president of the union local, informing him of the dissolution of Fieldston Growth Enterprises and the sale of its assets to cover debts. And O'Connell, the big dumb bastard, would bring it to Veasy for translation. "Hey, Al," he would say, "take a look at this," as though he already knew what it meant but felt it was his duty to let somebody else see the actual document. Not that it would do anybody any good by then.

Or now either. That was the trouble and always had been. Veasy could feel it as he walked away from the union hall, still wearing his clodhopper boots and a work shirt that the sweat had dried on hours ago. He could smell himself. The wise guys in their perfectly fitted three-piece suits and their Italian shoes always ended up with everything. The best the ordinary working man could hope for was sometimes to figure out how they'd done it, and then make one or two of them uncomfortable. Slow them down was what it amounted to. If it hadn't been Fieldston Growth Enterprises it would have been something else that sounded just as substantial and ended up just the same. The money gone and nobody, no person, who could be forced to give it back.

He kicked at a stone on the gravel parking lot. There probably wasn't even any point in going to the government about it. The courts and the bureaucrats and commissions. Veasy snorted. All of them made up of the same wise guys in the three-piece suits, so much alike you couldn't tell them from each other or from the crooks, except maybe the crooks were a little better at it, at getting money without working for it, and they smiled at you. The ones in the government didn't even have to smile at you, because they'd get their cut of it no matter what. But hell, what else could you do? You had to go through the motions. Sue Fieldston, just so it got on the record. A little machinists' union local in Ventura losing 70 percent of its pension fund to bad investments. It probably wouldn't even make the papers. But you had to try, even if all you could hope for was to make them a little more cautious next time, a little less greedy so they wouldn't try to take it all. And maybe make one or two of them sweat a little.

Veasy opened the door of his pickup truck and climbed in. He sat there for a minute, lit a cigarette, took a deep drag, and blew a puff out the window. "Jesus," he thought. "Nine o'clock. I wonder if Sue kept dinner for me." He looked at the lighted doorway of the union hall, where he could see the men filing out past the bulky shape of O'Connell, who was smiling and slapping somebody on the back. He would be saying something about how we don't know yet and that it's too early to panic. That's right, you big dumb bastard, thought Veasy. Keep calm, and you'll never know what hit you.

Veasy turned the key in the ignition and the whole world turned to fire and noise. The concussion threw O'Connell back against the clapboards of the union hall and disintegrated the front window. Then the parking lot was bathed in light as the billowing ball of flame tore up into the sky. Afterward a machinist named Lynley said pieces of the pickup truck went with it, but O'Connell said there wasn't anything to that. People always said things like that, especially when somebody actually got killed. Sure was a shame, though, and it was bad enough without making things up.

2

"Here's the daily gloom," said Padgett, tossing the sheaf of computer printouts on Elizabeth's desk. "Early today, and you're welcome to it."

"Thanks," said Elizabeth, not looking up from her calculations. She was still trying to figure out how that check had bounced. Even if the store had tried to cash it the next morning, the deposit should have been there at least twelve hours before. Eight fifteen, and the bank would open at nine thirty. She made a note to call. It was probably the post office, as usual. Anybody who couldn't deliver a piece of mail across town in two days ought to get into another business. They had sure delivered the notice of insufficient funds fast enough. One day.

Elizabeth put the checkbook and notice back in her purse and picked up the printout. "All those years of school for this," she thought. "Reading computerized obituaries for the Department of Justice for a living, and lucky to get it."

She started at the first sheet, going through the items one by one. "De Vitto, L. G. Male. Caucasian. 46. Apparent suicide. Shotgun, 12 gauge. Toledo, Ohio. Code number 79–8475." She marked the entry in pencil, maybe just because of the name that could mean Mafia, and maybe just because it was the first one, and the other prospects might be even less likely.

"Gale, D. R. Female. Caucasian. 34. Apparent murder. Revolver, .38. Suspects: Gale, P. G., 36; no prior arrests. Wichita, Kansas, code number 79–8476." No, just the usual thing, thought Elizabeth. Family argument and one of them picks up a gun. She went on down the list, searching for the unusual, the one that might not be one of the same old things.

"Veasy, A. E. Male. Caucasian. 35. Apparent murder. Dynamite. Ventura, California. Code number 79–8477." Dynamite? Murder by dynamite? Elizabeth marked this one. Maybe it wasn't anything for the Activity Report, but at least it wasn't the predictable, normal Friday night's random violence.

"Satterfield, R. J. Male. Afro-American. 26. Apparent murder/robbery. Revolver, .32. Washington, D.C. Code number 79–8478." No.

"Davidson, B. L. Female. Caucasian. 23. Apparent murder/rape. Knife. Carmel, California. Code number 79–8479." No again.

Down the printout she went, letting the sheets fall in front of her desk to re-form themselves into an accordion shape on the floor. Now and then she would make a check mark with her pencil beside an entry that didn't fall into the ten or twelve most common murder patterns. It was Monday, so she had to work fast to catch up. One thing Elizabeth had learned on this job was that a lot of people killed each other on weekends.

It was just after ten when she reached the final entry. "Stapleton, R. D. Male. Caucasian. 41. Apparent murder. Revolver, .45. Suspects: Stapleton, A. E., 38; no prior arrests. Buffalo, New York. Code number 79–102033." Padgett, the senior analyst in charge of analyzing reports, would be on his morning break, she thought. The timing was always wrong, somehow. Whenever you got to the stage where you needed somebody it was either lunchtime or a break. She picked up the printout and carried it across the office to the glass-walled room where the computer operators worked.

She was surprised to see Padgett at his desk behind the glass, frowning over a report. She rapped on the glass and he got up to open the door for her without putting down the papers he was reading.

"I thought you would be on your break, Roger," she said.

"Not today," said Padgett. "Must have been a big weekend. Four of our friends bought airline tickets in the last three days." He always called them "our friends," as though the years of scanning lists for familiar names had prompted a kind of affection.

"All to the same place?"

"No," he said. "Two to Las Vegas, one to Phoenix, and one to Los Angeles."

"It's probably the weather," said Elizabeth. "They don't like it any more than we do. You still have to scrape the snow off your car if it's a Rolls Royce."

He looked impatient. "Okay, love. What did you find?"

"Eight possibles. The numbers are marked. The rest are the usual weekend stuff—rapes, muggings, and arguments that went a little too far."

"I'll have Mary get the details to you as soon as they're printed out. Give her fifteen minutes. Take a break or something."

"Okay," she said, and walked out again into the large outer office. She saw that Brayer, her section head, was just putting a few papers into a file, then throwing on his sport coat.

"On a break, Elizabeth?" he asked.

"Yes," she said. "Can't do anything until the computer spits out the day's possibles."

"Come on," said Brayer. "I'll buy you a cup of coffee. I'm waiting on something myself." They walked down the hall and into the employees' lounge. Brayer poured two cups of coffee while Elizabeth staked her claim on a table in the far corner of the room.

Brayer sat down, sighing. "I sometimes get tired of this job. You never seem to get anything worthwhile, and you spend an awful lot of time analyzing data that doesn't form a pattern and wouldn't prove anything if it did. This morning I've been going over the field reports of last week's possibles. Nothing."

Elizabeth said, "Just what I needed—to hear my section chief talking like that on a Monday morning."

"I guess it's the logical flaw that bothers me," said Brayer. "You and I are looking for a pattern that will lead us to a professional killer, a hit man. So we pick out everything that doesn't seem routine and normal. The point about professional killers is that they don't do things to draw attention to themselves. What did you get this morning, for instance?"

"A shotgun suicide. One where they tortured a man and then cut his throat. One where a man was poisoned in a hotel dining room, one where the brakes failed on a new car. And a dynamite murder, and—"

"There!" said Brayer. "That's just what I was talking about. A dynamite murder. That's no hit man. It's a mental defective who saw a hit man do that on television. What we ought to be looking at is the ones that don't look unusual. The ones where the coroner says it was a natural death."

"You know why we don't," said Elizabeth.

"Sure. Too many of them. Thousands every day. But that's where our man will be. And you wouldn't be able to tell whether it was a hit man or pneumonia. Dynamite, shotguns, knives, hell. You don't have to hire a professional for that. You can find some junkie in half an hour who could do that for a couple of hundred."

"We help catch one now and then, you have to remember that."

"Yes, we do. You're right. We're not just wasting time. But there has to be a better way to do it. As it is, we find what we find, not what we're looking for. We catch lunatics, ax murderers, people like that. Once every few years an old Mafia soldier who wants to come in from the cold and can tell us who did what to whom in 1953. It's okay, but it's not what we're after."

"John, how many actual hit men do you suppose there are operating right now? The professionals we look for?"

"Oh, a hundred. Maybe two hundred if you count the semi-retired and the novices who have the knack. That's in the world. Not too many, is it?"

"No, not many when you're trying to find them by analyzing statistics. From another point of view it's plenty. I'd better go call my bank while I've got a minute. They bounced my check unjustly."

Brayer laughed. "Typical woman," he said. "Mathematical genius who can't add up her checkbook."

Elizabeth smiled her sweetest smile at him, the one that didn't show that her teeth were clenched. "Thanks for the coffee. I'll have the activity report in an hour or two." She got up and disappeared out the door of the lounge.

Brayer sat there alone, sipping the last half of his cup of coffee and feeling vaguely bereft. He liked to sit at a table with a pretty woman. That was about as far as he allowed it to go these days, he thought. It made him feel young.

"May I join you, or am I too ugly?" came a voice. Brayer looked up and saw Connors, the Organized Crime Division head, standing above him.

"You're perfect, Martin," said Brayer. "You being the boss, this being Monday, and you being ugly enough to fit right in. It's a pattern."

"Thanks," Connors said. "How are things going?"

"Rotten, I'm afraid. Elizabeth went back to pick out the second-stage possibles, of which there are several. None very promising, but they all take time. The field reports from last week are all blanks except the one from Tulsa, which is three days late and is probably just as blank."

"I almost hope so this morning," said Connors. "We've got just about every investigator in the field, and Padgett's airline reports say at least four of the people we keep an eye on bought tickets west this weekend."

"Anything in it?"

"Probably the usual. Old men like warm weather. At least I do. And Roncone and Neroni have investments out there. Legitimate businesses, or at least they would be if those two weren't in on them. But there's always a chance of a meeting."

"Maybe we'll get lucky," said Brayer without enthusiasm. "Well, I think I'll go see if Tulsa phoned in. I'd like to close the books on last week before Elizabeth comes up with today's massacres."

"How's she working out, anyway? It's been over a year."

Brayer sat back down and spoke in a low voice, "To tell you the truth, Martin, she's a real surprise. I think if I had to retire tomorrow, she'd be the one I'd pick to replace me."

"Come on, John," said Connors. "She can't possibly know enough yet. There's a difference between being clever and pretty and running an analysis section. She hasn't even been in any field investigation yet."

"But I think she's got the touch," said Brayer. "She's the only one in my section that's smarter than I am."

3

Two this week, he thought. Too many. After the next one, a vacation. At least a month. The old lady in front of him stepped aside to count her change, so he moved forward. "One way to Los Angeles, the three o'clock."

"Five fifty," said the weary ticket agent, running his hand over the bald spot on his head as though checking to be sure nothing had grown in there while he wasn't paying attention.

He paid the money and waited while the man filled in the ticket. It would be no problem. After something like Friday, a man buying a ticket on Saturday morning for someplace far away might have stuck. A man buying a ticket for Los Angeles on Monday afternoon was nothing. He wasn't leaving the vicinity of a crime. He was just leaving. This man behind the counter wouldn't remember him. Too many people in line buying the same ticket, as fast as he could write. Not even time to look at them all. Not the men, anyway.

He stepped aside and pocketed his ticket. The clock on the wall said 2:45. Almost time to board. Not much time to hang around the bus station and get stared at. No reason for anybody to remember having seen him, because they hadn't seen anybody in the first place. No chance they'd check on the motel either. He'd registered Friday afternoon three hours before the truck blew up, and the truck had been thirty miles away in Ventura. Another county. All clean and simple. From Los Angeles, you could take any kind of transport to anywhere. You practically had to set yourself on fire to attract a second glance in L. A.

On Monday, February twelfth, at 2:43 P.M., a man not fat, not thin, not young, not old, not tall, not short, not dark, not light, bought a bus ticket for Los Angeles at the Santa Barbara bus station. He was one of twenty or thirty that afternoon that you couldn't have told from one another, but that didn't matter because nobody looked at any of them. If the police were looking for someone in the area, it wasn't on a bus coming toward Ventura on its way to Los Angeles.

Elizabeth studied the second set of printouts on the day's possibles. The man who had been killed by the shotgun had left a note that satisfied his family and the coroner. The death by torture was linked to a religious cult that had been under investigation for a year and a half. The brake failure was officially attributed to incorrect assembly at the factory in Japan. That left the man poisoned in the hotel dining room and the victim of the dynamite murder.

The autopsy report on the unlucky diner convinced Elizabeth that there wasn't much point in following up with an investigation. Chances were that he hadn't even ingested the poison on the premises. It was a combination of drugs, all used for treatment of hypertension, and taken this time with a large amount of alcohol. Elizabeth moved on to the last one.

Veasy, Albert Edward. Machinist for a small company in Ventura, California, called Precision Tooling. Not very promising, really. Professional killers were an expensive service, and that meant powerful enemies. Machinists in Ventura didn't usually have that kind of enemy. Sexual jealousy? That might introduce him to somebody he wouldn't otherwise meet—somebody whose name turned up on Activity Reports now and then. Thirty-five years old, married for ten years, three kids. Still possible. Have to check his social habits, if it came to that.

Elizabeth scanned the narrative for the disqualifier, the one element that would make it clear that this one, too, was normal, just another instance of someone being murdered by someone who had a reason to do it, someone who at least knew him.

She noticed the location of the crime. Outside the headquarters of the Brotherhood of Machinists, Local 602, where he had been for a meeting. Her breath caught—a union meeting. Maybe a particularly nasty strike, or the first sign that one of the West Coast families was moving in on the union. She made a note to check it, and also the ownership of Precision Tooling. Maybe that was dirty money. Well what the hell, she thought. Might as well get all of it. Find out what they made, whom they sold it to, and tax summaries. She'd been expecting a busy day anyway, and the other possibles had already dissolved.

She moved down to the summary of the lab report. Explosives detonated by the ignition of the car. She made a note to ask for a list of the dynamite thefts during the last few months in California. She read further. "Explosive not dynamite, as earlier reported. Explosive 200 pounds of fertilizer carried in the bed of the victim's pickup truck." Elizabeth laughed involuntarily. Then she threw her pencil down, leaned back in her chair, and tore up her notes.

"What's up, Elizabeth?" asked Richardson, the analyst at the next desk. "You find a funny murder?"

Elizabeth said, "I can't help it. I think we've established today's pattern. My one possible blew himself up with a load of fertilizer. You should appreciate that. You're a connoisseur."

Richardson chuckled. "Let me see." He came up and looked over her shoulder at the printout. "Well, I guess it hit the fan this weekend," he said. "But that's a new one on me."

"Me too," said Elizabeth.

"How do you suppose it happened?"

"I don't know," said Elizabeth. "I've heard of sewers and septic tanks blowing up. I guess there's a lot of methane gas in animal waste."

"Oh yeah," said Richardson, suddenly pensive. "I remember reading about some guy who was going to parlay his chicken ranch into an energy empire. But you know what this means, don't you?"

"No."

"Brayer's a walking bomb. His pep talks at staff meetings could kill us."

Elizabeth giggled. "I knew I shouldn't have told you about this. I suppose I'll have to listen to a lot of infantile jokes now."

"No, I think I got them all out of my system for the present," said Richardson.

Elizabeth groaned. "Go back to your desk, you creep."

Richardson said, "I'm going. But you know what?"

"What?"

"I'd have this one checked out." Elizabeth made a face, but he held up his hand in the gesture he used to signal the return of the businesslike Richardson. "Seriously," he said.

"Checked out with whom?" asked Elizabeth, moving warily toward whatever absurdity he was anxious for her to elicit from him. "And why?"

"I'm not sure who. I guess the bomb squad. Maybe even somebody over in the Agriculture Department. Maybe this sort of thing happens all the time. Who knows? I'm a city boy myself. But if it does we ought to know about it. We might be sending agents out into the field once a week to find out some farmer blew himself up with his manure spreader."

Elizabeth studied his face, but he seemed serious. "I don't know if you're joking or not, but what you're saying makes sense. It'll take a few minutes to clear this up, and I've got some time on my hands this afternoon."

"Then do it," he said. "If only to cater to my curiosity."

In the Los Angeles airport there are some people who stand on the moving walkway, letting the long belt carry them to the end of the corridor. Others walk forward on it, combining muscle and machinery into something over a dead run; and others, probably the biggest group, don't use the machinery at all. This group consists of people who have spent too much time sitting down and know they'll soon be sitting again for a few hours, or people who arrived at the airport an hour earlier than they needed to. Among them was a man not tall or short, not young or old, not light or dark, with a one-way ticket to Denver in his breast pocket. When the flight attendant checks his boarding pass for the seat number a few minutes from now, she won't be able to decide whether he is on his way to one of the military bases in that area, or one of the ski resorts. And she certainly won't ask. After that she won't have time to notice. As soon as the lights go on she will be too busy to study faces. Once they are strapped in she will look mostly at their laps, where the trays and the drinks and the magazines will be.

The man at Treasury said, "That one's not in our bailiwick, I'm afraid. Have you tried the FBI?"

"Not yet," said Elizabeth. "I'd hoped to get something on it today."

The man chuckled. "Oh, you've noticed. But I'll tell you what you can do. There's a guy over there who knows just about everything about explosives. Name's Hart. Agent Robert E. Hart. If you call him direct you'll avoid all the referral forms and runarounds. He's the one you'd get to in the end anyway. He's at extension 3023. Write down that name and number, because it'll come in handy every now and then. Agent Hart."

"Thanks," said Elizabeth. "That'll save me a lot of time."

Elizabeth dialed the FBI number and waited. The female voice on the other end seemed to come from the soul of a melting candy bar: "Federal Bureau of Investigation." Elizabeth retaliated, making her voice go soft and whispery. "Extension 3023 please, dear."

That'll hold her, thought Elizabeth.

"Whom would you like to speak with, ma'am?" said the voice, now suddenly businesslike and mechanical.

"Agent Hart," said Elizabeth.

"I'll ring his office," said the voice.

The line clicked and there was that sound that seemed as though a door had opened on a physically larger space. "Hart," said a man's voice.

Elizabeth wondered if she had missed the ring. "This is Elizabeth Waring at Justice, Agent Hart. We have an explosives case and we need some information."

"Who told you to call me?"

"Treasury."

"Figures," he said, without emotion. "What do you want to know?"

"Anything you can tell me about fertilizer blowing up."

"About what?"

"Fertilizer. Er . . . manure. You know, fertilizer."

"Oh." There was silence on Hart's end.

Elizabeth waited. Then she said, "I assure you, Agent Hart, this isn't a—"

"I know," he said. "I was just thinking. What's the LEAA computer code designation?"

"Seven nine dash eight four seven seven."

"I'll take a look at it and call you back. What's your extension?"

"Two one two one. But does that happen? Have you heard of it before?"

"I'm not sure what we're talking about yet," said Hart. "I'll call you back in a few minutes." He hung up and Elizabeth said "Good-bye" into a dead phone.

She looked up and saw Padgett dash by with a cup of coffee in one hand and an open file in the other. Just then a loose sheet in the file peeled itself off in the breeze and wafted to the floor. He stopped and looked back at it in remorse.

"Got it," said Elizabeth, and sprang up to retrieve it for him.

"Thanks," said Padgett. "Too many things at once."

"Are your friends having a nice time out west?"

"Much better than I am," he said. "We've got to get a few investigators out there today before anything has a chance to happen, and I don't know where we're going to get them."

"You mean it might be something?"

"Probably not," he said, "but you never know. You can't take a chance of missing another Appalachin just because somebody's got the damned flu and somebody else is at an airport that's fogged in."

"How about holding the fort with technicians until the cavalry arrives? Locals even? Wiretaps and so on."

"You know what that mess is these days," said Padgett. "And we don't even have probable cause. Just four men we can't even prove know one another taking winter vacations within a couple hundred miles of one another. Want to go in front of a judge with that one? I don't, and I've been there."

"Well, good luck with it," said Elizabeth, not knowing what else to say. The telephone on her desk rang, and she answered it with relief. "Justice, Elizabeth Waring."

"Hart here," came the voice.

"Good," said Elizabeth. "What can you tell me?"

"It's pretty much what I figured," he said. "It's the fertilizer all right."

"You mean manure blows up?" she asked, a little louder than she had intended. She looked up and noticed that Richardson was watching her with a smirk on his face.

"No," Hart said. "Fertilizer. The kind they make in factories and sell in stores. A couple of the nitrate fertilizers are chemically similar to dynamite. If you know how to detonate them you can use them the same way. They're cheaper and you don't have to have a license to use them. If you run out you can go down to the store and buy all you want."

"That's incredible," said Elizabeth. "Do people know about this?"

"Sure," said Hart. "A lot of construction companies use fertilizer all the time. Been doing it for years."

"Then my case is closed, I guess," said Elizabeth. "The poor man probably just blew himself up by accident. But somebody ought to sue whoever makes that fertilizer. It could happen to anybody."

"No it couldn't," said Hart. "It doesn't blow up by accident. You have to use blasting caps and an electric charge. Theoretically the gasoline in Veasy's pickup truck is more dangerous than the fertilizer. More explosive power and easier to set off."

"So you think it was murder?"

"Or suicide. I haven't seen enough to tell, really, but I don't think it's likely he bought a bag of fertilizer for his garden and it just went off. I suppose if he was carrying blasting caps or shotgun shells or something, and the conditions were right, maybe. But the report says he was just sitting in a parking lot, not jolting along a country road, and something would have to set off whatever served as the detonator."

"So it is murder."

"I don't know. But if this is a case you're interested in I wouldn't write it off yet. I'd at least find out what he was carrying around in the bed of his pickup, and whether he even bought any fertilizer."

"Are you on this case, too? What I mean is, is the FBI interested?"

"No. At least I don't think so. If the explosive had turned out to be dynamite we would have been. There you have a federal statute having to do with a traceable substance. But as it is, unless it somehow ties in with another case, I doubt there'll be anyone on it. Local jurisdiction, no reason for the FBI to take an interest."

4

"Gentlemen, we're running this country like a goddamned poker game. The average man sees that he has nothing and somebody else has everything. He doesn't make trouble because he's optimistic enough to think that after the next hand he'll have everything. Watch out for the day when he figures out that the chips aren't changing hands the way they used to. And when he finds out that it's because the fellow with the chips is playing by different rules, we'd better be ready with our bags packed. You talk about a tax revolt, hell, there'll be a real revolt. See you next session, if there is one."

"It's the only game in town, Senator," said the senator from Illinois, putting his arm on the old man's shoulder and walking with him out of the committee hearing room. "Don't worry. We'll get a new tax bill passed next session. You put the fear of God into them."

They were walking down the quiet private hallway that led back under the street to the Senate office building. No one was now within earshot. The old man continued, "Hell, Billy. You're young yet. Boy senator from Illinois. But I may not even be alive next session. I'm seventy years old, you know. Six terms in the Senate. I'm not going to have a seventh, one way or the other, and when I go the chairmanship goes to—"

"I know, to Fairleigh. You watch seniority pretty closely if you don't have any yourself. But don't worry, Senator. Your tax bill is in the bag. Our esteemed colleagues aren't even dragging their feet anymore. Too much mail from home."

"I hope you're right, Billy," said the old man. "But I'd have felt a lot better about it if we could have gotten it all out on the floor this session. You know, I got a letter today from a woman who makes fifteen thousand dollars a year after twenty years working as a secretary. Her husband makes twenty-five thousand, so the first dollar she makes is taxed at forty-three percent. No tax shelters for them. By the time you figure state taxes, social security, and sales taxes that woman is losing over half her income. Maybe eight thousand dollars. Of the fifty richest people in my state, not one of them pays eight thousand a year in taxes. A lot of them don't pay anything and never have. And the recent tax bills gave the rich the biggest subsidy yet. We've got to make some changes."

"I know, Senator," said the younger man, patting him on the shoulder. "I've been with you on this since I got here. It's what got me elected. I said I'd try to work with you on income tax reforms that would help the average citizen, do whatever you wanted. They didn't vote for me, they voted for you."

"That's bullshit. You got here because you were the best governor they'd had in twenty-five years. And you'll get re-elected because you're the best senator for the last thirty. If something happens to me before we get this bill passed I'm counting on you to ramrod it. Remind a few people of what they promised us. You know who I mean."

"Well, here's my office," said the senator from Illinois. "Don't worry. We'll both be here to remind them, and we probably won't have to. Most of them will get an earful while they're home for the break. I leave myself in two hours. First speaking date is tonight."

"Oh, to be young again," said the old man. "See you in a few weeks, Billy." The younger man watched the older senator walk down the hallway toward his office. The familiar blue suit was hanging from the old man's stooped shoulders, but the white head was still held erect. The Honorable McKinley R. Claremont, senior senator from the great state of Colorado. He wasn't fooling anybody with that frail elder-statesman routine. Anybody who was

interested could check his schedule and see he had a press conference set for eight fifteen tonight in the Denver airport.

"You're sure about all this?" asked Brayer.

"Of course I'm sure," said Elizabeth. "I'm sure of the facts,
that is. I'm not sure about what interpretation to hang on them,
because there aren't enough of them. Veasy was carrying two
hundred-pound sacks of nitrate fertilizer in his pickup truck. He
must have bought them that day according to the Ventura police,
because nobody saw them before that. Somebody apparently came
along while he was in a union meeting and did something to the
fertilizer so it would explode. And the FBI agent said that was
perfectly possible for somebody who knew how."

Brayer leaned back in his chair and tapped his pencil absently
on the glass desktop. He stared off into space. Finally he turned to
her and said, "I'm afraid I don't know what to make of it either, but
it's sure not ordinary. Whoever did it was fast on his feet. He'd have
to ad lib, if the fertilizer was only bought that day."

"So what do we do now?" asked Elizabeth. "Does it warrant an
investigation or not?"

"I'm not sure I know what warrants an investigation these
days. We're supposed to be keeping an eye on organized crime, not
giving an Academy Award for the most imaginative performance
by a murderer. Do you have any reason to believe this fellow Veasy
might have had anything to do with the Mafia?"

"He didn't have a record, if that's what you mean, and his
name didn't come up when I had Padgett run the Who's Who
program on the computer. But who knows? Maybe he borrowed
money, maybe he smuggled something for them—Ventura's got a
harbor. Maybe anything. It could even have had something to do
with the union. We just don't have anything to go on."

"Except the fact that whoever snuffed him was clever about it."

"Right," said Elizabeth. "Clever enough to be a professional?"

"I don't know. Maybe a world-class amateur, maybe a lunatic
with beginner's luck. But there's always the chance it's the real

thing. Lunatics and beginners usually spend some time planning. They're not up to working with what they find."

"So you're going to dispatch an investigator?"

"I'm not sure yet. I'm not even sure if I have anybody I can send right now. What was that FBI agent's name, again?"

"Hart. Robert E. Hart. Extension 3023. Why?"

"I'll see if I can con his boss into sending him. If he's as good as the Treasury man said and I haven't heard of him, he's young enough and new enough to be eligible for legwork." He picked up the phone, then looked at her expectantly.

"You mean I have to leave?" she asked.

" 'Fraid so. It's hard to lie, cheat, and steal in front of an audience. Close the door on your way out."

5

Just one more before payday, and then a little vacation. Sometimes he wondered how long he would keep it up. At the beginning he'd thought five years was a long time, but now it had been six—no, almost seven, and still going strong. Living in motels and rent-by-the-week cottages could get to be pretty old after a month. It would be nice to be back in Tucson, where he could relax a little and get the old edge back. Eating in fast-food places and spending half your time traveling wasn't so good for your body. It had to catch up with you sooner or later.

Denver wasn't bad this time of year, though. Cold and clear. Later he'd take a walk down Colfax Avenue and see a movie. The plane wouldn't arrive until tonight, and the press conference would make the eleven o'clock news. For the first day or two the old guy'd be surrounded by reporters and hometown minor-league political hacks anyway. After that, when the rosy glow faded, there'd be time to work something out. Just a matter of seeing your best shot and taking it, like pool.

He turned off the television and walked to the dresser. He leaned over his suitcase and peered at the face in the mirror. A little tired from the plane ride is all. No lines, nothing, he thought. It would be ten years yet before it was the kind of face people remembered.

Brayer opened the door of his office and beckoned to Elizabeth, who was sitting at her desk glancing at a newspaper. She brought it with her into Brayer's office.

"Get down to Disbursement and pick up your travel vouchers," Brayer said. "There's a plane at eight that'll get you to L.A. International by ten o'clock Pacific time, and a hop to Ventura that'll get you in by eleven."

"Me?"

"Do you see anybody else?"

"But I'm an analyst, remember? Good old Elizabeth? I'm no investigator. I haven't been out of this office since—"

"You're going, Elizabeth," he said. "You've got the rating and the qualifications. Just because you haven't done it before doesn't mean you can't do it, or if it comes to that, that I can't order you to. I checked it with Martin Connors. So you're going."

"So the FBI wouldn't do it?" she smiled slyly.

"Yes, they will. But they'll only guarantee to let us use Hart for two days. They can pull him back any time after five o'clock Wednesday afternoon. And they'll only send him if he's there to investigate explosions, not handle the whole case by himself. Now get down there to your friendly local travel agent in Disbursement so they have some chance of getting you both on that eight-o'clock plane."

"I'm on my way," she said, heading for the door. "I hate snow anyway."

"If you come back with a tan anywhere but on your face I'll skin it off you and nail it to the wall," said Brayer. "You're not on a vacation, Waring."

She stopped in the doorway and said, "I thought the usual thing was the Death of a Thousand Cuts?"

"Get going," he said. To himself he thought, Damn. The best I've got. Maybe the best data analyst outside the National Security Agency, off on a wild-goose chase. The worst part was that he had needed to convince Connors to arrange it. He tried to remind himself there was no need to worry. The case and the timing could hardly be better for starting her in the field. It was the longest kind of long shot, complete with a trail that was already cold. She'd have little chance to put herself in harm's way before she was ready, getting in on armed surveillance or arrests. With four of the capos suddenly showing up in the West on the same day, it hadn't been hard to convince Connors that it was time to try Elizabeth in the field. The department really did need seasoned field investigators, and if she worked out, who could tell? A female with her brains out in the field—hell, it might make a difference some time. But, he thought, if Connors ever got around to reading the preliminary reports and saw the kind of case he'd sent two people out to investigate, Brayer would have some explaining to do. He consoled himself by planning what he'd say to Grosvenor, when and if he finally bothered to report in from Tulsa.

As Elizabeth stood in the elevator she was glad Brayer had said that about the suntan. California would be warm. It wouldn't do to show up wearing a heavy overcoat and wool skirts. It wasn't a vacation, as he'd said, but there was nothing in the rules that said you had to humiliate yourself in front of strangers, looking as though you'd arrived in California by walking over the North Pole. Besides, the bathing suit she had in mind didn't take up much room.

At the United Airlines desk there were two men. One sat drinking coffee, looking impatient, while the other did all the work. When Elizabeth reached the head of the line and handed the man her travel voucher, he nodded to the other and said, "Miss Waring, Mr. Hart is here waiting for you."

Hart dropped his cup in a basket and stepped around the desk to help her with the suitcase. "Good to meet you," he said, looking at the suitcase instead of at her.

"Same to you," she said. For once she meant it. He was tall and thin with a kind of delicacy about his hands and a rather unruly shock of light brown hair that probably made him look younger than he was. He guided her away from the desk to a line of seats facing the loading gate like a man conducting a lady off a dance floor. This wasn't going to be so terrible after all.

When they were seated she noticed that he had somehow managed to pick a spot that looked as though it was in the middle of things, but wasn't close enough to anyone so they couldn't talk.

He said, "Before I forget, are you carrying a weapon?"

"Yes," she said. "They admitted there wasn't any reason, but regulations say field investigators have to. Are you?"

"Yes," he said. "Same regulation. We'll have to board early so we don't attract too much attention when they wave us through the metal detectors."

"I'm glad you came," said Elizabeth, venturing onto the most dangerous ground first so she wouldn't have it in front of her later. "What made the FBI decide to get involved?"

"Your Mr. Brayer. He asked for cooperation and the Bureau is being very cooperative these days. Ten years of bad press, all the political stuff, massive housecleaning after Hoover died—you can imagine. Brayer offered a fairly straightforward murder case with a chance of something bigger, and all he needed was two days of legwork."

"So the Bureau jumped at it? I hope it's not a waste of your time," said Elizabeth.

"No," said Hart. "The Bureau is reestablishing its usefulness, doing favors. So either way it's no loss to the organization. As for me," he said, and Elizabeth could see he was going to step out on the tightrope, "I've been on assignments that didn't pan out before, and none of them involved flying to Southern California with a pretty lady."

Nicely managed, she thought, if a little clumsy. So he, too, liked to cover the hard part first. She rewarded him with the best smile she could risk. No sense in setting him up for some kind of embarrassment, but at least let him know we're friends.

The voice in the air said, "United Flight 452 arriving at Gate 23," and Hart looked at his ticket. "That's us," he said.

They sat in silence and watched the rest of the passengers filing in and getting settled. Then the door slammed with a pneumatic thump and the engines wound themselves up to a high whine and the plane began to taxi out away from the buildings into the night. At the end of the apron it spun around and faced into the wind, the engines screamed, and they shot down the runway into the sky.

Elizabeth said, "You had your job long?"

"Four years, about," said Hart. "You?"

"Only a little over a year. It's interesting, though. What made you decide to work over there?"

"Came back from the service, went to an undistinguished law school where I earned an undistinguished record," he smiled. "Seemed like a good idea at the time. Either that or spend the next twenty years researching precedents and hoping to become a junior partner somewhere. This sounded like more fun."

"Sounds familiar," said Elizabeth.

"You too?"

"With variations. For me it was Business Administration, and the twenty years would have been spent doing market analyses," said Elizabeth, and turned to look out the window. They were above the clouds now, and she wondered how long she could keep looking out there before he remembered that all she could see was the tip of the wing.

Movies were always a good way to spend those early hours of the evening in a strange town. A large crowd, a dark place, and a built-in etiquette that kept people from looking too closely at one another or starting a conversation. By the time the lights came up in the theater and he joined the file of people pouring out onto the sidewalk, he was hungry.

Years ago Eddie Mastrewski had told him always to forget he was using a cover. You should be whatever you pretended to be, all the time except when you were actually working. That way there were only a few hours a year when anything could happen to you. The rest of the time you really were an insurance salesman or a truck driver or a policeman, and you weren't in any more jeopardy than anybody else. If you slipped once your other life would go a long way toward saving your ass. Besides, it gave you something else to think about. Eddie was a butcher.

Of course that had all happened in the days before the trade got so busy. Nobody had that kind of time anymore. You were crazy if you passed up the kind of business you could get. It was easier now, too. Everybody was a stranger, and everybody traveled. The only cover you needed was to look like the others and do what they did when they did it. Right now people were eating. He walked down Colfax looking for a restaurant that was crowded enough.

"Don't be a jackass, Carlson," said the old man. "If I'm in any danger it's not from some guy with a gun, it's from some big corporation afraid of a bill that would take away its tax advantage. Criminals don't give a good goddamn about tax reforms because they don't pay any taxes."

"What I'm saying, Senator, is that things aren't that simple or predictable," said Carlson, a man in his thirties who was so tastefully dressed and well groomed as to appear abnormal. "You're a national figure now. Your picture is on the television every night. The exact composition of your politics isn't what we're talking about. It's the visibility in the media. That alone makes you a target. If your picture happens to be on the screen at the moment some borderline case finally gets his big headache, you're going to need security."

"Fine," Claremont said. "Get me some security, then. Meanwhile get the hell out of my way and let me do my job."

"Right, Senator," said Carlson, opening the door of the limousine for Claremont and climbing in after him, still talking.

The black automobile moved away from the curb and into the traffic so quickly that it looked as though the two men had barely caught it in time.

The plane touched down at Los Angeles International and Elizabeth began to prepare herself for whatever came next. Five hours in the air after a full day of work, and now at least one more hour before she could be alone and take her shoes off. She wondered what she must look like by now, then put it out of her mind. She probably looked like a woman who had just worked a thirteen-hour day, she thought, and there wasn't a whole lot she could do to hide it.

Elizabeth went over the notes she had taken during the long flight. First stop in the morning would be the Ventura police. Hart would handle the postmortem on the remains of the truck and the lab reports and the interview with the technicians. Elizabeth would read through the full report and interview whoever had written it, then follow whatever leads looked promising.

As the no-smoking light flickered and the engine wound down she wrote an additional note on her pad: *bank records.* If Veasy had a business relationship with organized crime there would be something that didn't fit. He would have made some surprising deposits or some surprising withdrawals. Or if not, there would be a discrepancy between the bank accounts and the way he had lived—maybe a sign that he had a source of money that didn't pass through the accounts. She added *safe-deposit box?* to her notes, then put the pad in her purse.

Elizabeth was glad to be able to move again. Airplane seats are small for a woman five feet five. She wondered what it must be like for Hart.

They joined the line of passengers moving past the flight attendants and out the door into the movable corridor that carried them to the terminal. Then they were in an airport lobby. Hart led her down another corridor to a second lobby, where there was a check-in desk for Golden West Airlines. He had a few words with the desk manager and then waited while the man picked up a telephone and turned his back. He hung up and said, "You can board at nine fifty-five at Gate Forty-one, Mr. Hart. Your bags will be transferred automatically, of course."

As Elizabeth and Hart wandered across the lobby, she checked the big wall clock: nine thirty. Not enough time to relax, too much time to wait comfortably in one of those blue plastic chairs. She was glad when Hart said, "How about a drink while we're waiting?"

They sat in a dark corner of the bar with their backs to the wall. The traffic was fairly thin, so the waitress was there for their order immediately. She scurried off to get them their drinks. She was back so fast that they hadn't said anything to each other.

"I've been thinking about this case," said Elizabeth. "It's going to be a little bewildering."

"They always are," said Hart. "This one is going to be more than that. You'll be better off if you think of it as preliminary research instead of a case of its own."

"What do you mean?"

"You're looking for professional touches. If you find any, that's about all you'll find, most likely. There's not much chance we'll make any arrests. If it's a professional there won't be anything to connect him with Veasy, and more likely than not we've never heard of him before. And this time there isn't even a case on record of anyone who works that way, so if it's a pattern this is the first of the series."

"So I shouldn't get my hopes up," said Elizabeth. "I haven't."

"Oh I don't know," said Hart. "Hope doesn't cost anything. But we've got very little this time. In a truck explosion like that there can't be any fingerprints. But there may be something connected with the method or the circumstances that'll be useful later."

"I've got a few ideas to start with," said Elizabeth. "Maybe we'll get lucky."

He nodded and sipped his drink. "Maybe, if we're thorough and careful and don't make any mistakes ourselves. But the best thing to do at the start of it is to forget about looking for anything in particular. Just look and write down everything you see or hear. It may make sense to somebody a year from now."

Elizabeth smiled to herself. He was a man all right—telling her not to get her hopes up, and then suggesting that it would all work out in a way that was too far off for anybody to predict. The endless replay of John Wayne handing the woman a pistol and saying ominously, "Save the last bullet for yourself" before he climbs over the stockade with a knife clenched in his teeth.

Elizabeth picked up her purse. "Nine fifty. Time to go."

He bolted the last inch of his Scotch, tossed some money on the table, and followed her out into the lobby. One more short flight, she thought, and then the chance for some rest.

He walked out of the restaurant and bought a *Denver Post* from the vending machine at the curb. Time to start doing some research on him. If they didn't publish his schedule, at least they might have a picture of him. You had to start somewhere. He remembered hearing a story about Dave Burton trying to collect on a next-door neighbor once. Probably not true, but you never knew. Things like that could happen if you weren't careful, and the big ones like this were worth taking a little extra time with. For that kind of money, why not? And this was the last one for a while. Another one of Eddie Mastrewski's proverbs. Always take it slow when you're tired. The police can be dumb as gorillas, make a million mistakes, but at the end of it they still get paid and go home to watch television. You make one and you're dead. If the police don't get you the client will because he'll get scared.

Getting out had to be the simplest part this time. He'd thought of that part right away, as soon as he'd heard the timing. A charter flight to Las Vegas, booked in advance. There was some kind of rule about that. Charter flights had to be advance booking, so the police wouldn't look closely for fugitives there. If you couldn't leave from another town, a charter flight wasn't bad.

Elizabeth held her exhaustion in abeyance while the little plane flew along the coast toward Ventura. At first she could see the incredible lighted expanse below her, stretching down the long valley to fade into a feeble fluttering like stars. Then the plane moved out across the coastal range and over the water, and there was only darkness and calm on her side of the cabin.

It seemed like only a few minutes before the little airplane began to descend. The Ventura airport wasn't much. They put a short wooden staircase next to the fuselage for people to step on, and there was an eager young man in a gold sportcoat that seemed to belong to an absent older brother to serve as spotter for the deplaning passengers. He smiled and hovered, his hands held out silently announcing his intention to catch any passenger who might begin to fall.

The night was calm and warm, like late spring. The airport reminded her of a small-town bus station, but they managed to find a cab driver lounging out front who knew the Ocean Sands Motel, where Disbursement had made their reservations. She was pleasantly surprised to see the sprawling, vaguely Spanish stucco building half-buried in luxuriant, unfamiliar vegetation. She wondered at first if Disbursement had made a mistake, but then remembered that the economies were always inconsistent: the leather-bound notepads with the cheap, thin paper in the office told it all.

Hart took charge and registered for them. Elizabeth couldn't help wondering if it was just his faintly antiquated courtesy again, or if his experience of hotels was all of the sort where the woman didn't sign her own name. She didn't think about it for long, because as soon as the key to her room was in her hand she was on her way toward the cool, clean sheets. When she was lying there it occurred to her that she probably hadn't bothered to say goodnight to him. She didn't think about that for long either.

He always made a point of staying away from women when he was traveling. It wasn't that any of the ones he was likely to meet would suddenly become suspicious and make inquiries to the police, or anything like that. It was just that it was too damned complicated. You had to make up something to tell them about yourself, maybe even make up a fake address and phone number, agree to be someplace at a particular time. Things like that took most of the fun out of it anyway, and added an element of danger.

So he walked more slowly to keep from catching up with the one ahead of him on the sidewalk. She was definitely trolling for someone—maybe him. He couldn't see her face, but her way of walking—her back arched slightly and her hips rolling a little as she strolled down Colfax Avenue—he had seen a thousand times. Women almost always walked fast when they were alone, especially on this kind of street. When they didn't, it was usually to say, I'm not going anywhere in particular and don't have anything to do: I've got all the time in the world. Another time, he thought as he watched her, his eyes moving irresistibly to the round, firm buttocks. A week from now it would be different.

She turned then and he knew that she was aware of him. She stopped to look in a store window, but he knew she was studying his reflection. He fixed his eyes in front of him and walked purposefully ahead at the same pace. As he passed her she began to walk again. If anyone else had seen it, it must have looked like an accident. A pretty lady window shopping, a man on his way to the parking ramp down the street to pick up his car. He heard her say, "If you like it, maybe you should try it." The voice was soft and confident at the same time, perfectly modulated to establish a kind of intimacy that said I know everything you feel and desire: I know you. He felt a wave of resentment well and pass over him at the violation, the casual assumption of knowledge like an assertion of possession.

He slowed and said, "Excuse me?" feigning a look of surprise.

She smiled the satisfied-cat smile they always had, with the lips closed and the amused eyes. Then she said, "If you're lonely, I'm not doing anything."

In one part of his mind he was thinking she was extremely tempting—huge, bright blue eyes that seemed to peep out from behind a veil of heavy brown hair. In another part all the danger signals were reminding him that this was neither the time nor the place. To have anything to do with her now would put him in jeopardy: she was risking his life and he was angry about it. So he said, "Oh, I'm sorry, Miss. I'm a married man." He did his best to look flustered, to make her think she'd been wrong this time, to convince her that this time she'd picked a man who hadn't even seen her. And then he quickened his pace, behaving like a frightened businessman who wanted nothing more at the moment than to escape the place where he'd been embarrassed, but after thinking it over and smoothing out the rough edges, wouldn't be able to resist telling his wife and one or two close friends about it because he thought it magnified him: a real prostitute came up to me on the street and . . . well, she offered herself to me. I couldn't believe it.

He turned off on a side street and kept going, moving along in his preoccupied businessman's stride. Then he turned again onto a narrow street that ran parallel with Colfax—almost an alley, really. It was darker, and on one side were the backs of stores and taverns and restaurants, nestled together and indistinguishable from one another with their steel fire doors and loading docks and navy-blue Dumpsters piled with cardboard boxes.

The girl had put him into a bad mood, reminded him of how impatient he was for this trip to end so he could go back to Tucson and relax. It wasn't easy to live for days at a time without so much as talking to anybody, and for weeks without saying more than "What's the soup of the day?"

He glanced at his watch. A little after ten. Time to head for the motel and read the paper while he waited for the eleven-o'clock news. Then the watch disappeared in a flash of pain, and he was aware that he had heard the sound of whatever had crashed into his skull even while he felt it. But he was on the ground now and his left kneecap seemed to hurt, too. Dimly he could see a rock the size of two fists beside him as he rolled in the gravel. He didn't have time to decide whether that was what hit him. He just scooped it in and had his arm cocked when he saw a human figure bending toward him for the next blow. With all of his strength he hurled it into the darkness where the face must be, pushing off the ground with his right foot at the same time. There was a sickening thump as it hit, and a high, tentative half-scream that never got all the way out before the shape crumpled.

He was up and moving now, whirling around because the other one would be behind him. This time he wasn't quite fast enough. A blow across his back with something long like a club electrified him with pain and terror, and he wasn't sure he could move himself. But then something hit him in the face and he was on the ground again and the other one was winding up for a kick. He grabbed the stable leg with one hand, pulling the man off balance, and punched up into the groin with the other—a quick, hard jab. This time there was no cry of pain, only the sound of the air leaving the man's lungs. Then the man lay on the ground doubled up like a fetus, rocking and grunting.

He stood up and looked for the others, but no, there had only been two. Muggers, he thought. Jesus! He looked down at them. The first one was probably dead. He wondered what he should do about the other. He didn't have anything with him— not even a knife. He couldn't leave them this way. They had almost certainly gotten a good look before they'd done anything. He walked over to the first one, picked up the bloody rock that lay by his head, and brought it down once, hard. Then he did the same to the other one. He dragged them by the ankles into the shadows behind the Dumpster and moved away down the alley, limping from the pain in his left knee. His back was throbbing and he could feel a thin trickle of blood warming his right cheek, but he couldn't tell if it was his head or his face. The face worried him. Muggers. Jesus.

The senator sat back in his chair and watched a commercial for new cars. There wasn't really anything in it about cars, but there was a small Japanese car there, and a lot of enthusiastic

Americans cavorting around it, showing surprise and pleasure and amazement to a spirited musical score.

Then the news came on. Carlson went over and turned the volume up a little. Not enough so the senator would have to take notice of the fact that Carlson knew he was old and probably didn't hear as well as he used to. Just enough to make explicit the view they shared, that commercials were a kind of atmospheric interference but the speech at the airport was the very essence of importance.

A newsman was saying, "Congress ended its regular session today and began its midsession break. We'll have footage of Senator McKinley Claremont's return to Denver. There was a brief flareup of fighting in the Middle East, an earthquake shook Central America, and New England is racked in the worst snowstorm in twenty years. More about these and other stories in a moment."

The Japanese car commercial came on again. "It's the same commercial exactly," said the senator, peering at the screen in amazement as the enthusiastic Americans mugged and pantomimed their way through the song again. "Carlson! When did they start doing that?"

"Doing what, Senator?"

"Playing the same damned commercial twice in a row?"

"Are they? I didn't notice," said Carlson.

6

He moved as quickly as he could. There'd be plenty of time to baby the bumps and bruises later when there wasn't anybody to watch him do it, but now the important thing was to get back to the motel room and out of sight before anybody found the bodies. He made a quick inventory as he walked—there was a tear in the left knee of his pants, and the whole suit was dusty. With effort he brushed himself off. There was definitely blood on his face, but that was easily taken care of. He pulled out his handkerchief and brought it to his right cheek, but had to stifle a yelp at the pain.

"Damn," he muttered, wishing vaguely that there was something more he could do to them. There was no question it would show: by morning there would be a bruise, and the swelling had already started. He just hoped there wouldn't be a scar. Maybe all the blood was coming from beyond the hairline. "Damn!" he said again, under his breath. "Stupid. Rocks and clubs, like animals. Baboons!"

Down the alley he could see the pool of light of the motel parking lot. He stopped to listen for a car coming his way, but there was nothing. He was surprised to see that he still had his newspaper. He didn't remember picking it up. But a wave of relief washed over him. He opened the paper as though he had been reading it since he parked his car down the alley. Then he took a deep breath and came around the corner of the motel, heading for the back stairway. He heard a door somewhere in the other wing slamming but he kept on going, trying hard not to limp. His ears picked up the sound of keys jangling and muffled voices, but he kept on going, gritting his teeth against the pain. Up the stairs he climbed, using the handrail to keep the weight off the leg. He swung around with the paper under his arm, keeping his left side to the light as long as he could, then pressing his face so close to the wall it almost touched while he unlocked the door.

He was inside, and breathing hard. He carefully stripped off his clothes, leaving them in a pile on the floor, then walked into the bathroom. The mirrored wall told him what he had feared. He stared at it, and what stared back at him was a thin, nondescript man in his early thirties who looked as if he'd walked away from an airplane crash. The right side of his face was already beginning to blacken and swell, and a thin trickle of blood was beginning to snake down from his temple. He watched it saturate the sideburn and then quickly curve down the cheek to the chin. As he leaned closer to search the face, the drop reached the point of his chin and fell, making a bright blotch in the sink. He carefully washed his face, then ran the water in the bathtub.

He sat on the edge of the tub and stared at his knee while he waited. A scrape, a cut with a little dirt in it maybe. He flexed the leg, studying the pain as though he were fine-tuning it. No cracks or chips, he thought. Just a scratch is all. But the face—he wasn't ready to think about that yet. He padded out into the other room and turned on the television. The news was just coming on. He caught sight of himself in the other mirror, sitting naked on the bed. A small, whitish animal with a few tufts of hair. And hurt, too. As he watched, the injured face in the mirror contracted a little, seemed to clench and compress itself into a mask of despair. A sigh like a strangled squeak escaped from its throat. He said aloud to the face, "You sorry little bastard." And then the moment was gone. The people on the television screen seemed to be dancing around, celebrating something having to do with a little car parked behind them. He wished them all dead.

Then the newsman came on. He padded back into the bathroom to check the water. It was beginning to get deep enough now, so he turned the tap off and tested the temperature. Too hot: time enough to watch the news.

When he got back to the bed, Claremont and his aide were descending the ladder of the plane. It was pretty much what he'd pictured—a white-haired, stiff-necked old coot in a three-piece banker's suit of the sort you could hardly buy in a store anymore, followed closely by a neat, short-haired, milk-complexioned young man who appeared to be the prototype of a new doll.

He studied their moves as they approached the terminal. The senator looked old and frail and a little tired. Then there was a different scene, at a podium bristling with microphones. He was saying, "We're going to fight it through this time to the end. We've got key people from both parties working very hard in Washington and in their home districts."

Claremont looked old and vulnerable all right. Too old to run or fight, probably too old to even make much noise. He had that sharp-eyed hawk-face look that old people got sometimes, and his temples were marbled with blue veins. The picture changed and the newsman was talking about something having to do with some dark, intense little men in olive-drab fatigues. He switched off the television, went into the bathroom, and slowly settled himself into the hot tub. He studied the knee again, watching the tiny pink cloud swirl away from the cut like liquid smoke. Then he settled back, relaxing every muscle in his body. In a minute he would submerge his head and try to clean those wounds, too. That would hurt but it had to be done. No sense getting an infection.

He tried to think the situation through. He couldn't travel with a face like that. People remembered things like black eyes and bruised faces. And in the morning they'd find the two bodies, and start looking for somebody who'd been in a fight. The first place they'd look would be in the hotels and motels around here, starting with the cheapest first. It would look like a gang fight, but not enough like one to keep them from checking out transients right away while they could still put their hands on them. He'd paid in cash for the room, three days in advance, like always. And then there was the charter flight for Las Vegas—paid in advance, too. But that didn't leave until Thursday night. Too soon for the face to get back to normal, and too long to wait while the police looked for a man who'd been in a fight. So it had to be tonight. There was no other way. He had to be somewhere else before they knew what they were looking for. And then his mind stopped dead. There was still the senator. How could he do the senator and get out of Denver in one night with a face like that? He thought again about the two men in the alley. If only they hadn't picked him out, or picked that alley, or had thought of it another night. But there wasn't much he could do about it now. He started again from the beginning. How can I travel with a face like this?

McKinley Claremont sipped the last of his bourbon and watched the film of the Arab gun crew expertly loading and firing at a distant hillside. He wondered if it was stock footage, or if they were really getting that organized. In '67 he'd been to Egypt on a fact-finding tour and it hadn't been like that. After a couple of rounds, the ammunition they had with them had turned out to be the wrong size, so the crew he was with just sat down and started eating and drinking. Two hours later a captain told him they were waiting for the supply lines to get untangled, or for further orders, whichever happened first. Meanwhile they sat in the sun behind their useless cannon, waiting.

Carlson interrupted his thoughts. "I'd say it came off very well, wouldn't you, Senator?"

"All right, I guess," said the senator. "On television they don't get the chance to spell your name wrong, anyway."

"Big day tomorrow," said Carlson tactfully.

"Right," said the old man. He set down his glass and raised himself slowly from his chair. "Call me at eight and while we're having breakfast we'll try to figure out what's got to be done. That is, if we've got time for breakfast?"

"Yes sir," said Carlson. "First appointment isn't until ten."

"Fine, see you in the morning then."

"Good night, Senator," said Carlson, already halfway out the door. "My room is right next door if you need anything. Four oh eight." The door shut.

Claremont shuffled over to the closet and brought out his pajamas. He tossed them on the bed and then took off his suit, carefully hanging it up so it wouldn't get wrinkled. If he didn't hate the idea of losing his privacy, he'd get a valet, he thought. Living out of a suitcase half of each year was bad enough. Then you had to decide whether to spend your time worrying about wrinkles or give up the few minutes of solitude you ever had.

He eased himself into the strange bed and tried out a couple of positions for comfort. Politics wasn't so bad for the young fellows, he thought. Trouble was, by the time you knew anything and had enough seniority to make anybody listen to it, you were too old. He peered through the darkness at his teeth soaking in the glass on the nightstand. Those things were older than some of the men in the House of Representatives. He chuckled to himself. Still plenty of bite to them, though.

He felt the water around him loosening the taut muscles and soaking some of the hurt out of him. He began to feel stronger. Now and then he would take a deep breath and lean back with his chin tucked into his chest to submerge his whole head. Then he would wait until his breath came back and do it again for as long as he could. Finally he sat up, took the soap between his hands, worked it into a lather, then rubbed soap over his head and face. It was as though dozens of hornets were stinging his scalp, his cheek, his temple. He gasped to fill his lungs again and ducked under. Slowly the pain went away.

He waited a few seconds, then climbed out of the tub and began toweling himself off, gingerly. When he came to his knee he dried around it. No telling what germs there were on a hotel towel, and no sense leaving bloodstains. He looked in the mirror again. This time the face didn't seem quite so bad, with the hair combed and no clot of blood on it. It was the cheek and the eye that'd give trouble, but with the right pair of sunglasses, maybe not so much, at least until tomorrow night.

He knew what he had to do now. There just wasn't any other way. As he dried himself he walked out into the bedroom. He picked up his watch from the dresser and put it on. Eleven thirty-nine. It would be a long night, no matter what. If only this had happened when he was working on something normal. He could call them and ask them to send somebody else, or even farm it out himself to someone he knew—Eddie Mastrewski had done that with him a couple of times. That reminded him of something Eddie had said, and it brought back the nervous anxiety: "Never work when you're hurt, kid. If you don't feel good you won't think straight, either. And if people can see it they'll remember it. I don't mean major surgery either. I wouldn't work with a pimple." Eddie was full of reasons not to work.

He put on clean clothes and carefully combed his wet hair. There was one consolation, he thought. If anybody saw him and he did get away, what they'd remember about him was the bumps and bruises, and they'd be gone in two weeks with any luck.

The whole thing would have to be changed now. He had planned to get a high-powered rifle with a scope, and get him through a window in his hotel. That was the way the crazies whose fantasies didn't include getting their pictures in the newspapers all did it. There wasn't time for that now, and he didn't have a gun, and—no use even thinking about it. He'd just have to live with the situation as it was.

He went to his suitcase and rummaged around for a few seconds, collecting some things. A pocketknife, a ballpoint pen, a clean handkerchief, a pair of sunglasses. He tried on the sunglasses and studied his reflection. It wasn't great, but it was something. He made a mental note to get a pair with bigger lenses, maybe the wraparound kind. Then he sat down to read the newspaper.

There was an article on the front page about the senator's return. He studied it, but could find nothing that would tell him where the old man was staying tonight. He flipped through the paper until he came to a second article. This one had pictures of the old man and his aide getting out of a limousine in front of a building. Only part of the facade was visible, but it was a hotel, all right. They had said the old man had never lived in Denver. He had started out as a state assemblyman in Pueblo and still owned a place there. He studied the picture for clues. There was a doorman wearing one of those ridiculous comic-opera costumes, but no insignia on it, and nothing on the marble facade of the building except a number. He smiled. That would do it. 1905.

He picked up the telephone book and leafed through it until he came to a page marked *Hospitals—Hotels*. There were dozens, but it didn't take him long. The Constellation Hotel. 1905 19th Street. He went through the rest of the list to see if there was another one with a 1905 number—he had been the victim of enough coincidences for one day—but there wasn't. So that was it. He studied the section carefully, looking for the hotel's ad. There wasn't any. So he turned to *Restaurants*. In a few seconds he'd found what he needed.

He got up and packed his suitcase, then tore his bed up a little. He set the key on the dresser, and looked around one last time to see if he'd left anything before he turned out the lights. He walked down the back stairs and through the alley. The cold made his knee stiffen up a little, but he was walking better now. A few blocks down there was another motel, and a telephone booth at the gas station across the street.

When he came to it, he called a cab company.

"I'd like a cab, please."

"Where are you now?"

He read the sign across the street. "The Wee Hours Motel on Colfax."

"Where do you want to go?"

"The Pirate's Cove Restaurant on Alameda." He'd almost said Alameda and 19th. Never work tired or hurt.

"Right. He'll be there in about five minutes."

They always said five minutes, he thought. Now the suitcase. He couldn't ditch it here. The police might not recognize the rock as the weapon and go around to all the trash cans looking for something else. Never overestimate the police, count on them figuring out the obvious. He decided to hold on to the suitcase for the moment. The worst thing the cabdriver could think was that he was skipping out on a motel bill in the middle of the night.

He saw the cab pull up in front of the motel across the street. The driver was staring at the office window for his fare, so he didn't see the man with the suitcase until he was almost to the car. When he did he reached behind him, swung the back door open, and said, "Pirate's Cove?"

"Yep, that's me."

The cab was fitted with an oversized heater that blew a continuous rush of hot, impure air into the back seat. After the cold outside he figured he could tolerate it for a few minutes. He sat in the driver's blind spot.

The driver said, "Hell of a cold night, ain't it?" as he pulled away from the curb.

"Sure is. Glad you got here so quick."

"Not much business this time of night. Mostly dedicated lushes who've lost their licenses. A few old folks out visiting each other. Now and then a whore or two."

"Must be hard to break even."

"Not too bad, really. When it gets slow we hang around the airport for the late flights. Nobody wants to call Aunt Mary to come pick them up at two A.M."

"I guess not."

They sat in silence for a while. He could see one advantage to the late shift. Even on Colfax the traffic was light, and the cab was able to glide down the street catching each signal just at the moment when it turned green. He looked at his watch again. Just a little after midnight. He resented the way time was passing. He was going to need as much as he could get. At the Pirate's Cove he reached over the seat and gave the driver a bill. "Ten cover it?" he said, facing downward away from the light.

"Sure," said the driver. "Thanks." He'd tipped generously but not enough to be remembered.

" 'Night," he said and quickly got out, heading toward the glass door of the restaurant. When he heard the cab pull away he bent down to tie his shoe until the car was too far away for the driver to see him. Then he straightened up and moved off down the street toward the Constellation Hotel.

It was seven stories, shaped like a cereal box. He went around the block to approach it from the rear. There was a parking ramp and a broad loading dock. To the left of the dock he could see that one part of the back wall was pierced with ventilators and fans with screens over them and a number of pipes—the kitchen. Just in front of it he noticed a small wooden stockade. He walked up to it, opened the gate, and looked inside. There were two large garbage Dumpsters. He opened the first, and the smell of it nearly gagged him. He tried the other, and it seemed to be mostly cardboard boxes flattened to save space. He set the suitcase on top and closed the cover, then made his way to the back entrance of the parking ramp.

There was an elevator, so he entered it and studied the panel of buttons, then pushed *Lobby*, and waited. He hoped it wasn't too empty. The way he looked he couldn't afford much company, but if he were alone it would be worse. When the doors opened he stepped out quickly, keeping his head down and moving across the lobby at a slight angle from the front desk toward the only doorway he could see. There were two young couples, well dressed, lounging in the oasis of furniture in the center of the room. One of the women had her shoes off and was rubbing her toes wearily. The man with her said something about a nightcap and she rolled her eyes in distaste.

He knew exactly what he was looking for, but had no way of knowing if the hypothesis was correct. As he came abreast of the front desk he quickly stared at the mailboxes. Room 406, unquestionably, he thought. He had to try it, anyway. The person most likely to have written messages pile up in his mailbox this late at night in a hotel would be the senator. He kept on going out the front door to the street, then walked around to the parking ramp again and pushed the elevator button for the fourth floor. This would be the hard part.

When the door opened he was prepared to see a uniformed guard, but the corridor was empty. As he searched for 406, part of his mind was taking note of which rooms seemed to be occupied. He heard voices behind one door, the background music from a television show behind another. There were Do Not Disturb signs hanging from some of the doorknobs. He went past 406 and down the corridor to take a look at the other elevator and the stairway. He had to get out of here afterward.

At the end of the hallway there was a room where the sign said, *Please Make Up the Room*. He wondered—it could just be somebody who'd reversed the sign by accident, meaning to leave the *Do Not Disturb* side out. He stopped and listened. There was no sound. He decided to chance it.

He took out his wallet and selected a credit card, then carefully slipped it into the door latch, easing the door open and waiting for the chain to catch. The door wasn't chained, so he moved inside and stood still, his back to the door, listening. He waited for his eyes to get used to the light, trying to sense whether there was anyone asleep in the bed. He crouched, trying to line up the surface of the bed with the dim glow of the window. When he succeeded he was sure. The silhouette of the bed was flat.

Quickly he walked to the window and out to the balcony. The senator's balcony would be the fifth one over. He wondered if he could even do it now, tired and hurt and cold. He studied the row of identical, iron-railed balconies. Yes, he thought, that was the way in. They were far enough away from one another so a fat-ass architect would assume no one could make it from one to the other.

He went back into the room and closed the window. He looked around for something long enough to reach. There was a long, low table along one wall. He studied it—no, it was bolted down too securely, and it was too heavy to handle alone. Then he noticed the closet. It was a double closet, huge, for a hotel room. He looked inside and saw the shelf. Perfect, he thought. It was a good ten inches wide and eight or nine feet long. Thank God for good, substantial hotels. And it was screwed in, too. Working rapidly, he used his pocketknife to take out the screws, then brought the shelf out with him to the balcony.

He stopped to take one last look at the layout of the room, memorizing the location, size, and shape of each piece of furniture. Then he slowly and carefully extended the board across the void between his balcony and the next one. It reached, the other end making a light tap on the railing as he set it down. He lifted his right leg up and got his knee on the board, then the other one. He winced with pain. He had forgotten that. It would be a long, hard crawl. The shelf bowed in the middle as he eased his weight onto it, but it seemed safe enough. Four floors below him he could see the little fence with the garbage Dumpsters in it, a tiny square in the corner of the parking lot. He thought about falling all that way; lying there in the cold, smashed on the pavement. But then he was at the end of the board. He swung his legs down to the balcony and turned to pull the shelf behind him. One down, four to go.

One after another he took them, not thinking about the rest of it now, not thinking about anything but crossing the cold, empty space that separated him from the fifth balcony. And then he was there. He leaned the shelf against the wall, then thought better of it. There might be some vantage, from some other building, where somebody could see it. He laid it down flat on the balcony, then ran his hand along the edge of the sliding window to feel for the latch. There wasn't one on the outside. Another security feature, he thought. Then he went to the other end of the window and checked that, hopelessly.

He would have to take the chance of leaving a sign. He opened his knife and slipped the blade under the rubber molding a few inches below the level of the inside latch, then slowly brought it up. The glass shifted minutely. He smiled, and kept smiling even though it hurt. It was just as he'd hoped. The latch was secure, but the glass wasn't fitted tightly to the aluminum frame. Using a gentle, steady pressure of his fingertips, he slid the large pane as far as it would go away from the latch, then stuffed his handkerchief into the crack to hold it there. He studied his accomplishment. He had about an eighth of an inch to work with now. Using his knife as a pry, he bent the aluminum frame a little to gain a few more thousandths of an inch. Then he took the knife and pointed the blade up under the latch. The spring was strong, but he managed to lift the hook clear of the catch and slide the window free. He stopped for a moment with the window open a hair, and pressed the molding and frame back into shape. He whisked his hand-kerchief over the glass and the frame, just in case. They wouldn't put it in the papers, he thought, but they'd send somebody to do it even if they thought he died of old age.

He took out the ballpoint pen he'd brought with him and held it up out of the deep shadows. He took out the clear plastic refill and looked at it. To any other eye it looked like nothing, a refill that only had about a third of its ink left. But the last two thirds were a clear liquid, like water only thicker.

Touching the window with his handkerchief, he quietly slid it aside and slipped into the room, closing it behind him and moving away from the light. He stood there, silent and unmoving, studying the room. Claremont was sound asleep, his slow, regular breathing faintly audible.

Now to find just the right thing, he thought. A bottle of pills, maybe. Or a laxative. Old people make a big deal out of taking a shit. He saw a glass on the coffee table, so he went over and sniffed it—liquor. That wouldn't do now. He could feel the seconds slipping past him, seconds he needed. He moved into the bathroom straining his eyes to find something for his purpose, but no—it was too dark. He thought of just forgetting the whole thing and smothering him with a pillow, but that was too dangerous and chancy. The bed was next to the wall, and all the old bastard would have to do was pound it once or twice in the struggle and that would be that. Old or not, he could make noise. He came out of the bathroom and stared at the sleeping figure. There was nothing—only the bed, the nightstand with the lamp and the glass. The liquor would have been great if he'd managed to get here in time to help with the mixing, he thought, but not now. And then he realized it wasn't the same glass. The liquor glass was on the coffee table.

Slowly and carefully, he drifted over to the bed and stared at the nightstand. He had to look a little to the side to discern anything much in the darkness. He brought his face close to the glass and then almost laughed out loud. Of course, he thought. False teeth! He slowly reached over and poured the contents of the pen refill into the glass.

Then he drifted back out to the balcony and closed the sliding window behind him. In a few seconds he was already on the third balcony and putting down his portable bridge to the second. He looked down again, this time elated by the height, but he held himself in check. Always work slowly when you're tired, he reminded himself. He channeled his concentration into his work, moving along the shelf and then pulling it after him, setting it on the next shelf and easing himself onto it. And then he was there. He slipped back into the room and closed the window, this time letting it lock. Then he went to the closet and set the shelf back on its supports. For a second he considered just leaving it, but no. Later he'd regret it. He took out his knife and carefully replaced the screws. Then he forced himself to stand quietly for a moment. Did he have everything? Was anything out of place? He reached into his coat pocket and screwed his pen back together. Then he took a few deep breaths, listened, and stepped out into the hallway.

At the elevator he pressed the button for the parking garage. The doors sighed and opened immediately. That was a good sign, he thought. In all that time since he'd come up, nobody had used that elevator. He glanced at his watch. It was only one fifteen. And then he realized he was getting an erection. It struck him as funny, but he didn't dare laugh yet.

When the elevator doors opened again and he felt the cold night air he forgot about it. He moved across the parking ramp and out to the lot. At the fenced-in Dumpsters he stopped and re-trieved his suitcase, then kept on going. At the first public trash can he came to, he broke his pen in two and threw it in among the crumpled cups and napkins and bottles and cans. He moved again, nursing his injured knee into exactly the right pace for a man disappearing into the night.

The senator stirred, then woke up. The room seemed awfully cold. The Constellation hadn't been the same since they'd re-modeled it in 1972, he thought. It was those damned fancy win-dows and balconies and things. The workmanship just wasn't any good anymore. People didn't take pride in their work. But then he reminded himself that he was an old man, a cranky one at that, and it was probably just his bad circulation. He rolled over and com-posed himself to go back to sleep. "A goose probably just walked over my grave."

THE KILLERS

Ernest Hemingway

The door of Henry's lunchroom opened and two men
came in. They sat down at the counter.

"What's yours?" George asked them.

"I don't know," one of the men said. "What do you want to eat, Al?"

"I don't know," said Al. "I don't know what I want to eat."

Outside it was getting dark. The streetlight came on outside the window. The two men at the counter read the menu. From the other end of the counter Nick Adams watched them. He had been talking to George when they came in.

"I'll have a roast pork tenderloin with apple sauce and mashed potatoes," the first man said.

"It isn't ready yet."

"What the hell do you put it on the card for?"

"That's the dinner," George explained. "You can get that at six o'clock."

George looked at the clock on the wall behind the counter.

"It's five o'clock."

"The clock says twenty minutes past five," the second man said.

"It's twenty minutes fast."

"Oh, to hell with the clock," the first man said. "What have you got to eat?"

"I can give you any kind of sandwiches," George said. "You can have ham and eggs, bacon and eggs, liver and bacon, or a steak."

"Give me chicken croquettes with green peas and cream sauce and mashed potatoes."

"That's the dinner."

"Everything we want's the dinner, eh? That's the way you work it."

"I can give you ham and eggs, bacon and eggs, liver—"

"I'll take ham and eggs," the man called Al said. He wore a derby hat and a black overcoat buttoned across the chest. His face was small and white and he had tight lips. He wore a silk muffler and gloves.

"Give me bacon and eggs," said the other man. He was about the same size as Al. Their faces were different, but they were dressed like twins. Both wore overcoats too tight for them. They sat leaning forward, their elbows on the counter.

"Got anything to drink?" Al asked.

"Silver beer, bevo, ginger ale," George said.

"I mean you got anything to *drink*?"

"Just those I said."

"This is a hot town," said the other. "What do they call it?"

"Summit."

"Ever hear of it?" Al asked his friend.

"No," said the friend.

"What do you do here nights?" Al asked.

"They eat the dinner," his friend said. "They all come here and eat the big dinner."

"That's right," George said.

"So you think that's right?" Al asked George.

"Sure."

"You're a pretty bright boy, aren't you?"

"Sure," said George.

"Well, you're not," said the other little man. "Is he, Al?"

"He's dumb," said Al. He turned to Nick. "What's your name?"

"Adams."

"Another bright boy," Al said. "Ain't he a bright boy, Max?"

"The town's full of bright boys," Max said.

George put the two platters, one of ham and eggs, the other of bacon and eggs, on the counter. He set down two side dishes of fried potatoes and closed the wicket into the kitchen.

"Which is yours?" he asked Al.

"Don't you remember?"

"Ham and eggs."

"Just a bright boy," Max said. He leaned forward and took the ham and eggs. Both men ate with their gloves on. George watched them eat.

"What are *you* looking it?" Max looked at George.

"Nothing."

"The hell you were. You were looking at me."

"Maybe the boy meant it for a joke, Max," Al said.

George laughed.

"*You* don't have to laugh," Max said to him. "*You* don't have to laugh at all, see?"

"All right," said George.

"So he thinks it's all right." Max turned to Al. "He thinks it's all right. That's a good one."

"Oh, he's a thinker," Al said. They went on eating.

"What's the bright boy's name down the counter?" Al asked Max.

"Hey, bright boy," Max said to Nick. "You go around on the other side of the counter with your boyfriend."

"What's the idea?" Nick asked.

"There isn't any idea."

"You better go around, bright boy," Al said. Nick went around behind the counter.

"What's the idea?" George asked.

"None of your damn business," Al said. "Who's out in the kitchen?"

"The nigger."

"What do you mean the nigger?"

"The nigger that cooks."

"Tell him to come in."

"What's the idea?"

"Tell him to come in."

"Where do you think you are?"

"We know damn well where we are," the man called Max said. "Do we look silly?"

"You talk silly," Al said to him. "What the hell do you argue with this kid for? Listen," he said to George, "tell the nigger to come out here."

"What are you going to do to him?"

"Nothing. Use your head, bright boy. What would we do to a nigger?"

George opened the slit that opened back into the kitchen. "Sam," he called. "Come in here a minute."

The door to the kitchen opened and the nigger came in. "What was it?" he asked. The two men at the counter took a look at him.

"All right, nigger. You stand right there," Al said.

Sam, the nigger, standing in his apron, looked at the two men sitting at the counter. "Yes, sir," he said. Al got down from his stool.

"I'm going back to the kitchen with the nigger and bright boy," he said. "Go on back to the kitchen, nigger. You go with him, bright boy." The little man walked after Nick and Sam, the cook, back into the kitchen. The door shut after them. The man called Max sat at the counter opposite George. He didn't look at George but looked in the mirror that ran along back of the counter. Henry's had been made over from a saloon into a lunch counter.

"Well, bright boy," Max said, looking into the mirror, "why don't you say something?"

"What's it all about?"

"Hey, Al," Max called, "bright boy wants to know what it's all about."

"Why don't you tell him?" Al's voice came from the kitchen.

"What do you think it's all about?"

"I don't know."

"What do you think?"

Max looked into the mirror all the time he was talking.

"I wouldn't say."

"Hey, Al, bright boy says he wouldn't say what he thinks it's all about."

"I can hear you, all right," Al said from the kitchen. He had propped open the slit that dishes passed through into the kitchen with a catsup bottle. "Listen, bright boy," he said from the kitchen to George. "Stand a little further along the bar. You move a little to the left, Max." He was like a photographer arranging for a group picture.

"Talk to me, bright boy," Max said. "What do you think's going to happen?"

George did not say anything.

"I'll tell you," Max said. "We're going to kill a Swede. Do you know a big Swede named Ole Andreson?"

"Yes."

"He comes here to eat every night, don't he?"

"Sometimes he comes here."

"He comes here at six o'clock, don't he?"

"If he comes."

"We know all that, bright boy," Max said. "Talk about something else. Ever go to the movies?"

"Once in a while."

"You ought to go to the movies more. The movies are fine for a bright boy like you."

"What are you going to kill Ole Andreson for? What did he ever do to you?"

"He never had a chance to do anything to us. He never even seen us."

"And he's only going to see us once," Al said from the kitchen.

"What are you going to kill him for, then?" George asked.

"We're killing him for a friend. Just to oblige a friend, bright boy."

"Shut up," said Al from the kitchen. "You talk too goddam much."

"Well, I got to keep bright boy amused. Don't I, bright boy?"

"You talk too damn much," Al said. "The nigger and my bright boy are amused by themselves. I got them tied up like a couple of girlfriends in the convent."

"I suppose you were in a convent?"

"You never know."

"You were in a kosher convent. That's where you were."

George looked up at the clock.

"If anybody comes in you tell them the cook is off, and if they keep after it, you tell them you'll go back and cook yourself. Do you get that, bright boy?"

"All right," George said. "What you going to do with us afterward?"

"That'll depend," Max said. "That's one of those things you never know at the time."

George looked up at the clock. It was a quarter past six. The door from the street opened. A street-car motorman came in.

"Hello, George," he said. "Can I get supper?"

"Sam's gone out," George said. "He'll be back in about half an hour."

"I'd better go up the street," the motorman said. George looked at the clock. It was twenty minutes past six.

"That was nice, bright boy," Max said. "You're a regular little gentleman."

"He knew I'd blow his head off," Al said from the kitchen.

"No," said Max. "It ain't that. Bright boy is nice. He's a nice boy. I like him."

At six-fifty-five George said: "He's not coming."

Two other people had been in the lunchroom. Once George had gone out to the kitchen and made a ham-and-egg sandwich "to go" that a man wanted to take with him. Inside the kitchen he saw Al, his derby hat tipped back, sitting on a stool beside the wicket with the muzzle of a sawed-off shotgun resting on the ledge. Nick and the cook were back to back in the corner, a towel tied in each of their mouths. George had cooked the sandwich, wrapped it up in oiled paper, put it in a bag, brought it in, and the man had paid for it and gone out.

"Bright boy can do everything," Max said. "He can cook and everything. You'd make some girl a nice wife, bright boy."

"Yes?" George said. "Your friend, Ole Andreson, isn't going to come."

"We'll give him ten minutes," Max said.

Max watched the mirror and the clock. The hands of the clock marked seven o'clock, and then five minutes past seven.

"Come on, Al," said Max. "We better go. He's not coming."

"Better give him five minutes," Al said from the kitchen.

In the five minutes a man came in, and George explained that the cook was sick.

"Why the hell don't you get another cook?" the man asked. "Aren't you running a lunch counter?" He went out.

"Come on, Al," Max said.

"What about the two bright boys and the nigger?"

"They're all right."

"You think so?"

"Sure. We're through with it."

"I don't like it," said Al. "It's sloppy. You talk too much."

"Oh, what the hell," said Max. "We got to keep amused, haven't we?"

"You talk too much, all the same," Al said. He came out from the kitchen. The cutoff barrels of the shotgun made a slight bulge under the waist of his too tight-fitting overcoat. He straightened his coat with his gloved hands.

"So long, bright boy," he said to George. "You got a lot of luck."

"That's the truth," Max said. "You ought to play the races, bright boy."

The two of them went out the door. George watched them, through the window, pass under the arc-light and cross the street. In their tight overcoats and derby hats they looked like a vaudeville team. George went back through the swinging-door into the kitchen and untied Nick and the cook.

"I don't want any more of that," said Sam, the cook. "I don't want any more of that."

Nick stood up. He had never had a towel in his mouth before.

"Say," he said. "What the hell?" He was trying to swagger it off.

"They were going to kill Ole Andreson," George said. "They were going to shoot him when he came in to eat."

"Ole Andreson?"

"Sure."

The cook felt the corners of his mouth with his thumbs.

"They all gone?" he asked.

"Yeah," said George. "They're gone now."

"I don't like it," said the cook. "I don't like any of it at all."

"Listen," George said to Nick. "You better go see Ole Andreson."

"All right."

"You better not have anything to do with it at all," Sam, the cook, said. "You better stay way out of it."

"Don't go if you don't want to," George said.

"Mixing up in this ain't going to get you anywhere," the cook said. "You stay out of it."

"I'll go see him," Nick said to George. "Where does he live?"

The cook turned away.

"Little boys always know what they want to do," he said.

"He lives up at Hirsch's rooming house," George said to Nick.

"I'll go up there."

Outside the arc-light shone through the bare branches of a tree. Nick walked up the street beside the car-tracks and turned at the next arc-light down a side street. Three houses up the street was Hirsch's rooming house. Nick walked up the two steps and pushed the bell. A woman came to the door.

"Is Ole Andreson here?"

"Do you want to see him?"

"Yes, if he's in."

Nick followed the woman up a flight of stairs and back to the end of a corridor. She knocked on the door.

"Who is it?"

"It's somebody to see you, Mr. Andreson," the woman said.

"It's Nick Adams."

"Come in."

Nick opened the door and went into the room. Ole Andreson was lying on the bed with all his clothes on. He had been a heavyweight prizefighter and he was too long for the bed. He lay with his head on two pillows. He did not look at Nick.

"What was it?" he asked.

"I was up at Henry's," Nick said, "and two fellows came in and tied up me and the cook, and they said they were going to kill you."

It sounded silly when he said it. Ole Andreson said nothing.

"They put us out in the kitchen," Nick went on. "They were going to shoot you when you came in to supper."

Ole Andreson looked at the wall and did not say anything.

"George thought I better come and tell you about it."

"There isn't anything I can do about it," Ole Andreson said.

"I'll tell you what they were like."

"I don't want to know what they were like," Ole Andreson said. He looked at the wall. "Thanks for coming to tell me about it."

"That's all right."

Nick looked at the big man lying on the bed.

"Don't you want me to go and see the police?"

"No," Ole Andreson said. "That wouldn't do any good."

"Isn't there something I could do?"

"No. There ain't anything to do."

"Maybe it was just a bluff."

"No. It ain't just a bluff."

Ole Andreson rolled over toward the wall.

"The only thing is," he said, talking toward the wall, "I just can't make up my mind to go out. I been in here all day."

"Couldn't you get out of town?"

"No," Ole Andreson said. "I'm through with all that running around."

He looked at the wall.

"There ain't anything to do now."

"Couldn't you fix it up some way?"

"No. I got in wrong." He talked in the same flat voice. "There ain't anything to do. After a while I'll make up my mind to go out."

"I better go back and see George," Nick said.

"So long," said Ole Andreson. He did not look toward Nick. "Thanks for coming around."

Nick went out. As he shut the door he saw Ole Andreson with all his clothes on, lying on the bed looking at the wall.

"He's been in his room all day," the landlady said downstairs. "I guess he don't feel well. I said to him: 'Mr. Andreson, you ought to go out and take a walk on a nice fall day like this,' but he didn't feel like it."

"He doesn't want to go out."

"I'm sorry he don't feel well," the woman said. "He's an awfully nice man. He was in the ring, you know."

"I know it."

"You'd never know it except from the way his face is," the woman said. They stood talking just inside the street door. "He's just as gentle."

"Well, good-night, Mrs. Hirsch," Nick said.

"I'm not Mrs. Hirsch," the woman said. "She owns the place. I just look after it for her. I'm Mrs. Bell."

"Well, good-night, Mrs. Bell," Nick said.

"Good-night," the woman said.

Nick walked up the dark street to the corner under the arc-light, and then along the car-tracks to Henry's eating house. George was inside, back of the counter.

"Did you see Ole?"

"Yes," said Nick. "He's in his room and he won't go out."

The cook opened the door from the kitchen when he heard Nick's voice.

"I don't even listen to it," he said and shut the door.

"Did you tell him about it?" George asked.

"Sure. I told him but he knows what it's all about."

"What's he going to do?"

"Nothing."

"They'll kill him."

"I guess they will."

"He must have got mixed up in something in Chicago."

"I guess so," said Nick.

"It's a hell of a thing."

"It's an awful thing," Nick said.

They did not say anything. George reached down for a towel and wiped the counter.

"I wonder what he did?" Nick said.

"Double-crossed somebody. That's what they kill them for."

"I'm going to get out of this town," Nick said.

"Yes," said George. "That's a good thing to do."

"I can't stand to think about him waiting in the room and knowing he's going to get it. It's too damned awful."

"Well," said George, "you better not think about it."

SCREEN IMAGE: (Royal Emerald Hotel, Nassau)

Mark Rudman

Viciousness incarnate. Meanness engraved.
Boneless, atomic, he leaned on the swivel

stool. His back to the bar.
To the gilded mirrors inhabited

by a jagged skyline, bottles;
gold labels: Chivas, Cointreau, Cutty Sark. . . .

Anyone would have noted this presence
even if the man had been

no one, but with his initials
in red on shirt cuffs, cuff links,

lapels, blazer breast pocket, and socks,
it seemed almost disingenuous

for the boy to ask "Are you—?"—
but it was the best he could do.

Sloe-eyed, conspiratorial, the actor spoke
out of the side of his mouth

but his gravelly menacing bass
carried kind words. "Pleased to meet you

son. Would you—mind—if I—bought—you a drink?
Bartender—get the boy a—'Shirley'—"

and then he winked!—a—'Roy Rogers.' "
They drank in dark and blissful silence.

"Just do me a favor, son; don't tell anyone
you saw me. I'm here . . . to get away."

The warm and intimate way the actor delivered these words
made the boy keen to keep a vow . . . of silence;

to ignore his chance to shine in the rec-room among the jaded kids
who'd waste no time making sure everyone who could know
        would know;

no, he would not tell that freckled snot from Great Neck
who came to Nassau with his own Ping-Pong racquet. . . .

The actor's equally glamorous friends,
who'd entered without a sound,

pressed the rims of cocktail glasses to their lips;
knocked down their martinis in one

gulp; hissed: retracted their chins like cobras.
The leather armrests on the bar let out a gasp

which led the two women to exchange quick
I didn't do it, did you? glances,

as if their rigid posture and breathless
diaphragms betrayed them, along

with their volitionless nylon rustling. . . .
They were prisoners anyway:

of masklike makeup; tintinnabulating bracelets;
minuscule purses without shoulder straps

and strapless, tight-waisted dresses; umbrella-spined
         bras;
nylons, garters, girdles, high heels: glued hair.

(Was the woman who was "with" the actor
reciting a silent mantra

that he himself would never do anything
like hurl boiling coffee in her face

as he did to Gloria Graham
in *The Big Heat?*)

Silken and silver were the hair and suit and voice
of the man who uttered the actor's first name.

Wouldn't "our table's ready" have been sufficient?
The actor dispersed like liquid mercury—

too early in time to draw some wry pleasure
from the uncanny resemblance

between the "special effect" on celluloid
and his own flesh and blood.

The boy did not move but eyed the party
through the speckled mirror; and though

he was as aware as any American
that whatever the hadn't done

in real life or was yet to do,
like push the future

President out of a speeding coupe in *The Killers* . . .
that he owed his renown to the brazen, indomitable cop

he played on *M-Squad*, the boy saw him repeatedly
as the itinerant cruelty in *The Missouri Traveller*

who lashed that boy's back in the heat-stricken barn
for feeding the skeletal horses extra hay.

He couldn't remember why he and his father
had gone to this bleak, obscure "sleeper" anyway,

unless, alone together in a place he could not remember,
they had time to kill.

THE SAME ONLY DIFFERENT!

Jiri Kajanë

The Ministry of Slogans seemed on the verge of closing for good. Even from my small office tucked away in the rear of the building it was easy to feel the mood shifting, everything changing, the frenetic pace of the previous months possibly dwindling to the lazy resignation of one last day. Clearly, the work generated by our department had not produced the desired results. Many young apprentices sulked in the hallways, and an even greater number of their superiors joined them, confidence now gone, roles suddenly undefined. It was no longer feasible to change the spirit of the people with a few catchy words placed in a memorable order.

Strangely, I, the deputy creative director of slogans, a person supposedly with much to lose, felt no dread at all. I was entirely calm, almost looking forward to the transformation that the coming days would bring to both the city and to my own life. I began cleaning the office with a great attention to detail—repairing the stapler, sharpening pencils, carefully alphabetizing scattered file folders. When I finished, the room looked nearly identical to the one I'd walked into that first summer morning many years back. Gone were all of my personal effects—the maps that had once decorated the walls, a pair of soccer trophies, even the graying photo of my father dressed in his favorite sweater.

It was still early, but outside toward the square, people had begun assembling—just as they'd done all week—their kinetic energy a sharp contrast to me in the office, quietly organizing obsolete files. Unlike me, the protestors seemed frantic in their fight against a government that no longer seemed to exist.

From my office window, I could see some of them making their way down to join in. Among the crowd was a lone figure I recognized, Altin Leka, an old acquaintance from the university. He was pushing a shiny white cart, preparing to sell ice cream. Soon the people passed him by, leaving Altin ambling along the road alone.

Ten minutes later, I was down there myself, headed in the opposite direction toward the line of buses. I'd planned on taking a day trip to visit my father, but soon discovered, one by one, that the bus doors were locked and the vehicles empty. The drivers had probably gone and joined the celebration, knowing that few if any passengers could be recruited today. As I began thinking of alternate plans, other ways I could reach my father's, I noticed my young friend Leni up the street, huddled in an apartment doorway with a taller, older woman. The way they were standing so closely, both wearing sizable coats, seemed quite strange for such a hot day.

"Hello," Leni yelled with an exaggerated wave, as if we had not met only a few hours earlier for lunch.

"Hello," I yelled back, trying to match his enthusiasm. As I walked toward them, the woman whispered something into Leni's ear, and then, rather discreetly, concealed a light blue paper bag she'd been holding.

"This is Mila," Leni said as I approached. "We were just heading back to the hotel."

"Please join us," she said, smiling. Her awkward accent and long round face made me think that she might be from the North.

There was a short pause as I glanced at Leni for some advice, some hint as to the answer he expected from me. Since gaining his restaurant position in the Hotel Dajti, he'd specialized in making the acquaintance of female guests. I did not want to interfere.

"I'm sure my friend has other matters to attend to," Leni quickly said. This was one of his standard lines, but the tone of his voice seemed shaky, hollow, and this surprised me. At that moment, Mila's eyes met mine, focused and warm, and I realized she seemed far closer to my age than Leni's. In the past, he'd offered many times to match me up with women like her, older women from the hotel. Why had he forgotten that offer now? During the first few years after my separation from Ana, I'd refused his help. But less than a month ago, I had finally succumbed to the idea.

"No, no, your friend must join us," Mila said firmly, taking me with one arm and Leni with the other. "Come."

As she pulled us toward the hotel, I noticed how tall and wide she was. In comparison, Leni and his small size seemed almost comical tucked beneath her strong arm. Yet for all of this strength, there was also a fragileness in Mila that I detected. She had a solid profile, very striking, that reminded me of the Italian television stars I had seen on Leni's brother's television. But something about her lips, how the upper one was as full as the lower, and how the tiny gap between her teeth appeared only when she smiled, all seemed to relax me.

"Do you feel like having a drink?" she said as we entered the familiar lobby of the Hotel Dajti. I expected Leni to somehow signal me to decline, but instead he merely answered, "Okay."

Leni gestured to his co-workers and soon a jug of wine materialized. I hadn't eaten since early that afternoon—a pair of stale ematurs—so after finishing the first glass, my face was rather flushed. It felt hot, but good.

"Today was probably his final day of work," Leni said, tilting the ceramic mug in my direction.

"Oh?" she asked.

"Yes," I said, refilling my glass, "until three o'clock today, I was employed by the Ministry of Slogans." There was a brief silence, and it seemed to be a long while before I returned the carafe to its spot on the table. It occurred to me how strange this must have appeared to Mila—me pouring the wine so slowly and precisely, as if it were something valuable like gasoline. I guess I was a little self-conscious because a long time had passed since I'd been around someone like her. I felt strangely drawn to her. "Well, I haven't actually been notified of my firing yet, but that's just a formality. We all know what's happening."

"What will you do now?" Mila said.

"Maybe he will get a job with me," Leni said, and he smiled to let me know he was not joking. Until that moment, I hadn't actually thought about what I would do once the Ministry's closure became official. I'd merely been thinking about its ultimate collapse, counting down the days.

"At least it's not like someone else is replacing you, right?" Mila said. She smiled, flashing the tiny gap between her teeth. "It's not like you yourself lost the job."

"True. I guess it's not so bad when you consider that."

"A job like Akey's, that's what we should all have," Leni said. "Working with cars and trucks."

I nodded.

"We need some more wine." Mila pointed to our empty carafe. "I'm going to see what I can do."

As she started toward the front of the restaurant, I leaned across the table and whispered to Leni, "She just grabbed my arm, what could I do?"

"Yes," he said. "But she is not for you, believe me."

"Mila seems so much older than you, Leni. Not once have I seen you with a woman even near her age."

"Yes, she's not for me, either."

"I don't understand—"

At that moment, Mila returned with a waiter close behind. The man put a fresh carafe of wine on the table and removed the empty one, giving Leni a subtle, quizzical look as if to say, "Who is this woman, and why does she act so aggressively?"

"Would you care for another?" he said instead, using a distant, professional voice.

"Just water for me," I said, and then watched as he refilled their glasses.

I looked around the room at the faded, flaking red wallpaper, the spots of orange and green peaking through from previous paint jobs. It was hard not to sit in the Dajti's lobby and stare, imagining the opulent place it had once been. The fixtures and flooring, the sculpted tables and chairs all managed to retain a faint glow from a more prosperous era that had now been lost beneath a wave of defects. Outside, there was only the dull roar of the crowd, rising and falling faintly in the distance.

"Maybe when things get settled, there will be more work for you," Mila said. A look of concern came upon her face, and for the first time that night, I did not see the tiny gap between her teeth as she smiled. "You know, the changes might actually bring along something better."

"Of course," I said.

"Things will fall into place," Leni said in a somewhat less convincing tone.

"Really, I'm not concerned. There will be time for that. I just want to relax now—I can worry later."

I looked over at Leni, who was idly staring out a window. Normally on a night like this, we would be at his brother Nossi's house, watching Italian television. "Why don't we go down to the square and see what's happening," he finally said.

"Yes, that might be fun," Mila responded. "But first let me finish my drink."

Later, as we walked along the river, I thought about finding the right moment to make a polite exit, to leave Leni and Mila alone together. Of course, she was charming and alluring, entirely appealing, yet at the same time, my loyalty to Leni, my loyalty to our friendship, stopped me from continuing in this manner, stopped me from thinking this way any longer. I just couldn't operate that way, my conscience would not allow it. Yet, despite this, Mila's arm remained locked in mine the entire time, as if she'd known me for years—and as if she knew I was thinking about leaving.

"Is anyone hungry?" Leni asked, veering toward the busy marketplace. He led us through the crowd to a stand where various overripe fruit had been spread out across a large table in an effort to make the supply look more plentiful. The vendor wore an outfit identical to that I'd seen earlier on Altin Leka, though maybe a bit less greasy and rumpled. After a few minutes, I selected a soft, brown apple, and it temporarily solved the problem of my empty stomach, helping me regain a bit of focus that the wine had eliminated earlier. Leni was far ahead now, wading through the crowd and motioning for us to follow. After Mila finished eating, she returned her arm to mine, smiled, and we quickened our pace.

"Where are you from?" I asked her.

"The North," she said. "I am here on business." The tone of her voice was a little flat, and I thought maybe she wanted to let it go at that, so I did.

"That fruit wasn't too bad," I said, changing the subject in such a clumsy way that it made her smile.

"I like you," she said.

Across the boulevard, at the other end of the fountain, we caught up with Leni. I stopped for a second and looked down to where the water had once flowed. Without luck, I tried imagining my reflection the way I'd always seen it as a child. When we began moving again, Leni was leading us toward Altin Leka's shiny white pushcart.

"Ah, friend," he said with some hesitation, obviously unable to recall my name. "A cold ice cream, perhaps?"

"Yes," I said, out of politeness rather than hunger. My appetite, which had been quite strong only a few moments earlier, had somehow gotten lost in the interesting combination of smells emanating from Altin's coat. It seemed to be a sweet flavor of cheap *raki* mixed with thawing winter dampness and early spring sweat.

"The flavor is almond," Altin offered, and for a moment I thought he was referring to a mystery ingredient embedded in his coat.

"Thank you," I said.

"People here in the square have been rowdy," he said, "but this is safer than I had expected. I do not have to worry about thieves at all. Everyone is happy." The subdued tone of his voice seemed to contradict the words he spoke, and it almost felt like he was patronizing us, or, at the very least, reading from some sort of government-sanctioned script.

"Yes," I responded uncomfortably.

"It is nice to see you, Leni."

Leni nodded a return greeting, and then introduced our new northern friend. "Altin, this is my cousin Mila, up visiting from Gjirokaster." As she moved to shake his hand, I wondered why Leni had gone to the trouble of lying about her. Clearly, things were not as simple as they'd seemed. I pulled a few leks from my pocket and announced that I was buying everyone ice cream. Leni smiled lightly and took me up on the offer, but Mila declined, saying that she'd had too much wine. As she spoke, she did not look up. Her eyes remained on Altin, watching him hand me and Leni the neatly scooped ice creams.

I looked around at all the people. How excited they seemed, how happy. I wanted to feel that way, too, and yet I could only summon a vague sensation of relief.

"For all the people out here, I don't recognize anyone," I said loudly, not realizing that only Leni was standing next to me. Mila and Altin had somehow drifted off into the crowd.

"Many outsiders," Leni remarked, so as not to leave my comment hanging. "Young people, too." His tone made me think that he did not view himself this way, that he felt connected instead to an older generation—my generation, I guessed. Mine and Mila's. I looked over and noticed her moving back in our direction, although she still seemed to be watching Altin Leka thirty meters ahead, slicing through the crowd, ignoring any possible customers.

"What is it about Altin that interests you so much?" I wanted to ask her. Or maybe, "Mila, why do you stare at him so?" I thought I should explain about his bitter and sullen personality, about his pettiness and arrogance. I wanted to tell her all this before she got involved any further, before she somehow found him attractive in his own peculiar way. Maybe I should talk about Altin's suspiciously rapid political demise or even his equally suspicious reappearance as a common vendor. Instead though, I said nothing. I just watched her, watching him.

A roar went up from the crowd, and Mila turned back, no longer chasing Altin, who had somehow disappeared. She caught my eye for a second, smiled, and then headed toward me. "Where's Leni?"

I looked around but could not see him anywhere. Mila gently put her arm in mine like before, and I quickly led the two of us forward. Where had Leni gone? As we searched, heading through all of the people, I noticed my assistants conducting a small group of children in song. The two of them stood at the front, strutting around like parade leaders, while the children followed behind, trying to imitate them. "And the stars in the sky, we only see them at night, but we know that they are always there." As they were singing this, one of my assistants recognized me, and a look of indecision came across his face, as if I was still his supervisor and we were still at the office. I smiled to relax him a little, and he smiled, too, then went back to the children. As we left, I examined the group more closely, trying to figure out which of the boys and girls belonged to him. Maybe none, maybe all, I couldn't tell. Then my mind returned to Leni, who was nowhere in sight.

The next morning, I awoke in a large, luxurious bed at the Hotel Dajti, high up in one of the top-story rooms. Mila had already gone, and so I rolled back the curtains and stared at the city. It was still early, and the square was empty now, looking no different than it had the week before, maybe even the month before that, and perhaps every day of the previous year. I suppose I'd expected to find it changed like the rest of us, but other than the scattered garbage, it remained entirely the same. I continued staring, entranced by the strange, almost foreign view offered by Mila's top-floor window. If I squinted my eyes in just the right way, I could imagine a postcard: "Greetings from Albania."

Before she'd left that morning, Mila offered an explanation of her errand in town. Strangely, I hadn't even asked—still following her cue about that from the night before. So it surprised me when she said, "I have to run out and meet some Italians about real estate. I'll be back later, okay?" And then she kissed me twice on the mouth and disappeared out the door. Obviously, she had lied. If she really were in town for some land negotiation, why all the vagueness, the secrecy? Why would Leni call her his cousin? Why would she brush aside any questions the night before? From the way she'd spoken that morning, I'd gotten the feeling that this bit about the Italians and real estate was simply meant to put my mind at ease, that she'd offered this explanation as a way of alleviating my worries—and as a way of fending off my inevitable questions. Perhaps she realized that our night together would somehow chip away at my ability to be discreet. Of course, this was not true. I'd learned long beforehand to keep quiet when necessary. The party taught me that—the party and my ex-wife Ana.

The last time Ana and I had been together, we'd already been separated for a while, but I'd gone back over to the apartment hoping for a reconciliation. Little was solved that night; each moment I spoke, I seemed only to make things worse. Yet, for the first time in a long while, we found ourselves drawn to each other with an odd intensity. And so, the talking stopped. Ana confessed to me later that she'd been in a bad state that particular evening and cautioned that it would never happen again. I didn't believe her at the time, but, in the end, she turned out to be speaking the truth.

I sat up in bed and counted the berries on the patterned wallpaper in Mila's room. Raspberries and blackberries alternated with small sprigs of holly. Leni had once shown me a handful of the Dajti's suites and most of them were alike, but this was the first one I could remember with such an unusual design covering the walls. Of course, the upper part of the building was set aside for high-ranking party officials, so perhaps this was some delineation of luxury, these berries. I was not sure. Either way, I thought, Mila must have been doing well in her business—whatever it was—if she could afford such a room.

I showered, dressed, and headed downstairs for some breakfast, but not before leaving Mila a brief note with the street address of my apartment. I mentioned that we could meet later that afternoon or evening, whenever she had completed her "business."

The hotel restaurant was nearly empty and unusually solemn, so I headed toward the Kafe Quristi. As I crossed the boulevard, I suddenly pictured Mila again—the way she'd looked the night before as we walked together in the square, and the way she'd asked why I was in such a big hurry to find Leni. There had been a strange feeling of innocence at that moment, as if she seriously expected an answer to her question. As if I would say to her, "The hurry is that he is my friend, and he is lost up ahead somewhere, and we need to find him." Yet, at the same time, I knew this was not what she had meant for me to say at all. It was a moment where my friendship with Leni was expected to bend a little. I suppose if I'd thought about it then like I was now, things might have ended up differently. Mila and I would have found Leni, and eventually, I would have walked back to my small apartment alone, taken off my suit, and gone to bed early like I'd done on so many other nights.

I was the only customer in the cafe when Ivan Quristi brought over my coffee. "I suppose everyone was out rather late last night," he said, indicating the empty restaurant with his outstretched hands, then wandering back into the kitchen without waiting for a reply. A few minutes later, Leni arrived, looking tired and carrying a small loaf of slightly burned raisin bread—from the hotel, I suspected. He sat down and signaled to Ivan for another cup.

"I'm glad I found you here so early," he said, taking off his thin jacket. "Listen, I'm sorry about disappearing last night. But I ran into Kosi, and we began talking."

Ivan appeared with coffee, poured, and then stood waiting. Leni handed him the bread. "Fresh from the oven, as I promised," Leni offered, smiling. Ivan thanked him, and headed back to the kitchen, only to return a few seconds later with buttered slices for the two of us.

"I've already eaten," Leni explained, pushing his slice on top of mine. "Go ahead."

"So, you were telling me about Kosi . . ." I said, trailing off. I wanted to get him started on the subject again, and keep his attention away from Mila.

"Yes, Kosi," he said. "I cannot help things when I see her, you know. It's out of my control." I nodded and bit into the blackened raisin bread.

"Every time that I do, it is wonderful," he continued. "Yet, I have to rely on coincidence to bring us together. There is something in her that tells me if I wrote a letter or telephoned, you know, to ask for a proper meeting, she would not allow it."

"Maybe she is afraid," I said.

"No, she just seems to prefer the spontaneity. To her, I think even the smallest plans are too official." He paused for a second and drank a sip of his coffee. "That's okay, though. I don't really mind."

"I'm envious," I said. "It sounds like the exact opposite of Ana." As I said this, I realized that my night with Mila had been this way, too—spontaneous and seemingly nonchalant. "Not like Ana at all."

"Yes," Leni said, but not in such a way as to agree with me too strongly. He knew it was all right for me to criticize Ana, but he was always careful about doing that himself.

At that moment, it seemed to be my turn, and although Leni expected me to explain what, if anything, had happened after he disappeared, it was not his style to ask. I could let the entire thing go and move on to a different topic of conversation—the state of the Ministry, the latest reports on the demonstrations, or even just gossip about someone like Altin Leka, passing along more vague rumors about his underground position—but that did not seem right. Just as it'd never been Leni's style to ask, it was not my style to keep things from him. Besides, now that I knew he really wasn't interested in Mila—at least not in the way he was interested in Kosi—there didn't seem to be much of a problem. Perhaps when he had spoken less than positively about her the day before, when he'd said she was not for me, it was part of a little game—a theory of reverse persuasion. I had only recently succumbed to his never-ending offers of matchmaking, and so possibly he had thought it was time to turn the tables, catching me off guard. "You do not want Mila," I could hear him saying. "Yes, Leni, I do," I would've answered. "But she is not right for you." "Yes, yes, she is. Believe me!"

Mr. Kruchnik, a high-ranking party official and Leni's sometime boss, appeared in the doorway. "Good morning, gentlemen," he said. "May I join you?"

Kruchnik was carrying a small leather satchel, and he loudly dropped it onto the seat across from me before sitting next to Leni. As if on cue, Ivan Quristi appeared from the kitchen with another pot of coffee and an extra cup. I sat there for a moment trying to figure out if Kruchnik was a party official who I still needed to worry about. Probably not, but it did seem strange the way the rest of the customers, the handful of people who had entered after Leni, quieted a bit as Kruchnik sat down.

He poured himself some coffee, then leaned across the table and refilled our cups. "It has been a strange couple of weeks," Kruchnik said, breaking the silence. "Now, it is the others who must worry." He laughed a little at his own remark.

"Yes," I said, not really committing myself one way or the other.

Kruchnik smiled back and took a large, gurgling sip of his coffee. He was a younger man, I don't mean as young as Leni, but still young, and his meteoric rise within the party was well-known. Even his detractors were amazed by the fact that he had accomplished so much at such an early age. Yet, Kruchnik's success was actually justified. Although I had never seen anything in writing, I knew of his ability to make quick, ruthless decisions that always left him on the right end of things.

"Well, this is a wonderful day," Kruchnik began again, maintaining his jovial mood. Leni and I forced polite smiles, and Kruchnik seemed to take no notice of our uneasiness; instead, he continued laughing and called Ivan Quristi to bring out some fancy pastries.

"Allow me to select something for you both," Kruchnik said, eyeing the cart Ivan had rolled out from the kitchen. "I'm usually pretty good at making decisions." There were three large, crusty fruit tarts, all cramped together in the middle of the platter. One of them would have been enough to split among us. "We'll take all three," Kruchnik said loudly. Ivan nodded slightly and asked if we wanted them heated.

"Of course!" Kruchnik moaned, before adjusting himself in the chair.

"Thank you, sir," Leni managed.

"Here," Kruchnik said, his tone suddenly subdued and businesslike. He reached into his satchel, pulled out a light blue paper bag, and handed it across the table to Leni, who remained silent. Some crisp lira notes and a few tattered dinars, all of high denominations, dribbled out of the bag momentarily before Leni quickly crammed them back inside. He glanced over at me and I looked down at my empty coffee cup, trying not to let him know I'd seen the money.

"So what's this?" Kruchnik said, noticing our exchange, Leni's look of anxiety, me averting my eyes. Neither of us answered, perhaps a little dumbfounded at his acknowledgment of a moment that should have been ignored. Kruchnik sat back in his chair and a sly smile came over his face, the first time I'd ever seen such an expression.

"Have either of you ever heard the story about the two fish swimming in the Drina?" he said, leaning back in his chair.

"No," Leni said.

"Well, this is one from my childhood, from way way back. These two fish had grown up together, you see . . . had been spawned together. Brothers. And when they got older, one got bigger than the other all of a sudden. But the two of them ignored this difference between them. Instead, they made every effort to remain equal, and every effort to remain friends."

At that moment, Ivan returned with our heated pastries. "Ah, good, good," Kruchnik said. As the old cafe owner set down our plates, I looked over at Leni sitting there, silent, expressionless, as quiet as I'd seen him in years.

"And so everything was fine," Kruchnik said, hacking off a piece of his tart. "They just did their best not to address the massive physical difference between them. But then one day the head fish—the mayor I guess you could say—approached the larger brother with an errand. The mayor wanted the large one to protect him, to serve as his bodyguard. In exchange for these services, the large fish would be introduced to the mayor's daughter, a beautiful guppy."

"Did he take the job?" Leni said.

"Well, he thought about it for many days, until finally he went to ask Mila, the goddess of the sea, for advice," Kruchnik answered, and as he said this last part, his eyes widened, the whites of them grossly clear—as if we weren't making the painfully obvious connections here. "And so while he was away, the smaller brother swam around the Drina alone, wondering where his large brother had gone." Kruchnik's voice was hushed now, almost sinister, and a knowing look formed on his face. He stared at both of us for a moment and then continued his story.

"One morning, the smaller brother, still swimming on his own in the lovely Drina, came upon a beautiful young guppy, scanning the bottom of the riverbed for food. 'I have plenty of food,' the smaller brother said, 'Would you like to share?' And so the beautiful guppy, the mayor's daughter, went with the smaller brother to eat." Kruchnik smiled as he said this last part, and then put down his fork. "So do you know what happened next?" he said in my direction.

"No," I said. "What happened?" I was grumpy now.

"The mayor's daughter fell in love with the smaller brother?" Leni said.

"Aha," Kruchnik said. "I see you have heard this one before. Why did you not stop me earlier? Now I feel as if I have made a fool of myself." Of course, Kruchnik did not feel this way in the slightest. If he had, he never would've admitted it. Besides, I was fairly certain that he had made the whole thing up anyway, and probably even as he was telling it.

"Well," Kruchnik said, slyly laughing and examining each of our expressions. "Seems as if we have come to the end." He then deliberately took the package of money out of Leni's hands and plopped it on the table directly in front of me. Studying our expressions, he cut a large portion of his strawberry tart and stuffed it into his mouth, emitting a small gushing sound as he chewed. How strangely things had twisted. There was my young friend Leni, who hardly knew anything of my evening with Mila, and then there was Kruchnik, who seemed aware of everything.

I wanted time to think about the money and what Mila could have done to earn it. Clearly, her hotel room had been arranged by Kruchnik, which explained how she had secured such a fancy suite, yet I didn't have even the slightest indication why.

"See," Kruchnik finally said, leaning back in his chair and gesturing toward the cafe's crowd, "while other officials are losing power, I'm gaining it by the minute." He smiled widely, opening his mouth just a bit as if to release a silent laugh. For a moment, I suspected he might burp. "Last week, or last night for that matter, I might have been afraid to dine in public, to be seen spreading money around like this. But how quickly things can change, I tell you. It's an amazing thing."

"Yes, it is," Leni said cautiously.

"Ah, my young friend," Kruchnik said to him, taking hold of his hand, "there is nothing to worry about. Believe me! You've done your part."

Both of Kruchnik's hands were clasped on Leni's now, cupping them much like a father might as he consoled his troubled son. In the background, other customers in the cafe sat up and began leaving, some even before they had finished their meals. The expression on Leni's face remained unchanged.

Although they managed to create a good deal of noise, the crowd gathering in the square was nowhere near as large as it had been the previous day. Perhaps people were finally running out of energy, their stamina waning. The longer a celebration lasts, I figured, the harder it must be to maintain the frenetic pace, the constant revelry. Recapturing the energy of that first day seemed nearly impossible now. Clearly, the gatherings were no longer the result of an impulse, a spontaneous force within the people. As the days continued, the immediacy and passion could not help but fade.

Kruchnik had instructed me to meet Mila back at the Dajti sometime that afternoon, so I lingered in the square only for a few minutes. Across from the Ministry building, still silent and deserted, I saw Altin's white pushcart, neatly planted in the exact spot it had been the afternoon before, but no Altin Leka to be found. Instead, a group of children were gathered around it, and one of them, his head buried from view, was handing ice creams out from the storage compartment. Altin's smelly coat lay across the back of his chair, with important-looking documents sprouting from the inside pocket. I stood there staring.

"The almond man's not coming back," a young girl said to me. She was carrying a small bag with a loaf of bread leaning out of the top.

"What?" I said, kneeling down to her.

"The almond man won't be back."

At that moment, the girl's mother showed up and the two of them held hands.

"They sent somebody to find his family."

"Why?"

The mother and daughter looked at each other for a second, a sullen expression on their faces, and they remained silent. "I suppose somebody should do something about those little thieves," the mother finally said, indicating the children raiding Altin's cart.

"Yes, somebody should," I mumbled back, not sure what else I could say. The three of us stood there for a moment, staring at one another. Then I ran over to the cart yelling, and the kids fled in every direction, scattering and screaming, but without fear in the voices. It was more like laughter, as if we'd been playing a grand game. I flipped the top of each compartment closed, fastened the partitions on Altin's vehicle, and rolled it into the shade by the Ministry building. Up the street, the woman and her daughter continued watching me. I guess they wanted to make sure I wasn't going to steal anything myself.

"All fine," I yelled toward them, waving. They did not call back to me or make any motion. They just stood there, watching as before. I wanted to walk over and demand a detailed explanation of Altin's fate, but I knew that was not possible. Even the slightest of my questions, I fearfully imagined, would be met with more stone-faced looks, sinister glances that might say, "Of course, you know what happened to Altin. And didn't you have a part in it, too?"

Quickly arriving home, I went through the apartment and looked for potential money-hiding places. From the Italian crime shows I'd seen on Nossi's TV, I remembered two or three good spots to do this: behind a painting, under a floorboard, or in the hollow pipe of a brass bedpost. But I didn't have any of these things in my place—they were back at the old house with Ana—and so I took the money and sat on the bed, trying to figure a solution. I did have one picture up, but it was just an unframed print of boats resting in the Adriatic.

The light blue money bag was next to me, and I held it with both hands, squeezing it again and again. Then I dumped it out across the blanket, letting everything come free. For a moment, seeing it all there, I genuinely thought about taking it for myself. I was surprised at the nice feeling it gave me. Freedom. Of course, even if I could convince myself, I knew that this one bag was not nearly enough to take me beyond the range of its consequences.

I gathered the bills into small piles and paused a couple of times to look at the currency itself, the strange green and purple etchings of Ruđer Bošković, his hair tied back in the old-style ponytail, the ruffles of his shirt helping to balance out a slight double chin. Scientific spatial models, spheres, equations rested above his left shoulder. I couldn't remember what they were, what he'd done. I once knew the answer to this, I suppose, as a child, back when there was time and reason to know such things—long before I'd become a member of the Ministry.

I went to my desk and pulled out the large bottom drawer completely, setting it to the side. There was a good four inches of space between the floor and the rail that held the drawer in position. Before reconfiguring the currency into three-inch piles, I wiped the area out with a towel, then lined the money inside. There was something slightly gratifying about seeing it neatly tucked into this hiding spot, and as I replaced the drawer, I felt strange having so much cash concealed within my desk.

After that, I immersed myself in routine housework—washing the dishes, soaking my work shirts, darning some socks, even scrubbing the floor. I tried—without success—to reach my father by telephone to explain the lack of transportation, why I wasn't coming. Of course there were other reasons, too, but they had surfaced afterward. Truly, the buses had stopped me.

I replayed the moment Mila insisted I join her and Leni for a drink at the hotel; the way we lost Leni in the crowd; the look on the desk clerk's face as the two of us headed up to Mila's room; and even Kruchnik handing me the light blue money bag with such showy self-assuredness. To be honest, I was embarrassed at how easily I'd been drawn into such a scheme. Yet, I wasn't ready to disentangle myself from whatever it was, whatever it would be. Even if my part was merely that of the naive fool, it was still infinitely more interesting than anything I had done in a long while.

I began preparing for Mila's arrival, planning what I would be doing when she appeared, what the best way would be for her to see me. Reading the paper on the couch, the front door slightly cracked? Hunched over the stove, preparing dinner? Or even leaning on the small balcony, studying the night sky? My mind raced on to other considerations, too. Was there enough food in the kitchen if she agreed to stay? Were my clothes appropriate? And yes, the sheets on the bed—were they clean?

I knew how foolish this was; clearly it was causing my small seed of hope to multiply upon itself. But then, I pictured Mila as my ex-wife Ana, and imagined how successful my initial scheming had been with her. That first night, many years ago, Ana had come to my apartment planning to visit for only a moment, but gradually I had convinced her to stay. At first, it was the warmth of my burning fireplace, and then later impeccable cooking and well-planned conversation. It worked for a long time, nearly ten years, before she decided that, yes, she really must go.

I decided to await Mila's arrival on the couch, reading the news journal and glancing over some of my old papers from work. I was able to spend a long while in this position, anxiously listening for that knock on the door. Eventually, though, I grew bored and moved into the kitchen. For about an hour, I dawdled around the stove and counter, mindlessly preparing one of Ana's old recipes. From there, I went outside to the porch and listened intently for Mila's solid footsteps along the dirt street. Inevitably, the cold night air and a growing sense of disappointment forced me back to the warm couch where I drifted into a light sleep.

The next morning, without thinking, I ate breakfast, put on my work clothes, and headed off toward the Ministry of Slogans.

The warm sunshine distracted me from the setback of the previous night, just as recent events had helped me overlook the fact that I would soon lose my job.

As I walked across the boulevard toward the city center, I noticed a small group of people heading in my direction. My old boss Hansa Splite and his wife Katarina were leading the spectacle, arm-in-arm and dressed in their blackest of black clothes. Beside them was Hansa's sister, Lena, and she was crying inconsolably. As they got closer, a small horse cart pulling a casket appeared, followed by a meager, slightly underdressed and seemingly uninterested group of mourners. Altin Leka was no longer missing.

Though I hadn't cared for him much, seeing Altin's mother Lena in tears made me reconsider him for a moment. Even figuring his supposedly swift decline in power, it seemed rather odd that there was not one uniformed party official in the procession. This almost seemed to confirm the rumors of his shadow position.

Up ahead in the square, the large crowds of the past few days had entirely subsided, giving me the distinct impression that all of the changes that had taken place would no longer be detectable to the human eye. If things had indeed changed, maybe now they were simply of the mind and of the mood—something outsiders might easily overlook.

The front door to the Ministry was unlocked and propped open by a large brick. Inside, I unexpectedly found apprentices and managers alike moving about the place in a flurry of activity. They were carrying reports and diagrams back and forth across the office, much in the same way as they had the week before, but now there was a palpable sense of eagerness and almost giddy optimism among the workers. I stood in the foyer, somewhat entranced by the action. After a while, however, I felt strange and began the trek upstairs, through the corridor, and across the wing to my corner office, seeking the comfort of my routine. Along the way, I watched other workers, hoping to gain clues as to my approaching fate. But there was nothing—no frowns of dread, looks of sympathy, or even glances of morbid curiosity.

Through the distorted glass of my office door, I could see people moving inside. I entered with a bit of trepidation and was relieved to find my two assistants arranging large stacks of paper across my desk.

"Good morning," they said in unison.

"Good morning," I responded. Then there was a strange moment of silence, as if both parties were waiting for the other to make some important declaration. Yet, nobody spoke.

"Okay then," I finally offered, trying to ease the tension.

"I'm glad you're here," the younger one said.

"We have a lot of work," the senior assistant added, straightening one of the piles. "I have placed the most important items—those that require immediate action—on the left. The secondary documents have been divided into three stacks atop the rear table."

"Action," I said, sliding down into my old chair. "Action is good."

It occurred to me that the desk drawers were empty and my box of personal possessions was sitting across the room, exactly where I'd left it. I considered ways of walking around the desk to retrieve it without betraying my recent uncertainty, but then reconsidered.

"There's also been a delivery for you this morning," the older assistant said with some hesitance. He had very thin lips and an extremely short haircut that made him appear quite young. The other assistant, ruddy-faced and eager, pointed toward a basket of fruit.

I quickly moved to open the tiny card pinned to the front. A fancy wax seal embossed with the letter "K" held the envelope together. Inside, I found a simple piece of paper imprinted with the words "Thank you." From the concerned looks on their faces, I could tell that my assistants had recognized Kruchnik's stationery. I smiled, quickly relieving their apprehension, and then tossed them each a pale melon from the basket.

"Okay," I said, allowing the commotion to resume.

"Well, sir," the senior assistant began, his thin lips clicking lightly, "I believe you'll be quite pleased to hear what we've discovered this morning."

"Yes?" I said, easing back into my comfortable chair.

"Now, while the new slogan campaign we've been contracted to produce is entirely different from anything we've ever created, I think you'll agree that—with only some minor modifications—we can reuse a great deal of our old material."

"Well," I said, "that is good news."

I pictured banners and murals that had been painted on our behalf, the "Ministry of Slogans" in glossy red, tempered slightly with sensible olive, and how each would now be cut and pasted to fit with the latest direction. "All for Success, Success for All" would become "Success at Last!" "A body in motion stays in motion" would now be "A body at rest can spend a week in Durrës!" Even "Workers Unite!" would be up for grabs.

"Let's schedule a meeting," I said.

"When?" the younger assistant asked excitedly.

"How about in half an hour?"

"Yes, sir."

Then the two of them left to write the meeting time down on the calendar out front, sharpen the pencils, collect the various papers, and send the requisite memo to the file announcing the meeting. Thirty minutes later, they would return and the meeting would proceed.

At that moment, my friend Leni was probably trying to get me a position at the hotel kitchen, or perhaps one in the service area registering guests and sending telegrams. What a strange and sudden twist in my situation. Earlier, it hadn't occurred to me how confusing things would be once everyone, even high-ranking officials, had been excused from work. I pictured myself lining up to compete with other former Ministry directors and assistant directors and managers and supervisors, all vying for a single bellcap's job. Perhaps then, the former State Director would wind up as the one lucky enough to land the position. I pictured a big grin appearing across his face while the rest of us congratulated him and pointed him downstage to collect the flowers and chocolates thrown by admirers from the audience.

"May I come in?" Mila said, cracking open my office door slightly. Her northern accent jarred me for a moment.

"Yes," I said.

"I heard you might be here." She walked over, removed her coat before I could offer help, then leaned back and gave me a quick kiss on the cheek.

"I expected you sooner—last night," I said.

"Your office is much larger than I imagined," she said.

"You like it?"

"Yes. May I sit down?"

"Please."

"And two assistants of your own," she said.

"Yes, I am lucky, I suppose."

"So you still have your job, then."

"It seems that way. Just some adjustments to make, that's all."

"Now I'm not so sure what to think about the things you told me earlier."

"What?"

"You know, how you were losing your job, and all that," she said with a knowing smile. "Maybe you were attempting to elicit some pity?"

"Really?" I blurted out.

"Well, yesterday you had no job, your life was on the brink of ruin, your future uncertain. Today, it's business as usual. Nothing seems to have happened."

"Yes," I admitted. Thinking about it that way did make me appear overly dramatic. I quickly tried to remember other parts, conversations of the last day or so, and how foolish they made me appear now. My box of possessions next to the door only seemed to confirm this.

Of course, my colleagues might disagree with all this, claiming the recent changes had been both sudden and drastic; and yet realistically, I knew Mila was probably right—the only truly irreversible act of the past few days was the one she had performed herself.

"Still, I suppose it added a little extra something to our night together," she said. She meant it, but I felt a little strange, unbalanced. It was a different sort of feeling than the usual nervousness I expected to have around her, the nervousness I had felt in my apartment the night before.

She had her back to me now, examining the other parts of my office. I tried picturing her as someone dangerous, someone I couldn't trust. Yet, I had already seen her lie once, and so what? I'd gone with her anyway. Strangely enough, knowing what I knew about her hadn't changed much of anything. Again, I loved a woman I couldn't exactly depend on.

"I still have something for you," I said, attempting nonchalance.

"Oh?" she said coyly, looking over her shoulder.

"Yes."

"Well then," Mila declared, now speaking quite loudly, as if she wanted to be heard by some imaginary people hiding behind the walls. "As you know, I'm very fond of presents."

"Yes," I said in an equally loud voice, "yes, you are." And I thought of the small stacks of money hidden under my big desk drawer.

Relaxing a bit, I added, "It's waiting for you at my apartment. We can go there now if you like. Let me just tell my assistants."

Mila nodded, still gazing out the window and onto the square. As I moved around the desk toward the door, she grabbed my shoulders and pulled me close. Her lips parted just the slightest before she suddenly propped my chin down and kissed me on the forehead. As we stood there, embracing awkwardly, my head under her jaw, pressed against her throat, and my body buried in her strong arms, I could hear my assistants behind the door, arguing over one of the new slogans.

"In sameness, only difference," the older one said, nearly yelling.

"For difference, cultivate the same," the other replied. I could not tell whether they were serious.

I stopped for a second and closed my eyes, absorbing the sun as it burst through my office window. How weird. How strange! Until that moment, I hadn't even considered Ana, hadn't even thought of a reconciliation. It gave me a good, exuberant feeling to know that, but at the same time, it concerned me. Rarely a day went by that I did not wake up and think immediately of our impending reunion. I tried recalling our last attempt to talk, reach some understanding, patch things up, but could only picture our wedding day—me in the pale suit borrowed from my brother, and she in a gown furnished by the state. Oddly, it had not occurred to me until that moment that Mila was the first woman I'd been with since Ana, the first since our separation. And now, regardless of what might happen, I knew that I'd always remember her in that exact way.

She walked over to the window where I was standing, staring out onto the square. Her skin smelled soapy, even waxy, but it was a pleasant smell that appealed to me more than any flowery perfume ever could. I ran my hand along her shirt and leaned up to kiss her. She hesitated for a second, then pressed herself closer, her strong arms folding me in. Now, she was easing into her role, and I, into mine. With a clumsy twist of my arm, I managed to slide the door bolt shut. Outside, the deliberations continued.

"Similar, yet dissimilar."

"Identical, but unique!"

Through the window, on the street below, I could see the buses lined up as always, though this time a large, jovial crowd of would-be passengers stood alongside, waiting for their driver to appear.

Translated by Kevin Phelan and Bill U'Ren

HIT MAN

Charles Bukowski

Ronnie was to meet the two men at the German bar in the Silverlake district. It was 7:15 P.M. He sat there drinking the dark beer at the table by himself. The barmaid was blond, fine ass, and her breasts looked as if they were going to fall out of her blouse.

Ronnie liked blondes. It was like ice-skating and roller-skating. The blondes were ice-skating, the rest were roller-skating. The blondes even smelled different. But women meant trouble, and for him the trouble often outweighed the joy. In other words, the price was too high.

Yet a man needed a woman now and then, if for no other reason than to prove he could get one. The sex was secondary. It wasn't a lover's world, it never would be.

7:20. He waved her over for another beer. She came smiling, carrying the beer out in front of her breasts. You couldn't help liking her like that.

"You like working here?" he asked her.

"Oh yes, I meet a lot of men."

"Nice men?"

"Nice men and the other kind."

"How can you tell them apart?"

"I can tell by looking."

"What kind of man am I?"

"Oh," she laughed, "nice, of course."

"You've earned your tip," said Ronnie.

7:25. They'd said seven. Then he looked up. It was Curt. Curt had the guy with him. They came over and sat down. Curt waved for a pitcher.

"The Rams ain't worth shit," said Curt, "I've lost an even $500 on them this season."

"You think Prothro's finished?"

"Yeah, it's over for him," said Curt. "Oh, this is Bill. Bill, this is Ronnie."

They shook hands. The barmaid arrived with the pitcher.

"Gentlemen," said Ronnie, "this is Kathy."

"Oh," said Bill.

"Oh, yes," said Curt.

The barmaid laughed and wiggled off.

"It's good beer," said Ronnie. "I've been here since seven o'clock, waiting. I ought to know."

"You don't want to get drunk," said Curt.

"Is he reliable?" asked Bill.

"He's got the best references," said Curt.

"Look," said Bill, "I don't want comedy. It's my money."

"How do I know you're not a pig?" asked Ronnie.

"How do I know you won't cut with the $2500?"

"Three grand."

"Curt said two and one half."

"I just upped it. I don't like you."

"I don't care too much for your ass either. I've got a good mind to call it off."

"You won't. You guys never do."

"Do you do this regular?"

"Yes. Do you?"

"All right, gentlemen," said Curt, "I don't care what you settle for. I get my grand for the contract."

"You're the lucky one, Curt," said Bill.

"Yeah," said Ronnie.

"Each man is an expert in his own line," said Curt, lighting a cigarette.

"Curt, how do I know this guy won't cut with the three grand?"

"He won't or he's out of business. It's the only kind of work he can do."

"That's horrible," said Bill.

"What's horrible about it? You need him, don't you?"

"Well, yes."

"Other people need him, too. They say each man is good at something. He's good at that."

Somebody put some money in the juke and they sat listening to the music and drinking the beer.

"I'd really like to give it to that blonde," said Ronnie. "I'd like to give her about six hours of turkeyneck."

"I would, too," said Curt, "if I had it."

"Let's get another pitcher," said Bill. "I'm nervous."

"There's nothing to worry about," said Curt. He waved for another pitcher of beer. "That $500 I dropped on the Rams, I'll get it back at Anita. They open December twenty-sixth. I'll be there."

"Is the Shoe going to ride in the meet?" asked Bill.

"I haven't read the papers. I'd imagine he will. He can't quit. It's in his blood."

"Longden quit," said Ronnie.

"Well, he had to; they had to strap the old man in the saddle."

"He won his last race."

"Campus pulled the other horse."

"I don't think you can beat the horses," said Bill.

"A smart man can beat anything he puts his mind to," said Curt. "I've never worked in my life."

"Yeah," said Ronnie, "but I gotta work tonight."

"Be sure you do a good job, baby," said Curt.

"I always do a good job."

They were quiet and sat drinking their beer. Then Ronnie said, "All right, where's the goddamned money?"

"You'll get it, you'll get it," said Bill. "It's lucky I brought an extra $500."

"I want it now. All of it."

"Give him the money, Bill. And while you're at it, give me mine."

It was all in hundreds. Bill counted it under the table. Ronnie got his first, then Curt got his. They checked it. Okay.

"Where's it at?" asked Ronnie.

"Here," said Bill, handing him an envelope. "The address and key are inside."

"How far away is it?"

"Thirty minutes. You take the Ventura freeway."

"Can I ask you one thing?"

"Sure."

"Why?"

"Why?"

"Yes, why?"

"Do you care?"

"No."

"Then why ask?"

"Too much beer, I guess."

"Maybe you better get going," said Curt.

"Just one more pitcher of beer," said Ronnie.

"No," said Curt, "get going."

"Well, shit, all right."

Ronnie moved around the table, got out, walked to the exit. Curt and Bill sat there looking at him. He walked outside. Night. Stars. Moon. Traffic. His car. He unlocked it, got in, drove off.

Ronnie checked the street carefully and the address more carefully. He parked a block and a half away and walked back. The key fit the door. He opened it and walked in. There was a TV set going in the front room. He walked across the rug.

"Bill?" somebody asked. He listened for the voice. She was in the bathroom. "Bill?" she said again. He pushed the door open and there she sat in the tub, very blond, very white, young. She screamed.

He got his hands around her throat and pushed her under the water. His sleeves were soaked. She kicked and struggled violently. It got so bad that he had to get in the tub with her, clothes and all. He had to hold her down. Finally she was still and he let her go.

Bill's clothes didn't quite fit him but at least they were dry. The wallet was wet but he kept the wallet. Then he got out of there, walked the block and one half to his car and drove off.

THE DEATH OF MRS. SHEER

Joyce Carol Oates

One afternoon not long ago, on a red-streaked dirt
road in the Eden Valley, two men in an open jalopy were driving
along in such a hurry that anyone watching could have guessed
they had business ahead. The jalopy was without species: it bore no
insignia or features to identify it with other cars or jalopies, but
many to distinguish itself in the memory—jingling behind was a
battered license plate, last year's and now five months outdated,
hanging down straight from a twist of wire, and other twists of this
wire (which was not even chicken fence wire, but new shiny copper
wire), professional and concise, held the trunk door nearly closed
and both doors permanently closed. Dirty string and clothesline
laced important parts of the car together, too, notably the hood
and the left front fender, the only fender remaining. Though parts
here and there creaked and the lone fender shuddered, everything
really moved in harmony, including the men who nodded in
agreement with the rapid progression of scrubland. Their nods
were solemn, prudent, and innocently calculating. They looked

vaguely alike, as if their original faces had been identical and a brush stroke here, a flattening as with a mallet there, had turned them into Jeremiah and Sweet Gum.

Jeremiah, who drove, was about thirty-four. He was a tall thick-chested man, with a dark beard ragged about his face and pleased-looking lips shut tight as if he had a secret he wouldn't tell, not even to Sweet Gum. His forehead was innocent of wrinkles or thought. It was true that his hair was matted and made him look something like one of the larger land animals—most people were put in mind of a buffalo, even those who had never seen buffaloes but had only looked at pictures of them. But his eyes were clear and alert and looked intelligent, especially when anyone was talking to him. Jeremiah, years ago, had passed up through all grades except seventh, his last, just by gazing at his teacher with that look and sometimes nodding, as he did now. They were approaching an old wooden bridge and Jeremiah nodded as if he had known it was coming.

Sweet Gum's throat jumped at the sight of that bridge: Sweet Gum was only twenty and had never been this far from home, except to the army and back (he told the story that he had decided against the army, even after they gave him supper there, because he didn't like all the niggers around). He had a fair roundish face, that of a cherub dashed out of his element and so baffled and sullen for life. His hair, bleached by the sun, grew down shabby and long on his neck, though the ridge where the bowl had been and his mother had stopped cutting was still visible, jutting out two or three inches up his head, so that he looked ruffled and distorted. He had pale eyes, probably blue, and soft-looking eye-brows that were really one eyebrow, grown gently together over his nose. His cheeks were plump, freckled, his lips moist and always parted (at night there was wet anywhere he put his head, after a while). Like his cousin Jeremiah he wore a suit in spite of the heat—it was about ninety-eight—with a colored shirt open at the throat. Sweet Gum's suit was still too big for him, a hand-down that was wearing out before he grew into it, and Jeremiah's suit, a pure, dead black, was shiny and smelled like the attic. Ever since Jeremiah had appeared wearing it, Sweet Gum had been glancing at him strangely, as if he weren't sure whether this was his cousin Jeremiah or some other Jeremiah.

They clattered onto the bridge. "Whooee," Jeremiah laughed without enthusiasm, as boards clanked and jumped behind them and the old rusted rails jerked up as if caught by surprise. The bridge spanned nothing—just dried-up, cracked ground with dying weeds—and both men stared down at it with all their features run together into one blur of consternation. Then Jeremiah said, "All passed. All passed," and they were safe again.

"*God* taken hold of us there," Sweet Gum said, so frightened by the bridge that he forgot Jeremiah always laughed at remarks like that. But Jeremiah did not seem to notice. "God's saving us for our promise," he muttered, so that Jeremiah could hear it or not, just as he wanted. Back in his mind, and even coming out when his lips moved, was the thought: "First promise to do. First promise." If the Devil himself were to come and take Sweet Gum out into the desert with him, or up on a mountain, or pyramid, or anywhere, and tempt him to break his promise to his uncle Simon, Sweet Gum would shout "No!" at him—"No!" to the Devil himself.

As if to mock Sweet Gum's thoughts, Jeremiah twitched and rubbed his nose suddenly. "Christ, boy," he said, "I got a itch—Am I going to kiss a fool all the way out here?"

Sweet Gum turned red. "You keep your goddamn kissing to yourself!" he snarled, as if Jeremiah were no one to be afraid of. Had the duty of fulfilling a promise already begun to change him? He felt Jeremiah's surprise with pride. "Nobody's going to kiss *me*," Sweet Gum said with venom.

Probably no one on Main Street in Plain Dealing saw Jeremiah and Sweet Gum leave, though many would see them leave for the last time a few days later. By now Sweet Gum sat in a real sweat of anticipation, his suit drenched and his eyes squinting past a haze of sweat as if peering out of a disguise. As soon as the startling sign

PLAIN DEALING appeared by the ditch, Jeremiah said quietly, "Now, I don't want no upstart rambunctiousness ruining our plans. You remember that." Sweet Gum was embarrassed and angry, yet at the same time he knew Jeremiah was right. Behind Jeremiah his family stretched out of sight: all the Coke family, grandfathers and fathers, sons, cousins, brothers, women all over; it made Sweet Gum and his mother and little brother look like a joke someone had played. Of course maybe someone had played a joke—Sweet Gum's mother was not married, and through years of furious shame he had gathered that his father, whoever he was, was not even the father of his brother. *That* bothered Sweet Gum as much as not knowing who his father was.

They drove through town. It was larger than they had expected. The main street was wide and paved; at either side long strips of reddish dirt stretched out to buildings and fields far from the road. There were open-air markets for vegetables and fruit and poultry, a schoolhouse (without a flag on its flagpole), a gas station and general store and post office put together (groups of boys and young men straggled about in front of this building, and Sweet Gum stared at them as if trying to recognize someone), houses (all built up on blocks, perched off the ground), and, even, catching the eye of both men, a movie house—in a Quonset hut with a roof painted shiny orange and a bright, poster-covered front. Sweet Gum stared as they drove by.

Jeremiah shortly turned the car into a driveway. Sweet Gum wanted to grab his arm in surprise. "This place is where *he* stays, you found it so fast?" he said faintly. "Hell, no," Jeremiah said. "Can't you read? This is a 'hotel.' We got to stay overnight, don't we?" "Overnight?" said Sweet Gum, looking around. "You mean in a room? Somebody else's room?" "They fix them for you. You get the key to the door and go in and out all you want," Jeremiah said. He had parked the car on a bumpy incline before an old, wide-verandaed house—peeling white, with pillars and vines and two old men, like twins, sitting in chairs as if somebody had placed them there. "Why are we staying overnight? *That's* what I don't

like," Sweet Gum said. "It ain't for you to like, then," Jeremiah said
with a sneer. He had climbed with elastic energy out of the car and
now began smoothing his suit and hair and face. Out of his pocket
he took a necktie: a precise-striped, urban tie, of a conservative
gray color. "You ain't going to leave me, are you?" Sweet Gum said,
climbing awkwardly out of the car.

They went to the counter inside and stood with their hands
out on it, as if waiting to be fed. A middle-aged woman with a sour
face stared back at them. "No luggage, then pay in advance," she
said. "Pay?" said Sweet Gum. Jeremiah jabbed him in the ribs.
"How much is it?" Jeremiah said carefully, making a little bow with
his head. "Three for the two of you," the woman said. Sweet Gum
hoped that Jeremiah would roar with laughter at this; but instead
he took out of his pocket a billfold and money, and counted it out to
the woman. One dollar bill and many coins. "Might's well sleep in
the car as pay all that," Sweet Gum muttered. No one glanced at
him. Jeremiah was staring at the woman strangely—standing at his
full height, six foot three or so—so that when the woman turned to
give him the key she froze and stared right back at him. Jeremiah
smiled, dipped his head as if pleased. The woman withdrew from
the counter; little prickly wrinkles had appeared on her face.
"Ma'am," Jeremiah said formally, "maybe I could put to you a little
question? As how we're guests here and everything?" "Maybe,"
said the woman. Jeremiah paused and wiggled his short beard, as if
he were suddenly shy. Sweet Gum waited in an agony of embarrassment, looking at the floor. But finally Jeremiah said, rushing the
words out: "Where's *he* live? Where's *his* house?"

His words vibrated in the hot musty air. Jeremiah's face was
wet with new perspiration as he listened to them with disbelief.
The woman only stared; her lips parted. Sweet Gum, sensing error,
wanted to run outside and climb in the car and wait for Jeremiah,
but his legs were frozen. Finally the woman whispered, "*He?* Who
do you mean, *he?* My husband? My husband's right—" "No, hell!"
Jeremiah said. "I mean *Motley.*" With a clumsy try at secrecy he
leaned forward on the counter, craned his neck, and whispered:

"Motley. Nathan Motley. *Him.*" "Why, Nathan Motley," stammered the woman, "he lives around here somewheres. He—You relatives of his, back country? Why do you want to see him?"

Sweet Gum could bear it no longer. "Who says there's a why about it?" he snarled. "Why? Why what? What why? *You* said there was a why about it, we never did! We just drove into town five minutes ago! Where's there a *why* about—"

Jeremiah brought his arm around and struck Sweet Gum in the chest. Not with his fist or elbow, but just with his arm; somehow that was degrading, as if Sweet Gum were not worth being hit properly. "That'll do," Jeremiah said. The woman was staring at them. "Get outside and get the *things*," he whispered to Sweet Gum contemptuously, "while I see to this woman here, you scairt-like-any-goddamn-back-country bastard."

Outside, four or five young men of Sweet Gum's age stood around the jalopy. They had hands pushed in their pockets, elbows idle, feet prodding at lumps of dried mud. Sweet Gum, glowering and muttering to himself, walked right down to the car. They made way for him. "How far you come in this thing?" one boy giggled. Sweet Gum leaned over and got the satchel out of the car. He pretended to be checking the lock, as if it had a lock. "Going to lose your license plates back here," somebody said. "This making way to fall off. Then the cops'll get you." Sweet Gum whirled around. "Cops? What the hell do I care about cops?" He lifted his lip. The boys all wore straw hats that looked alike, as if bought in the same store. Sweet Gum had the idea, staring at them, that their deaths—if they should fall over dead right now, one after the other—would mean no more than the random deaths in a woods of skunks and woodchucks and rabbits and squirrels. Somehow this pleased him. "Ain't worrying my young head over *cops*," Sweet Gum said. He knew they were watching as he strode back up to the hotel. Someone yelled out daringly, "Backwoods!" but Sweet Gum did not even glance around.

In a tavern that night Sweet Gum had to keep going back and forth to the outside and stand trembling on the seashell gravel, waiting to get sick; then if he did get sick, good enough, it was over for a while; if not, he went back inside. Each time the fresh air revived him and made him furious at Jeremiah, who sat slouched at the bar talking to a woman, his big knees out in opposite directions. Sweet Gum wanted to grab Jeremiah and say it was time they were about their business. But when he did speak, his voice always came out in a whine: "Ain't we going to locate him tonight? What about that room they got waiting for us? That woman—" Jeremiah turned away from the conversation he was having—with a strange thick black-haired woman, always smiling—and, with his eyes shut tight, said, "You see to your own bus'ness. I'm finding out about *him*." "But—" "Find out some yourself, go over there," Jeremiah said, his eyes still shut, and waving vaguely behind Sweet Gum. Then he turned away. Sweet Gum drank beer faster and faster. Once in a while he would sniff sadly, wipe his nose, and take out the black cloth change purse in which he had put the money Uncle Simon had given him for "food." Despair touched him: had he not already betrayed his uncle by drinking instead of eating, by wasting time here, by getting sick so that by now people laughed when he got up to hurry outside? If he *did* have a father, maybe that man would be ashamed of him; and what then? Sweet Gum sometimes dreamt of this—a strange man revealing himself to be his father, and then saying plainly that he was disappointed in his son. A man back from the navy, or from a ranch farther west. Sweet Gum wanted to begin, to go to Motley, to find him somewhere—where would he be hiding, up in an attic? crawled under a house?—and get it over with and return home, have his uncle proud of him and give him the reward, and turn, in two days, into a man. His chest glowed with the thought: he would become a man. But his inspiration was distracted by Jeremiah's big, sweating indifferent back and Sweet Gum's own faint, sickish gasey feeling. "Goin' outside, ain't comin' back," he muttered, purposely low so that Jeremiah would not hear and would wonder, later, where he was. He stumbled down from the stool and wavered through the crowd. Someone poked him, Sweet Gum looked around expecting to find a friend, found nothing instead—faces—and someone laughed. A woman some-where laughed. Sweet Gum's stomach jerked with anger and he had to run to the door.

When Sweet Gum woke, lying flat on his stomach in the gravel, he could tell by the smell of the night that it was late. Everything was quiet: the tavern was closed and looked dark and harmless, like an abandoned house. Sweet Gum spat and got up. A thought touched him, really a recollection; and, with sweet memories of abandoned houses, he groped for a handful of seashells and pebbles and threw them at the window nearest him. It did not break and he threw again, more energetically: this time the window shattered. Sweet Gum nodded and went out to the road.

He went back to the hotel but found the door to the room locked. He could hear Jeremiah snoring inside. Yet instead of being angry, he felt strangely pleased, even pacified, and lay down on the floor outside. As he fell asleep he thought of Jeremiah, one of his many cousins, a Coke rightfully enough—a Coke who had killed a man before he was twenty-five and whose clever talk made all the girls whoop with laughter and look around at one another, as they never did with Sweet Gum.

After breakfast the next morning Jeremiah and Sweet Gum and the black-haired woman drove in Jeremiah's car through town. The woman sat by the door, where Sweet Gum wanted to sit, and as they drove up and down Main Street she shrieked and waved and roared with laughter at people on the street. "Don't know 'em!" she yelled at someone, a man, and shrugged her shoulders high. "Never seen 'em before!" Even Jeremiah thought that was funny. But after a while, when they had driven back and forth several times, Jeremiah announced that they had to be about their busi-ness: they were on a proposition and their time wasn't all their own. "Hell, just one more time around," said the woman loudly. She had a broad, splendid face, so shiny with lipstick and makeup and pencil lines that Sweet Gum's eye slid around helplessly and could not focus on any single part. "Ain't got time for it," Jeremiah said, "we got to be about our business. Which way is it?" "Drive on. Straight," the woman said sullenly. She had a big head of hair, a big body, and a hard, red, waxen mouth that fascinated Sweet Gum, but whenever he looked at her she was looking at something else; she never noticed him. All she did was push him away with her elbow and thigh, trying to make more room for herself but doing it without glancing at him, as if she didn't really know he was there. "Keep straight. A mile or two," she said, yawning.

A few minutes later, out in the country, they stopped in front of a house. It was a small single-story house, covered with ripped brown siding, set up on wobbly blocks. "He don't do no work that *I* know of," the woman said. "He's got his finger in some backwoods whiskey—y'know, whiskey from the backwoods." She winked at Jeremiah. Sweet Gum's heart was pounding; Jeremiah kept jiggling his beard. In the cinder driveway an old brown dog lay as if exhausted and watched them, getting ready to bark. There was a wild field next to the house on the right, and an old decaying orchard—pear trees—on the left. Across the road, a quarter mile away, was a small farm: Sweet Gum could see cows grazing by a creek. "All right, honey," Jeremiah said, "you can start back now." "Walk back?" said the woman. "Yes, we got bus'ness here, between men. Ain't I explained that?" "What kind of bus'ness?" said the woman. "Men's business," Jeremiah said, but kindly; and he reached past Sweet Gum and put his big hairy hand on the woman's arm. "You start walking back and like's not we'll catch up in a few minutes and ride you back. Don't worry Jeremiah now, honey." The woman hesitated, though Sweet Gum knew she had already made up her mind. "Well," she said, "all right, if it's men's bus'ness. But don't . . . maybe don't tell Nathan it was me put you on him." "We won't never do that," Jeremiah said.

Jeremiah wasted more time by waving at the woman and blowing kisses as she walked away, but finally he calmed down and got out of the car and straightened his clothes and pressed down on his hair; he took out the necktie once more and tied it around his neck. Sweet Gum, carrying the satchel, climbed over the door on Jeremiah's side and jumped to the ground. The dog's ears shifted but the dog itself did not move. On the porch of the house sat a child, and behind him were piles of junk—firewood, old boxes, barrels, coils of rusted wire. The screen door opened and another child came out, a boy of about eight. He wore jeans and was barefoot. He and the smaller child and the dog watched Jeremiah and Sweet Gum arrange their clothing, slick down their hair by spitting into their palms and rubbing their heads viciously, and stare straight before them as if each were alone. Finally it was time: they crossed the ditch to the house.

The dog whimpered. "Son," cried Jeremiah to the older boy, "is your pa anywheres handy?" The boy's toes twitched on the edge of the steps. He began stepping backward, cautiously, and the other boy scrambled to his feet and backed up, too, retreating behind the piles of junk. "Tell your pa we're here to see him," said Jeremiah. He walked ahead; Sweet Gum, hugging the satchel, followed close. Faces appeared at a window, another child or a woman. Then the screen door opened cautiously and a man stepped out.

He was about forty, gone to fat now, with a reddish apologetic face. The way he scratched the underside of his jaw made Sweet Gum know that he was apologetic about something. "You Nathan Motley?" Jeremiah cried. "What's that to you?" the man said, clearing his throat. Behind the piles of junk the two boys crouched, watching. "Here, boy," Jeremiah said to Sweet Gum, "open it up." Sweet Gum opened up the satchel and Jeremiah took out his pistol, an old rust-streaked revolver that had belonged to his father. He aimed it at the man and fired. Someone screamed. But when Sweet Gum could see again, the porch was empty even of children—the screen door had fallen shut. "Goddamn," said Jeremiah, still holding the pistol aloft, "you spose I *missed* him?"

Sweet Gum had his pistol now—not his own yet, but it would be when he returned home. "I'm going around here," Sweet Gum said. He ran around the house. In the driveway the dog had drawn its muddy feet up to its body and lay watching them with wet, alert eyes. Sweet Gum had just rounded the back corner when he saw someone diving into a clump of bushes in the wild field behind the house. Sweet Gum let out a yodel: this was all familiar to him, nothing frightening about it, it was exactly like the games he had played as a child. "Here! Back here!" he yelled. He fired wildly at the clump of bushes. Behind him, in the house, there were screams and shrieks—Jeremiah was stomping through the house, bellowing. When he appeared running out of the back door his tie was thrown back over his shoulder as if someone had playfully pulled it there, and he still looked surprised. "This is hot weather for a hunt," he said when he caught up to Sweet Gum. They ran through the stiff grass, in brilliant sunshine, and about them birds flew up in terror. The field smelled of sunburned grass. "I'm headed this way, you keep straight," Jeremiah grunted. Sweet Gum ran on, slashing through bushes, pushing aside tree branches with his gun. "You, Motley!" he cried in despair. "Where you hiding at?" Something stumbled on the far side of a clump of bushes; Sweet Gum fired into it. In a moment Jeremiah appeared, mouth open and sucking for breath, as if he were swimming through the foliage. "Where's that bastard? He ain't over on my side, I swear it," Jeremiah said.

"If he gets away it ain't my fault," Sweet Gum cried. He was so angry he wanted to dance around. "He was standing there for you and you missed! Uncle Simon asks me, I got to tell the truth!"

Jeremiah scratched his head. "I got a feeling he's over this way. Let's track him over here." "I never seen him on my side," Sweet Gum said sullenly. "Nor me on *mine*," Jeremiah answered. They walked along, slashing at the tops of weeds with their guns. Birds sang airily about them. After a minute or two they slowed to a stop. Jeremiah scratched his beard with the barrel of the gun. "Spose we went back to the house," he said suddenly. "He's got to come back for supper, don't he? Or to sleep tonight?" Sweet Gum wished he had thought of that, but did not let on. "Hell of a idea," he grumbled. "First you miss him at that close, then want to quit tracking him." "You track him, I'll go back alone," Jeremiah said. "Naw," said Sweet Gum, hiding his alarm, "I ain't staying back here alone." They turned and followed their paths back through the field.

Then something fortunate happened: Sweet Gum happened to see a hen pheasant start up in a panic. Off to their left, in a big long stretch of high grass. Sweet Gum fired into the grass. "There he is, he's hiding in there! He's hiding in there!" Jeremiah started forward, yelling, "Where do you see him? Do you see him?" He pushed past Sweet Gum, who fired again into the weeds. "He's laid flat," Sweet Gum said, "crawling around on the ground—" In the silence that followed, however, they heard only the usual country noises, insects and birds. "Motley, are you in there?" Jeremiah asked. His voice had a touch of impatience. "Where are you?" They waited. Then, incredibly, a voice lifted—"What do you want?" Sweet Gum fired at once. Both he and Jeremiah ran forward. "Which way was it? Was it this way?" Sweet Gum cried. He and Jeremiah collided. Jeremiah even swung his gun around and hit Sweet Gum, hard, on the chest. Sweet Gum sobbed with pain and anger. "*I* found him! *I* saw the pheasant go up!" he snarled. "Shut your mouth and keep it shut!" Jeremiah said.

"But what do you want?" the voice cried again. It was forlorn, a ghostly voice; it seemed to come out of the air. Sweet Gum was so confused he did not even fire. "Let's talk. Can't we talk?" Jeremiah stood, staring furiously into the grass. His face was red. "Ain't nothing to talk about," he said sullenly, as if he suspected a joke. "We got a job to do." "Somebody hired you?" the voice said. Sweet Gum lifted his gun but Jeremiah made a signal for him to wait. "Hired us for sure. What do you think?" Jeremiah said. "Somebody wants me kilt, then?" said the voice. "Somebody paying you for it?" "I just explained that!" Jeremiah said. "You having a joke with me?" And he lifted his pistol and took a step into the high grass. "No, no," the voice cried, "I'm not joking—I . . . I want to hire you, too—I got a job for you to do . . . both of you—I'll pay—" "*How* can he pay, if he's dead?" Sweet Gum yelled furiously. "He's making fun of us!" "He ain't either, you goddamn backwoods idiot," Jeremiah said. "Shut your mouth. Now, mister, what's this-here job you got for us?"

The patch of weeds stirred. "A job for two men that can shoot straight," the voice said slowly. It paused. "That take in you two?" "Takes in me," Jeremiah said. "Me too," Sweet Gum heard his voice say—with surprise. "How much you paying?" said Jeremiah. "Fifty dollars a man," the voice said without hesitation. "Hell, that ain't enough," Sweet Gum said, raising his pistol. "No, no, a hunnert a man," the voice cried. Sweet Gum's arm froze. He and Jeremiah looked at each other. "A hunnert a man," Jeremiah said solemnly. "Uncle Simon's giving us fifty both, and a gun for Sweet Gum—that's him there—and a horse for me that I always liked; spose you can't thow in no horse, can you?" "And no gun neither!" Sweet Gum said in disgust. "Can't thow in no gun, and I'm purely fond of this one!" "But you can have the gun," said the voice, "after he's dead—and the horse, too—Why couldn't you keep them, after he's dead? Didn't he promise them to you?"

Jeremiah scratched his nose. "Well," he said.

The patch moved. A man's head appeared—balding red hair, pop eyes, a mouth that kept opening and closing—and then his shoulders and arms and the rest of him. He looked from Jeremiah to Sweet Gum. "You two are good men, then?" His arms were loose at his sides. What was happening? Sweet Gum stood as if in a dream, a daze; he could not believe he had betrayed his uncle. "Aw, let's shoot him," he said suddenly, feverishly. "We come all this ways to do it—"

"*Shut* your mouth."

"But Uncle Simon—"

There was silence. The man brushed himself calmly. He knew enough to address Jeremiah when he spoke. "You two are good men, then? Can be trusted?"

"Ain't you trusting us now?" Jeremiah said with a wink.

The man smiled politely. "What experience you got?"

At this, Sweet Gum looked down; his face went hot. "*I* got it," Jeremiah said, but slowly, as if he felt sorry for Sweet Gum. "Got put on trial for killing two men and found Not Guilty."

"When was this?"

"Few years," Jeremiah said. "I'm not saying whether I done it or not—was cautioned what to say. I don't know if the time is up yet. Two state troopers come and arrested me that hadn't any bus'ness in the Rapids—where we're from—and I got jailed and put on trial; for killing two storekeepers somewhere and taking seven hundred dollars. Was put on trial," Jeremiah said with a sigh, "and different people come to talk, one at a time, the jury come back and said Not Guilty for robbery; so it went for the other, too—murder, too. *But* they didn't let me keep the seven hundred dollars; they kept that themselves and fixed up the schoolhouse. New windows and the bathrooms cleaned and something else. Makes me proud when I go past—I got lots of cousins in the school."

"You were Not Guilty? How was that?"

Jeremiah shrugged. "They decided so."

The man now turned to Sweet Gum. But Sweet Gum, ashamed, could hardly look up. He could see his uncle, with that big wide face and false teeth, watching him and Jeremiah as they stood in this field betraying him. "What about you, son?" the man said gently. "This ain't your first job, is it?" Sweet Gum nodded without looking up. "Well, I like to see young people given a chance," the man said—and Sweet Gum, in spite of his shame, did feel a pang of satisfaction at this. "I like to see young ones and experience go together," the man said.

He turned to Jeremiah and put out his hand. Jeremiah shook hands with him solemnly; both men's faces looked alike. Sweet Gum stumbled through the grass to get to them and put his hand right in the middle. His eyes stung and he looked from man to man as if he thought they might explain the miracle of why he was acting as he was. But Motley, with color returning unevenly to his face, just grinned and said, "Let's go back to the house now."

An hour later Jeremiah and Sweet Gum were heading out of town. Jeremiah drove faster than before and kept twitching and shifting around in the seat, pressing his big belly against the steering wheel. "No one of us mislikes it more than me," he said finally, "but you know Uncle Simon ain't much expecting to live too long. Three-four years." With his mouth open, Sweet Gum stared at the road. There was a small dry hole in the side of his head into which Jeremiah's words droned, and Sweet Gum had no choice but to accept them. Inside, the words became entangled with the shouting and cursing with which Uncle Simon blessed this ride. The old man sat in his rocking chair on the porch, stains of chewing-tobacco juice etched permanently down the sides of his chin, glaring at Jeremiah and Sweet Gum who, thirty and forty years younger than he, were rushing along hot dirt roads to hurry him out of his life. And his teeth were new: not more than five years old. Sweet Gum remembered when Uncle Simon had got the teeth from a city and had shown the family how they worked, biting into apples and chewing with a malicious look of triumph. Uncle Simon! Sweet Gum felt as if the old man had put his bony hand on his shoulder.

"Boy, what's wrong with you?" Jeremiah said nervously.

"Sent us out after something and we ain't preformed it," Sweet Gum said. He wiped his nose on the back of his hand.

Jeremiah considered this. Then he said, after a moment, "But kin don't mean nothing. Being kin to somebody is just a accident; you got to think it through, what other ones mean to you. Uncles or what not. Or brothers, or grandmas, or anything."

Sweet Gum blinked. "Even a man with his father? If he had a father?"

That was the thing about Sweet Gum: he would always get onto this subject sooner or later. Usually whoever it was he spoke to would shrug his shoulders and look embarrassed—but Jeremiah just glanced over at him as if something had shocked him. "A father's maybe different," Jeremiah said, and let Sweet Gum know by the hard set of his jaw that he was finished talking.

They made so many turns, followed so many twisting roads, that the sun leaped back and forth across the sky. Sweet Gum could always tell the time at home, but out on the road it might as well be nine o'clock as three o'clock; nothing stayed still, nothing could be trusted. The old car was covered with dust and it got into their noses and mouths, making them choke. Sweet Gum wondered if his punishment for betraying his uncle had already begun, or if this wouldn't count because the murder hadn't taken place yet. "Remember this turn, don't you?" Jeremiah said, trying to be cheerful. Sweet Gum showed by his empty stare that he did not remember having seen this patch of hot scrubby land before—he recognized nothing on the return trip, as if he were really someone else.

As soon as they crossed the bridge to the Rapids, Sweet Gum gulped, "I can't do it."

Some boys were running in the road after the car, shouting and tossing stones. "Hey, you, Jeremiah Coke, you give us a ride!" they yelled. But Jeremiah was so surprised by Sweet Gum that he did not even glance around. "Hell, what's wrong now? Ain't we decided what to do?"

Sweet Gum's lips trembled. "Sent us out and we ain't preformed it for him," he said.

"Goddamn it, didn't you shake hands with Motley? Come loping acrost the weeds to stick your hand in, didn't you? Hired yourself out for a hunnert dollars. Do you do that much bus'ness every day?"

"No," said Sweet Gum, wiping his nose.

"Ain't a man his own bus'ness? Christ Himself was a bus'ness; he was selling stuff. Wasn't He? He never took money for it, wanted other things instead—more important things—a person's life, is that cheap? Everybody's a bus'ness trying for something and you got to farm yourself out to the richest one that wants you. Goddamn it, boy," Jeremiah said, "are you going back on Motley when you just now gave him your word?"

"Gone back on Uncle Simon," Sweet Gum said.

"That'll do on him. I'm asking you something else. The least thing you do after you break one promise is to keep the next one. A man is allowed one change of mind."

Sweet Gum, already won, liked to keep Jeremiah's attention so fiercely on him. When Jeremiah looked at him he felt warm, even hot: but it was a good feeling. "Well," said Sweet Gum, sighing. They were just then turning off onto their uncle's lane.

There the old house was, back past a clump of weedlike willows, with the old barns and the new aluminum-roofed barn behind it. Sweet Gum was surprised that he didn't feel frightened: but everything seemed familiar, as it did when he was chasing Motley, and strangely correct—even righteous—along with being familiar.

The car rolled to a stop. Jeremiah took his pistol out of the satchel and shoved it into the top of his trousers, past his big stomach; it looked uncomfortable but Jeremiah wouldn't admit it by taking it out. Sweet Gum climbed over the door and stood in the lane. The dirt quivered beneath his feet; he felt unreal. He giggled as he followed Jeremiah back the lane. They crossed to a field, half wild grass, half trees. When Jeremiah got down on his hands and knees, Sweet Gum did the same. They crawled along, Sweet Gum with his head hanging limply down, staring at the bottoms of Jeremiah's boots. If Jeremiah had wanted to crawl back and forth all day in the field Sweet Gum would have followed him.

Jeremiah stopped. "There he is. Sitting there." He pulled some weeds aside for Sweet Gum to look out, but Sweet Gum nodded immediately; he did not have to be shown. His brain was throbbing. "Here, aim at him," Jeremiah whispered. He pulled Sweet Gum's arm up. "I'll say the word and both fire at once. Then lay low; we can crawl back to the car and drive up and ask them what-all went on." Sweet Gum saw that Jeremiah's face was mottled, red and gray, like Motley's had been. Jeremiah aimed through the weeds, waited, and then, queerly, turned back to Sweet Gum. "You ain't aiming right! Don't want to shoot, do you? Have me do it all, you little bastard!"

"I ain't one of them!" Sweet Gum screamed.

The scream was astounding. A mile away, even, a bird must have heard it and now, in the following silence, questioned it—

three bright notes and a trill. Sweet Gum was so numb he couldn't think of the name of that bird. Jeremiah was staring at Sweet Gum; their faces were so close that their breathing surely got mixed up. That was why, Sweet Gum thought, he felt dizzy—old dirty air coming out of Jeremiah and getting sucked into him. Rocked in inertia, dazzled by the sunshine and the silence, the two men stared at each other. "No, I ain't one of them," Sweet Gum whispered. "Please, I ain't." Then a voice sailed over that Sweet Gum recognized at once.

"Who's over there? Who's in the field? Goddamn it if I don't hear somebody there." There was a furious rapping noise: Uncle Simon slamming the porch floor with his old-fashioned thick-heeled boots, angry enough to break into a jig. Jeremiah and Sweet Gum crouched together, sweating. They heard the old man talking with his wife, then his mutter rising without hesitation into another series of shouts: "Who is it? Stand up. Stand up and face me. Who's hiding there? I'll have my gun out in a minute.—Get the hell out of here, Ma, go back inside. I *said*—"

Jeremiah, sighing mightily, got to his feet. "Hiya, Uncle Simon," he said, waving the pistol. "It's Sweet Gum here, and me." He helped Sweet Gum get to his feet. Across the lane the old man stood on the edge of his porch with one fist in the air. Was that the Uncle Simon who had cursed them all day, hovering over the car like a ghost? The old man looked younger than Sweet Gum remembered. "Just us over here," Jeremiah said, smiling foolishly.

"What the hell are you up to?" Uncle Simon yelled. At this, the old woman came out again, her hands wiping each other on her apron as always. "Jeremiah himself and Sweet Gum hiding over there, playing at guns with their own Uncle Simon," the old man said viciously. "A man with three-four years to go and not a month more. See them there?"

The old woman, almost blind, nodded sullenly just the same. Sweet Gum wanted to run over to her and have her embrace him, smell the damp clean odor of her smooth-cracked hands, be told that everything was all right—as she had told him when two cousins of his, boys hardly older than he, had been arrested for killing a government agent one Hallowe'en night. And that *had* turned out all right, for the judge could not get a jury—everyone liked the boys or were related to them—and so the case was dismissed. "Like niggers in a field! Look at them there, crawling around like niggers in a field!" Uncle Simon yelled.

Jeremiah was the first to break down. Big hot tears exploded out of his eyes, tumbled down his face and were lost in his beard. "*He* talked us into it," he said, "me and Sweet Gum was trapped by him. *He* talked us all kinds of fast words, and long sentences like at church; and explained it to us that he would tell the state police. I had enough trouble with them once, Uncle Simon, didn't I?—And he tole us it would be a hunnert a man and we could keep the horse and the gun anyways. We got so mixed up hearing it all, and them police at the back of my mind—" Jeremiah's voice ran down suddenly. Sweet Gum stared at his feet, hoping he would not be expected to continue.

"Who? Motley? A hunnert a man?" What was strange was that Uncle Simon stared at them like that—his rage frozen on his face, and something new taking over. "A hunnert a man?"

"And to keep the horse and the gun anyways," Jeremiah said in a croaking voice.

The old man put his little finger to his eye and scratched it, just once. Then he yelled: "All right. Get back in that car. Goddamn you both, get in it and turn it around and get back to Plain Dealing! I'll plain-deal you! I'll ambush you! Use your brains—tell that Motley bastard you took care of it out here—shot your poor old uncle—and want the reward from him now. Say you want your reward, can you remember that? Jeremiah, you stay back; don't you come on my lane. You stay back in the field. I don't want to see your goddamn faces again till you do the job right. Do I have to go all that ways myself, a man sixty-five or more years old, would be retired like they do in the city if I was a regular man? Yes, would be retired with money coming in, a check, every month—Ma, *you* stay back, this ain't anything of yours! And say to Motley you want your reward, and let him give it to you—one hunnert a man—then fire at him and that's that. How much money you make from it?"

Sweet Gum said, so fast he surprised himself, "A hunnert a man."

"*How* much?"

Sweet Gum's brain reeled and clicked. "A hunnert-fifty a man and a gun for me. And a horse for Jeremiah."

"Put in a horse for you and another one for Jeremiah. That's that." The old man spat maliciously toward them. "Now, get the hell back to the car. You got some work to do with Motley."

"Yes, thank you, that's right, Uncle Simon," Jeremiah said. He gulped at air. "We're on the way to do it. Two horses? Which one is the other? The red mare or what?"

"Your pick," the old man said. He turned sullenly away as if he had forgotten about them. Sweet Gum wanted to laugh out loud—it had been so easy. He did laugh, he heard himself with alarm, and felt at the same time something begin to twitch in his face. It twitched again: a muscle around his eye. Nothing like that had ever happened to him before, yet he understood that the twitch, and probably the breathless giggle, would be with him for life.

Jeremiah's jalopy broke down on the return trip, without drama: it just rolled to a stop as if it had died. Jeremiah got out and kicked it in a fury and tore off the fender and part of the bumper; but Sweet Gum just stood quietly and watched, and by and by Jeremiah joined him. They strolled along the road for a while. Sweet Gum noticed how Jeremiah's fingers kept twitching.

Though they were on a U.S. highway, there was not much traffic—when a car appeared Sweet Gum would stand diffidently by the road and put up his hand, without apparent purpose, as if he were ready to withdraw it at any moment. After an hour or two an automobile stopped, as if by magic; the man said he was driving right through Plain Dealing.

When they arrived in front of Motley's house it was suppertime. Sweet Gum and Jeremiah went up the driveway; Jeremiah took out his pistol and looked at it, for some reason, and Sweet

Gum did the same—he noticed that he had one bullet left. Hiding a yawn, Jeremiah approached the porch and peered in the window: there the family sat, or at least the woman and children, arguing about something so that their faces took on slanted, vicious expressions. Jeremiah stood staring in the window until someone—the oldest boy—happened to see him. The boy's face jerked, his features blurred together, his bony arm jerked up as if he were accusing Jeremiah of something. Then the woman caught sight of him and, pulling her dress somehow, straightening the skirt, came to the door. "Whatcha got there? He's in town right now. You them clowns come out here before, ain't you?" The woman looked ready to laugh. "Nat told me about you; says you were kidding him with play-guns. How come I don't know you? Nat says—"

"Where is he?" said Jeremiah.

"In town," the woman said. "He's at the club, probably. That's the Five Aces Club, acrost from the bank. He tole me not to wait on him tonight so I didn't, but he never tole me to expeck some guests for supper. As a fact, he never tells me much," she laughed. "Bet you tell your wife where you are or whatcha doing or who's coming out for supper. Bet you—"

"How do you spell that?" Jeremiah said patiently.

"Spell it? Huh? Spell what?"

"The place he's at."

"Acrost from the bank, the Five Aces—I don't know, how do you spell five? It's a number five, they got it on a sign; you know how five looks? That's it." Both Jeremiah and Sweet Gum nodded. "Then 'Aces,' that's out there too—begins with A, A S or A C, then S on the end—it's more than one. Acrost from the bank. But why don't you come in and wait, he'll be—"

"We surely thank you," Jeremiah said with a faint smile, "but we got bus'ness to attend to. Maybe later on."

It took them a while to walk back to town. Jeremiah's fingers were busier than ever. Most of the time they were scratching at his head, then darting into his ears or nose and darting back out again. Sweet Gum walked behind so that his giggling would not annoy

Jeremiah. They passed houses, farmers' markets, a gas station with an old model-T out front filled with tires. They passed a diner that was boarded up, and the movie house, in front of which the boys with straw hats stood around smoking. When Sweet Gum and Jeremiah passed, the boys stared in silence; even the smoke from their cigarettes stiffened in the air.

Town began suddenly: a drug store, an old country store on a corner. In a clapboard shanty, a dentist's office advertised in bright green paint. There were no sidewalks, so Jeremiah and Sweet Gum walked at the side of the road. "Down there looks like the bank," Jeremiah said, waving his pistol at something ahead; Sweet Gum did not see it. They walked on. "We come a long way," Jeremiah said in a strange remote voice, like a man embarking on a speech. "Done a lot this past week or however long it's been. I never known till now that I was born for this life—did you? Thought it'd be for me like anyone else—a farm and cows maybe and a fambly to raise up and maybe chickens, the wife could take care of them; I mostly had the wife picked out, too. Won't tell you which one. But now I know different. Now I see it was in me all along, from before I kilt them two men even—I thought I done that by *accident*, had too much to drink—something in a dream—but no, now I know better; now I got it clear." A few cars passed them: people out for after-supper rides. A girl of about two, with thin blond hair, leaned out a window and waved sweetly at Sweet Gum. "Now I know," Jeremiah said, so strangely that Sweet Gum felt embarrassed in spite of his confusion, "that there isn't a person but wouldn't like to do that, what I did. Or to set a place afire, say—any place—their own house even. Set it all afire, house and grass and trees alike, all the same. Was there ever a difference between a house people live in and trees outside that they name? Them trees *make* you name them, think up names for them as soon as you see them, what choice does a man have! Never no choice! Get rid of it all, fire it all up, all the things that bother you, that keep you from yourself, and people, too—and people, too—Sweet Gum, I got to tell you now, with us both coming so far like we did, that I'm your pa here, *I* am, Jeremiah your pa after all these years, all the way from the beginning!"

They continued walking. Sweet Gum blinked once or twice. Jeremiah's words bored through that tiny hole in the side of his head, flipped themselves around right side up to make sense: but Sweet Gum only hid a sudden laugh with his hand, stared at the sweaty back of Jeremiah's old funeral suit, and thought aloud, "Is that so." "That so, boy, all the way from the beginning," Jeremiah said, stifling a yawn. "This-here is your own pa walking right in front of you."

Sweet Gum should have said something, but he could not think of it and so let it pass. They were approaching the 5 Aces Club now, heading toward it as if it were a magnet. Sweet Gum heard voices behind him and glanced around: the group of boys was following them, idly and at a distance; a man in overalls had joined them, looking sour and disapproving. Sweet Gum forgot them as soon as he turned again. They passed a Laundromat with orange signs: OPEN 24 HOURS EACH DAY WASH 20¢ DRY 10¢. A few people were inside in spite of the heat. In the doorway children kicked at one another and did not even glance up at Jeremiah and Sweet Gum. Then there was a 5¢ 10¢ 25¢ AND $1.00 STORE, gold letters on a red background, windows crowded and stuffed with merchandise; but it was closed. Then the club itself, coming so fast Sweet Gum's eye twitched more than ever and he had to hold onto it with his palm to keep it from jumping out of his head. "Spose he's in there," Sweet Gum whimpered, "spose he gets to talking. Don't let him talk. Please. Don't let him. Shoot him right off. If I hear talk of horses or gun or twice as much money—"

The club had had a window at one time, a big square window like something in a shoe store, but now it was completely hidden by tin foil. There were advertisements for beer and cigarettes everywhere: beautiful pink-cheeked girls, men with black hair and big chests and clean white gleaming teeth. Long muscular thighs, smooth legs, slender ankles, silver-painted toenails, tatooed arms and backs of hands; and curly-haired chests and dimpled chests,

chests bare and bronze in the sun, chests demurely proud in red polka-dot halters—everything mixed together! Faces channeled themselves out of blue skies and rushed at Sweet Gum with their fixed serene smiles. That *there* is heaven, Sweet Gum thought suddenly, with a certainty he had never before felt about life—as if, about to leave it, he might pass judgment on it. His stomach ached with silent sobs, as much for that lost heaven as for the duties of this familiar, demanding world.

Jeremiah had opened the door to the tavern. "You, Motley, come out here a minute." Someone answered inside but Jeremiah went on patiently, "Motley. Some bus'ness outside."

Jeremiah let the door close. Sweet Gum clutched at him. "Is he coming? Is he? Was that him inside?" he said. "Don't let him talk none. Shoot him first or let me—shoot him—"

"We ain't going to shoot him yet."

"But what if he talks of more horses or another gun? What if—"

"He ain't. Get back, now—"

"I'm going to shoot him—"

"Goddamn you, boy, you stand back," Jeremiah shouted. "Why's it always you at the center of trouble? Any goddamn thing that bothers me these days, *you're* in the middle!"

"Don't let him talk none. If he—"

"We got to talk to him. Got to tell him we come for the reward."

"Reward?" Sweet Gum's sobs broke through to the surface. "Reward? I don't remember none, what reward? What? He's going to talk, going to—"

Jeremiah pushed him away and opened the door again. "Motley!" he yelled. Sweet Gum's head was so clamoring with voices that he could not be sure if he heard anyone answer. "He's coming, guess it's him," Jeremiah said vaguely. "Stand back now, boy, and don't you do no reckless shooting your pa will have to clean up after—"

"I'm going to shoot him," Sweet Gum cried, "or he'll talk like before—If he talks and we hear him we got to go back and be in the field again. We got to hide there. And Aunt Clarey, I always loved her so, how it's for *her* to see us hiding there? Even if she can't see much. If he comes out and talks we got to—"

"Boy, I'm telling you!"

"Don't you call me boy!"

The door opened suddenly, angrily. Sweet Gum raised his pistol, took a giant step backward, and was about to shoot when a stranger appeared in the doorway, a big pot-bellied bald man with a towel used for an apron tucked in his belt. "What the *hell*—" the man roared.

Sweet Gum, shocked, staggered back. Inside his head the clamoring arose to a mighty scream and, in defense, he turned to Jeremiah. Everything focused on Jeremiah, the sun itself seemed to glare on his bulging eyes. Sweet Gum cried: "*You!* It was *you* I been hunting these twenty years!" But somehow in his confusion he had turned around, or half around, and when he fired he did not shoot Jeremiah at all, or any man at all, but instead a woman—a stranger, a stocky woman with a sunburned, pleasant, bossy face, dressed in jeans and a man's dirty white shirt. She fell right onto the basket of damp laundry she was carrying. Blood burst out of nowhere, onto the clothes, and also out of nowhere appeared two children, shrieking and screaming.

Sweet Gum backed away. A crowd, an untidy circle, was gathering about the fallen woman. Sweet Gum, dazed, put the barrel of the pistol to his lips and stared, still backing away, stumbling. He had been cheated: he could not get things clear: his whole life had flooded up to this moment and now was dammed and could not get past, everything was over. He could have wept for the end of his young life (mistakenly, as it turned out, for in less than three years he would be working downriver at the tomato canning factory, making good money), spilled here on the dirt road, splashing and sucked away, while everyone stood around gawking.

MEMORIES OF WEST STREET AND LEPKE

Robert Lowell

Only teaching on Tuesdays, book-worming
in pajamas fresh from the washer each morning,
I hog a whole house on Boston's
"hardly passionate Marlborough Street,"
where even the man
scavenging filth in the back alley trash cans,
has two children, a beach wagon, a helpmate,
and is a "young Republican."
I have a nine months' daughter,
young enough to be my granddaughter.
Like the sun she rises in her flame-flamingo infants' wear.

These are the tranquillized Fifties,
and I am forty. Ought I to regret my seedtime?
I was a fire-breathing Catholic C.O.,
and made my manic statement,
telling off the state and president, and then

sat waiting sentence in the bull pen
beside a Negro boy with curlicues
of marijuana in his hair.

Given a year,
I walked on the roof of the West Street Jail, a short
enclosure like my school soccer court,
and saw the Hudson River once a day
through sooty clothesline entanglements
and bleaching khaki tenements.
Strolling, I yammered metaphysics with Abramowitz,
a jaundice-yellow ("it's really tan")
and fly-weight pacifist,
so vegetarian,
he wore rope shoes and preferred fallen fruit.
He tried to convert Bioff and Brown,
the Hollywood pimps, to his diet.
Hairy, muscular, suburban,
wearing chocolate double-breasted suits,
they blew their tops and beat him black and blue.

I was so out of things, I'd never heard
of the Jehovah's Witnesses.
"Are you a C.O.?" I asked a fellow jailbird.
"No," he answered, "I'm a J.W."
He taught me the "hospital tuck,"
and pointed out the T-shirted back
of *Murder Incorporated's* czar Lepke,
there piling towels on a rack,
or dawdling off to his little segregated cell full
of things forbidden the common man:
a portable radio, a dresser, two toy American
flags tied together with a ribbon of Easter palm.
Flabby, bald, lobotomized,
he drifted in a sheepish calm,

where no agonizing reappraisal
jarred his concentration on the electric chair—
hanging like an oasis in his air
of lost connections. . . .

CAIN

Andrew Vachss

1

"Look at my Buster . . . look what they did to him."

The old man pointed a shaking finger at the dog, a big German shepherd. The animal was cowering in a corner of the kitchen of the railroad flat—his fine head was lopsided, a piece of his skull missing under the ragged fur. A deep pocket of scar tissue glowed white where one eye had been, the other was cataract-milky, fire-dotted with fear. The dog's tail hung behind him at a demented angle, one front paw hung useless in a plaster cast.

"Who did it?"

The old man wasn't listening, not finished yet. Squeezing the wound to get the pus out. "Buster guards out back, where the chicken wire is. They tormented him, threw stuff at him, made him crazy. Then they cut the lock. Two of them. One had a baseball bat, the other had a piece of pipe. My Buster . . . he wouldn't hurt anyone. They beat on him, over and over, laughing. I

ran downstairs to stop them . . . they just slapped me, like I was
a fly. They did my Buster so bad, it even hurts him when I try and
rub him."

The old man sat crying at his kitchen table.

The dog watched me, a thin whine coming from his open
mouth. Half his teeth were missing.

"You know who did it," I said. It wasn't a question. He didn't
know, he wouldn't have called me—I'm no private eye.

"I called . . . I called the cops. 911. They never came. I went
down to the precinct. The man at the desk, he said to call the
ASPCA."

"You know who they are?"

"I don't know their names. Two men, young men. One has big
muscles, the other's skinny."

"They're from around here?"

"I don't know. They're always together—I've seen them before.
Everybody knows them. They have their heads shaved, too."

"Everybody knows them?"

"Everybody. They beat other dogs, too. They make the dogs
bark at them, then they . . ." He was crying again.

I waited, watching the dog.

"They come back. I see them walking down the alley. Almost
every day. I can't leave Buster outside anymore—can't even take
him for a walk. I have to clean up after him now."

"What do you want?"

"What do I want?"

"You called me. You got my name from somewhere. You know
what I do."

The old man got up, knelt next to his dog. Put his hand
gently on the dog's head. "Buster used to be the toughest dog
in the world—wasn't afraid of nothing. I had him ever since
he was a pup. He won't even look out the back window with
me now."

"What do you want?" I asked him again.

They both looked at me. "You know," the old man said.

2

A freestanding brick building in Red Hook, not far from the waterfront, surrounded by a chain-link fence topped with razor wire. I rang the bell. A dog snarled a warning. I looked into the mirrored glass, knowing they could see me. The steel door opened. A man in a white T-shirt over floppy black trousers opened the door. He was barefoot, dark hair cropped close, body so smooth it might have been extruded from rubber. He bowed slightly. I returned his bow, followed him inside.

A rectangular room, roughened wood floor. A canvas-wrapped heavy bag swung from the ceiling in one corner. In another, a car tire was suspended from a thick rope. A pair of long wood staves hung on hooks.

"I'll get him," the man said.

I waited, standing in one spot.

He returned, leading a dog by a chain. A broad-chested pit bull, all white except for a black patch over one eye. The dog watched me, cobra-calm.

"Here he is," the man said.

"You sure he'll do it?"

"Guaranteed."

"What's his name?"

"Cain."

I squatted down, said the dog's name, scratched him behind his erect ears when he came to me.

"You want to practice with him?"

"Yeah, I'd better. I know the commands you gave me, but . . ."

"Wait here."

I played with Cain, putting him through standard-obedience paces. He was a machine, perfect.

The trainer came back into the room. Two other men with him, dressed in full agitator's suits, leather-lined and padded. Masks on their faces, like hockey goalies wear.

"Let's do it," he said.

3

I walked down the alley behind the old man's building, Cain on a thin leather leash, held lightly in my left hand. The dog knew the route by now—it was our fifth straight day.

They turned the corner fifty feet from me. The smaller one had a baseball bat over his shoulder, the muscleman slapped a piece of lead pipe into one palm.

They closed in. I stepped aside to let them pass, pulling Cain close to my leg.

They didn't walk past. The smaller one planted his feet, looking into my eyes.

"Hey, man. That's a pit bull, right? Pretty tough dogs, I heard."

"No, he's not tough," I said, a catch in my voice. "He's just a pet."

"He looks like a bad dog to me," the big guy said, poking the lead pipe into the dog's face, stabbing. Cain stepped out of the way.

"Please don't hurt my dog," I begged them, pulling up on the leash.

Cain leaped into my arms, his face against my chest. I could feel the bunched muscles in his legs, all four paws flat against me.

"Aw, is your dog *scared*, man?" the big one sneered, stepping close to me, slapping the dog's back with the pipe.

"Leave us alone," I said, stepping back as they closed in.

"Put the dog down, faggot!"

I put my mouth close to Cain's ear, whispered "Go!" as I threw open my arms. The pit bull launched himself off my chest without a sound, his alligator teeth locking on the big guy's face. A scream bubbled out. The big man fell to the ground, clawing at Cain's back. Pieces of his face flew off, red and white. He spasmed like he was in the electric chair, but the dog held on, wouldn't drop the bite. The smaller guy stood there, rooted, mouth open, no sound coming out, his pants turning dark at the crotch.

"Out!" I snapped at the dog. Cain stepped away, his mouth foamy with bloody gristle.

"Your turn," I said to the smaller guy. He took off, running for his life. Cain caught him, running right up his spine, locking onto the back of his neck.

I called him off when I heard a snap.

As we turned to walk back down the alley, I glanced up.

The old man was at the window. Buster next to him, the plaster cast on his paw draped over the sill.

WHEN THIS MAN DIES

Lawrence Block

The night before the first letter came, he had Speckled Band in the feature at Saratoga. The horse went off at nine-to-two from the number one pole and Edgar Kraft had two hundred dollars on him, half to win and half to place. Speckled Band went to the front and stayed there. The odds-on favorite, a four-year-old named Sheila's Kid, challenged around the clubhouse turn and got hung up on the outside. Kraft was counting his money. In the stretch, Speckled Band broke stride, galloped home madly, was summarily disqualified, and placed fourth. Kraft tore up his tickets and went home.

So he was in no mood for jokes that morning. He opened five of the six letters that came in the morning mail, and all five were bills, none of which he had any prospect of paying in the immediate future. He put them in a drawer in his desk. There were already several bills in that drawer. He opened the final letter and was at first relieved to discover that it was not a bill, not a notice of payment due, not a threat to repossess car or furniture. It was, instead, a very simple message typed in the center of a large sheet of plain typing paper.

First a name:

Mr. Joseph H. Neimann

And, below that:

When this man dies
You will receive
Five hundred dollars.

He was in no mood for jokes. Trotters that lead all the way, and then break in the stretch, do not contribute to a man's sense of humor. He looked at the sheet of paper, turned it over to see if there was anything further on its reverse, turned it over again to read the message once more, picked up the envelope, saw nothing on it but his own name and a local postmark, said something unprintable about some idiots and their idea of a joke, and tore everything up and threw it away, message and envelope and all.

In the course of the next week he thought about the letter once, maybe twice. No more than that. He had problems of his own. He had never heard of anyone named Joseph H. Neimann and entertained no hopes of receiving five hundred dollars in the event of the man's death. He did not mention the cryptic message to his wife. When the man from Superior Finance called to ask him if he had any hopes of meeting his note on time, he did not say anything about the legacy that Mr. Neimann meant to leave him.

He went on doing his work from one day to the next, working with the quiet desperation of a man who knows his income, while better than nothing, will never quite get around to equaling his expenditures. He went to the track twice, won thirty dollars one night, lost twenty-three the next. He came quite close to forgetting entirely about Mr. Joseph H. Neimann and the mysterious correspondent.

Then the second letter came. He opened it mechanically, unfolded a large sheet of plain white paper. Ten fresh fifty dollar bills fluttered down upon the top of his desk. In the center of the sheet of paper someone had typed:

Thank you

Edgar Kraft did not make the connection immediately. He tried to think what he might have done that would merit anyone's thanks, not to mention anyone's five hundred dollars. It took him a moment, and then he recalled that other letter and rushed out of his office and down the street to a drugstore. He bought a morning paper, turned to the obituaries. Joseph Henry Neimann, 67, of 413 Park Place, had died the previous afternoon in County Hospital after an illness of several months' duration. He left a widow, three children, and four grandchildren. Funeral services would be private, flowers were please to be omitted.

He put three hundred dollars in his checking account and two hundred dollars in his wallet. He made his payment on the car, paid his rent, cleared up a handful of small bills. The mess in his desk drawer was substantially less baleful, although by no means completely cleared up. He still owed money, but he owed less now than before the timely death of Joseph Henry Neimann. The man from Superior Finance had been appeased by a partial payment; he would stop making a nuisance of himself, at least for the time being.

That night, Kraft took his wife to the track. He even let her make a couple impossible hunch bets. He lost forty dollars and it hardly bothered him at all.

When the next letter came he did not tear it up. He recognized the typing on the envelope, and he turned it over in his hands for a few moments before opening it, like a child with a wrapped present. He was somewhat more apprehensive than a child with a present, however; he couldn't help feeling that the mysterious benefactor would want something in return for his five hundred dollars.

He opened the letter. No demands, however. Just the usual sheet of plain paper, with another name typed in its center:

Mr. Raymond Andersen

And, below that:

When this man dies
You will receive
Seven hundred fifty dollars.

For the next few days he kept telling himself that he did not wish anything unpleasant for Mr. Raymond Andersen. He didn't know the man, he had never heard of him, and he was not the sort to wish death upon some total stranger. And yet—

Each morning he bought a paper and turned at once to the death notices, searching almost against his will for the name of Mr. Raymond Andersen. *I don't wish him harm*, he would think each time. But seven hundred fifty dollars was a happy sum. If something were going to happen to Mr. Raymond Andersen, he might as well profit by it. It wasn't as though he was doing anything to cause Andersen's death. He was even unwilling to wish for it. But if something happened . . .

Something happened. Five days after the letter came, he found Andersen's obituary in the morning paper. Andersen was an old man, a very old man, and he had died in his bed at a home for the aged after a long illness. His heart jumped when he read the notice with a combination of excitement and guilt. But what was there to feel guilty about? He hadn't done anything. And death, for a sick old man like Raymond Andersen, was more a cause for relief than grief, more a blessing than a tragedy.

But why would anyone want to pay him seven hundred fifty dollars?

Nevertheless, someone did.

The letter came the following morning, after a wretched night during which Kraft tossed and turned and batted two possibilities back and forth—that the letter would come and that it would not. It did come, and it brought the promised seven hundred fifty dollars in fifties and hundreds. And the same message:

Thank You

For what? He had not the slightest idea. But he looked at the two-word message again before putting it carefully away.

You're welcome, he thought. *You're entirely welcome.*

For two weeks no letter came. He kept waiting for the mail, kept hoping for another windfall like the two that had come so far. There were times when he would sit at his desk for twenty or thirty minutes at a time, staring off into space and thinking about the letters and the money. He would have done better keeping his mind on his work, but this was not easy. His job brought him five thousand dollars a year, and for that sum he had to work forty to fifty hours a week. His anonymous pen pal had thus far brought him a quarter as much as he earned in a year, and he had done nothing at all for the money.

The seven fifty had helped, but he was still in hot water. On a sudden female whim his wife had had the living room recarpeted. The rent was due. There was another payment due on the car. He had one very good night at the track, but a few other visits took back his winnings and more.

And then the letter came, along with a circular inviting him to buy a dehumidifier for his basement and an appeal for funds from some dubious charity. He swept the circular and appeal into his wastebasket and tore open the plain white envelope. The message was the usual sort:

Mr. Claude Pierce

And, below the name:

When this man dies
You will receive
One thousand dollars.

Kraft's hands were shaking slightly as he put the envelope and letter away in his desk. One thousand dollars—the price had gone up again, this time to a fairly staggering figure. Mr. Claude Pierce. Did he know anyone named Claude Pierce? He did not. Was Claude Pierce sick? Was he a lonely old man, dying somewhere of a terminal illness?

Kraft hoped so. He hated himself for the wish, but he could not smother it.

He hoped Claude Pierce was dying.

This time he did a little research. He thumbed through the phone book until he found a listing for a Claude Pierce on Honeydale Drive. He closed the book then and tried to put the whole business out of his mind, an enterprise foredoomed to failure.

Finally he gave up, looked up the listing once more, looked at the man's name and thought that this man was going to die. It was inevitable, wasn't it? They sent him some man's name in the mail, and then the man died, and then Edgar Kraft was paid. Obviously, Claude Pierce was a doomed man.

He called Pierce's number. A woman answered, and Kraft asked if Mr. Pierce was in.

"Mr. Pierce is in the hospital," the woman said. "Who's calling, please?"

"Thank you," Kraft said.

Of course, he thought. They, whoever they were, simply found people in hospitals who were about to die, and they paid money to Edgar Kraft when the inevitable occurred, and that was all. The why of it was impenetrable. But so few things made sense in Kraft's life that he did not want to question the whole affair too closely. Perhaps his unknown correspondent was like that lunatic on television who gave away a million dollars every week. If someone wanted to give Kraft money, Kraft wouldn't argue with him.

That afternoon he called the hospital. Claude Pierce had been admitted two days ago for major surgery, a nurse told Kraft. His condition was listed as *good*.

Well, he would have a relapse, Kraft thought. He was doomed— the letter-writer had ordained his death. He felt momentarily sorry for Claude Pierce, and then he turned his attention to the entries at Saratoga. There was a horse named Orange Pips which Kraft had been watching for some time. The horse had a good post now, and if he was ever going to win, this was the time.

Kraft went to the track. Orange Pips ran out of the money. In the morning Kraft failed to find Pierce's obituary. When he called the hospital, the nurse told him that Pierce was recovering very nicely.

Impossible, Kraft thought.

For three weeks Claude Pierce lay in his hospital bed, and for three weeks Edgar Kraft followed his condition with more interest than Pierce's doctor could have displayed. Once Pierce took a turn for the worse and slipped into a coma. The nurse's voice was grave over the phone, and Kraft bowed his head, resigned to the inevitable. A day later Pierce had rallied remarkably. The nurse sounded positively cheerful, and Kraft fought off a sudden wave of rage that threatened to overwhelm him.

From that point on, Pierce improved steadily. He was released, finally, a whole man again, and Kraft could not understand quite what had happened. Something had gone wrong. When Pierce died, he was to receive a thousand dollars. Pierce had been sick, Pierce had been close to death, and then, inexplicably, Pierce had been snatched from the very jaws of death, with a thousand dollars simultaneously snatched from Edgar Kraft.

He waited for another letter. No letter came.

With the rent two weeks overdue, with a payment on the car past due, with the man from Superior Finance calling him far too often, Kraft's mind began to work against him. *When this man dies,* the letter had said. There had been no strings attached, no time limit on Pierce's death. After all, Pierce could not live forever. No one did. And whenever Pierce did happen to draw his last breath, he would get that thousand dollars.

Suppose something happened to Pierce—

He thought it over against his own will. It would not be hard, he kept telling himself. No one knew that he had any interest whatsoever in Claude Pierce. If he picked his time well, if he did the dirty business and got it done with and hurried off into the night, no one would know. The police would never think of him in the same breath with Claude Pierce, if police were in the habit of thinking in breaths. He did not know Pierce, he had no obvious motive for killing Pierce, and—

He couldn't do it, he told himself. He simply could not do it. He was no killer. And something as senseless as this, something so thoroughly absurd, was unthinkable.

He would manage without the thousand dollars. Somehow, he would live without the money. True, he had already spent it a dozen times over in his mind. True, he had been counting and recounting it when Pierce lay in a coma. But he would get along without it. What else could he do?

The next morning headlines shrieked Pierce's name at Edgar Kraft. The previous night someone had broken into the Pierce home on Honeydale Drive and had knifed Claude Pierce in his bed. The murderer had escaped unseen. No possible motive for the slaying of Pierce could be established. The police were baffled.

Kraft got slightly sick to his stomach as he read the story. His first reaction was a pure and simple onrush of unbearable guilt, as though he had been the man with the knife, as though he himself had broken in during the night to stab silently and flee promptly, mission accomplished. He could not shake this guilt away. He knew well enough that he had done nothing, that he had killed no one. But he had conceived of the act, he had willed that it be done, and he could not escape the feeling that he was a murderer, at heart if not in fact.

His blood money came on schedule. One thousand dollars, ten fresh hundreds this time. And the message. *Thank you.*

Don't thank me, he thought, holding the bills in his hand, holding them tenderly. Don't thank me!

> *Mr. Leon Dennison*
> *When this man dies*
> *You will receive*
> *Fifteen hundred dollars.*

Kraft did not keep the letter. He was breathing heavily when he read it, his heart pounding. He read it twice through, and then he took it and the envelope it had come in, and all the other letters and envelopes that he had so carefully saved, and he tore them all into little bits and flushed them down the toilet.

He had a headache. He took aspirin, but it did not help his headache at all. He sat at his desk and did no work until lunchtime. He went to the luncheonette around the corner and ate lunch without tasting his food. During the afternoon he found that, for the first time, he could not make head or tails out of the list of entries at Saratoga. He couldn't concentrate on a thing, and he left the office early and took a long walk.

Mr. Leon Dennison.

Dennison lived in an apartment on Cadbury Avenue. No one answered his phone. Dennison was an attorney, and he had an office listing. When Kraft called it a secretary answered and told him that Mr. Dennison was in conference. Would he care to leave his name?

When this man dies.

But Dennison would not die, he thought. Not in a hospital bed, at any rate. Dennison was perfectly all right, he was at work, and the person who had written all those letters knew very well that Dennison was all right, that he was not sick.

Fifteen hundred dollars.

But how? he wondered. He did not own a gun and had not the slightest idea how to get one. A knife? Someone had used a knife on Claude Pierce, he remembered. And a knife would probably not be hard to get his hands on. But a knife seemed somehow unnatural to him.

How, then? By automobile? He could do it that way, he could lie in wait for Dennison and run him down in his car. It would not be difficult, and it would probably be certain enough. Still, the police were supposed to be able to find hit and run drivers fairly easily. There was something about paint scrapings, or blood on your own bumper, or something. He didn't know the details, but they always did seem to catch hit and run drivers.

Forget it, he told himself. You are not a killer.

He didn't forget it. For two days he tried to think of other things and failed miserably. He thought about Dennison, and he thought about fifteen hundred dollars, and he thought about murder.

When this man dies—

One time he got up early in the morning and drove to Cadbury Avenue. He watched Leon Dennison's apartment, and he saw Dennison emerge, and when Dennison crossed the street toward his parked car Kraft settled his own foot on the accelerator and ached to put the pedal on the floor and send the car hurtling toward Leon Dennison. But he didn't do it. He waited.

So clever. Suppose he were caught in the act? Nothing linked him with the person who wrote him the letters. He hadn't even kept the letters, but even if he had, they were untraceable.

Fifteen hundred dollars—

On a Thursday afternoon he called his wife and told her he was going directly to Saratoga. She complained mechanically before bowing to the inevitable. He drove to Cadbury Avenue and parked his car. When the doorman slipped down to the corner for a cup of coffee, Kraft ducked into the building and found Leon Dennison's apartment. The door was locked, but he managed to spring the lock with the blade of a pen knife. He was sweating freely as he worked on the lock, expecting every moment someone to come up behind him and lay a hand on his shoulder. The lock gave, and he went inside and closed it after him.

But something happened the moment he entered the apartment. All the fear, all the anxiety, all of this suddenly left Edgar Kraft. He was mysteriously calm now. Everything was prearranged, he told himself. Joseph H. Neimann had been doomed, and Raymond Andersen had been doomed, and Claude Pierce had been doomed, and each of them had died. Now Leon Dennison was similarly doomed, and he, too, would die.

It seemed very simple. And Edgar Kraft himself was nothing but a part of this grand design, nothing but a cog in a gigantic machine. He would do his part without worrying about it. Everything could only go according to plan.

Everything did. He waited three hours for Leon Dennison to come home, waited in calm silence. When a key turned in the lock, he stepped swiftly and noiselessly to the side of the door, a fireplace andiron held high overhead. The door opened and Leon Dennison entered, quite alone.

The andiron descended.

Leon Dennison fell without a murmur. He collapsed, lay still. The andiron rose and fell twice more, just for insurance, and Leon Dennison never moved and never uttered a sound. Kraft had only to wipe off the andiron and a few other surfaces to eliminate any fingerprints he might have left behind. He left the building by the service entrance. No one saw him.

He waited all that night for the rush of guilt. He was surprised when it failed to come. But he had already been a murderer—by wishing for Andersen's death, by planning Pierce's murder. The simple translation of his impulses from thought to deed was no impetus for further guilt.

There was no letter the next day. The following morning the usual envelope was waiting for him. It was quite bulky; it was filled with fifteen hundred dollar bills.

The note was different. It said *Thank you,* of course. But beneath that there was another line:

How do you like your new job?

from
RIPLEY'S GAME

Patricia Highsmith

1

"There's no such thing as a perfect murder," Tom
said to Reeves. "That's just a parlor game, trying to dream one up.
Of course you could say there are a lot of unsolved murders. That's
different." Tom was bored. He walked up and down in front of his
big fireplace, where a small but cozy fire crackled. Tom felt he had
spoken in a stuffy, pontificating way. But the point was he couldn't
help Reeves, and he'd already told him that.

"Yes, sure," said Reeves. He was sitting in one of the yellow silk
armchairs, his lean figure hunched forward; hands clasped between his knees. He had a bony face, short light brown hair, cold
gray eyes—not a pleasant face but a face that might have been
rather handsome if it hadn't borne a scar that traveled five inches
from his right temple across his cheek almost to his mouth. Slightly
pinker than the rest of his face, the scar looked like a bad job of
stitching, or as if perhaps it had never been stitched. Tom had never

asked about the scar, but Reeves had volunteered once, "A girl did it with her compact. Can you imagine?" (No. Tom couldn't.) Reeves had given Tom a quick, sad smile, one of the few smiles Tom could recall from Reeves. And, on another occasion, "I was thrown from a horse—dragged by the stirrup for a few yards." Reeves had said that to someone else, but Tom had been present. Tom suspected a dull knife in a very nasty fight somewhere.

Now Reeves wanted Tom to provide someone—suggest someone—to do one or perhaps two "simple murders" and perhaps one theft, also safe and simple. Reeves had come from Hamburg to Villeperce to talk to Tom, and he was going to stay the night and go to Paris tomorrow to talk to someone else, then return to his home in Hamburg, presumably to do some more thinking if he failed. Reeves was primarily a fence, but lately he had been dabbling in the illegal gambling world of Hamburg, which he was now undertaking to protect. Protect from what? Italian sharks who wanted to come in. One Italian in Hamburg was a Mafia button man, sent out as a feeler, Reeves thought, and the other might be one—from a different family. By eliminating one or both of these intruders, Reeves hoped to discourage further Mafia attempts, and also to draw the attention of the Hamburg police to a Mafia threat. Then let the police handle the rest; which was to say, throw the Mafia out. "These Hamburg boys are a decent batch," Reeves had declared fervently. "Maybe what they're doing is illegal, running a couple of private casinos, but as clubs they're not illegal, and they're not taking outrageous profits. It's not like Las Vegas, *all* Mafia-controlled, and right under the noses of the American cops!"

Tom took the poker, pushed the fire together, and put another neatly cut third of a log on. It was nearly six. Soon be time for a drink. And why not now? "Would you—"

Mme. Annette, the Ripleys' housekeeper, came in from the kitchen hall. "Excuse me, Messieurs. Would you like your drinks now, M. Tome, since the gentleman has not wanted any tea?"

"Yes, thank you, Mme. Annette. Just what I was thinking. And ask Mme. Héloïse to join us, would you?" Tom wanted Héloïse to lighten the atmosphere a little. He had said to Héloïse, before he went to Orly at three to fetch Reeves, that Reeves wanted to talk to him about something, so Héloïse had puttered about in the garden or stayed upstairs all afternoon.

"You wouldn't consider taking it on yourself?" Reeves said with a last-minute urgency and hope. "You're not connected, you see, and that's what we want. Safety. And after all, the money—ninety-six thousand bucks—isn't bad."

Tom shook his head. "I'm connected with *you*—in a way." Dammit, he'd done little jobs for Reeves Minot, such as mailing small stolen items, or recovering tiny objects like microfilm rolls from toothpaste tubes where Reeves had planted them. "How much of this cloak-and-dagger stuff do you think I can get away with? I've got my reputation to protect, you know." Tom felt like smiling at that, but at the same time his heart had quickened with genuine feeling, and he stood taller, conscious of the fine house in which he lived, of his secure existence now, six whole months after the Derwatt episode, a near catastrophe from which he had escaped with no worse than a bit of suspicion upon him. Thin ice, yes, but the ice hadn't broken through. Tom had accompanied the English Inspector Webster and a couple of forensic men to the Salzburg woods where he had cremated the body of the man presumed to be the painter Derwatt. Why had he crushed the skull? the police had asked. Tom still winced when he thought of it, because he had done it to try to scatter and hide the upper teeth. The lower jaw had come away easily, and Tom had buried it at a distance. But the upper teeth—some of them had been gathered by one of the forensic men. Fortunately there had been no record of Derwatt's teeth with any dentist in London, Derwatt having been living (it was believed) in Mexico for the preceding six years. "It seemed part of the cremation, part of the idea of reducing him to ashes," Tom had replied. The cremated body had been Bernard's. Yes, Tom could still shudder, as much at the danger of that moment as at the horror of his act, dropping a big stone on the charred skull. But he hadn't killed Bernard. Bernard Tufts had been a suicide.

Tom said, "Surely among all the people you know, you can find somebody who can do it."

"Yes, and that would be a connection—more than you. Oh, the people I know are sort of known," Reeves said with sad defeat in his voice. "You know a lot of respectable people, Tom, people really in the clear, people above reproach."

Tom laughed. "How're you going to *get* such people? Sometimes I think you're out of your mind, Reeves."

"No! You know what I mean. Someone who'd do it for the money, just the money. They don't have to be experts. We'd prepare the way. It'd be like—public assassinations. Someone who, if he was questioned, would look—absolutely incapable of doing such a thing."

Mme. Annette came in with the bar cart. The silver ice bucket shone. The cart squeaked slightly. Tom had been meaning to oil it for weeks. Tom might have gone on bantering with Reeves because Mme. Annette, bless her soul, didn't understand English, but Tom was tired of the subject, and delighted by Mme. Annette's interruption. Mme. Annette was in her sixties, from a Normandy family, fine of feature and sturdy of body, a gem of a servant. Tom could not imagine Belle Ombre functioning without her.

Then Héloïse came in from the garden, and Reeves got to his feet. Héloïse was wearing bell-bottom pink-and-red striped dungarees with LEVI printed vertically on all the stripes. Her blond hair swung long and loose. Tom saw the firelight glow in it and thought, What purity compared to what we've been talking about! The light in her hair was gold, however, which made Tom think of money. Well, he didn't really need any more money, even if the Derwatt picture sales, of which he got a percentage, would soon come to an end because there would be no more pictures. He still got a percentage from the Derwatt Art Supplies Company, and that would continue. Then there was the modest but slowly increasing income from the Greenleaf securities that he had inherited in a will forged by Tom himself. Not to mention Héloïse's generous allowance from her father. No use being greedy. Tom detested murder unless it was absolutely necessary.

"Did you have a good talk?" Héloïse asked in English, and fell back gracefully onto the yellow sofa.

"Yes, thank you," said Reeves.

The rest of the conversation was in French, because Héloïse was not comfortable in English. Reeves did not know much French but he got along, and they were not talking about anything important: the garden, the mild winter, which seemed really to have passed because here it was early March and the daffodils were opening. Tom poured champagne for Héloïse from one of the little bottles on the cart.

"How ees eet in Hambourg?" Héloïse ventured again in English, and Tom saw amusement in her eyes as Reeves struggled to get out a conventional response in French.

It was not too cold in Hamburg, either, and Reeves added that he had a garden also, as his *petite maison* found itself on the Alster, which was water; that was to say, a sort of bay where many people had homes with gardens and water, meaning they could have small boats if they wished.

Tom knew that Héloïse disliked Reeves Minot, distrusted him, that Reeves was the kind of person Héloïse wanted Tom to avoid. Tom reflected with satisfaction that he could honestly say to Héloïse tonight that he had declined to cooperate in the scheme that Reeves had proposed. Héloïse was always worried about what her father would say. Her father, Jacques Plissot, was a millionaire pharmaceutical manufacturer, a Gaullist, the essence of French respectability. And he had never cared for Tom. "My father will not stand for much more!" Héloïse often warned Tom, but Tom knew she was more interested in his own safety than in hanging on to the allowance her father gave her—an allowance he frequently threatened to cut off, according to Héloïse. She had lunch with her parents at their home in Chantilly once a week, usually Friday. If her father ever severed her allowance, they could not quite make it at Belle Ombre, Tom knew.

The dinner menu was *médaillons de boeuf,* preceded by cold artichokes with Mme. Annette's own sauce. Héloïse had changed into a simple dress of pale blue. She sensed already, Tom thought, that Reeves had not got what he had come for. Before they all retired, Tom made sure that Reeves had everything he needed, and at what hour he would like tea or coffee brought to his room. Coffee at eight, Reeves said. Reeves had the guest room in the left center of the house, which gave him the bathroom that was usually Héloïse's, but from which Mme. Annette had already removed Héloïse's toothbrush to Tom's bathroom, off his room.

"I am glad he is going tomorrow. Why is he so tense?" Héloïse asked while brushing her teeth.

"He's always tense." Tom turned off the shower, stepped out, and quickly enveloped himself in a big yellow towel. "That's why he's thin—maybe." They were speaking in English, because Héloïse was not shy about speaking English with him.

"How did you meet him?"

Tom couldn't remember. When? Maybe five or six years ago. In Rome? Who was Reeves a friend of? Tom was too tired to think hard, and it didn't matter. He had five or six such acquaintances, and would have been hard pressed to say where he had met each one.

"What did he want from you?"

Tom put his arm around Héloïse's waist, pressing the loose nightdress close to her body. He kissed her cool cheek. "Something impossible. I said no. You can see that. He is disappointed."

That night there was an owl, a lonely owl calling somewhere in the pines of the communal forest behind Belle Ombre. Tom lay with his left arm under Héloïse's neck, thinking. She fell asleep, and her breathing became slow and soft. Tom sighed, and went on thinking. But he was not thinking in a logical, constructive way. His second coffee was keeping him awake. He was remembering a party he had been to a month ago in Fontainebleau, an informal birthday party for a Mme.—who? It was her husband's name that Tom was interested in, an English name that might come to him in a few seconds. The man, the host, had been in his early thirties, and they had a small son. The house was a straight-up-and-down three-story, on a residential street in Fontainebleau, a patch of garden behind it. The man was a picture framer; that was why Tom had been dragged along by Pierre Gauthier, who had an art-supply shop in the Rue Grande, where Tom bought his paints and brushes. Gauthier had said, "Oh, come along with me, M. Reeply. Bring your wife! He wants a lot of people. He's a little depressed. . . . And anyway, since he makes frames, you might give him some business."

Tom blinked in the darkness, and moved his head back a little so his eyelashes would not touch Héloïse's shoulder. He recalled a tall blond Englishman with a certain resentment and dislike, because in the kitchen—that gloomy kitchen with worn-out linoleum and a smoke-stained tin ceiling with a nineteenth-century bas-relief pattern—this man had made an unpleasant remark to Tom. The man—Trewbridge, Tewksbury?—had said, in an almost sneering way, "Oh, yes, I've heard of you." Tom had said, "I'm Tom Ripley. I live in Villeperce," and Tom had been about to ask him how long he'd been in Fontainebleau, thinking that perhaps an Englishman with a French wife might like to make acquaintance with an American with a French wife living not far away, but Tom's venture had been met with rudeness. Trevanny? Wasn't that his name? Blond straight hair, rather Dutch-looking—but then the English often looked Dutch and vice versa.

What Tom was thinking of now, however, was what Gauthier had said later the same evening: "He's depressed. He doesn't mean to be unfriendly. He's got some kind of blood disease—leukemia, I think. Pretty serious. Also, as you can see from the house, he's not doing too well." Gauthier had a glass eye of a curious yellow-green color, obviously an attempt to match the real one, but a failure. In fact, Gauthier's false eye suggested the eye of a dead cat. You avoided looking at it, yet you were hypnotically drawn to it. Gauthier's gloomy words, combined with the glass eye, had made a strong impression of death upon Tom, and Tom had not forgotten.

Oh, yes, I've heard of you. Did that mean that Trevanny, or whatever his name was, thought he was responsible for Bernard

Tufts's death, and before that Dickie Greenleaf's? Or was the Englishman merely embittered against everyone because of his ailment? Dyspeptic, like a man with a constant stomachache? Now Tom recalled Trevanny's wife, not pretty, but rather an interesting-looking woman with chestnut hair, friendly and outgoing, making an effort at that party in the small living room and the kitchen where no one sat down on the few chairs available.

Tom was thinking. Would this man take on such a job as Reeves was proposing? An interesting approach to Trevanny had occurred to Tom. It was an approach that might work with any man, if one prepared the ground, but in this case the ground was already prepared. Trevanny was seriously worried about his health. Tom's idea was nothing more than a practical joke, he thought, a nasty one, but the man had been nasty to him. The joke might not last more than a day or so, until Trevanny could consult his doctor.

Tom was amused by his thoughts, and eased himself gently from Héloïse, so that if he shook with repressed laughter for an instant he wouldn't awaken her. Suppose Trevanny was vulnerable, and carried out Reeves's plan like a soldier, like a dream? Was it worth a try? Yes, because Tom had nothing to lose. Neither had Trevanny. Trevanny might gain. Reeves might gain—according to Reeves, but let Reeves figure that out, because what Reeves wanted seemed as vague to Tom as Reeves's microfilm activities, which presumably had to do with international spying. Were governments aware of the insane antics of some of their spies? Of those whimsical, half-demented men flitting from Bucharest to Moscow and Washington with guns and microfilm—men who might with the same enthusiasm have put their energies into stamp-collecting, or acquiring secrets of miniature electric trains?

2

So it was that some ten days later, Jonathan Trevanny, who lived in the Rue Saint-Merry, Fontainebleau, received a curious letter from his good friend Alan McNear. Alan, a Paris representative of an English electronics firm, had written the letter just before leaving for New York on a business assignment, and oddly the day after he had visited the Trevannys in Fontainebleau. Jonathan had expected—or, rather, not expected—a sort of thank-you letter from Alan for the send-off party Jonathan and Simone had given him, and Alan did write a few words of appreciation, but the paragraph that puzzled Jonathan went:

Jon, I was shocked at the news in regard to the old blood ailment, and am even now hoping it isn't so. I was told that you knew but weren't telling any of your friends. Very noble of you, but what are friends for? You needn't think we'll avoid you or that we'll think you'll become so melancholy that we won't want to see you. Your friends (and I'm one) are here— always. But I can't write anything I want to say, really. I'll do better when I see you next, in a couple of months when I wangle myself a vacation, so forgive these inadequate words.

What was Alan talking about? Had his doctor, Périer, said something to his friends, something he wouldn't tell him? Something about not living much longer? Dr. Périer hadn't been to the party for Alan, but could Dr. Périer have said something to someone else?

Had Dr. Périer spoken to Simone? And was Simone keeping it from him, too?

As Jonathan thought of these possibilities, he was standing in his garden, at eight-thirty in the morning, chilly under his sweater, his fingers smudged with earth. He'd best speak with Dr. Périer today. No use with Simone. She might put on an act. *But, darling, what're you talking about?* Jonathan wasn't sure he'd be able to tell if she was putting on an act or not.

And Dr. Périer—could he trust him? Dr. Périer was always bouncing with optimism, which was fine if you had something minor—you felt fifty percent better, even cured. But Jonathan knew he didn't have anything minor. He had myelocytic leukemia, characterized by an excess of yellow matter in the bone marrow. In the past five years, he'd had at least four blood transfusions per year. Every time he felt weak, he was supposed to get to his doctor, or to the Fontainebleau hospital, for a transfusion. Dr. Périer had said (and so had a specialist in Paris) that there would come a time when the decline might be swift, when transfusions wouldn't do the trick any longer. Jonathan had read enough about his ailment to know that himself. No doctor had yet come up with a cure for myelocytic leukemia. On the average, you died after six to twelve years, or even six to eight. Jonathan was entering his sixth year.

Jonathan set his fork back in the little brick structure, formerly an outside toilet, that served as a tool shed, then walked to his back steps. He paused with one foot on the first step and drew the fresh morning air into his lungs, thinking, How many weeks will I have to enjoy such mornings? He remembered thinking the same thing last spring, however. Buck up, he told himself, he'd known for six years that he might not live to see thirty-five. Jonathan mounted the iron steps with a firm tread, thinking that it was already eight-fifty-two, and that he was due in his shop at nine or a few minutes after.

Simone had gone off with Georges to the École Maternelle, and the house was empty. Jonathan washed his hands at the sink and made use of the vegetable brush, which Simone would not have approved of, but he left the brush clean. The only other sink was in the bathroom on the top floor. There was no telephone in the house. He'd ring Dr. Périer from his shop the first thing.

Jonathan walked to the Rue de la Paroisse and turned left, then went on to the Rue des Sablons, which crossed it. In his shop, Jonathan dialed Dr. Périer's number, which he knew by heart.

The nurse said the doctor was booked up today, which Jonathan had expected.

"But this is urgent. It's something that won't take long. Just a question, really—but I must see him."

"You are feeling weak, M. Trevanny?"

"Yes, I am," Jonathan said at once.

He got an appointment for twelve noon. The hour had a certain doom about it.

Jonathan was a picture framer. He cut mats and glass, made frames, chose frames from his stock for clients who were undecided, and once in a blue moon, when buying old frames at auctions and from junk dealers, he got a picture that was of some interest with the frame, a picture which he could clean and put in his window and sell. But it wasn't a lucrative business. He scraped along. Seven years ago he'd had a partner, another Englishman, from Manchester, and they had started an antique shop in Fontainebleau, dealing mainly in junk which they refurbished and sold. This hadn't paid enough for two, and Roy had pushed off and got a job as a garage mechanic somewhere near Paris. Shortly after that, a Paris doctor had said the same thing that a London doctor had told Jonathan: "You're inclined to anemia. You'd better have frequent checkups, and it's best if you don't do any heavy work." So from handling armoires and sofas, Jonathan had turned to the lighter work of handling picture frames and glass. Before Jonathan had married Simone, he had told her that he might not live more than another six years, because just at the time he met Simone, he'd had it confirmed by two doctors that his periodic weakness was caused by myelocytic leukemia.

Now, Jonathan thought as he calmly, very calmly, began his day, Simone might remarry if he died. Simone worked five afternoons a week from two-thirty until six-thirty at a shoe shop in the Avenue Franklin Roosevelt, which was within walking distance of their house. She had begun working only in the past year, when Georges had been old enough to be put into the French equivalent of kindergarten. They needed the two hundred francs a week that Simone earned, but Jonathan was irked by the thought that Brezard, her boss, was a bit of a lecher, liked to pinch his employees' behinds, and doubtless to try his luck in the back room where the stock was. Simone was a married woman, as Brezard well knew, so there was a limit as to how far he could go, Jonathan supposed, but that never stopped his type from trying. Simone was not at all a flirt; she had a curious shyness, in fact, that suggested she thought herself not attractive to men. It was a quality that endeared her to Jonathan. In Jonathan's opinion, Simone was supercharged with sex appeal, though of the kind that might not be apparent to the average man, and it especially annoyed Jonathan that that swine Brezard must have become aware of Simone's very different kind of attractiveness and wanted some of it for himself. Not that Simone talked much about Brezard. Once she had mentioned that he tried it on with his women employees—two besides Simone. For an instant that morning, as Jonathan presented a framed watercolor to a client, he imagined Simone, after a discreet interval, succumbing to the odious Brezard, who, after all, was a bachelor and financially better off than Jonathan. Absurd, Jonathan thought. Simone hated his type.

"Oh, it's lovely! Excellent!" said the young woman holding the watercolor at arm's length.

Jonathan's long, serious face slowly smiled, as if a small and private sun had come out of clouds and begun to shine within him. She was so genuinely pleased! Jonathan didn't know her; in fact, she was picking up the picture that an older woman, perhaps her mother, had brought in. The price should have been twenty francs more than he had first estimated, because the framing was not the same kind the older woman had chosen (Jonathan had not had enough in stock), but he didn't mention this and accepted the eighty francs agreed upon.

Then Jonathan pushed a broom over his wooden floor, and feather-dusted the three or four pictures in his small front window. His shop was positively shabby, Jonathan thought that morning. No color anywhere, frames of all sizes leaning against unpainted walls, samples of frame wood hanging from the ceiling, a counter with an order book, ruler, pencils. At the back of the shop stood a long wooden table where Jonathan worked with his miter boxes, saws, and glass cutters. Also on the big table were his carefully protected sheets of matboard, a great roll of brown paper, string, wire, pots of glue, and boxes of variously sized nails, and above the table on the walls were racks of knives and hammers. In principle, Jonathan liked the nineteenth-century atmosphere, the lack of commercial frou-frou. He wanted his shop to look as if a good craftsman ran it, and in that he had succeeded, he thought. He never overcharged; he did his work on time, or if he was going to be late, he notified his clients by postcard or a telephone call. People appreciated that, Jonathan had found.

At eleven-thirty-five, having framed two small pictures and fixed their owners' names to them, Jonathan washed his hands and face at the cold-water tap in his sink, combed his hair, stood up straight, and tried to brace himself for the worst. Dr. Périer's office was not far away in the Rue Grande. Jonathan turned his door card to OUVERT at 14:30, locked his front door, and set out.

Jonathan had to wait in Dr. Périer's front room with its sickly, dusty rose laurel plant. The plant never flowered; it didn't die, and never grew, never changed. Jonathan identified himself with the plant. Again and again his eyes were drawn to it, though he tried to think of other things. There were copies of *Paris-Match* on the oval table, out of date and much thumbed; Jonathan found them more depressing than the laurel plant. Dr. Périer also worked at the big Hôpital de Fontainebleau, Jonathan reminded himself; otherwise it would have seemed an absurdity to entrust one's life to, to believe a life-or-death diagnosis of, a doctor who worked in such a wretched little place as this looked.

The nurse came out and beckoned.

"Well, well, how's the interesting patient, my most interesting patient?" said Dr. Périer, rubbing his hands, then extending one to Jonathan.

Jonathan shook his hand. "I feel quite all right, thank you. But what this is about—I mean the tests of two months ago. I understand they are not favorable?"

Dr. Périer looked blank, and Jonathan watched him intently. Then Dr. Périer smiled, showing yellowish teeth under his carelessly trimmed mustache.

"What do you mean unfavorable? You saw the results."

"But—you know I'm not an expert in understanding them—perhaps."

"But I explained them to you. Now, what is the matter? You're feeling tired again?"

"In fact, no." Since Jonathan knew the doctor wanted to get away for lunch, he said hastily, "To tell the truth, a friend of mine has learned somewhere that—I'm due for a crisis. Maybe I haven't long to live. Naturally, I thought this information must have come from you."

Dr. Périer shook his head, then laughed, hopped about like a bird, and came to rest with his skinny arms lightly outspread on the top of a glass-enclosed bookcase. "My dear sir— first of all, if it were true, I would not have said it to anybody. That is not ethical. Second, it is not true, as far as I know from the last test. . . . Do you want another test today? Late this afternoon at the hospital, maybe I—"

"Not necessarily. What I really wanted to know is—is it true? You wouldn't just not tell me?" Jonathan said, with a laugh. "Just to make me feel better?"

"What nonsense! Do you think I'm that kind of a doctor?"

Yes, Jonathan thought, looking Dr. Périer straight in the eye. And God bless him, maybe, in some cases, but Jonathan thought he deserved the facts; because he was the kind of man who could face the facts. Jonathan bit his underlip. He could go to the lab in Paris, he thought, insist on seeing the specialist Moussu again. Also he might get something out of Simone today at lunchtime.

Dr. Périer was patting his arm. "Your friend—and I won't ask who he is!—is either mistaken or not a very nice friend, I think. Now, then, you should tell me when and if you become tired. *That* is what counts."

Twenty minutes later, Jonathan was climbing the front steps of his house, carrying an apple tart and a long loaf of bread. He let himself in with his key and walked down the hall to the kitchen. He smelled frying potatoes, a mouth-watering smell signifying lunch, not dinner, and Simone's potatoes would be in long slender pieces, not short chunks like the chips in England. Why had he thought of English chips?

Simone was at the stove, wearing an apron over her dress, wielding a long fork. "Hello, Jon. You're late."

Jonathan put an arm around her and kissed her cheek, then held up the paper box and swung it toward Georges, who was sitting at the table, blond head bent, cutting out parts for a mobile from an empty box of cornflakes.

"Ah, a cake! What kind?" Georges asked.

"Apple." Jonathan set the box on the table.

They had a small steak each, the delicious fried potatoes, a green salad.

"Brezard is starting inventory," Simone said. "The summer stock comes in next week, so he wants to have a sale Friday and Saturday. I might be a little late tonight."

She had warmed the apple tart on the asbestos plate. Jonathan waited impatiently for Georges to go in the living room, where a lot of his toys were, or out to the garden.

When Georges left finally, Jonathan said, "I had a funny letter today from Alan."

"Alan? Funny how?"

"He wrote it just before he went to New York. It seems he's heard—" Should he show her Alan's letter? She could read English well enough. Jonathan decided to go on. "He's heard somewhere that I'm worse, due for a bad crisis—or something. Do you know anything about it?" Jonathan watched her eyes.

Simone looked genuinely surprised. "Why, no, Jon. How would I hear—except from you?"

"I spoke with Dr. Périer just now. That's why I was late. Périer says he doesn't know of any change in the situation, but you know Périer!" Jonathan smiled, still watching Simone anxiously. "Well, here's the letter," he said, pulling it from his back pocket. He translated the paragraph.

"*Mon Dieu!* Well, where did *he* hear it from?"

"Yes, that's the question. I'll write him and ask, don't you think?" Jonathan smiled again, a more genuine smile. He was sure Simone didn't know anything about it.

Jonathan carried a second cup of coffee into the small square living room where Georges was now sprawled on the floor with his cut-outs. Jonathan sat down at the writing desk, which always made him feel like a giant. It was a rather dainty French *écritoire*, a present from Simone's family. Jonathan was careful not to put too much weight on the writing shelf. He addressed an airmail letter to Alan McNear at the Hotel New Yorker, began the letter breezily enough, and wrote a second paragraph:

> I don't know quite what you mean in your letter about the news (about me) which shocked you. I feel all right, but this morning spoke with my doctor here to see if he was giving me the whole story. He disclaims any knowledge of a worse condition. So, dear Alan, what does interest me is where did you hear it? Could you possibly drop me a line soon? It sounds like a misunderstanding, and I'd be delighted to forget it, but I hope you can understand my curiosity as to where you heard it.

He dropped the letter in a mailbox en route to his shop. It would probably be a week before he heard from Alan.

That afternoon, Jonathan's hand was as steady as ever as he pulled his razor knife down the edge of his steel ruler. He thought of his letter, making its progress to Orly airport maybe by this evening, maybe by tomorrow morning. He thought of his age, thirty-four, and of how pitifully little he would have done if he were to die in another couple of months. He'd produced a son, and that was something, but hardly an achievement worthy of special praise. He would not leave Simone very secure. If anything, he had lowered her standard of living slightly. Her father was only a coal merchant, but somehow over the years her family had gathered a few conveniences around them—a car, for instance, and decent furniture. They vacationed in June or July down south in a villa which they rented, and last year they had paid a month's rent so that Jonathan and Simone could go there with Georges. Jonathan had not done as well as his brother Philip, two years older than himself, though Philip had looked physically weaker and had been a dull, plodding type all his life. Philip was a professor of anthropology at Bristol University—not brilliant, Jonathan was sure, but a good solid man with a solid career, a wife, and two children. Jonathan's mother, a widow now, had a happy existence with her brother and sister-in-law in Oxfordshire, taking care of the big garden there and doing all the shopping and cooking. Jonathan felt himself the failure of his family, both physically and as to his work. He had first wanted to be an actor. At eighteen he'd gone to a drama school for two years. He didn't have a bad face for an actor, he thought—not too handsome, with his big nose and wide mouth, but good-looking enough to play romantic roles and heavy enough to play heavier roles in time. What pipedreams! He'd hardly got two walk-on parts in the three years he'd hung around London and Manchester theatres— supporting himself by odd jobs, including one as a veterinary's assistant. "You take up a lot of space and you're not even sure of yourself," a director once said to him. And then, working for an antique dealer in another of his odd jobs, Jonathan had thought he might like the antique business. He had learned all he could from his boss, Andrew Mott. Then the grand move to France with his friend Roy Johnson, who had had enthusiasm, if not much knowledge, about starting an antique shop via the junk trade. Jonathan remembered his dreams of glory and adventure in a new country, France; dreams of freedom, of success. And instead of success, instead of a series of educational mistresses, instead of making friends with bohemians, or with some stratum of French society which Jonathan had imagined existed but perhaps didn't—instead of all this, Jonathan had continued to limp along, no better off really than when he'd been trying to get jobs as an actor and had supported himself any old way.

The only successful thing in his whole life was his marriage to Simone, Jonathan thought. The news of his disease had come in the same month he had met Simone Foussadier. He'd begun to feel strangely weak, and had romantically thought that it might be due to falling in love. But a little extra rest hadn't shaken the weakness; he had fainted once in a street in Nemours, so he had gone to a doctor—Dr. Périer in Fontainebleau, who had suspected a blood condition and sent him to a specialist in Paris. The specialist, Dr. Moussu, after two days of tests, had confirmed myelocytic leukemia, and said that he might have from six to eight—or, with luck, twelve—years to live. There would be an enlargement of the spleen, which in fact Jonathan already had without having noticed it. Thus Jonathan's proposal to Simone had been a declaration of love and death in the same awkward speech. It would have been enough to put most young women off, or to have made them say they needed some time to think about it. Simone had said yes, she loved him, too. "It is the love that is important, not the time," Simone had said. None of the calculation that Jonathan had associated with the French, and with Latins in general. Simone said she had already spoken to her family. And this after they had known each other only two weeks. Jonathan felt himself suddenly in a world more secure than any he had ever known. Love—in a real and not a merely romantic sense, love that he had no control over— had miraculously rescued him. In a way, he felt that it had rescued him from death, but he realized that he meant that love had taken the terror out of death. And here was death six years later, as Dr. Moussu in Paris had predicted. Perhaps. Jonathan didn't know what to believe.

He must make another visit to Moussu in Paris, he thought. Three years ago, Jonathan had had a complete change of blood under Dr. Moussu's supervision in a Paris hospital. The treatment was called Vincainestine, the idea or the hope being that the excess of white with accompanying yellow components would not return to the blood. But the yellow excess had reappeared in about eight months.

Before he made an appointment with Dr. Moussu, however, Jonathan preferred to wait for a letter from Alan McNear. Alan would write at once, Jonathan felt sure. One could count on Alan.

Jonathan, before he left his shop, cast one desperate glance around its Dickensian interior. It wasn't really dusty; it was just that the walls needed repainting. He wondered if he should make an effort to spruce the place up, start soaking his customers as so many picture framers did, sell lacquered brass items with big markups? Jonathan winced. He wasn't the type.

That day was Wednesday. On Friday, while bending over a stubborn screw eye that had been in an oak frame for perhaps a hundred and fifty years and had no intention of yielding to his pliers, Jonathan suddenly had to drop the pliers and look for a seat. The seat was a wooden box against the wall. He got up almost at once and went to the sink to wet his face, bending as low as he could. In five minutes or so, the faintness passed, and by lunchtime he had forgotten about it. Such moments came every two or three months, and Jonathan was glad if they didn't catch him on the street.

On Tuesday, six days after he had posted his letter to Alan, he received a letter from the Hotel New Yorker.

Saturday, March 25th
Dear Jon,

Believe me, I'm glad you spoke with your doctor and that the news is good! The person who told me you were in a serious way was a little balding fellow with a mustache and a glass eye—early forties, maybe. He seemed really concerned, and perhaps you shouldn't hold it too much against him, as he may have heard it from someone else.
I'm enjoying this town and wish you and Simone were here, esp. as I'm on an expense account. . . .

The man Alan meant was obviously Pierre Gauthier, who had the art-supply shop in the Rue Grande. He was not a friend of Jonathan's, just an acquaintance. Gauthier often sent people to Jonathan to have their pictures framed. He had been at the house the night of Alan's send-off party, Jonathan remembered distinctly, and must have spoken to Alan then. It was out of the question that Gauthier had spoken maliciously. Jonathan was only a little surprised that Gauthier even knew he had a blood ailment, though word did get around, Jonathan realized. Jonathan thought the thing to do was speak to Gauthier and ask him where he'd heard the story.

It was ten to nine. Jonathan had waited for the mail, as he had yesterday morning. His impulse was to go straight to Gauthier, but he felt this would show unseemly anxiety, and that he'd better get his bearings by going to his shop and opening as usual.

Because of three or four customers, Jonathan didn't have a break till ten-thirty. He left his clock card in the glass of his door indicating that he would be open again at eleven.

When Jonathan entered the art-supply shop, Gauthier was busy with two women customers. Jonathan pretended to browse among racks of paintbrushes until Gauthier was free. Then he said, "M. Gauthier! How goes it?" and extended a hand.

Gauthier clasped Jonathan's hand in both his own and smiled. "And you, my friend?"

"Well enough, thank you. . . . *Écoutez.* I don't want to take your time—but there is something I would like to ask you."

"Yes? What's that?"

Jonathan beckoned Gauthier farther away from the door, which might open at any minute. There was not much standing room in the little shop. "I heard from a friend—my friend Alan, you remember? The Englishman. At the party at my house a few weeks ago."

"Yes! Your friend the Englishman. Alain." Gauthier remembered and looked attentive.

Jonathan tried to avoid even glancing at Gauthier's false eye by concentrating on the other eye. "Well, it seems you told Alan that you'd heard I was very ill, maybe not going to live much longer."

Gauthier's soft face grew solemn. He nodded. "Yes, M'sieur, I did hear that. I hope it's not true. I remember Alain, because you introduced him to me as your best friend. So I assumed he knew. Perhaps I should have said nothing. I am sorry. It was perhaps tactless. I thought you were—in the English style—putting on a brave face."

"It's nothing serious, M. Gauthier, because as far as I know, it's not true! I've just spoken with my doctor. But—"

"Ah, *bon!* Ah, well, that's different! I'm delighted to hear that, M. Trevanny! Ha! Ha!" Pierre Gauthier gave a peal of laughter as if a ghost had been laid and he found not only Jonathan but himself back among the living.

"But I'd like to know where you heard this. Who told you I was so ill?"

"Ah-yes!" Gauthier pressed a finger to his lips, thinking. "Who? A man. Yes—of *course!*" He had it, but he paused.

Jonathan waited.

"But I remember he said he wasn't sure. He'd heard it, he said. An incurable blood disease, he said."

Jonathan felt warm with anxiety again, as he had felt several times in the past week. He wet his lips. "But who? How did he hear it? Didn't he say?"

Gauthier again hesitated. "Since it isn't true—shouldn't we best forget it?"

"Someone you know very well?"

"No! Not at all well, I assure you."

"A customer?"

"Yes. Yes, he is. A nice man, a gentleman. But since he *said* he wasn't sure— Really, M'sieur, you shouldn't bear a resentment, although I can understand how you could resent such a remark."

"Which leads to the interesting question of how the gentleman came to hear I was very ill," Jonathan went on, laughing now.

"Yes. Exactly. Well, the point is, it isn't true. Isn't that the main thing?"

Jonathan saw in Gauthier a French politeness, and unwilling-ness to alienate a customer, and—which was to be expected—an aversion to the subject of death. "You're right. That's the main thing." Jonathan shook hands with Gauthier, both of them smiling now, and bade him adieu.

That very day at lunch, Simone asked Jonathan if he had heard from Alan. Jonathan said yes.

"It was Gauthier who said something to Alan."

"Gauthier? The art-shop man?"

"Yes." Jonathan was lighting a cigarette over his coffee. Georges had gone out into the garden. "I went to see Gauthier this morning and I asked him where he'd heard it. He said from a customer. A man. . . . Funny, isn't it? Gauthier wouldn't tell me who, and I can't really blame him. It's some mistake, of course. Gauthier realizes that."

"But it's a shocking thing," said Simone.

Jonathan smiled, knowing Simone wasn't really shocked, since she knew Dr. Périer had given him rather good news. "As we say in English, one mustn't make a mountain out of a molehill."

In the following week, Jonathan bumped into Dr. Périer in the Rue Grande, the doctor in a hurry to enter the Société Gén-érale before it shut at twelve sharp. But he paused to ask him how he was.

"Quite well, thank you," said Jonathan, whose mind was on buying a plunger for the toilet from a shop, a hundred yards away, which also shut at noon.

"M. Trevanny." Dr. Périer paused with one hand on the big knob of the bank's door. He moved away from the door, closer to Jonathan. "In regard to what we were talking about the other day, no doctor can be *sure*, you know. In a situation like yours. I don't want you to think I've given you a guarantee of perfect health, immunity for years. You know yourself—"

"Oh, I didn't assume that!" Jonathan interrupted.

"Then you understand," said Dr. Périer, smiling, and dashed at once into his bank.

Jonathan trotted on in quest of the plunger. It was the kitchen sink that was stopped up, not the toilet, he remembered, and Simone had lent a neighbor their plunger months ago and . . . Jonathan was thinking of what Dr. Périer had said. *Did* he know something, suspect something from the last test, something not sufficiently definite to warrant telling him about?

At the door of the *droguerie*, Jonathan encountered a smiling, dark-haired girl who was just locking up, removing the outside door handle.

"I'm sorry. It's five minutes past twelve," she said.

3

Tom, during the last week in March, was engaged in painting a full-length portrait of Héloïse horizontal on the yellow satin sofa. And Héloïse seldom agreed to pose. But the sofa stayed still, and Tom had it satisfactorily on his canvas. He had also made seven or eight sketches of Héloïse with her head propped upon her left hand, her right hand resting on a big art book. He kept the two best sketches and threw the others away.

Reeves Minot had written him a letter asking if he had come up with a helpful idea—as to a person, Reeves meant. The letter had arrived a couple of days after Tom had spoken with Gauthier, from whom Tom usually bought his paints. Tom had replied to Reeves: "Am trying to think, but meanwhile you should go ahead with your own ideas, if you have any." The "am trying to think" was merely polite, even false, like a lot of phrases that served to oil the machinery of social intercourse, as Emily Post might say. Reeves hardly kept Belle Ombre oiled financially; in fact, Reeves's payments to Tom for occasional services as go-between and fence would hardly cover the dry-cleaning bills, but it never hurt to maintain friendly relations. Reeves had procured a false passport for Tom and had got it to Paris fast when Tom had needed it to help defend the Derwatt industry. Tom might one day need Reeves again.

The business with Jonathan Trevanny was merely a game for Tom. He was not doing it for Reeves's gambling interests. Tom happened to dislike gambling and had no respect for people who chose to earn their living, or even part of their living, from it. It was pimping, of a sort. Tom had started the Trevanny game out of curiosity, and because Trevanny had once sneered at him—and because Tom wanted to see if his own wild shot would find its mark, and make Jonathan Trevanny, who Tom sensed was priggish and self-righteous, uneasy for a time. Then Reeves could offer his bait, hammering in the point that Trevanny was soon to die anyway. Tom doubted that Trevanny would bite, but it would be a period of discomfort for the man, certainly. Unfortunately Tom couldn't guess how soon the rumor would get to Jonathan Trevanny's ears. Gauthier was gossipy enough, but it just might happen, even if Gauthier told two or three people, that no one would have the courage to broach the subject to Trevanny himself.

So Tom, although he was busy as usual with his painting, his spring planting, his German and French studies (Schiller and Molière now), plus supervising a crew of three masons who were constructing a greenhouse along the right side of Belle Ombre's back lawn, still counted the passing days and imagined what might have happened after that afternoon in the middle of March when he had said to Gauthier that he'd heard Trevanny wasn't long for this world. Not too likely that Gauthier would speak to Trevanny directly, unless they were closer than Tom thought. Gauthier would more likely tell someone else about it. Tom counted on the fact (he was sure it was a fact) that the possibility of anyone's imminent death was a fascinating subject to everyone.

Tom went to Fontainebleau, some twelve miles from Villeperce, every two weeks or so. Fontainebleau was better than Moret for shopping, for having suede coats cleaned, for buying radio batteries and the rarer things that Mme. Annette wanted for her cuisine. Jonathan Trevanny had a telephone in his shop, Tom had noted in the directory, but apparently not in his house in the Rue Saint-Merry. Tom had been trying to look up the house number, although he thought he would recognize the house when he saw it. Around the end of March, Tom became curious to see Trevanny again—from a distance, of course. So on a trip to Fontainebleau one morning, a market day, for the purpose of buying two round terra-cotta flower tubs, Tom, after putting these items in the back of the green Renault station wagon, walked through the Rue des Sablons where Trevanny's shop was. It was nearly noon.

Trevanny's shop looked in need of paint and a bit depressing, as if it belonged to an old man, Tom thought. Tom had never patronized Trevanny, because there was a good framer in Moret, closer to Tom. The little shop with "Encadrement" in fading red letters on the wood over the door stood in a row of shops—a launderette, a cobbler's, a modest travel agency—with its door on the left side and to the right a square window with assorted frames and two or three paintings with handwritten price tags on them. Tom crossed the street casually, glanced into the shop, and saw Trevanny's tall, Nordic-looking figure behind the counter some twenty feet away. Trevanny was showing a man a length of frame, slapping it into his palm, talking. Then Trevanny glanced at the window, saw Tom for an instant, but continued talking to the customer with no change in his expression.

Tom strolled on. Trevanny hadn't recognized him. Tom turned right, in to the Rue de France, the second important street after the Rue Grande, and continued till he came to the Rue Saint-Merry, where he turned right. Or had Trevanny's house been to the left? No, right.

Yes, there it was, surely, the narrow, cramped-looking gray house with slender black handrails going up the front steps. The tiny areas on either side of the steps were cemented, and no flowerpots relieved the barrenness. But there was a garden behind, Tom recalled. The windows, though sparkling clean, showed rather limp curtains. Yes, this was where he'd come on the invitation of Gauthier that evening in February. There was a narrow passage on the left side of the house that must lead to the garden beyond. A green plastic garbage bin stood in front of the padlocked iron gate to the garden, and Tom imagined that the Trevannys usually got to the garden via the back door off the kitchen, which Tom remembered.

Tom was on the other side of the street, walking slowly, but careful not to appear to be loitering, because he couldn't be sure that the wife, or someone else, was not even now looking out one of the windows.

Was there anything else he needed to buy? Zinc white. He was nearly out of it. And that purchase would take him to Gauthier, the art-supply man. Tom quickened his step, congratulating himself because his need of zinc white was a real need, so he'd be entering Gauthier's on a real errand, while at the same time he might be able to satisfy his curiosity.

Gauthier was alone in the shop.

"*Bonjour,* M. Gauthier!" said Tom.

"*Bonjour,* M. Reepley!" Gauthier replied, smiling. "And how are you?"

"Very well, thank you, and you? . . . I find I need some zinc white."

"Zinc white." Gauthier pulled a flat drawer from his cabinet against a wall. "Here they are. And you like the Rembrandt, as I recall."

Tom did. Derwatt zinc white and other Derwatt-made colors were available, too, their tubes emblazoned with the bold, downward-slanting signature of Derwatt in black on the label, but somehow Tom didn't want to paint at home with the name Derwatt catching his eye every time he reached for a tube of anything.

Tom paid, and as Gauthier was handing him his change and the little bag with the zinc white in it, Gauthier said, "Ah, M. Reepley, you recall M. Trevanny, the framer in the Rue Saint-Merry?"

"Yes, of course," said Tom, who had been wondering how to bring Trevanny up.

"Well, the rumor that you heard, that he is going to die soon, is not true at all." Gauthier smiled.

"No? Well, very good! I'm glad to hear that."

"Yes. M. Trevanny went to see his doctor, even. I think he was a bit upset. Who wouldn't be, eh? Ha-ha! But you said somebody told *you*, M. Reepley?"

"Yes. A man who was at the party—in February. Mme. Trevanny's birthday party. So I assumed it was a fact and everybody knew it, you see."

Gauthier looked thoughtful.

"You spoke to M. Trevanny?" Tom asked.

"No-no. But I did speak to his best friend one evening, another evening at the Trevannys' house, this month. Evidently he spoke to M. Trevanny. How these things get around!"

"His best friend?" Tom asked with an air of innocence.

"An Englishman. Alain something. He was going to America the next day. But—do you recall who told *you*, M. Reepley?"

Tom shook his head slowly. "Can't recall his name, not even how he looked. There were so many people that night."

"Because"—Gauthier bent closer and whispered, as if there were someone else present—"M. Trevanny asked *me*, you see, who had told me. Of course I didn't say it was *you*. These things can be misinterpreted. I didn't want to get *you* into trouble. Ha!" Gauthier's shiny glass eye did not laugh but looked out from his head with a bold stare, as if there were a different brain controlling that eye, a computer kind of brain that would know everything at once, if someone just programmed it properly.

"I thank you for that, because it is not nice to make remarks that are not true about people's health, eh?" Tom was grinning now, ready to take his leave, but he added, "M. Trevanny does have a blood condition, however, didn't you say?"

"That is true. I think it's leukemia. But that's something he lives with. He once told me he'd had it for years."

Tom nodded. "At any rate, I'm glad he's not in danger. À *bientôt*, M. Gauthier. Many thanks."

Tom walked in the direction of his car. Trevanny's shock, though it may have lasted only a few hours until he consulted his doctor, must at least have put a little crack in his self-confidence. A few people had believed—and maybe Trevanny himself had believed—that he was not going to live more than a few weeks. That was because such a possibility wasn't out of the question for a man with Trevanny's ailment. A pity Trevanny was now reassured, but that little crack might be all that Reeves needed. The game could now enter its second stage. Trevanny would probably say no to Reeves. End of game, in that case. On the other hand, Reeves would approach him as if he was a doomed man. It would be amusing if Trevanny weakened. That day after lunch with Héloïse and her Paris friend Noëlle, who was going to stay overnight, Tom left the ladies and wrote a letter to Reeves on his typewriter.

March 28th

Dear Reeves,

I have an idea for you, in case you have not yet found what you are looking for. His name is Jonathan Trevanny, early thirties, English, a picture framer, married to Frenchwoman with small son. [Here Tom gave Trevanny's home and shop addresses and shop telephone number.] He looks as if he could use some money, and although he may not be the *type* you want, he looks the picture of decency and innocence, and, what is more important for you, I have found out that he has only a few months or weeks to live. He's got leukemia, and has just heard the bad news. He might be willing to take on a dangerous job to earn some money now.

I don't know Trevanny personally. Need I emphasize that I don't wish to make his acquaintance, nor do I wish you to mention my name? My suggestion is if you want to sound him out, come to F'bleau, put yourself up at a charming hostelry called L'Aigle Noir for a couple of days, ring Trevanny at his shop, make an appointment, and talk it over. And do I have to tell you to give another name besides your own?

Tom felt a sudden optimism about the project. The vision of Reeves with his disarming air of uncertainty and anxiety—almost suggestive of probity—laying such an idea before Trevanny, who looked as upright as a saint, made Tom laugh. Did he dare occupy a table in L'Aigle Noir's dining room or bar when Reeves made his date with Trevanny? No, that would be too much. This reminded him of another point, and he added to his letter:

> If you come to F'bleau, please don't telephone or write a note
> to me under any circumstances. Destroy my letter now,
> please.
> Yours ever,
> Tom

4

The telephone rang in Jonathan's shop on Friday afternoon, March 31st. He was just gluing brown paper to the back of a large picture, and he had to find suitable weights—an old sandstone saying LONDON, the glue pot itself, a wooden mallet—before he could lift the telephone.

"Hello?"

"*Bonjour,* M'sieur. M. Trevanny? . . . You speak English, I think. My name is Stephen Wister, W-i-s-t-e-r. I'm in Fontainebleau for a couple of days, and I wonder if you could find a few minutes to talk with me about something—something that I think would interest you."

The man had an American accent. "I don't buy pictures," Jonathan said. "I'm a framer."

"I didn't want to see you about anything connected with your work. It's something I can't explain over the phone. . . . I'm staying at the Aigle Noir."

"Oh?"

"I was wondering if you have a few minutes this evening after you close your shop. Around seven? Six-thirty? We could have a drink or a coffee."

"But—I'd like to know why you want to see me." A woman had come into the shop—Mme. Tissot, Tissaud?—to pick up a picture. Jonathan smiled apologetically to her.

"I'll have to explain when I see you," said the soft, earnest voice. "It'll take only ten minutes. Have you any time? At seven today, for instance?"

Jonathan shifted. "Six-thirty would be all right."

"I'll meet you in the lobby. I'm wearing a gray plaid suit. But I'll speak to the porter. It won't be difficult."

Jonathan usually closed around six-thirty. At six-fifteen, he stood at his cold-water sink, scrubbing his hands. It was a mild day, and Jonathan had worn a polo-neck sweater with an old beige corduroy jacket, not elegant enough for L'Aigle Noir, and the addition of his second-best mack would have made things worse. Why should he care? The man wanted to sell him something. It couldn't be anything else.

The hotel was only a five-minute walk from the shop. It had a small front court enclosed by high iron gates, and a few steps led up to its front door.

Jonathan saw a slender, tense-looking man with crew-cut hair move toward him with a faint uncertainty, and Jonathan said, "Mr. Wister?"

"Yes." Reeves gave a twitch of a smile and extended his hand. "Shall we have a drink in the bar here, or do you prefer somewhere else?"

The bar was pleasant and quiet. Jonathan shrugged. "As you like." He noticed an awful scar the length of Wister's cheek.

They went to the wide door of the hotel's bar, which was empty except for a man and a woman at a small table.

Wister turned away as if put off by the quietude, and said, "Let's try somewhere else."

They walked out of the hotel and turned right. Jonathan knew the next bar, the Café du Sport or some such, roistering at this hour with boys at the pinball machines and workmen at the counter. On the threshold of the bar-café, Wister stopped as if he had come unexpectedly upon a battlefield in action.

"Would you mind," Wister said, turning away, "coming up to my room? It's quiet and we can have something sent up."

They went back to the hotel, climbed a flight of stairs, and entered an attractive room in Spanish décor—black ironwork, a raspberry-colored bedspread, a pale green carpet. A suitcase on the rack was the only sign of the room's occupancy. Wister had entered without a key.

"What'll you have?" Wister went to the telephone. "Scotch?"

"Fine."

The man ordered in clumsy French. He asked for the bottle to be brought up, and for plenty of ice, please.

Then there was a silence. Why was the man uneasy, Jonathan wondered. Jonathan stood by the window where he had been looking out. Evidently Wister didn't want to talk until the drinks arrived. Jonathan heard a discreet tap at the door.

A white-jacketed waiter came in with a tray and a friendly smile. Stephen Wister poured generous drinks.

"Are you interested in making some money?"

Jonathan smiled, settled in a comfortable armchair now, with the huge iced Scotch in his hand. "Who isn't?"

"I have a dangerous job in mind—well, an important job—for which I'm prepared to pay quite well."

Jonathan thought of drugs: the man probably wanted something delivered or held. "What business are you in?" Jonathan inquired politely.

"Several. Just now one you might call—gambling. . . . Do you gamble?"

"No." Jonathan smiled.

"I don't, either. That's not the point." The man got up from the side of the bed and walked slowly about the room. "I live in Hamburg."

"Oh?"

"Gambling isn't legal in the city limits, but it goes on in private clubs. However, whether it's legal or not is not the point. I need a person eliminated, possibly two—and maybe a theft done. Now, that's putting my cards on the table." He looked at Jonathan with a serious, hopeful expression.

Killed, the man meant. Jonathan was startled; then he smiled and shook his head. "I wonder where you got my name!"

Stephen Wister didn't smile. "Never mind that." He continued walking up and down with his drink in his hand, and his gray eyes glanced at Jonathan and away again. "I wonder if you're interested in ninety-six thousand dollars? That's about forty thousand pounds, and about four hundred and eighty thousand francs—new francs. Just for shooting a man—maybe two; we'll have to see how it goes. It'll be an arrangement that's safe and foolproof for you."

Jonathan shook his head again. "I don't know where you heard that I'm a—a gunman. You've got me confused with someone else."

"No. Not at all."

Jonathan's smile faded under the man's intense stare. "It's a mistake. Do you mind telling me how you came to ring me?"

"Well, you're—" Wister looked more pained than ever. "You're not going to live more than a few months. You know that. You've got a wife and a small son—haven't you? Wouldn't you like to leave them a little something when you're gone?"

Jonathan felt the blood drain from his face. How did Wister know so much? Then he realized it was all connected, that whoever told Gauthier he was going to die soon knew this man, was connected with him somehow. Jonathan was not going to mention Gauthier. Gauthier was an honest man, and Wister was a crook. Suddenly Jonathan's Scotch didn't taste so good. "There was a crazy rumor—recently—"

Now Wister shook his head. "It is not a crazy rumor. It may be that your doctor hasn't told you the truth."

"And you know more than my doctor? My doctor doesn't lie to me. It's true I have a blood disease, but I'm in no worse state now—"

Jonathan broke off. "The essential thing is, I'm afraid I can't help you, Mr. Wister."

As Wister bit his underlip, the long scar moved in a distasteful way, like a live worm.

Jonathan looked away from him. Was Dr. Périer lying, after all? Jonathan thought he should ring up the Paris laboratory tomorrow morning and ask some questions, or simply go to Paris and demand another examination.

"Mr. Trevanny, I'm sorry to say it's evidently you who aren't informed. At least you've heard what you call the rumor, so I'm not the bearer of bad tidings. It's your own choice, but under the circumstances, a considerable sum like this, I would think, should sound rather pleasant. You could stop working and enjoy your— Well, for instance, you could take a cruise around the world with your family and still leave your wife—"

Jonathan felt slightly faint. He stood up and took a deep breath. The sensation passed, but he preferred to be on his feet. Wister was talking, but Jonathan barely listened.

". . . my idea. There're a few men in Hamburg who would contribute toward the ninety-six thousand dollars. The man, or men, we want out of the way are Mafia men."

Jonathan had only half recovered. "Thanks, I am not a killer. You may as well get off the subject."

Wister went on. "But exactly what we want is someone not connected with any of us, or with Hamburg. Although the first man, only a button man, must be shot in Hamburg. The reason is that we want the police to think that two Mafia gangs are fighting each other in Hamburg. In fact, we want the police to step in on our side." He continued to walk up and down, looking at the floor mostly. "The first man ought to be shot in a crowd, a U-bahn crowd. That's our subway—'underground' you'd call it. The gun would be dropped at once, the—the assassin blends into the crowd and vanishes. An Italian gun, with no fingerprints on it. No clues." He brought his hands down like a conductor finishing.

Jonathan moved back to the chair, in need of it for a few seconds. "Sorry. No." He would walk to the door as soon as he got his strength back.

"I'm here all tomorrow, and probably till late Sunday afternoon. I wish you'd think about it. . . . Another Scotch? Might do you good."

"No, thanks." Jonathan hauled himself up. "I'll be pushing off." Wister nodded, looking disappointed.

"And thanks for the drink."

"Don't mention it." Wister opened the door for Jonathan.

Jonathan went out. He had expected Wister to press a card with his name and address into his hand. Jonathan was glad he hadn't.

The streetlights had come on in the Rue de France. Seven twenty-two. Had Simone asked him to buy anything? Bread, perhaps. Jonathan went into a *boulangerie* and bought a long stick. The familiar chore was comforting.

The supper consisted of vegetable soup, a couple of slices of leftover fromage de tête, a salad of tomatoes and onions. Simone talked about a wallpaper sale at a shop near where she worked. For a hundred francs, they could paper the bedroom, and she had seen a beautiful mauve and green pattern, very light and art nouveau.

"With only one window, that bedroom's very dark, you know, Jon."

"Sounds fine," Jonathan said. "Especially if it's a sale."

"It *is* a sale. Not one of these silly sales where they reduce something five percent—like my stingy boss." She wiped bread crust in her salad oil and popped it into her mouth. "You're worried about something? Something happened today?"

Jonathan smiled suddenly. He wasn't worried about anything. He was glad Simone hadn't noticed he was a little late, and that he'd had a big drink. "No, darling. Nothing happened. The end of the week, maybe. Almost the end."

"You feel tired?"

It was like a question from a doctor, routine now. "No. I've got to telephone a customer tonight between eight and nine." It was eight thirty-seven. "I may as well do it now, dear. Maybe I'll have some coffee later."

"Can I go with you?" Georges asked, dropping his fork, sitting back ready to leap out of his chair.

"Not tonight, *mon petit copain*. I'm in a hurry. And you just want to play the pinball machines—I know you."

"Hollywood Chewing Gum!" Georges shouted, pronouncing it in the French manner, "Ollyvoo Schvang Gom!"

Jonathan winced as he lifted his jacket from the hall hook. Hollywood Chewing Gum, whose green and white wrappers littered the gutters and occasionally Jonathan's garden, had mysterious attractions for infants of the French nation. "*Oui*, M'sieur," Jonathan said, and went out the door.

Dr. Périer had a home number in the directory, and Jonathan hoped he was in tonight. A certain *bar-tabac*, which had a telephone, was closer than Jonathan's shop. Panic was taking hold of him, and he began to trot toward the slanting lighted red cylinder that marked the tabac two streets away. He would insist on the truth. Jonathan nodded a greeting to the young man behind the bar, whom he knew slightly, and pointed to the telephone and also to the shelf where the directories lay. "*Fontainebleau!*" Jonathan shouted. The place was noisy, and the jukebox was going. Jonathan searched out the number and dialed.

Dr. Périer answered and recognized Jonathan's voice.

"I would like to have another test. Even tonight. Now—if you could take a sample."

"Tonight?"

"I could come to see you at once. In five minutes."

"Are you—You are weak?"

"Well—I thought if the test went to Paris tomorrow—" Jonathan knew that Dr. Périer was in the habit of sending various samples to Paris on Saturday mornings. "If you could take a sample either tonight or early tomorrow morning—"

"I am not in my office tomorrow morning. I have visits to make. If you are so upset, M. Trevanny, come to my house now."

Jonathan paid for his call, and remembered just before he went out the door to buy two packages of Hollywood Chewing Gum. Périer lived way over on the Boulevard Maginot, which would take nearly ten minutes. Jonathan trotted and walked. He had never been to the doctor's house.

It was a big, gloomy building, and the concierge was an old, slow, skinny woman who was watching television in a little glass-enclosed room full of plastic plants.

While Jonathan waited for the lift to descend into the rickety cage, the concierge crept into the hall and asked curiously, "Your wife is having a baby, M'sieur?"

"No. No," Jonathan said, smiling, and recalled that Dr. Périer was a general practitioner.

He rode up.

"Now what is the matter?" Dr. Périer asked, beckoning him through the dining room. "Come into this room."

The apartment was dimly lighted. The television set was on somewhere. The room they went into was like a little office, with medical books on the shelves, and a desk on which the doctor's black bag now sat.

"*Mon Dieu,* one would think you are on the brink of collapse. You've just been running, obviously, and your cheeks are pink. Don't tell me you've heard another rumor that you're on the edge of the grave!"

Jonathan made an effort to sound calm. "It's just that I want to be sure. I don't feel so splendid, to tell the truth. I know it's been only two months since the last test but—since the next is due the end of April, what's the harm—" He broke off, shrugging. "Since it's easy to take some marrow, and since it can go off tomorrow early—" Jonathan was aware that his French was clumsy at that moment, aware of the word *moelle,* marrow, which had become revolting, especially when Jonathan thought of his as being abnormally yellow. He sensed Dr. Périer's attitude of humoring his patient.

"Yes, I can take the sample. The result will probably be the same as last time. You can never have complete assurance from medical men, M. Trevanny. . . ." The doctor continued to talk while Jonathan removed his sweater, obeyed Dr. Périer's gesture, and lay down on an old leather sofa. The doctor jabbed the anesthetizing needle in. "But I can appreciate your anxiety," Dr. Périer said seconds later, pressing and tapping on the tube that was going into Jonathan's sternum.

Jonathan disliked the crunching sound of it, but found the slight pain quite bearable. This time, perhaps, he'd learn something. Jonathan could not refrain from saying before he left, "I must know the truth, Dr. Périer. You don't think that the laboratory might not be giving us a proper summing up? I'm ready to believe their *figures* are correct—"

"This summing up or prediction is what you can't get, my dear young man!"

Jonathan then walked home. He thought of telling Simone that he'd gone to see Périer, that he again felt anxious, but he couldn't: he'd put Simone through enough. What could she say if he told her? She would only become a little more anxious herself.

Georges was already in bed upstairs, and Simone was reading to him. Asterix again. Georges, propped against his pillows, and Simone, on a low stool under the lamplight, were like a *tableau vivant* of domesticity. The year might have been 1880, Jonathan thought, except for Simone's slacks. Georges's hair was as yellow as corn silk under the light.

"Le schvang gom?" Georges asked, grinning.

Jonathan smiled and produced one packet. The other could wait for another occasion.

"You were gone a long time," said Simone.

"I had a beer at the café," Jonathan said.

The next afternoon between four-thirty and five, as Dr. Périer had told him to do, Jonathan telephoned the Ebberle-Valent Laboratoires in Neuilly. He gave his name and spelled it and said he was a patient of Dr. Périer's in Fontainebleau. Then he waited to be connected with the right department, while the telephone gave a *blup* every minute for the pay units. Jonathan had pen and paper ready. Could he spell his name again, please? Then a woman's voice began to read the report, and Jonathan jotted figures down quickly. Hyperleukocytose 190,000. Wasn't that bigger than before?

"We shall, of course, send a written report to your doctor, which he should receive by Tuesday."

"This report is less favorable than the last, is it not?"

"I have not the previous report here, M'sieur."

"Is there a doctor there? Could I speak with a doctor, perhaps?"

"I am a doctor, M'sieur."

"Oh. Then this report—whether you have the old one or not—is not a good one, is it?"

Like a textbook, she said, "This is a potentially dangerous condition involving lowered resistance. . . ."

Jonathan had telephoned from his shop. He had turned his sign to FERMÉ and drawn his door curtain, though he had been visible through the window. Now, as he went to remove the sign, he realized he hadn't locked his door. Since no one else was due to call for a picture that afternoon, Jonathan thought he could afford to close. It was five to five.

He walked to Dr. Périer's office, prepared to wait more than an hour if he had to. Saturday was a busy day, because most people didn't work and were free to see the doctor. There were three people ahead of Jonathan, but the nurse asked if he would be long, Jonathan said no, and the nurse squeezed him in with an apology to the next patient. Had Dr. Périer spoken to his nurse about him? Jonathan wondered.

Dr. Périer raised his black eyebrows at Jonathan's scribbled notes, and said, "But this is incomplete."

"I know, but it tells something, doesn't it? It's slightly worse—isn't it?"

"One would think you want to get worse!" Dr. Périer said with his customary cheer, which now Jonathan mistrusted. "Frankly, yes, it is worse, but only a little worse. It is not crucial."

"In percentage—ten percent worse, would you say?"

"M. Trevanny, you are not an automobile! Now, it is not reasonable for me to make a remark until I get the full report Tuesday."

Jonathan walked homeward rather slowly, walked through the Rue des Sablons just in case he saw someone who wanted to go into his shop. There wasn't anyone. Only the launderette was doing a brisk business. People with bundles of laundry were bumping into each other at the door. It was nearly six. Simone would be quitting the shoe shop sometime after seven, later than usual, because Brezard wanted to take in every franc possible before closing for Sunday and Monday. And Wister was still at L'Aigle Noir. Was he only waiting for him, waiting for him to change his mind and say yes? Wouldn't it be funny if Dr. Périer was in conspiracy with Stephen Wister, if between them they might have fixed the Ebberle-Valent Laboratoires to give him a bad report? And if Gauthier were in on it, too, the little messenger of bad tidings? Like a nightmare in which the strangest elements join forces against—against the dreamer. But Jonathan knew he wasn't dreaming. He knew that Dr. Périer wasn't in the pay of Stephen Wister. Nor was Ebberle-Valent. And it was not a dream that his condition was worse, that death was a little closer, or sooner, than he had thought. It was, however, true of everyone who lived one more day, Jonathan reminded himself. Jonathan thought of death, and the process of aging, as a decline, literally a downward path. Most people had a chance to take it slowly, starting at fifty-five or whenever they slowed up, descending until seventy or whatever year was their number. Jonathan realized that his death was going to be like falling over a cliff. When he tried to "prepare" himself, his mind wavered and dodged. His attitude, or his spirit, was still thirty-four years old and wanted to live.

The Trevannys' narrow house, blue-gray in the dusk, showed no lights. It was a rather somber house, and that fact had amused Jonathan and Simone when they had bought it five years ago. "The Sherlock Holmes house," Jonathan used to call it when they were debating against another in Fontainebleau. "I still prefer the Sherlock Holmes house," Jonathan remembered saying once. The house had an 1890 air, suggestive of gaslights and polished banisters, though none of the wood anywhere had been polished when they moved in. The house had looked as if it could be made into something with turn-of-the-century charm, however. The rooms were small but interestingly arranged, the garden a rectangular patch full of wildly overgrown rosebushes, but at least the rosebushes were there, and all the garden had needed was a clearing out. And the scalloped glass portico over the back steps, its little glass-enclosed porch, had made Jonathan think of Vuillard, Bonnard. Now it struck Jonathan that five years of occupancy hadn't really defeated the gloom. New wallpaper would brighten the bedroom, yes, but that was only one room. The house wasn't yet paid for: they had three more years to go on the mortgage. An apartment such as they'd had in the first year of their marriage would have been cheaper, but Simone was used to a house with a bit of garden—she'd had a garden all her life in Nemours—and as an Englishman, Jonathan liked a bit of garden, too. He had never regretted that the house took such a hunk of their income.

What Jonathan was thinking of as he climbed the front steps was not so much the remaining mortgage but the fact that he was probably going to die in this house. More than likely, he would never know another, more cheerful house with Simone. He was thinking that the Sherlock Holmes house had been standing for decades before he had been born, and that it would stand for decades after his death. It had been his fate to choose this house, he felt. One day they would carry him out feet first, maybe still alive but dying, and he would never enter the house again.

To Jonathan's surprise, Simone was in the kitchen playing some kind of card game with Georges. She looked up, smiling; then Jonathan saw her remember: the Paris laboratory this afternoon. He had told her he was going to call, to try to speak to Moussu again. But she couldn't mention that in front of Georges.

"The old creep closed early today," Simone said. "No business."

"Good!" Jonathan said brightly. "What goes on in this gambling den?"

"I'm winning!" Georges said in French.

Simone got up and followed Jonathan into the hall as he hung his raincoat. She looked at him inquiringly.

"Nothing to worry about," Jonathan said, but she beckoned him farther down the hall to the living room. "It seems to be a trifle worse, but I don't feel worse, so what the hell? I'm sick of it. Let's have a Cinzano."

"You were worried because of that story, weren't you, Jon?"

"Yes. That's true."

"I wish I knew who started it." Her eyes narrowed bitterly. "It's a nasty story. Gauthier never told you who said it?"

"No. As Gauthier said, there was some mistake somewhere, some kind of exaggeration." Jonathan was repeating what he had said to Simone before. But he knew it was no mistake, that it was a quite calculated story.

5

Jonathan stood at the first floor bedroom window, watching Simone hang the wash on the garden line. There were pillowcases, Georges's sleep suits, a dozen pairs of Georges's and Jonathan's socks, two white nightdresses, bras, Jonathan's beige work trousers—everything except sheets, which Simone sent to the laundry, because well-ironed sheets were important to her. Simone wore tweed slacks and a thin red sweater that clung to her body. Her back looked strong and supple as she bent over the big oval basket, pegging out dish-cloths now. It was a fine, sunny morning with a hint of summer in the breeze.

Jonathan had wriggled out of going to Nemours to have lunch with Simone's parents, the Foussadiers. He and Simone went every other Sunday as a rule. Unless Simone's brother Gérard fetched them, they took the bus to Nemours. Then, at the Foussadiers' house, they had a big lunch with Gérard and his wife and two children, who also lived in Nemours. Simone's parents always made a fuss over Georges, always had a present for him. Around three, Simone's father, Jean-Noël, would turn on the TV. Jonathan was frequently bored, but he went with Simone because it was the correct thing to do, and because he respected the closeness of French families.

"Do you feel all right?" Simone had asked when Jonathan had begged off.

"Yes, darling. It's just that I'm not in the mood today, and I'd also like to get that patch ready for the tomatoes. So why don't you go with Georges?"

So Simone and Georges went on the bus at noon. Simone had put the remains of a boeuf bourguignon into a small red casserole on the stove, and all Jonathan had to do was heat it when he felt hungry.

Jonathan had wanted to be alone. He was thinking about the mysterious Stephen Wister and his proposal. Jonathan was very much aware that Wister was still there, at L'Aigle Noir, not three hundred yards away. He certainly had no intention of getting in touch with Wister, though the idea was curiously exciting and disturbing, a bolt from the blue, a shaft of color in his uneventful existence, and he wanted to observe it—to enjoy it, in a sense. Jonathan also had the feeling (it had been proved quite often) that Simone could read his thoughts, or at least knew when something was preoccupying him. If he appeared absentminded that Sunday, he didn't want Simone to notice it and ask him what was the matter. So Jonathan gardened with a will, and daydreamed. He thought of forty thousand pounds, a sum which meant the mortgage could be paid off at once, a couple of installment items taken care of, the interior of their house painted where it needed it, a television set acquired, a nest egg put aside for Georges's university, a few new clothes for Simone and himself—ah, mental ease! Simply freedom from anxiety! He thought of one—maybe two Mafia figures—burly, dark-haired thugs exploding in death, arms flailing, their bodies falling. What Jonathan was incapable of imagining, as his spade sank into the earth of his garden, was himself pulling a trigger, having aimed a gun at a man's back, perhaps. More interesting, more mysterious, more dangerous was how Wister had got hold of his name. There was a plot against him in Fontainebleau, and it had somehow got to Hamburg. Impossible that Wister had him mixed up with someone else, because even Wister had spoken of his illness, of his wife and small son. Someone, Jonathan thought, whom he considered a friend, or at least a friendly acquaintance, was not friendly at all toward him.

Wister would probably leave Fontainebleau around five this afternoon, Jonathan thought. By three, Jonathan had eaten his lunch, and had tidied up papers and old receipts in the catchall drawer of the round table in the center of the living room. Then— he was happily aware that he was not tired at all—he tackled with broom and dustpan the exterior of the pipes and the floor around their oil furnace.

A little after five, as Jonathan was scrubbing soot from his hands at the kitchen sink, Simone arrived with Georges, her brother Gérard, and his wife Yvonne, and they all had a drink in the kitchen. Georges had been presented by his grandparents with a round box of Easter goodies, including an egg wrapped in gold foil, a chocolate rabbit, and colored gumdrops—all under yellow cellophane and as yet unopened because Simone had forbade him to open it, in view of the other sweets he had eaten in Nemours. Georges went with the Foussadier children into the garden.

"Don't step on the soft part, Georges!" Jonathan shouted. He had raked the turned ground smooth, but left the pebbles for Georges to pick up. Georges would probably get his two friends to help him fill the red wagon. Jonathan gave him fifty centimes for a wagonful of pebbles—not ever full, but full enough to cover the bottom.

It was starting to rain. Jonathan had brought the laundry in a few minutes ago.

"The garden looks marvelous!" Simone said. "Look, Gérard!" She beckoned her brother onto the little back porch.

By now, Jonathan thought, Wister was probably on a train from Fontainebleau to Paris, or maybe he'd taken a taxi from

Fontainebleau to Orly, considering the money he seemed to have. Maybe he was already in the air, en route to Hamburg. Simone's presence, the voices of Gérard and Yvonne seemed to erase Wister from the Hôtel de L'Aigle Noir, seemed to turn Wister almost into a quirk of Jonathan's imagination. Jonathan felt a mild triumph in the fact that he had not telephoned Wister, as if by not telephoning him he had successfully resisted some kind of temptation.

Gérard Foussadier, an electrician, was a neat, serious man a little older than Simone, with fairer hair than hers, and a carefully clipped brown mustache. His hobby was naval history, and he made model nineteenth-century and eighteenth-century frigates in which he installed miniature electric lights that he could put completely or partially on by a switch in his living room. Gérard himself laughed at the anachronism of electric lights in his frigates, but the effect was beautiful when all the other lights in the house were turned out and eight or ten ships seemed to be sailing on a dark sea around the living room.

"Simone said you were a little worried—as to your health, Jon," Gérard said earnestly. "I am sorry."

"Not particularly. Just another checkup," Jonathan said. "The report's about the same." Jonathan was used to these clichés, which were like saying, "Very well, thank you," when someone asked you how you felt. What Jonathan said seemed to satisfy Gérard, so evidently Simone had not said much.

Yvonne and Simone were talking about linoleum. The kitchen linoleum was wearing out in front of the stove and the sink. It hadn't been new when they bought the house.

"You're really feeling all right, darling?" Simone asked Jonathan when the Foussadiers had left.

"Better than all right. I even attacked the boiler room. The soot." Jonathan smiled.

"You are mad. . . . Tonight you'll have a decent dinner, at least. Mama insisted that I bring home three *paupiettes* from lunch and they're delicious!"

Then close to eleven, as they were about to go to bed, Jonathan felt a sudden depression, as if his legs, his whole body had sunk into something viscous, as if he were walking hip-deep in mud. Was he simply tired? But it seemed more mental than physical. He was glad when the light was turned out, when he could relax with his arms around Simone, her arms around him, as they always lay when they fell asleep. He thought of Stephen Wister (was that his real name?) maybe flying eastward now, his thin figure stretched out in an airplane seat. Jonathan imagined Wister's face with the pinkish scar, puzzled, tense; but Wister would no longer be thinking of Jonathan Trevanny. He'd be thinking of someone else. He must have two or three more prospects, Jonathan thought.

The morning was chill and foggy. Just after eight, Simone went off with Georges to the École Maternelle, and Jonathan stood in the kitchen, warming his fingers on a second bowl of café au lait. The heating system wasn't adequate. They'd got rather uncomfortably through another winter, and even now in spring the house was chilly in the morning. The furnace had been in the house when they bought it, adequate for the five radiators downstairs, but not for the other five upstairs which they had hopefully installed. They'd been warned, Jonathan remembered, but a bigger furnace would have cost three thousand new francs, and they hadn't had the money.

Three letters had fallen through the slot in the front door. One was an electricity bill. Jonathan turned a square white envelope over and saw "Hôtel de L'Aigle Noir" on its back. He opened the envelope. A business card fell out and dropped. Jonathan picked it up and read "Stephen Wister *chez*," which had been written above:

> REEVES MINOT
> 159 AGNESSTRASSE
> WINTERHUDE (ALSTER)
> HAMBURG 56
> 629–6757

There was also a letter.

April 1st

Dear Mr. Trevanny,

I was sorry not to hear from you this morning, or so far this afternoon. In case you change your mind, I enclose a card with my address in Hamburg. If you have second thoughts about my proposition, please telephone me collect at any hour. Or come to talk to me in Hamburg. Your round-trip transportation can be wired to you at once if I hear from you. In fact, wouldn't it be a good idea to see a Hamburg specialist about your blood condition and get another opinion? This might make you feel more comfortable.

I am returning to Hamburg Sunday night.

Yours sincerely,

Stephen Wister

Jonathan was surprised, amused, annoyed all at once. *More comfortable.* That was a bit funny, since Wister was sure he was going to die soon. If a Hamburg specialist said, "*Ach, ja,* you have just one or two more months," would that make him feel more comfortable? Jonathan pushed the letter and the card into a back pocket of his trousers. A return trip to Hamburg gratis. Wister was thinking of every enticement. Interesting that he'd sent the letter Saturday afternoon, so that he would receive it early Monday, though Jonathan might have rung him at any time Sunday. There was no mailbox collection on Sunday.

It was 8:52 A.M. Jonathan thought of what he had to do. He needed more mat paper from a firm in Melun. There were at least two clients he should write a postcard to, because their pictures had been ready for more than a week. Jonathan usually went to his shop on Mondays and spent his time doing odds and ends, though the shop was not open since it was against French law to be open six days a week.

Jonathan got to his shop at nine-fifteen, drew the green shade of the door, and locked the door again, leaving the FERMÉ sign on it. He puttered about, still thinking about Hamburg. The opinion of a German specialist might be a good thing. Suppose he accepted Wister's offer of a round trip? (Jonathan was copying an address onto a postcard.) But then he'd be beholden to Wister. Jonathan realized he was toying with the idea of killing someone for Wister—not for Wister, but for the money. A Mafia member. They were all criminals themselves, weren't they? Of course, Jonathan reminded himself, he could always pay Wister back if he accepted his round-trip fare. The point was, Jonathan couldn't pay for the trip himself just now; there wasn't enough money in the bank. If he really wanted to make sure of his condition, Germany (or Switzerland, for that matter) could tell him. They still had the best doctors in the world, hadn't they? Jonathan put the card of the paper supplier of Melun beside his telephone to remind him to call tomorrow, because the paper place wasn't open today either. And who knew, mightn't Stephen Wister's proposal be feasible? For an instant, Jonathan saw himself blown to bits by the crossfire of German police officers: they'd caught him just after he fired on the Italian. But even if he was dead, Simone and Georges would get the forty thousand quid. Jonathan came back to reality. He wasn't going to kill anybody, no. But Hamburg—going to Hamburg seemed a lark, a break, even if he learned some bad news. He'd learn *facts*, anyway. And if Wister paid now, Jonathan could pay him back in a matter of three months, if he scrimped, didn't buy any clothes—not even a beer in a café. Jonathan rather dreaded telling Simone, though she'd agree, of course, since it had to do with seeing another doctor, presumably an excellent doctor. The scrimping would come out of Jonathan's own pocket.

Around eleven, Jonathan put in a call to Wister's number in Hamburg, direct, not collect. Three or four minutes later, his telephone rang, and Jonathan had a clear connection, much better than the one to Paris usually sounded.

". . . Yes, this is Wister," Wister said, in his light, tense voice.

"I had your letter this morning," Jonathan began. "The idea of going to Hamburg—"

"Yes, why not?" said Wister casually.

"But I mean the idea of seeing a specialist—"

"I'll cable you the money right away. You can pick it up at the Fontainebleau post office. It should be there in a couple of hours."

"That's—that's kind of you. Once I'm there, I can—"

"Can you come today? This evening? There's room here for you to stay."

"I don't know about today." And yet why not?

"Call me again when you've got your ticket. Tell me what time you're coming in. I'll be in all day."

Jonathan's heart was beating a little fast when he hung up.

At home during lunchtime, Jonathan went upstairs to the bedroom to see if his suitcase was handy. It was, on top of the wardrobe where it had been since their last holiday, nearly a year ago, in Arles.

He said to Simone, "Darling, something important. I've decided to go to Hamburg and see a specialist."

"Oh, yes? . . . Périer suggested it?"

"Well—in fact, no. My idea. I wouldn't mind having a German doctor's opinion. I know it's an expense."

"Oh, Jon! Expense! . . . Did you have any news this morning? The laboratory report comes tomorrow, doesn't it?"

"Yes. What they say is always the same, darling. I want a fresh opinion."

"When do you want to go?"

"Soon. This week."

Just before five, Jonathan called at the Fontainebleau post office. The money had arrived. Jonathan presented his *carte d'identité* and received six hundred francs. He went from the post office to the Syndicate d'Initiative in the Avenue Franklin Roosevelt, just a couple of streets away, and bought a round-trip ticket to Hamburg on a plane that left Orly airport at 9:25 P.M. that evening. He would have to hurry, he realized, and he liked that, because it precluded thinking, hesitating. He went to his shop and telephoned Hamburg, this time collect.

Wister again answered. "Oh, that's fine. At eleven fifty-five, right. Take the airport bus to the city terminus, would you? I'll meet you there."

Then Jonathan made a telephone call to a client who had an important picture to pick up, and said that he would be closed Tuesday and Wednesday for "family reasons," a common excuse. He'd have to leave a sign to that effect in his door for a couple of days. Not a very unusual matter, Jonathan thought, since shop-keepers in town frequently closed for a few days for one reason or another. Jonathan had once seen a sign saying, "Closed because of hangover."

Jonathan shut up shop and went home to pack. It would be a two-day stay at most, he thought, unless the Hamburg hospital or whatever insisted that he stay longer for tests. He had checked the trains to Paris, and there was one around 7 P.M. that would do nicely. He had to get to Paris, then to Les Invalides for a bus to Orly. When Simone came home with Georges, Jonathan had his suit-case downstairs.

"Tonight?" Simone said.

"The sooner the better, darling. I had an impulse. I'll be back Wednesday, maybe even tomorrow night."

"But—where can I reach you? You arranged for a hotel?"

"No. I'll have to telegraph you, darling. Don't worry."

"You've got everything arranged with the doctor? Who is the doctor?"

"I don't know yet. I only know the hospital." Jonathan dropped his passport as he tried to stick it into the inside pocket of his jacket.

"I never saw you like this," said Simone.

Jonathan smiled at her. "At least—I'm not collapsing!"

Simone wanted to go with him to the Fontainebleau-Avon station, and take the bus back, but Jonathan begged her not to.

"I'll telegraph right away," Jonathan said.

"Where is Hamburg?" Georges demanded for the second time.

"*Allemagne!* Germany!" Jonathan said.

Jonathan found a taxi in the Rue de France luckily. The train was pulling into the Fontainebleau-Avon station as he arrived, and he barely had time to buy his ticket and hop on. He took a taxi from the Gare de Lyon to Les Invalides. Jonathan had some money left from the six hundred francs. For a while, he was not going to worry about money.

On the plane, he half slept, with a magazine in his lap. He was imagining being another person. The rush of the plane seemed to be rushing this new person away from the man left behind in the dark gray house in the Rue Saint-Merry. He imagined another Jonathan helping Simone with the dishes at this moment, chatting about boring things such as the price of linoleum for the kitchen floor.

The plane touched down. The air was sharp and much colder. There was a long lighted speedway, then the city's streets, massive buildings looming up into the night sky, streetlights of different color and shape from those of France.

And there was Wister smiling, walking toward him with his right hand extended. "Welcome, Mr. Trevanny! Have a good trip? . . . My car is just outside. Hope you didn't mind coming to the terminus. My driver—not my driver but one I use sometimes— was tied up till just a few minutes ago."

They were walking out to the curb. Wister droned on in his American accent. Except for his scar, nothing about Wister suggested violence. He was, Jonathan decided, overly calm, which from a psychiatric point of view might be ominous. Or was he merely nursing an ulcer? Wister stopped beside a well-polished black Mercedes-Benz. An older man, wearing no cap, took care of Jonathan's medium-sized suitcase and held the door for him and Wister.

"This is Karl," Wister said.

"Evening," Jonathan said.

Karl smiled, and murmured something in German.

It was quite a long drive. Wister pointed out the Rathaus, "the oldest in all Europe, and the bombs didn't get it," and a great church or cathedral whose name Jonathan didn't catch. He and Wister were sitting together in the back. They entered a part of town with a more country-like atmosphere, went over a bridge, and onto a darker road.

"Here we are," Wister said. "My place."

The car had turned onto a climbing driveway and stopped beside a large house with a few lighted windows and a lighted, well-kept entrance.

"It's an old house with four flats, and I have one," Wister explained. "Lots of such houses in Hamburg. Reconverted. Here I have a nice view of the Alster. It's the Aussenalster, the big one. You'll see more tomorrow."

They rode up in a modern lift, Karl taking Jonathan's suitcase. Karl pressed a bell, and a middle-aged woman in a black dress and white apron opened the door, smiling.

"This is Gaby," said Wister to Jonathan. "My part-time house-keeper. She works for another family in the house and sleeps with them, but I told her we might want some food tonight. Gaby, Herr Trevanny *aus Frankreich*."

The woman greeted Jonathan pleasantly and took his coat. She had a round, pudding-like face, and looked the soul of good will.

"Wash up in here, if you like," said Wister, gesturing to a bathroom whose light was already on. "I'll get you a Scotch. Are you hungry?"

When Jonathan came out of the bathroom, the lights—four lamps—were on in the big square living room. Wister was sitting on a green sofa, smoking a cigar. Two Scotches stood on the coffee table in front of him. Gaby came in at once with a tray of sand-wiches and a round pale yellow cheese.

"Ah, thank you, Gaby." Wister said to Jonathan, "It's late for Gaby, but when I told her I had a guest coming, she insisted on staying up to serve the sandwiches." Wister, though making a cheerful remark, didn't smile. In fact his straight eyebrows drew together anxiously as Gaby arranged the plates and the silverware.

When she departed, he said, "You're feeling all right? Now, the main thing is—the visit to the specialist. I have a good man in mind, Dr. Heinrich Wentzel, a hematologist at the Eppendorfer Krankenhaus, which is the principal hospital here. World famous. I've made an appointment for you for tomorrow at two, if that's agreeable."

"Certainly. Thank you," Jonathan said.

"That gives you a chance to catch up on your sleep. Your wife didn't mind your taking off on such short notice, I hope? . . . After all, it's only intelligent to consult more than one doctor about a serious ailment."

Jonathan felt a bit dazed, and he was also distracted by the décor, by the fact that it was all supposed to be *German*, and that it was the first time he'd been in Germany. The furnishings were quite conventional and more modern than antique, though there was a handsome Biedermeier desk against the wall opposite Jonathan. There were low bookshelves along all the walls, long green curtains at the windows, and the lamps in the corners spread the light pleasantly. A purple wooden box lay open on the glass coffee table, presenting a variety of cigars and cigarettes in compartments. The white fireplace had brass accessories, but there was no fire now. A rather interesting painting that looked like a Derwatt hung over the fireplace. And where was Reeves Minot? Wister was Minot, Jonathan supposed. Was Wister going to announce this, or assume that Jonathan realized it? It occurred to Jonathan that he and Simone ought to paint or paper their whole house white. He should discourage the idea of the art-nouveau wallpaper in the bedroom. If they wanted to achieve more light, white was the logical—

". . . You might've given some thought to the other proposition," Wister was saying, in his soft voice. "The idea I was talking about in Fontainebleau."

"I'm afraid I haven't changed my mind about that," Jonathan said. "And so this leads to—obviously I owe you six hundred francs." Jonathan forced a smile. Already he felt the Scotch, and as soon as he realized this, he nervously drank a little more from his glass. "I can repay you within three months. The specialist is the essential thing for me now. . . . First things first."

"Of course," said Wister. "And you mustn't think about repayment. That's absurd."

Jonathan didn't want to argue, but he felt vaguely ashamed. More than anything, Jonathan felt odd, as if he were dreaming, or somehow not himself. It's only the foreignness of everything, he thought.

"This Italian we want eliminated," Wister said, folding his hands behind his head and looking up at the ceiling, "has a routine job. Ha! That's funny! He only makes out that it's a regular job with regular hours. He hangs around the clubs off the Reeperbahn, pretending he has a taste for gambling, just as he's pretending he's an oenologist. I'm sure he has a friend at the—whatever they call the wine factory here. He goes to the wine factory every afternoon, but he spends his evenings in one or another of the private clubs, playing the tables a little and seeing who he can meet. Mornings he sleeps because he's up all night. Now, the point is," Wister said, sitting up, "he takes the U-bahn every afternoon to get home, home being a rented flat. He's got a six-month lease and a real six-month job with the wine place to make it look legitimate. . . . Have a sandwich!" Wister extended the plate as if he had just realized the sandwiches were there.

Jonathan took a tongue sandwich. There was also coleslaw and dill pickle.

"The important point is, he gets off the U-bahn at the Steinstrasse station every day around six-fifteen by himself, looking like any other businessman coming back from the office. That's the time we want to get him." Wister spread his bony hands palm downward. "The assassin fires once if you can get the middle of his back—twice for sure, maybe—drops the gun, and bob's your uncle, as the English say, isn't that right?"

The phrase was indeed familiar, out of the long-ago past. "If it's so easy, why do you need me?" Jonathan managed a polite smile. "I'm an amateur, to say the least. I'd botch it."

Wister might not have heard. "The crowd in the U-bahn *may* be rounded up. Some of them. Who can tell? Thirty, forty people, perhaps, if the cops get there fast enough. It's a huge station, the station for the main railway terminus. They might look people over. But suppose they look you over?" Wister shrugged. "You'll have dropped the gun. You'll have used a thin stocking over your hand, and you'll drop the stocking a few seconds after you fire. No powder marks on you, no fingerprints on the gun. You have no connection with the man who's dead. Oh, it really won't come to all that. But one look at your French identity card, the fact of your appointment with Dr. Wentzel—you're in the clear. My point is—*our* point—we don't want anyone connected with us or the clubs. . . ."

Jonathan listened and made no comment. On the day of the shooting, he was thinking, he would have to be in a hotel, he could hardly be a houseguest of Wister, in case a policeman asked him where he was staying. And what about Karl and the housekeeper? Did they know anything about this? Were they trustworthy? It's all a lot of nonsense, Jonathan thought, and wanted to smile, but he wasn't smiling.

"You're tired," Wister informed him. "Want to see your room? Gaby already took your suitcase in."

Fifteen minutes later, Jonathan was in pajamas after a hot shower. His room had a window on the front of the house like the living room, which had two windows on the front, and Jonathan looked out on a body of water with white lights along the near shore, and some red and green from the tied-up boats. It looked dark, peaceful, and spacious. A searchlight's beam swept protectively across the sky. His bed was a three-quarter width, neatly turned down. There was a glass of what looked like water on his bed table and a package of Gitanes maize, his brand, and an ashtray and matches. Jonathan took a sip from the glass and found that it was indeed water.

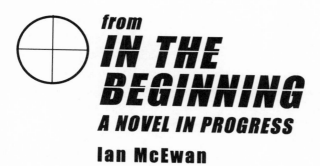

from
IN THE BEGINNING
A NOVEL IN PROGRESS
Ian McEwan

I arrived ten minutes late. The place was doing good lunchtime business. Conversation was at a roar, and stepping in from the street was like walking into a storm. You could imagine a single topic—an hour later, there would be. The professor was already seated, but Clarissa was on her feet, and I knew from across the room that she was in the mood for a fuss. A waiter was on his knees, praying style, wedging a table leg. Another was arranging a cushion on her chair to bring her up to height. When she saw me, she came skipping through the din and took my hand and led me to the table as though I were blind. If only. I associated these skittish impersonations of a child with celebration—and mayhem. And we had some cause to raise a glass. Professor Jocelyn Kale, Clarissa's godfather, had been appointed to an honorary position on the Human Genome Project. Clarissa had delivered her book the week before. I had just come from recording the last of my lectures. Three had been broadcast. Above all, it was Clarissa's birthday.

Before I sat down, I kissed her. Our tongues touched. Jocelyn half rose from his seat and shook my hand. At the same moment, champagne in an ice bucket was brought to the table, and we pitched our voices in with the roar. The ice bucket sat within a rhomboid of sunlight on the white tablecloth. The tall restaurant windows showed off rectangles of blue sky between the buildings. I had a hard-on from the kiss. In memory, it was all success, clarity, clatter. In memory, all the food they brought us first was red: the bresaola, the fat tongues of roasted peppers laid on goat's cheese, the radicchio, the white china bowl of radish coronets. When I think how we leaned in and shouted, I seem to be remembering an underwater event.

Jocelyn took from his pocket a small parcel done up in blue tissue. We drew down an imaginary silence on our table while Clarissa unwrapped it. Perhaps that was when I glanced to my left, at the table next to ours. A man, whose name I now know was Colin Tapp, was with his daughter and his father. Perhaps I noticed them later. Inside the tissue was a black box. Inside the box, on a cumulus of cotton wool, was a golden brooch. Still without speaking, Clarissa lifted it out, and we examined it on her palm.

Two gold bands were entwined in a double helix. Crossing between them were tiny silver rungs in groups of three, representing the base pairs—the four-letter alphabet that coded, in permutating triplets, all living things. Engraved on the helical bands were spherical designs, to suggest the twenty amino acids onto which the three-letter codons were mapped. In the full light gathered from the tabletop, it looked in Clarissa's hand like more than a representation. It could have been the thing itself, ready to cook up chains of amino acids which would be blended into protein molecules. It could have divided right there in her hand to make another gift. When Clarissa sighed Jocelyn's name, the sound of the restaurant surged back on us.

"Oh God, it's beautiful," she said and kissed him.

His weak yellow-blue eyes were moist. He said, "It was Gillian's, you know. She would have loved you to have it."

I was impatient to produce my own present, but we were still in the spell of Jocelyn's. Clarissa pinned the brooch on her gray silk blouse.

Would I remember the conversation now if I did not know what it preceded?

We began by joking that the Genome Project gave away such brooches by the dozen. Then Jocelyn talked about the discovery of DNA. Perhaps that was when I turned in my seat to ask a waiter to bring us water and noticed the two men and the girl. We emptied the champagne, and the antipasto was cleared away. I don't remember what food we ordered after that. Jocelyn began to tell us about Johann Friedrich Miescher, the Swiss chemist who identified DNA, in 1869. This was supposed to be one of the great missed chances in the history of science. Miescher had got himself a steady supply of pus-soaked bandages from a local hospital. (Rich in white blood cells, Jocelyn added for Clarissa's benefit.) Miescher was interested in the chemistry of the cell nucleus. In the nuclei he found phosphorous— an improbable substance, which didn't sit with current ideas. An extraordinary find, but his paper was blocked by his teacher, who spent two years repeating and confirming his student's results.

It was not boredom that let my attention shift, though I knew the Miescher story. It was pleasure. I was pleased with my last lecture, and I'd ridden out the fuss generated by the first three. My *tour d'horizon* of a hundred thousand religions—Neanderthal funerary rites to the leadership cults of certain socialist republics— had dismayed some by its evenhandedness. But anger rose against my assertion that, since religious practice was universal to all known societies, it must have a genetic base and therefore be the product of evolutionary pressure. I invoked E. O. Wilson: "Religions, like all other human institutions, evolve so as to enhance the persistence and influence of their practitioners." The bishops' anathemas, the millennial disgust of politicians and New Agers, a cranky death threat down the phone, the wounded letters to the press demonstrated that we do not live in a secular age. The death threat—a man's voice perhaps, pretending to be a woman's—

simply informed me that a congregation had paid for the hire of my killer. Briefly, I was demonized; I had my fifteen minutes. Then the public mind, like that of some giant, squalling baby, was distracted by a newer, brighter thing. I had survived.

I looked around. At the next table, the girl was being helped through the menu by her father. Like me, he had to slide his glasses down his nose to see the print. The girl leaned fondly against his arm. Would I ever have a child? Was it too late?

Meanwhile, Jocelyn, enjoying the triple privilege of age, eminence, and the bestower of a gift, told his story. Miescher pressed on. He assembled a team and set about working out the chemistry of what he called "nucleic acid." Then he found them, the substances that made up the four-letter alphabet in whose language all life is written—adenine and cytosine, guanine and thymine. But it meant nothing. And that was odd, especially as the years went by. Mendel's work on the laws of inheritance had been generally accepted. Chromosomes had been identified in the cell nucleus and were suspected of being the location of genetic information. Now, thanks to Miescher, it was known that DNA was in the chromosomes, and he had described its chemistry. In 1892, in a letter to his uncle, he had speculated that DNA might code for life, just as an alphabet codes for language and concepts.

"It was staring them in the face," Jocelyn said. "But they couldn't see, they wouldn't see. The problem, of course, was the chemists. . . ."

It was hard work, talking against the din. We waited while he drank his water. The story was for Clarissa, an embellishment on her present. While Jocelyn was resting his voice, there was movement behind me. I was obliged to pull in my chair to let the girl through. She went off in the direction of the lavatories. When I was next aware of her she was back in her seat.

"The chemists, you see. Very powerful, rather grand. The nineteenth had been a good century for them. They had authority, but they were a crusty lot. Take Phoebus Levene at the Rockefeller

Institute. He was absolutely certain that DNA was a boring, irrelevant molecule containing random sequences of those four letters, A, C, G, and T. He dismissed it, and then, in that peculiar human way, this became a matter of faith with him, deep faith. What he knew, he knew, and the molecule was insignificant. None of the younger chaps could get round him. It had to wait for years, until Griffiths's work on bacteria, in the twenties. Which Oswald Avery picked up in New York—Levene was old by then, of course. Oswald's work took forever, right up into the forties. Then Alexander Todd, working in Cambridge on the sugar-phosphate links; then in '52 and '53 Maurice Wilkins and Rosalind Franklin; and then Crick and Watson. You know what poor Rosalind said when they showed her the model they had built of the DNA molecule? She said it was simply too beautiful not to be true."

The accelerated roll call of names and his old chestnut—beauty in science—slowed Jocelyn into speechless reminiscence. He fumbled with his napkin. He was eighty-two. As student or colleague, he had known them all. And Gillian had worked with Crick, after the first great breakthrough, on adaptor molecules. Gillian, like Franklin herself, had died of leukemia.

I was a second or two slow on the uptake, but Jocelyn had lobbed me an excellent cue. I reached under my chair and could not resist the chocolate-box lines: "Beauty is truth, truth beauty. . . ." Clarissa smiled. She must have guessed that after all her labor and triumph she might be getting Keats, but she could not have dreamed of what was now in her hands, in plain brown paper. Even before the wrapping was off she recognized it and squealed. The girl at the next table turned in her seat to stare, until her father tapped her on the arm. Foolscap octavo in drab boards with back label. Condition—poor, foxed, slight water damage. A first edition of his first collection, "Poems," of 1817.

"What presents!" Clarissa said. She stood and put her arms around my neck. "It must have cost you thousands." Then she put her lips to my ear. "You're a bad boy to spend so much money. I'm going to make you fuck me all afternoon."

"Oh, all right," I said. "If it'll make you feel better."

It is a temptation to invent or embellish details about the table next to ours, to force memory to deliver what was never captured. But I did see the man, Colin Tapp, put his hand on his father's arm as he spoke, reassuring him, soothing him. It is also difficult to disentangle what I discovered later from what I sensed at the time. Tapp was in fact two years older than me, his daughter was twelve, and his father seventy-three. I did nothing so deliberate as speculate about their ages. By now my attention was not wandering—our own table was absorbing, we were having fun. But I must have assumed a good deal about the relationships of our neighbors, and done it barely consciously—out of the corner of my eye, wordlessly, in the preverbal language of instant thought that linguists call "mentalese." The prepubescent girl I did take in, however glancingly. She had that straightbacked poise some children adopt, self-possession attempting worldliness and disarmingly revealing its opposite. Her skin was dark, her black hair was cut in a bob, and the skin on her neck was paler than the rest—the haircut was recent. Or were these details I observed later, in the chaos, or in the time after the chaos?

At our table, Clarissa had resumed her seat, and the conversation concerned young men put down or otherwise blocked by older men—their fathers, teachers, mentors, or idols. The starting point had been Miescher and his teacher, Hopper Seyler, who had held up publication of his student's discovery of phosphorous in cell nuclei. Seyler also happened to be the editor of the journal to which Miescher's papers had been submitted. From there—and I've had time to trace our conversation backward—from Miescher and Seyler, we arrived at Keats and Wordsworth.

Clarissa was our main source now, although outside his subject Jocelyn knew a little about most things, and he knew the famous story of the young Keats going to visit the poet he revered. I knew of the visit from Clarissa's researches. In late 1817, Keats had been staying at an inn, the Fox & Hounds, by Box Hill on the North

Downs, where he finished his long poem "Endymion." He stayed on for a week and walked the downs in a daze of contentment. He was just twenty-two, he had written a long, serious, beautiful poem about being in love, and by the time he returned to London he was feeling high. There he heard the news and rejoiced: his hero, William Wordsworth, was in town. Keats had already sent his "Poems," with the inscription "To W. Wordsworth with the Author's sincere Reverence." (That would have been the one to give Clarissa. It's in the Princeton University Library; there are many uncut pages.) Keats had grown up on Wordsworth's poetry. He called "The Excursion" one of the "three things to rejoice at in this Age." He had taken from Wordsworth the idea of poetry as a sacred vocation, the most noble endeavor. Now he persuaded his painter friend Benjamin Robert Haydon to arrange a meeting. They set out together from Haydon's studio at Lisson Grove to walk to Queen Ann Street and call on the great genius. In his journal, Haydon noted that Keats expressed "the greatest, the purest, the most unalloyed pleasure at the prospect."

Wordsworth was a notorious grouch at that stage of his life—he was forty-seven—but he was friendly enough to Keats, and after a few minutes of small talk asked him what he'd been working on. Haydon jumped in and answered for him, and begged Keats to repeat the ode to Pan from "Endymion." So Keats walked up and down in front of the great man, reciting in "his usual half-chant (most touching). . . ."

It was at this point in the story that Clarissa fought the restaurant clamor and quoted:

> Be still the unimaginable lodge
> For solitary thinkings; such as dodge
> Conception to the very bourne of heaven,
> Then leave the naked brain.

And when the passionate young man was done, Wordsworth delivered into the silence his dryly dismissive verdict: "a Very pretty piece of Paganism"—which, according to Haydon, was "unfeeling and unworthy of his high Genius to a young Worshipper like Keats, and Keats felt it *deeply*," and never forgave him.

"But do we trust this story?" Jocelyn said. "Didn't I read somewhere that we shouldn't?"

"We don't." Clarissa counted off the reasons. Haydon wrote his account thirty years later, not long before he went completely mad. He wanted to get at Leigh Hunt, who was putting about his own version of the meeting even though he hadn't been there. By then Haydon also had a grudge against Wordsworth for not lending him money. Haydon didn't mention the story in the diary he kept at the time. Nor did Wordsworth. Keats made no reference to it in his letters, and a couple of weeks later he was reciting his poetry in front of Wordsworth again and eating dinner with him. And how much of an insult was it really? In those days, "pretty" retained the meanings of clever, or skillful, or well-turned. Dorothy wrote, in 1803, about her brother's use of the word getting him into trouble in Scotland.

If I had stood up while Clarissa was telling us this and turned toward the entrance, I would have seen, across half an acre of talking heads, two figures come in and talk to the maître d'. One of the men was tall, but I don't think I took that in. I knew it later, but a trick of memory has given me the image as if I had stood up then: the crowded room, the tall man, the maître d' nodding and gesturing vaguely in our direction. And then what, in fantasy, could I have done to persuade Clarissa and Jocelyn and the strangers at the next table to leave their meals and run with me up the stairs to find, by interconnecting doors, a way down into the street? On a score of sleepless nights I've been back to plead with them to leave. Look, you don't know me, but I know what is about to happen. I'm from a future tainted by grief. It was a mistake, it doesn't have to happen. We could choose another outcome. Put down your knives and forks and follow me, quick! No, really, please trust me. Just trust me. Let's go!

But they do not see or hear me. They go on eating and talking. And so did I.

I said, "But the story lives on. The famous put-down."

"Yes," Jocelyn said eagerly. "It isn't true, but we need it. A kind of myth."

We looked at Clarissa. I may have given the impression that she was the lecturing type, like those academic friends whose conversational style has been corrupted by years of teaching. But she wasn't like that. She may have been crazy now and then, playing tricks with her size, but she wasn't dull. She was reticent about what she knew really well. I once went down on drunken knees at a beach party to get her to recite "La Belle Dame sans Merci" from memory. But today we were celebrating; we were celebrating her, her birthday, her book, and the things she knew.

"It isn't true, but it tells the truth. Wordsworth was arrogant to the point of being loathsome about other writers. Gittings has a good line about his being in the difficult second half of a man's forties. When he got to fifty, he calmed down, brightened up, and everyone around him breathed. A year later, Keats was dead. There's always something delicious about young genius spurned by the powerful. You know, like The Man Who Turned Down the Beatles for Decca. We know that God, in the form of history, will have his revenge. . . ."

The two men were probably making their way between the tables toward us by then. I'm not sure. I have excavated that last half minute and I know two things for sure. One was that the waiter brought us sorbets. The other was that I slipped into a daydream. I often do. Almost by definition, daydreams leave no trace—they really do dodge conception to the very bourne of heaven, then leave the naked brain. But I've been back so many times, and I've retrieved it by remembering what triggered it: Clarissa's *A year later, Keats was dead.*

The words, the memento mori, floated me off. I was briefly gone. I saw them together, Wordsworth, Haydon, and Keats, in a room in Monkhouse's place on Queen Ann Street, and imagined the sum of their every sensation and thought, and all the stuff—the feel of clothes, the creak of chairs and floorboards, the resonance in their chests of their own voices, the little heat of reputation, the fit of their toes in their shoes and the things in their pockets, the separate assumptions about their recent pasts and what they would be doing next, the growing, tottering frame they each carried of where they were in the story of their lives— all this as luminously self-evident as this roaring restaurant, and all *gone.*

What takes a minute to describe took two seconds to experience. I returned, and compensated for my absence by telling a genius-spurned story. A retired-publisher friend had told me that back in the fifties he had turned down a novel called "Strangers from Within." (By then, the visitors must have been ten feet away, right behind our table. I don't think they even saw us.) The point about my friend was that he only discovered his error thirty years later when an old title turned up at the place where he used to work. He hadn't remembered the name on the typescript—he was reading dozens every month—and he did not read the book when it finally appeared. Or at least not at first. The author, William Golding, had renamed it "Lord of the Flies" and had excised the long, boring first chapter that had put my friend off.

I think I was about to draw my resounding conclusion—that time protects us from our worst mistakes—but Clarissa and Jocelyn were not listening. I too had been aware of movement to one side. Now I followed their sight lines and turned. The two men who had stopped by the table next to ours seemed to have suffered burns to the face. Their skin was a lifeless, prosthetic pink, the color of dolls, or of medical plasters—the color of no one's skin. They shared a robotic nullity of expression. Later, we learned about the latex masks, but at the time these men were a shocking sight, even before they acted. The arrival of the waiter with our desserts in stainless-steel bowls was temporarily soothing. Both men wore black coats that gave them a priestly look. There was ceremony in their stillness. The flavor of my sorbet was lime, just to the green side of white. I already had a spoon in my hand but I hadn't used it. Our table was staring shamelessly.

The intruders simply stood and looked down at our neighbors, who in turn looked back, puzzled, waiting. The young girl looked to her father and then back to the men. The older man put down his empty fork and seemed about to speak, but he said nothing. A variety of possibilities unspooled before me at speed: a student stunt; venders; that the man, Colin Tapp, was a doctor or a lawyer, and these were his patients or clients; some new version of the kissogram; crazy members of the family come to embarrass. Around us the lunchtime uproar, which had dipped locally, was back to level. When the taller man drew from his coat a black stick, a wand, I inclined to the kissogram. But who was his companion, now slowly turning to survey the room? He missed our table, it was so close. His eyes, piglike in the artificial skin, never met mine. The tall man, ready to cast his spell, pointed his wand at Colin Tapp.

And Tapp himself was suddenly a second ahead of us all. His face showed what we didn't understand about the spell. His puzzlement, congealed in terror, could not find a word to tell us, because there was no time. The bullet struck through his white shirt at his heart. He was lifted from his chair and smacked against the wall and thrown back down to catch another in the throat. The first high-velocity impact forced a fine spray, a blood mist, across our tablecloth, our desserts, our hands, our sight. My first impulse was simple and self-protective: I did not believe what I was seeing. Clichés are rooted in truth: I did not believe my eyes. Tapp flopped forward across the table. His father did not move, not a muscle in his face moved. As for his daughter, she did the only possible thing—she passed out. Her mind closed down on this atrocity. She slipped sideways in her chair toward Jocelyn, who put out a hand—the instincts of an old sportsman—and, though he could not prevent her fall, he caught her upper arm and saved her head from a bang.

Apart from that, we could not move. Or speak. And the men? They walked away. The tall one tucked the gun and silencer into his coat as he went. They moved swiftly toward the entrance.

Only two tables had witnessed the event. There may have been a scream, and then, for seconds on end, paralysis. Further off, no one heard a thing. The chatter, the chink of cutlery against plates, went stupidly on.

Then I looked at Clarissa. Her face was horribly rouged. She mouthed a single word at me which I did not catch, and if I had I would not have understood its significance. She was looking at me, communicating with a kind of pulsing, pleading silence, pushing me toward a simple fact. And then I got it, it came to me without effort, in the same neural flash of preverbal thought that comprehends relation and structure all at once, that knows the connection between things better than the things themselves. The unimaginable lodge. Our two tables—their composition, the numbers, the sexes, Clarissa's size, our relative ages, my glasses . . .

But I felt nothing. This was in the time before the invention of feeling, before the division of thought, before the panic and the guilt and all the choices. So we sat there, hopeless in shock, while around us the uproar subsided and understanding spread concentrically outward from our silence. Two waiters were hurrying toward us, their faces loopily amazed, and it was only when they reached us, and we began to talk, to blabber, that I learned that Clarissa's word was "telephone." The congregation had wasted its money on the wrong man.

THE ASSASSIN

David Ray

In the dream the assassin keeps forgetting
to do his chore, doing me in, though he has every intention
of keeping his contract. He just keeps dropping asleep, that's all.
He's an unemployed cabdriver, has grown a hobo's beard,
simply can't get it together. But he's got the fee
in hand, dirty crumpled-up cash, and he'll get round to it,
proving that sooner or later he can do something worthwhile.
Sure, he can do something right, give him time. His name is
    Bob.
As soon as he gets this done and gets himself a shave
he'll stand up straight, self-respecting,
stroking his smooth scented chin like a new man.

SHELTER

David Kost

Fade In:

Ext. New Jersey Turnpike Night

Snow lines the highway, as a dark sedan with New York plates veers slowly off at the New Brunswick exit.

Int. Sedan Night

Four tough and deadly serious men ride in the car. They are dressed in dark, expensive suits with black overcoats. SAL, a lean, muscular Italian-American with sharp features and a thin mustache, sits in the passenger seat, watching the town as it drifts by, while BENNIE, the driver, speaks nervously.

BENNIE

Jeez, Sal, I just can't picture you growin' up around here.

SAL

Me neither.

SAL seems far away. He watches solemnly as they roll past a high school and a church. In the back seat DENUNZIO loads a revolver as RICCI dozes.

cut to:

EXT. STREET NIGHT, MOMENTS LATER

SLAM-SLAM-SLAM!, the doors of the dark sedan close almost in unison, as the four men emerge. Their breath fogs, as they survey the quiet snowy street. Christmas lights adorn the tightly spaced row houses, and small apartment buildings.

SAL, the apparent leader, pops open the trunk, handing each man a suspiciously long and narrow box wrapped festively as a Christmas present. Closing the trunk, SAL starts across the street toward a narrow, four-story, brick apartment building. The others follow in tight formation.

At the entrance, SAL motions BENNIE to cover the front, and sends RICCI to the back. SAL and DENUNZIO steel themselves with a glance before heading up into the building.

INT. APT. STAIRWELL NIGHT

SAL and DENUNZIO go through two sets of glass doors, and up the first flight of stairs. They walk shoulder to shoulder, and cradle their packages anxiously. Their steps are almost in sync, and they create an ominous rhythm that echoes all up and down the stairwell.

Halfway across the third-floor landing, SAL halts DENUNZIO, and motions for him to be quiet. SAL listens intently, slowly leaning over the stairwell, looking down. DENUNZIO leans even further, trying to see what is concerning SAL.

Suddenly, SAL steps back, tearing open his package, but almost simultaneously, a shot rings out, and DENUNZIO is knocked up and back from the stairwell. SAL produces a heavy-gauge shotgun from his box, and pins himself to a wall. DENUNZIO falls at SAL's feet, his nose a bloody hole.

There are more shots outside, and voices all over the building. SAL thinks fast, sizing up the landing. There is an apartment door directly across from him, and another at the opposite end of the landing. On the floor above, a door opens, and SAL watches the ceiling as he listens to footsteps overhead. Out a window to his right, he sees three men with shotguns running through the building's narrow parking lot. Guns cock on the floor below. More footsteps above, and SAL has made up his mind. He blasts into the ceiling twice as he runs full bore for the apartment door directly across, lowering his shoulder.

INT. APT. NIGHT

CRASH!, and the door gives way, sending SAL to the ground of the dark and cluttered apartment. He struggles quickly back to his feet, looking around. The place is empty, and SAL kicks the door shut. Looking down out of the living-room window, he sees five men watching his car. He moves quickly toward the bedroom, but something in the kitchen gets his attention. He pulls a large carving knife from the dish rack and pockets it. Entering the bedroom, he locks the door and approaches the window. There is a fire escape leading down into a narrow, empty alley.

EXT. ALLEY NIGHT

Taking the fire escape too fast, SAL slips on the icy steps, and tumbles halfway down. He picks himself up, but before he gets to the next set of stairs, he freezes. Two GUNMEN appear at the rear corner of the building. SAL slowly presses himself against the second-floor window, sinking into shadow till only his fogging breath still shows.

One of the men stays at the corner, while the other walks slowly down the alley, directly beneath SAL. Suddenly, a light goes on in the bedroom behind him. Although the curtains are closed, SAL finds himself fully illuminated and a sitting duck. Keeping his cool, he pulls the kitchen knife from his pocket, holding it by the blade and checking it for balance. His throw is quick and strong, and the knife lands with a thunk in the back of the GUNMAN at the corner.

The wounded GUNMAN drops to the ground, coughing and gasping. His partner runs back to the corner, thinking the knife came from the rear of the building. He positions himself with his back to SAL, and aims his rifle around the corner. He sees nothing, but his wounded ally points weakly up behind him. Slowly he turns his head to see SAL standing at the edge of the fire escape aiming his rifle dead at him. He gulps. BLAM!, the GUNMAN goes down.

The curtain draws suddenly in the window behind SAL. He is startled not just by the movement, but by the near apparition of the hard and weathered BOSS gunman, who aims through the window with a .38 snub-nose, and burns through SAL with eyes like coals. SAL throws himself back over the railing, partly as a desperate escape, and partly out of sheer shock. A shot shatters the window as SAL flips backward, falling one story down, and landing noisily on metal trash cans.

A shot from above bangs wildly, ricocheting down through the steel of the fire escape. SAL struggles painfully to his feet and pins himself to the wall, breathing heavily and straining to see up through the framework. High above, men have followed him out the third-floor window, and are out on the fire escape. They loosen snow that filters down through the stairways and landings, and falls in clumps around SAL.

The BOSS gunman sees the men above and steps away from the window, exiting the room.

Realizing he is holding his side, SAL checks his hand and sees blood. Looking under his coat, he has apparently been grazed or cut by the shattering glass. He is shaken, but not seriously wounded. The men are starting down the fire escape, but SAL is pinned beneath, as he would be an easy target if he ran in either direction.

Men appear at the street end of the alley. SAL quickly squats using the metal trash cans as cover from their pistol fire. He must make a run for the back of the building. Decisively, he grabs a trash can and uses it as a shield as he backs out of the alley firing his shotgun wildly with one hand. Shots ricochet off the can, making strange echoing noises inside. As he reaches the corner, he trips backward over the bodies of the two gunmen he earlier dispatched and spills garbage over them. He rolls around the corner and is out of range.

EXT. REAR OF BUILDING NIGHT

He sprints to the other corner and peeks around looking up the parking lot side of the building, toward the street. The BOSS has just come out, and is yelling something to the men guarding SAL's car. He is unaware of SAL, who has him dead in his sights, but a pull of the trigger produces a meager "click." He is out of ammo. He throws down the weapon in disgust and runs for a low fence behind the building.

EXT. PARKING LOT NIGHT

SAL throws himself over the fence. There is a small hill on the other side sloping down to a vacant, white-blanketed parking lot. SAL tumbles down like an oversized snowball. Pulling himself up, he runs for the street, his overcoat flying behind him. He corners a building just as four rival gunmen get to the fence. Three follow SAL, and the last turns back.

cut to:

EXT. TRAIN OVERPASS NIGHT

A commuter train rattles noisily overhead, casting moving shadows on SAL who pauses trying to catch his breath. He looks around a corner, back in the direction he just came. The three gunmen are a few hundred yards behind, following his tracks in the virgin snow. He continues running.

cut to:

INT. APT. STAIRWELL NIGHT

The gunman from the fence, DOM, rushes past two men struggling to carry a body through the double-glass doors. The BOSS holds the inner door open for them.

DOM

(Out of breath)

The last one's givin' us a run, Boss, but I got three men on him. I don't think he'll get far.

The BOSS regards the body as it passes.

> BOSS
> *(growling at Dom)*
> I want everybody on the street . . .

cut to:

EXT. STREET NIGHT

SAL is in a more affluent neighborhood. The homes are larger, more spaced out, and more elaborately decorated. He is sauntering along where the snow has already been disturbed by numerous footsteps. He seems to have put a comfortable distance on his pursuers. Not too far away, CAROLERS sing "Silent night." He jogs across the street, stopping at two large granite pillars that mark the entrance to a cul-de-sac. There is something clearly familiar to SAL about these landmarks. He lights a cigarette, taking long calming drags, and glances up the cul-de-sac. The footsteps he's been following belong to a group of CAROLERS who sing in front of a large colonial home.

As they finish their song, they move on, and SAL approaches the large colonial. He stares at the place. He seems uncertain, nervous. The CAROLERS begin again, farther up the cul-de-sac. SAL takes a couple steps up the walkway and stops. Realizing how disheveled he is, he tries to straighten himself up. He pulls off his gloves, smooths down his black hair, and fixes his tie. Noticing that blood has soaked through to his right hand, he squats and scrubs his hand in the snow. Rising again, he looks back the way he came as if looking for some other route. There is none. He steels himself, straightens his overcoat, and walks to the porch.

EXT. PORCH NIGHT

SAL rings the bell, and savors one last drag before flicking away his cigarette. MRS. DOWNEY, a middle-aged woman with expensive beauty parlor looks answers the door.

> MRS. DOWNEY
> Yes? May I help you?

SAL smiles a broad "Eddie Haskel" smile.

SAL

Hello, Mrs. Downey.

MRS. DOWNEY's expression melts slowly into a grand smile.

MRS. DOWNEY

Salvatore? Oh my gosh—Salvatore!
> *(yelling back into the house)*

It's Salvatore. Salvatore Vaccionne. Do you believe it?
> *(back to Sal)*

Oh! I just can't believe it. Look at you. You look wonderful. You must be doing well. Come in, Come in, wait till
Bobby sees you.

INT. DOWNEY HOUSE DAY

SAL steps in closing the door. He seems slightly nervous, not
knowing what to do with his hands. MRS. DOWNEY yells upstairs.

MRS. DOWNEY

Bobby! . . . Bobby! . . . come down here. You won't believe who's here.

In the dining room adjoining the entry hall, Bobby's father and
brothers sit at the immaculately set holiday table. Her younger
brother, TED, smiles broadly and makes a waving gesture, while MR.
DOWNEY and JACK, her older brother, regard him with considerably
less enthusiasm. All are dressed in sweaters and ties. SAL smiles
weakly at them.

MRS. DOWNEY

Well what on earth brings you here, Salvatore?
> *(answering herself)*

You were with those carolers, weren't you? —How sweet!

SAL

Well—sort of, actually I was in town . . . uh . . . visiting
some friends, and . . .

He stops midsentence, when he sees BOBBY coming down the
stairs. She stops on the stairway, as soon as she sees SAL. She is SAL's
age, but she is still beautiful in a youthful way.

BOBBY
(to herself)

Sal . . .

They stare at each other a long moment, before BOBBY recovers,
stepping down to SAL. She takes both his hands and smiles
brightly at him. He returns the smile awkwardly, and she em-
braces him.

BOBBY

Sal, God it's great to see you.

SAL is slow to return the embrace, he is unnerved by the rest of her
family watching. JACK turns to TED shaking his head.

JACK
(under his breath)

I wonder what he wants.

TED returns him a dirty look. MRS. DOWNEY beams, watching the
couple, then turns to speak to JACK and TED.

MRS. DOWNEY

Don't just sit there, set an extra place for Salvatore.

SAL and BOBBY separate.

SAL

Oh no, I don't wanna impose, please.

MRS. DOWNEY

Don't be silly, we'd love to catch up with you.

JACK is displeased, he looks to MR. DOWNEY for support. MR. DOWNEY returns a shrug of pained resignation.

> SAL
> I just stopped by to . . . I mean, I was just in the area. I didn't mean to bust up your nice dinner here.

> BOBBY
> *(quietly to Sal)*
> Please, Sal, don't run, it's been so long.

SAL smiles, giving in.

cut to:

INT. APT. STAIRWELL NIGHT

The BOSS is loading his .38 as he exits the apartment that SAL broke through. DOM is waiting in the hallway.

> BOSS
> What?

DOM nods toward BENNIE who is kneeling at DENUNZIO's corpse.

> BENNIE
> The guy you're lookin' for grew up in this town.

A single drop of blood lands on the BOSS's forehead. They all look overhead seeing where SAL shot before busting down the door. He obviously got lucky, as blood now gathers around the splintery holes. The BOSS seethes silently as he dabs his forehead with DOM's kerchief.

> BOSS
> You get paid when this guy's dead.

The BOSS exits, not turning back. DOM follows.

                    BENNIE
Hey, I did my part.

                    (to himself)
Can't trust no one.

cut to:

INT. DOWNEY HOUSE NIGHT

SAL is in the study, directly across the entry hall from the dining room. The study is dominated by a large Christmas tree, whose lights flash on and off. SAL, popping a cigarette in his mouth, shields the phone from the open door, through which we can see BOBBY joining her brothers, as they set an extra place, and bring out food. A gruff voice comes on the phone.

                    VOICE OF CALABRESE
Hello, you have reached the Calabrese residence. Sorry, but no one is available to answer your call right now, but if you leave your name and number at the tone, your call will be returned as soon as possible.

SAL looks at the phone incredulously, his frustration mounting.

                    SAL
We got problems here. No delivery on them X-mas presents, and I lost all my elves tryin'. I'm okay, but I gotta get a lift outta here. I'm at this number . . .

He squints, reading the number off the phone.

                    SAL
                    (cont.)
2-0-1 area code, 8-5-7   4-3-0-9. Merry Christmas.

As he hangs up, SAL's frustration and anger slowly give way to nostalgia. His cigarette dangles limply from his lip.

                    SAL
                (to himself)
    8-5-7   4-3-0-9.

He smiles, looking back into the dining room. BOBBY straightens the flowers in the table's centerpiece.

cut to:

EXT. STREET NIGHT

The three men are still trailing SAL, though slowly. They seem confused by the numerous footsteps, but as they turn a corner they are at the large granite pillars of the cul-de-sac entry.

cut to:

INT. DOWNEY HOUSE BATHROOM

SAL inspects his side in the mirror, the blood is dried around the wound, as well as on his shirt. As he tucks the shirt back in, he adjusts the small automatic he keeps on his back.

    He checks that his suit jacket conceals the bloodstain, and then flicks his cigarette into the toilet, flushing. He splashes his face with cold water, taking a moment to look at himself coldly in the mirror.

cut to:

INT. BOSS'S CAR NIGHT

The BOSS sits in the back seat next to BENNIE, listening intently to a cellular phone. DOM is at the wheel, he monitors the BOSS's face with anticipation. The BOSS hangs up.

BOSS

Church and Cherry.

DOM throws it into gear.

cut to:

INT. DOWNEY HOUSE

MRS. DOWNEY brings the turkey out of the kitchen to a chorus of "oohs" and "ahs." She sets it in front of her husband, as SAL seats himself, smiling forcefully at everyone. TED and JACK sit across the table, and BOBBY takes the seat next to SAL. MR. DOWNEY carves the bird as his wife returns to the kitchen.

TED

So how yah been, Sal?

SAL

Good. Very good. What about you, Teddy?

TED proudly lifts the bottom of his sweater above the table, display-ing a large yellow "P."

SAL

What is that? — Princeton?
                    (*Ted nods*)
Hey, that's great.
                    (*to Jack*)
How about that, huh, the kid's at Princeton.
                    (*setting him up*)
Is that where you went, Jack?

JACK

No.

TED

Jack went to State. (*pause*)
Bobby went to Princeton though.

SAL turns and smiles to BOBBY who is slightly embarrassed.

> SAL
> I remember, but we always knew she would do well.
> *(back to Jack)*
> Right?

> MR. DOWNEY
> What about you, Mr. Vaccionne, you look like your doing
> pretty well for yourself, did you ever go on in school?

MR. DOWNEY has apparently noticed SAL's expensive suit, gold
watch, and rings.

> SAL
> As a matter-a-fact, I've been doin' pretty good. No
> thanks to higher education though.

> MR. DOWNEY
> Oh? What line of work are you in?

> SAL
> Uhh, contracting.
> *(he smiles)*

> JACK
> *(smugly)*
> Oh, a trade.

> SAL
> Not really, I'm on the management side . . . trouble
> shooting.

> JACK
> *(incredulously)*
> —And no special training is required for that?

> SAL
> Nothing you could learn in school.

SAL is clearly enjoying his charade. Out of the kitchen, MRS. DOWNEY sits at the opposite end of the table from her husband.

> MRS. DOWNEY
> Well, why don't we have Salvatore say grace, since he's our guest.

SAL seems put on the spot.

> MR. DOWNEY
> Not too Catholic now Sal.

> BOBBY
> Daddy!

> MRS. DOWNEY
> It doesn't matter, Salvatore, go right ahead.

Everyone grasps hands and bows their heads. SAL thinks fast, he is obviously out of practice.

> SAL
> Well, bless this meal, this house, and . . . uh . . . all who are in it . . .

SAL looks at BOBBY's hand in his, she is doing the same, and they catch each other looking.

> SAL
> *(cont.)*
> . . . Protect us from harm. Deliver us from evil. *(pause)* In the name of the Father, the Son, The Holy Ghost, Amen.

> EVERYONE TOGETHER
> Amen.

cut to:

EXT. STREET NIGHT

The BOSS, DOM, and a score of other men are walking the cul-de-sac, there are tracks everywhere, but they seem confident he is around somewhere.

cut to:

INT. DOWNEY HOUSE NIGHT

Dinner is under way. Platters and serving bowls circulate around the table, as some begin to eat.

> BOBBY
> I'm sorry we lost touch, Sal. I wondered what you were up to all these years.

> TED
> *(laughing)*
> I remember Dad used to say you were probably in jail.

> MR. DOWNEY
> *(smiling weakly)*
> I was joking.

BOBBY and TED both look at him dubiously.

> SAL
> *(laughing it off)*
> If I hadn't wised up, I might'a ended up there. I was always gettin' into trouble those days.
> *(to Bobby)*
> How'd you ever put up with it?

BOBBY smiles warmly.

> MRS. DOWNEY
> Love.

The strength of the word takes everyone aback.

> MRS. DOWNEY
> (cont.)
> I know you were just teenagers, but I know love when I
> see it.

She winks to her husband. MR. DOWNEY smiles weakly as he chews.
SAL seems genuinely embarrassed.

> BOBBY
> Mom, that was a long time ago, we're both adults now,
> we're different people.

SAL seems somewhat relieved by this statement.

cut to:

EXT. DOWNEY HOUSE NIGHT

The BOSS stops in front of the large colonial. He regards it with no
special attention, until something catches his eye. He steps up onto
the walkway and slowly squats. He dabs his finger into a small patch
of pink snow. It is where SAL cleaned his hand. The BOSS looks up at
the house. He knows.

cut to:

INT. DOWNEY HOUSE NIGHT

MRS. DOWNEY is up from the table, as the others continue eating.

> JACK
> (shouting)
> Mother! Come back to dinner.
> (to Mr. Downey)
> Father—please.

> MR. DOWNEY
> C'mon, dear, that'll wait, let's eat first.

MRS. DOWNEY enters carrying a photo album.

> MRS. DOWNEY
> See that, it took two seconds.

She leans in between BOBBY and SAL, opening the album on the table between their plates.

> MRS. DOWNEY
> *(cont.)*
> Ah-huh, there it is.

MRS. DOWNEY points at a picture of SAL and BOBBY at the prom. BOBBY wears a frilly pink dress, and SAL wears a light blue tux, complete with wide lapels, and tinted ruffle shirt. They both laugh at themselves. TED strains to see across the table.

> TED
> What? What is it?

BAM! BAM! BAM! The happy moment is cut by a loud knocking at the door. SAL tenses. MRS. DOWNEY turns to the door.

> MRS. DOWNEY
> Well now, who can this be?

BOBBIE holds up the picture for her brothers and father. SAL slowly reaches around his back.

> BOBBY
> Is this funny or what?

SAL pays no attention to the album, he is focused on MRS. DOWNEY, who goes out of view, as she goes into the entry hall. His hand curls around his gun. He doesn't blink. MRS. DOWNEY pokes her head back out from the entry hall, smiling.

> MRS. DOWNEY
> Salvatore, it's for you.

SAL is frozen. JACK looks at him suspiciously.

>   BOBBY
> Who is it, Sal?

SAL shrugs weakly. Everyone turns toward the entry hall. BENNIE steps into view.

>   BENNIE
> Sal!

SAL's face lights up. He is overwhelmed to see the comrade he thought was dead.

>   SAL
> B-bennie, Jesus, I can't believe it. How did you get—I mean, well—I just didn't expect to see you.

SAL gets up, heading for BENNIE. BENNIE smiles broadly.

>   BENNIE
> Here I am.

They meet, shaking hands. SAL is almost checking to see that BENNIE is real.

>   SAL
>   *(quietly)*
> I don't understand.

>   BENNIE
>   *(under his breath)*
> I'll explain later. Let's get outta here.

>   MRS. DOWNEY
> Are you going to introduce us to your friend, Sal?

>   SAL
> Uh . . . yeah, this is Bennie. Bennie Saducci. He's a . . . friend a mine. A friend a mine from work.

MRS. DOWNEY moves to greet BENNIE.

MRS. DOWNEY

Oh, how nice, was he caroling with you?

BENNIE has no idea what's going on.

SAL

Sure—well, we were visitin' some business associates in
the area . . . and I wanted to stop by here,

(to Bennie)

but I didn't think I was gonna be seein' you again.

TED

Ahem.

TED reminds SAL to introduce the rest of the family with a gesture.

SAL

Bennie, this is the Downeys; Mrs. Downey, Mr. Downey,
Jack, Ted, and Bobby. *(pause)* Bobby and I used to go out
in high school.

BENNIE

No kidding.

(he smiles to Bobby)

That's nice. So Sal, you ready to go?

MRS. DOWNEY

Nonsense, we just started dinner, and you're going to join
us.

She motions to TED and JACK to set another place. TED hops to, but
JACK rises begrudgingly.

BENNIE

No-uh, we really should be goin'.

SAL is already pushing him toward the table.

SAL
(making a point)

We got plenty a time.

BENNIE
(slightly bewildered)

Maybe a quick bite.

MRS. DOWNEY seats him between JACK and TED, and JACK sets a dish down loudly in front of him. BENNIE seems very uncomfortable. SAL takes his seat as BOBBY shows BENNIE the prom picture.

BENNIE
(disbelieving)

That's you, Sal?

JACK and TED take their seats, as BENNIE's tittering turns to snorting guffaws. He tries to share the joke, showing the picture to TED who chuckles with him, and JACK who looks at him like he's crazy. SAL is not so amused.

MR. DOWNEY

So, you're in contracting Bennie?

BENNIE
(recovering)

Huh?

MR. DOWNEY

Sal was telling us about your work.

BENNIE looks panicked, having no idea what SAL has told them. TED passes him the stuffing, which seems to fluster him more. SAL is looking worried as well.

MR. DOWNEY
(cont.)

What is it that you do?

> BENNIE

Me?

> SAL
> *(covering)*

He works with me.

> BOBBY

Like an assistant?

> SAL

Yeah, exactly. He's one of my assistants.

SAL smiles, and BOBBY smiles as well, proud that SAL rates enough to have assistants. BENNIE sighs with relief, and dishes himself up some stuffing.

> MRS. DOWNEY

My! You must be very important to have all those assistants.

> JACK
> *(incredulously)*

Just how many assistants do you have?

> SAL

Nine.

> BENNIE

Seven.

> SAL

Yeah, seven. A couple just got . . . well . . . actually, the competition got 'em.

> MR. DOWNEY

It can get pretty cut throat out there.

> SAL

You said it!

> *(pause)*
You're still in insurance?

MR. DOWNEY nods, as BENNIE drops a fork full of mashed potatoes back onto his plate.

> BENNIE
> *(enthusiastically)*
We got lotsa experience in insurance.

> SAL
> *(scowling at Bennie)*
We dabbled in it a while ago.

JACK is becoming increasingly suspicious.

> JACK
Insurance? Contracting? What kind of company do you work for?

SAL and BENNIE exchange a worried glance.

> SAL
Jack! I'm sorry, I've been ignoring you. What kind of work have you been doing?

JACK wants an answer to his question, but can't resist the invitation to talk about himself.

> JACK
Well . . . I've been . . .
> *(he smiles)*
I'm a CPA now and I just started my own firm in Paramus.

> SAL
A bean-counter, no kidding, well that must be your Mercedes out front.

> BOBBY

Ahem.

BOBBY indicates that it is her car.

> SAL

The Chrysler?

MR. DOWNEY raises his hand as he chews.

> TED
> *(chuckling)*

Yugo.

> JACK

There's nothing funny about economy.

BENNIE laughs as well, he is beginning to enjoy SAL's ruse as well as the meal. SAL turns to BOBBY.

> SAL

Mercedes, huh. What've you been doin'?

> BOBBY

I've been teaching. The Mercedes I got in the settlement.

> SAL

Settlement?

> MRS. DOWNEY
> *(whispering it like a dirty word)*

Divorce.

> SAL

Divorce. You didn't even say you were married.

> BOBBY

Well I'm not—anymore. Thank God.

SAL

When did all this happen?

BOBBY

College. After we broke up, I started seeing Gerald.

SAL
(disgusted)

Gerald?

TED

He was a jerk.

JACK

He was rich.

MR. DOWNEY

He was a rich jerk.

MRS. DOWNEY

He was very nice, but I don't think Bobby loved him.

BOBBY
(embarrassed)

Eight years. I guess I was kidding myself.

The statement hits SAL strongly. BENNIE heaps more stuffing onto his plate.

BENNIE

Good stuffing, Mrs. D.

MRS. DOWNEY

Thank you, Benjamin.
(to Sal)
You're not married, are you, Salvatore?

SAL

No.

The phone rings as SAL does a double take, getting Mrs. Downey's drift. She smiles, rising to get the phone.

> MR. DOWNEY
> (*directs his comment at Sal*)
> He took good care of Bobby.

> BOBBY
> (*indignant*)
> People need more than money and things, Daddy.

The tense moment is interrupted by MRS. DOWNEY, who holds up the phone receiver, and shouts in from the study.

> MRS. DOWNEY
> Salvatore, it's for you.

SAL starts to get up.

> JACK
> So, Bennie, tell us more about yourself.

BENNIE stops midchew, and shoots SAL a worried look. SAL thinks twice about leaving him alone with JACK, but he's got to answer the phone.

> BENNIE
> (*mouth still full*)
> I-I-I was always real curious about accounting.

SAL picks up the phone in the study, lighting himself a smoke. He glances worriedly back toward BENNIE at the table, before turning to shield his conversation.

> SAL
> Hello.

> VOICE OF CALABRESE
> Sallie, you okay there? What the hell happened?

                         SAL

Our little Christmas surprise was no surprise. Somebody
ratted out Santa.

                  VOICE OF CALABRESE

Impossible, Sal. Nobody knew about this except me and
you. Who else did you tell?

                         SAL

Nobody, just my . . .

As SAL speaks he turns to see BENNIE laughing in the other room.
The truth slowly dawns on him. He stares in silent shock a
moment.

                  VOICE OF CALABRESE

Sal? Sal, you there?

                         SAL

Yeah. Yeah, look I gotta change a plans here. I don't need
that lift yet. I gotta take care a somethin' first.

                  VOICE OF CALABRESE

Everything okay there, Sal?

                         SAL

Yeah, fine. I'll call when I need that ride, okay?

cut to:

INT. BOSS'S CAR NIGHT

The BOSS checks his watch impatiently, then speaks to DOM.

                         BOSS

I give him five more minutes,
                       (pause)
and we're goin' in.

cut to:

INT. DOWNEY HOUSE NIGHT

SAL is back at the dinner table. He looks morose.

> BOBBY
> Is everything okay, Sal?

> SAL
> Yeah. Yeah, fine.

> MR. DOWNEY
> Bennie here says you're quite a bigshot at your company.

BENNIE smiles proudly at SAL who barely manages a smile in return.

> MR. DOWNEY
> *(cont.)*
> Look, Sal, I think I owe you an apology. I used to think
> you were no good, but it's obvious there was more to you
> than I realized.

> SAL
> Look, I didn't want to have to deal with this now,
> *(pause)*
> but that call was . . . well, there's been a tragedy. I'm
> afraid I need to speak to Bennie alone.

A solemn hush hits the table. BOBBY places a sympathetic hand on
SAL's shoulder. BENNIE is confused at first, but catches on that SAL
wants to talk in private. The two men rise.

> MRS. DOWNEY
> Why don't you use the study. You can close the door.

> SAL
> Thanks. Please, go on with dinner.

SAL ushers BENNIE into the study, holding the door.

> MRS. DOWNEY
> I'll save you some dessert.

SAL smiles and nods, as he closes the door.

> BENNIE
>
> C'mon, Sal, let's get outta this town.

SAL is lighting a cigarette with his back to BENNIE as he admires the all-silver nativity scene on the fireplace mantel. He picks up a figure, weighing it, and packing it in his hand like a roll of coins.

> SAL
>
> Why such a hurry?

> BENNIE
>
> This town's hot. The sooner we get outta here, the better.

SAL walks slowly up to BENNIE. Face to face, he stares him in the eye. The Christmas tree blinks behind them.

> SAL
>
> What happens when I step out the door?

SAL stares him down, dragging slowly off his smoke. BENNIE's expression slowly melts into panic.

> BENNIE
>
> What-whatta ya mean?

SAL says nothing, exhaling smoke with a long hissing sound.

BOOM! SAL connects with a sharp blow to BENNIE's rib cage, and follows instantaneously with a two-handed uppercut that sends BENNIE up and back flattening a Christmas present as he lands.

SAL pauses to pick his cigarette back up off the carpet. BENNIE crawls toward the fireplace grabbing the Yule log and swinging back with it—connecting hard with SAL's ankle. SAL falls to his knees. BENNIE swings again, but SAL grabs the log, using it to throw himself into a sweeping roundhouse. SAL's loaded fist catches BENNIE's jaw, knocking him out cold.

MRS. DOWNEY
(through the door)
Is everything okay in there?

SAL grabs his cigarette from the floor again and limps to the door.
He opens it a crack, and speaks quietly to Mrs. Downey.

SAL
He's not taking it very well, I'm afraid. Give him a minute.

MRS. DOWNEY nods, and SAL closes the door.

MRS. DOWNEY
(to Bobby)
What a sweet man!

SAL throws the poinsettias from a vase, and splashes the water on
BENNIE's face. Grabbing him by the collar, he presses a sharp table
knife to the groggy man's neck.

SAL
How many men out there?

BENNIE
(fear making him more lucid)
Maybe . . . ten.

SAL
In back?

BENNIE
I don't know—I think they got a dog in back.

SAL thinks to himself a moment.

BENNIE
(desperately)
I didn't know he was gonna kill anybody, Sal. Lemme go
out there before he turns this place into a battleground.
Maybe I could . . .

SAL regards BENNIE with utter contempt. Covering BENNIE's mouth, he thrusts the knife into his windpipe.

SAL emerges from the study, closing the door behind him.

> SAL
> He really needs to be alone for a while.

He steps toward the table, struggling to hide a limp.

> BOBBY
> Of course.

> MRS. DOWNEY
> Some pie, Salvatore?

> SAL
> No thanks.

He leans to whisper into BOBBY's ear.

> SAL
> Take me upstairs, Bob, I'll explain later.

BOBBY finds the request odd, but thinks it's connected to "the tragedy." She rises from the table.

> BOBBY
> Excuse us, please, but I need to speak with Sal alone.
> We'll be upstairs.

SAL follows BOBBY up the staircase, suppressing a grimace with each step.

> JACK
> Upstairs?

> MRS. DOWNEY
> It's a little romantic. Isn't it?

cut to:

INT. DOWNEY HOUSE-UPSTAIRS

SAL and BOBBY are in the upstairs hallway. SAL points to a door.

> SAL
>
> Let's go in there.

> BOBBY
>
> That's my parents' room.

> SAL
>
> Trust me.

BOBBY opens the door, and they enter. SAL keeps BOBBY from flicking on the lights. She looks at him curiously.

> SAL
>
> Check and see if your dog's still in the backyard.

> BOBBY
>
> What?

> SAL
> *(emphatically)*
>
> Please.

BOBBY moves to the window drawing the curtains.

> BOBBY
>
> I really don't understand any of this, Sal.

> SAL
>
> The dog?

> BOBBY
>
> Yeah, he's there, asleep in his house.

> SAL
>
> Any footprints back there?

BOBBY

Just the dog's.

SAL seems relieved. He steps toward the window, and BOBBY meets him. Behind them on the wall are pictures of her and her brothers as kids.

SAL
(struggling)
Look, I lied about a lot of things here tonight.

BOBBY
(interrupting)
Sal, I don't care how much money you have.

SAL is taken aback by the statement.

SAL
I wish that's all it was. (pause) This is never gonna make any sense to you, but . . .

BOBBY
What, Sal?

SAL
There's people after me, and if I don't make a run for it, they'll tear this place apart.

BOBBY
You're being crazy.

SAL
I'm trying to be noble.

He lifts open the window, turning back to BOBBY.

SAL
Don't hate me.

BOBBY
(confused)

Sal, I—

SAL

Promise me.

She moves closer, taking SAL's hands.

BOBBY

Sal, I . . . I still love you.

She pulls closer, kissing SAL lightly. He is stunned. Every ounce of hate seems to drain from him. He can say nothing. He just turns slipping silently out the window. She watches as he slides down the sloping roof toward the yard. The dog awakens barking, and almost simultaneously MRS. DOWNEY screams shrilly downstairs.

cut to:

EXT. STREET NIGHT

The BOSS is sitting in his car, DOM at the wheel, when he hears the dog barking. He yells out the window to the men in front of the Downeys' house.

BOSS

He's going out the back. Get him!

(to Dom)

Head him off.

DOM swings the car around wildly, throwing chunks of gray ice at the men who scramble around the street.

cut to:

INT. DOWNEY HOUSE NIGHT

BOBBY sheds a silent tear as she consoles her mother by the stairs. The men regard the body in the study. MR. DOWNEY speaks as he dials the phone.

MR. DOWNEY
I guess the news was too much for him.

JACK looks at his father incredulously as TED regards the nativity scene.

TED
Where's Christ?

cut to:

EXT. STREET NIGHT

SAL runs lamely across the empty boulevard. As a gentle snow begins to fall, his tracks become clearer and clearer. In the distance, a train whistle breaks the silence. SAL cocks his head, and turns a corner with renewed vigor.

The tracks are only a block away. SAL runs down the middle of the broad white street, heading for a long flight of stairs that lead up to the train platform. The whistle sounds again, closer.

SCREEECH! The BOSS's car screams into an intersection several blocks directly behind SAL. He runs as fast as his bad leg will allow, but the car is closing fast.

SAL hits the stairs bounding, as the car slides to a stop.

SAL is halfway up, as the BOSS steps out. The train is pulling in as the BOSS takes aim. SAL is only steps away from the top.

BLAM! A single shot catches SAL just short of the platform.

SAL drags himself up the last steps and stumbles into the train as it pulls out.

INT. TRAIN NIGHT

Collapsing into a seat, SAL holds his gut with both hands. He struggles to catch his breath, as he leans his head limply against the window.

He lights himself a smoke, his bloody hands staining the cigarette. Out the window, scenes of New Brunswick glide by.

fade out

Appendix: HIT MAN MOVIES

The list of hit man movies that follows is by no means inclusive. There are hundreds of films in which the character of the hit man—or some approximation thereof—appears. Most are unwatchable. I have not, for example, included any of the countless action movies that feature some sort of assassin as they do not enrich the subgenre. Rather, I have included only those movies (fifteen, exactly) that are indispensable to understanding the character of the hired killer.

This Gun for Hire (1942).

Dir: Frank Tuttle. Starring: Alan Ladd, Robert Preston, Veronica Lake.

This movie features Alan Ladd in the role that made him a star. He is wonderful—if somewhat too good-looking; don't forget, in the book Graham Greene was very specific about his killer's ugliness—as Raven, the hit man who completes a job only to be double-crossed by those who hired him. Robert Wagner re-created the role forty-nine years later in a dismal made-for-television affair, but the original is vintage noir.

The Killers (1964).

Dir: Don Siegel. Starring: Lee Marvin, John Cassavetes, Angie Dickinson, Ronald Reagan.

This film, while very loosely based on the Hemingway short story, is excellent. It features Lee Marvin as the older member of a hit team who is puzzled by their latest victim's (John Cassavetes) willingness to die. He and his partner go to Miami in order to unravel the puzzle and get the money they believe he was killed for. Ronald Reagan is perfect as the slick criminal/businessman, as is Angie Dickinson, the beautiful bait. Also some interesting small performances by Norman Fell and Claude Akins.

The Day of the Jackal (1973).

Dir: Fred Zinnemann. Starring: Edward Fox, Alan Badel, Tony Britton, Cyril Cusack.

Beautifully written, if slightly overlong, this film features Edward Fox as the assassin hired to kill General Charles de Gaulle. The suspense is unrelenting and the film marks one of the few successful attempts to bring the character of the hired killer over into the thriller genre. Perhaps even more noteworthy is that while this piece is filled with action, its narrative integrity is never compromised.

Three Days of the Condor (1975).

Dir: Sydney Pollack. Starring: Robert Redford, Cliff Robertson, Max von Sydow, Faye Dunaway, John Houseman.

Another hit man/thriller film (perhaps the only other successful one of its kind), it features Robert Redford as a CIA bookworm who reads too much into something he shouldn't have. When his colleagues are murdered by a hit squad, he goes on the run, unsure of who his friends are, who is trying to kill him and why. The movie is saved from becoming another unremarkable entry in the mystery/espionage genre because it is superbly written and the performances—especially Faye Dunaway as the beautiful stranger Redford abducts in order to avoid capture and Max von Sydow as the hit man hired to kill him—are outstanding.

The Killing of a Chinese Bookie (1976).

Dir: John Cassavetes. Starring: Ben Gazzara, Seymour Cassel, Virginia Carrington, Azizi Johari.

This movie should have been better considering it was written and directed by John Cassavetes. It features Ben Gazzara as a luckless nightclub owner who is forced to work off a $23,000 gambling debt as a hit man. His mark is a Chinese crime boss who is at odds with the crime family he owes the money to. Despite the fact that it is the most accessible Cassavetes film, it is dull, overlong, and too dark for its own good. It is interesting mainly because it is the perfect cinematic example of *The Metamorphoses Tale.*

Andy Warhol's BAD (1977).

Dir: Jed Johnson. Starring: Carroll Baker, Perry King, Susan Tyrrell.

While not as bizarre as *Backtrack*, this movie has its moments. Carroll Baker plays the head of an all-girl hit man ring that she runs out of her home, the first floor of which doubles as a suburban electrolysis clinic. A young Perry King is the professional from out-of-town who boards with her while he waits for the go-ahead on a particularly lucrative job, the killing of a mentally retarded boy. In addition to any number of bizarre things—from the attempted assassination of a dog to a severed finger in a catsup bottle—this movie also features an incredibly disturbing falling-infant leitmotif.

The Hit (1984).

Dir: *Stephen Frears. Starring: John Hurt, Terrence Stamp, Tim Roth, Fernando Rey, Laura Del Sol, Bill Hunter.*

As a character study, this film is worth seeing. John Hurt is the icy professional sent to retrieve a Mafia informer (Terrence Stamp) who is living under witness protection in Spain. Tim Roth, one of those actors who seem particularly drawn to the character of the hired killer (along with Dennis Hopper and John Cassavetes, also directors of movies in the subgenre), plays the hit man's psychopathic sidekick. Though the piece is artfully shot and the acting is wonderful—the pace (this movie is dreadfully slow in places) tends to get in the way.

Prizzi's Honor (1985).

Dir: *John Huston. Starring: Jack Nicholson, Kathleen Turner, Robert Logia, John Randolph, William Hickey, Anjelica Huston.*

Based on the Richard Condon novel of the same name, this film features Jack Nicholson as the most respected hired gun of the Prizzi crime family and Kathleen Turner as the mysterious woman he falls for who, as it turns out, is also a professional killer. Perhaps the only hit man movie done intentionally as a comedy, it is undoubtedly the most successful black comedy ever made. Some of the dialogue (particularly that between Jack Nicholson and Anjelica Huston) is unmatchable.

Backtrack (1990).

Dir: *Dennis Hopper. Starring: Dennis Hopper, Jodie Foster, Dean Stockwell, Vincent Price, John Turturro, Fred Ward, Bob Dylan, Joe Pesci, Charlie Sheen.*

Interesting only because of its incredible cast, this is the most bizarre hit man movie ever made. Jodie Foster plays a visual artist who witnesses a Mafia execution, flees, and is then targeted herself. However, the hit man sent to kill her (a sexually repressed, tone deaf, saxophone-playing eccentric played by Dennis Hopper) falls in love with her and helps her escape. For all of the talent behind it, this movie is a grand and charmless failure.

Red Rock West (1993).

Dir: John Dahl. Starring: Nicolas Cage, Dennis Hopper, Lara Flynn Boyle, Timothy Carhart, J.T. Walsh.

Nicolas Cage plays a drifter with a good heart, which is precisely what gets him into so much trouble. Mistaken for a hit man by a bar owner who wants his wife dead, he accepts the contract with the intention of warning the victim and leaving town with the cash. Leaving town, however, is the one thing he can't do, especially when the bar owner turns out to be the sheriff and the real hit man (Dennis Hopper) comes to make good on the contract. *Red Rock West* is a dark labyrinth of a movie with each character more evil than the next. Interesting cameo by Dwight Yokum as well.

Shelter (1993).

Dir: Dave Kost. Starring: Ramsey Faragallah, Kelly Herman, Joe Ambrose, Louise Ventrella, Dave Kost.

This beautiful short film is one of the best in the subgenre. Dave Kost is perfect as Sal, the head of a group of hit men who are delivered to the henchmen of a rival crime family by one of their own members (Bennie, played by Ramsey Faragallah). When the hit on which they are set turns out to be a setup, Sal escapes to the home of an old high school sweetheart. The Christmas dinner scene which follows is a study in black comedy as well as the most apt example of a society that is allowed to keep its innocence, its state of grace, in the midst of the most unimaginable acts.

Bulletproof Heart (1994).

Dir: Mark Malone. Starring: Anthony LaPaglia, Mimi Rogers, Matt Craven, Peter Boyle.

This movie was conceived after director Mark Malone learned that organized crime bosses now prefer their professional killers to be nihilists instead of psychopaths. Anthony LaPaglia is brilliant as the hired killer who falls in love with his mark (Mimi Rogers), a woman who wants to be killed. The plot is fantastic as the audience is caught between hoping the woman will somehow find her way out of the mess she is in while, simultaneously, hoping that the hit man won't do anything to ruin his career. While the film is obviously inspired by John Huston's 1985 masterpiece, *Prizzi's Honor,* it is in no way derivative.

Little Odessa (1994).

Dir: James Gray. Starring: Tim Roth, Edward Furlong, Moira Kelly, Vanessa Redgrave, Maximilian Schell.

This movie is a beautiful illustration of how close and yet completely removed the margins are from the mainstream. Tim Roth plays the lost-son-turned-assassin who returns to his old neighborhood to do a hit. But when he attempts to enter the mainstream in a capacity other than that of the hired killer (he goes to see his mother [Vanessa Redgrave] who is desperately ill), he is thrown back into a world in which it is impossible for him to function. Though the acting is strong, the piece as a whole intelligent and artfully done, the movie has difficulty living up to its own opening—a brutal, matter-of-fact hit done at a bus stop.

Romeo is Bleeding (1994).

Dir: Peter Medak. Starring: Gary Oldman, Lena Olin, Annabella Sciorra, Juliette Lewis.

This film is interesting primarily because of Roy Scheider's cameo. Scheider plays the crime boss who has contracted the hit on Lena Olin and when Gary Oldman (in a role that has become all too familiar) comes to tell him things are not going as planned, he delivers a miniature soliloquy in which he mentions Robert Lowell's stay in the West Street Jail. It is worth noting that Scheider starred in an earlier hit man movie—*Cohen and Tate*—in 1989. A complete mess and a waste of his talent, it costarred Adam Baldwin as one of the most obnoxious hit men in the history of murder; a man only slightly more palatable than his intended victim, a whiny nine-year-old brat who, much to the audience's disappointment, comes through the ordeal alive.

The Professional (1994).

Dir: Luc Besson. Starring: Danny Aiello, Gary Oldman, Jean Reno, Natalie Portman, Peter Appel, Michael Badalucco, Ellen Greene.

Luc Besson's first American film since *La Femme Nikita* features Jean Reno as Leon, a hit man who takes in a little girl (Natalie Portman) after her family has been murdered by rogue police officers. Gary Oldman's character, the leader of the police gang with a lust for violence and Beethoven, is a tip of the hat to Alex of *A Clockwork Orange*. Unfortunately, the depth of the Burgess character is missing here, as is the chilling portrayal by Malcolm McDowell of that character in the Stanley Kubrick film of 1971.

Pulp Fiction (1994).

Dir: Quentin Tarantino. Starring: John Travolta, Samual L. Jackson, Uma Thurman, Harvey Keitel, Tim Roth, Amanda Plummer, Maria de Medeiros, Ving Rhames, Eric Stoltz, Rosanna Arquette, Christopher Walken, Bruce Willis.

Winner of Best Picture, 1994 Cannes Film Festival; the Golden Globe Award for Best Screenplay; Best Picture, Los Angeles Film Critics awards; Best Screenplay, New York Film Critics Circle awards; and Best Screenplay, Los Angeles Film Critics awards; this film features John Travolta and Samual L.